THE LOST TAVERN

A Pirate's Odyssey

By Kerry Brown and Chris Kelly

For Sarah,
a great colleague, friend, + teacher!
→ Kerry
Chris

authorHOUSE®

AuthorHouse™
1663 Liberty Drive
Bloomington, IN 47403
www.authorhouse.com
Phone: 1-800-839-8640

First published by AuthorHouse 1/13/2011

ISBN: 978-1-4520-8208-0 (sc)
ISBN: 978-1-4520-8209-7 (dj)
ISBN: 978-1-4520-8210-3 (e)

Library of Congress Control Number: 2010914417

Printed in the United States of America

This book is printed on acid-free paper.

Contents

Chapter One
Final Crossing
September, 1776

"the narrowing Cape that stretches its shrunk arm
out to all the winds and the relentless smiting of the
waves..."

After all these years the tavern was still there in the distance,
standing like a sentinel overlooking the bay and the nearby
inlets. When he was a young boy, he would awake on summer
mornings to the sounds of waves softly lapping against the sand and
to the sight of Mr. Samuel Smith's imposing tavern some three and
a half miles distant across the water. On clear days it had seemed so
close that if he tried, he could call "Hulloo" to whalers he knew on
the far beach and be heard -- or that he could smell the smoke of
the birch wood curling from the tavern's chimney. In those days the
tavern was another world for him, a world apart and one redolent of
young people, the smell of ale, hard labor, the allurements of danger,
and, as it was to turn out, painful betrayal.

From his small bayside cottage overlooking the mouth of Silver
Springs in Hither Billingsgate, the journey to the tavern on Great
Island was a twenty minute walk along the beach, past Fresh Brook
village to Blackfish Creek where his skiff was located, and then
another twenty minutes by sail across Grampus Bay to Smith's Cove
inside the curl of the island. When he was a boy, Isaac Doane had
loved this journey. He loved the feel of the sand left by an outgoing
tide, cool and wet under his feet, the southwesterly breeze warm on
his face and in his hair, the tight billow of the canvas sail as he made
a direct tack to the island. He loved the way the morning sunlight
glistened on the water's surface and inched up the Great Island
bluff as he rounded Lieutenant's Island and made his way across the
bay. He loved the sun's long slant of light along the tree tops in the
early morning, and he especially loved the creatures of the bay: the

complaining gulls, the indolent sunfish, the dark lobsters that would wash up on the beach, and the pilot whales -- the grampus and black fish -- that he and his companions would herd and drive to their destruction all along the beaches of Mr. Smith's island. These were the impressions of a boy whose skin was smooth and unscarred at fifteen, who was truly a child of the century -- having entered it in its first year -- and who knew the territory and its people as intimately as one might a loved one's smile.

Mapmakers and scholars originally named the land "Woods End," the place where the large hardwoods stopped at the sea's edge. But after men felled the oak, pine, birch, sassafras, holly, juniper, ash, and walnut for homes and warmth, after the cows and sheep had assured the disappearance of their roots, and after the winds and sea had finished the work, there were no more woods. Like the ever-diminishing Billingsgate Island to the south and west of the tavern, there was only sand blown fitfully by the winds, ultimately subsiding beneath the water's reach. There were, however, cod fish -- pastures of them in the neighboring sea -- and so the solitary spit of wind-blown sand jutting out like a flexed biceps into the ocean, assumed its rightful name: Cape Cod. Despite its reputation as the graveyard of the Atlantic due to the ever-migrating, riddling sands along the shoreline that claimed countless ships, this land was more temperate than inland cities during the winter and cooler than those same places in the summer months. And for Isaac there was no better place to live on earth than Cape Cod in September. He had held to that belief for the balance of a long life, and now more than sixty years after he had made his first journey by skiff to the distant island, he was once again on a tack toward Mr. Smith's island making what he knew would be his last visit to the place.

September heralded the closing of nature's accounts, something he knew in his mind and felt in his old bones. He was getting too old to handle the main sheet of even this small boat, and the brisk wind blowing down from the northern territories signaled that harsher winds and fading light would follow all too soon. The tobacco in his pipe flared for an instant as a gust of wind buffeted the skiff, and Isaac was once again reminded of how much he hated to say farewell to people and places he loved. As he surveyed the shoreline back towards Silver Springs and to his right along Lieutenant's Island, he saw a few scattered homesteads just above the shoreline. From there his eye was drawn across the bay to Great Island, where the tavern still stood although it had seen little use for years.

Instinctively, he looked to the left toward Beach Hill, but all that remained of the massive tower, which had been used to descry the arrival of whales, were a few shattered timbers propped against some scrub pines and bleaching in the sun. Well he could recall standing atop that thirty foot tower, which itself stood on a bluff fifty feet above the sea, as he called to the men below that the blackfish were just west of Billingsgate Island and coming on fast. At such moments he felt as if he were the most powerful boy in the world, as if, simply by identifying the darkened fields of the bay and hollering, "Whales off!" to those below, he could set the world in motion. And to some extent he could because upon hearing his cry, crews of young, muscular men would scramble for their equipment, leap into large dories, and begin rowing toward the approaching pods of whales. Later, when Isaac was himself powerful and careless of danger, he would hear the cry of a young boy in the nearby tower, race down from the tavern to the beached boats, lay his back into the first hard pulls on his oar, and glut himself on the taste of sweat and peril.

Someone inspecting the bay with a spyglass from the Duck Creek wharf on this September afternoon might have been surprised to see solitary old Isaac Doane making his way in his small skiff toward Mr. Smith's Island, harmless old Isaac who had lived alone all those years on the bluff overlooking Silver Springs, who needed no one and of whom few in town ever spoke. The young people simply disregarded the old man when he would shamble into town for provisions, and the older folks would avert their eyes from his scarred face, be it from disapproval of an old reprobate or some unspoken communal shame that they shared with him. Be that as it may, little would that distant wharf-bound observer have guessed at the images pushing one after another through the old man's imagination as he approached the spit at Beach Hill, bringing the bow of his skiff up into the wind, and tacking into the shallows.

The bay water was warm around his ankles when he slipped over the side of the boat into the shallows, and although it was difficult work for an old man, he was careful to pull the skiff as far as he could up the beach and then secure the bow line to a scrub oak nearby. On his journey across the bay he had determined to land on the Beach Hill side of the island because he wanted to take his time walking along the beach below the high escarpment from which Mr. Smith's tavern surveyed the surrounding waters. To Isaac the curving beach seemed desolate and eerily quiet until he realized that for days he had been imagining it the way it used to be -- filled with his old companions, the try works operating at full blast, and the air alive with the distant cries of strange men and women who were discovering the tavern for the first time.

The tavern in those days had been an outpost, an ongoing town meeting, the heart of a new and growing whaling industry, a den of pleasure and of thieves, a starting point. But that was sixty years ago. Now as he attempted to avoid stepping on broken, razor-sharp clam shells with his bare feet, he sensed in his sore muscles the essential loneliness of this place. Even the trees atop the high cliff had disappeared, victims of the need for homes, ship masts, fuel, and countless other human priorities. In their place was sand: sand sifting between his toes, sand shifting along the beach, sand slowly seeping down the cliffside, sand swirling around the abandoned tavern, sand slowly sinking beneath the water's surface on nearby Billingsgate Island, even massive storms of sand all the way up the Cape toward Provincetown. Years before, the town fathers of "Helltown," as Provincetown was known then, had tried to stem the inexorable loss of the land by not allowing cattle to graze on the grass; in its place, fish became a staple of their diet, and cows were rumored to gather along the shore in expectation of fish heads and frames that might be thrown their way by fishermen returning from their voyages.

Isaac smiled at the memory, but as he did, he suddenly became aware of a massive silhouette looming like a thunderhead in the distance where the island ended to the south. He recognized it immediately -- the Somerset, the British frigate -- because it had patrolled the waters of Barnstable Bay so often and raided the local towns at will. His chest rose and fell in a soft sigh as he thought of what that ship meant to him and to others: half of the town had moved away rather than defy the King's will, and the other half was fiercely resentful of the arrogance of the ship's crew and the monarch they represented. Isaac was aware that Nantucket had already become a safe harbor for British loyalists, and the sight of the three-masted warship aroused sharply varying responses from everyone who saw her from the neighboring beaches or the harbors. Isaac soon turned away from the sight, however, because he did not want this day's journey into the past to be disturbed by thoughts of the inevitable war to come – but, in part, the Somerset's very presence was a reason for the journey. He had planned his actions for too long, had anticipated their fulfillment so intensely, that he simply felt that he did not have time to contemplate the insult and injustice the ship represented for him.

As he resumed his walk up the beach, Isaac occasionally found remnants of the old tryworks where Mr. Smith's men would process the whales that Isaac and his compatriots had driven to their destruction. At the base of the bluff was a rusting caldron in which the blubber had been refined into oil, but missing were the spades, flensers, and other cutting tools used to butcher the whales into blankets of blubber; absent was the thick, noxious stench that filled the nostrils and seemed to linger in them for days. And gone were the people. In other earthly places men were carrying out these activities and would continue to do so for years to come: standing over the great pots, cutting, stirring, cursing, their faces illuminated by the infernal flames until they seemed to be stoking hell's fires. But on the quiet shores of Great Island this solitary September afternoon, they were gone, having left few traces, a pentimento, of the curious, wild, and savage rituals that bound them to the whales and to the sea.

Isaac made out the path, now overgrown with scrub oak, that led up to the tavern and wondered whether the sign that Mr. Smith had carved himself would still be standing. As he started up the path, there it was, weathered yet discernible:

"Sam Smith, he has good flip,
Good toddy if you please:
The way is near, and very clear
'Tis just beyond the trees."

Isaac knelt down, pushed aside the grasses that had grown up in front of it, grasped the top of the sign with both hands, and slowly began to push and pull until its stake came loose from the ground and he could lift it free. Isaac held the words before him for a last time and read them fondly, recalling when he and Running Water had first come upon the sign. He had passed the marker so many times on his way up to the tavern, but after today he knew no one would ever read these lines again. Then, without another thought, he grasped the stake firmly in both hands and with all his strength, whirled and flung the sign as far as he could into the underbrush, where it landed face down. No longer would strangers, or friends for that matter, have the promise of Samuel Smith's hospitality to guide them along the way. Isaac felt as if he had begun to repay a long-standing promise to Mr. Smith; in fact, on this day he would make good on his oath to Mr. Smith. Years before he had sworn to him that he would watch over the tavern and protect it from harm. Now the British warship represented a palpable threat: Never would the British establish an outpost in Samuel Smith's old tavern; never would the king's soldiers occupy the place. Isaac would see to it.

Isaac made his way up the path, and as he did so, he occasionally bent over to grab a handful of dried pine needles, in the same motion placing them in his left pocket so that it bulged out from his hip a little. As he made his way up the overgrown path, his face was tickled by a glistening cobweb, which he pushed aside, and his eye bleared from a stray twig that lashed across it. The way was not easy for an old man, and he had to lift his feet to avoid tripping over the clusters of grass in the path. The musky aroma of the low pines was still sweet to him after all these years, and he looked forward to seeing the dark outline of the tavern up ahead. After climbing for ten minutes, out of breath and weary, Isaac emerged from a copse of trees to discover that the area immediately surrounding the tavern was virtually barren. The broad porch was still there, but now showing the effects of years of neglect, and the second story of the building still stood high above the bay. The building had visibly sagged, however, as if the breath that had animated it had departed, and, in fact, most of those who had given it life were many years dead.

Two rough-hewn chairs, which he poignantly remembered, still remained on the porch, and Isaac settled wearily and gratefully into one of them. As he stared to the west, past Billingsgate Island and then towards Boston, his finger found the ridge of the scar that extended from his eye down to his jaw, and delicately massaged it as he would so often when his mind was preoccupied. Soon he entered a zone where the water below him, the vague ship in the distance, and the glistening horizon began to coalesce and merge together. Then his head slowly fell to his chest as his mind filled with faces: those of Samuel Smith, Running Water, Daniel Atwood, Reverend Treat, Cyprian Southack, John Julian, Sam Harding, and finally, looming last, those of Maria Hallett and Sam Bellamy.

Chapter Two
The Whaling Tavern
1690-1776

The tavern on the bluff of Great Island is as much a character in this narrative as any of the human beings who will live and breathe in the pages that follow. It was born in 1690 and died in 1776 when the British warship, Somerset, definitively ended whaling operations in the Billingsgate area. Mr. Samuel Smith (1641-1697) attended its birth by constructing the rambling building to support his interest in the local whaling industry. When Mr. Smith, a prosperous farmer and landowner in the area, died in 1697, the tavern passed to his brother, Daniel, who ran it for almost twenty years until Sam Smith's grandson took it over in 1714. Samuel Smith III was as energetic and visionary as his grandfather, inspiring the affection and devotion of the citizenry – Puritan and Indian alike – and, in particular, Isaac Doane.

A note on Samuel Smith III: Whereas his Puritan forbears were concerned with avoiding the heat of the spiritual inferno, Mr. Smith was occupied with stoking the inferno at his whale houses on Great Island and nearby Lieutenant's Island. These houses, also known as tryworks, were little more than high, elevated roofs supported by great timbers and, consequently, lacked enclosing walls. In these structures whalers stored their gear, but, more important, they processed whale blubber in a large vat that required countless cords of wood and steadfast men who could bear the heat and stench that rose from the boiling fats and oils. These men were frequently Indians from the nearby islands, and Sam Smith was both farsighted and pragmatic enough to make them an integral part of the local economy.

These were the people who had shared their knowledge of the land and the sea with the earliest colonists, and although his family did not arrive on the Mayflower, Sam Smith was the kind of practical New Englander who knew a good thing when he saw it.

As a consequence, he employed Indians in his whaling enterprises, he entertained them in his tavern, and he protected their property rights throughout the area. The income that accrued to him from his tavern and from his whaling enterprises enabled him to add to the holdings that had come to him from his father and grandfather and contributed to his becoming a major landholder on Cape Cod. Mr. Smith was also open-hearted to those in need, and his generosity to Isaac Doane and his mother was only one instance of many that made him one of the most respected men on the outer Cape.

In its prime, from 1700 to 1740, the tavern was a state of mind, a place where work was done, deals were transacted, and good ale was always flowing. By 1740, now middle-aged, the tavern performed more sporadically: Because whaling activity had moved from the bay to the vaster ocean, the tryworks closed down, and the tavern only opened on demand when vagrant whaling and merchant vessels returned to Barnstable Bay. By 1788, twenty years after Sam Smith III died, the nexus of the whaling industry was in Nantucket, and the number of whaling vessels that regularly set sail from what is now known as Wellfleet Harbor was reduced from forty to four. In 1768, the large door of the tavern closed, only to open when a fitful wind might blow it ajar.

In 1970, almost two hundred years later, seeking any secrets the tavern's grave might be concealing, excavators unearthed a soiled treasure, a memento mori, that has considerable importance to the outcome of this story. For the time being, however, suffice it to say that the Smith family's tavern is the stage on which all of our principal figures walked and where many of the climactic events of this narrative occurred. Just as local residents breathed in the aromas of spilt beer, sizzling beef, hempen tobaccos, and human warmth, so the tavern itself seemed to breathe until its final exhalation in the first year of our country's independence. Of the countless whalemen, sailors, laborers, revelers, wayfarers, and weathered women who crossed its threshold, only Isaac Doane, who knew the tavern most intimately, bore witness to its death.

Chapter Three
First Encounter
December, 1714

Isaac shivered. It was mid-December, and the bare branches of the trees were spread out against the sky like fans composed of dark lace. It had been uncommonly cold for two weeks, and the thickening ice on the kettle ponds reflected the pewter shades of the sky. Isaac reflexively curled his shoulders into his neck and contemplated doing once again what he had done so many times when he was younger -- venturing as far out on the ice as he could before he heard it begin to crack.

When he was a boy of six, the deep sound, rumbling and ominous, had thrilled him as he would carefully place one foot in front of another to avoid falling to the hard surface --- and perhaps through it. He loved the shimmering darkness of the ice and the danger it promised. Now fifteen years old and more aware of the danger, he sat at the edge of Great Pond strapping his new skating blades to his snow encrusted boots. For weeks he had waited for the chance to try out the skates, ever since Elias Crowell had fashioned them for him at his forge in Eastham. Now the time had come, and as he ran this thumb along the sharp edge of the blade, he envisioned himself cutting silently through the north wind, creating long white threads on the dark surface. His blue fingers moved quickly to secure the leather straps around his boots, and soon after, he was launching himself outward toward the center of the pond.

Free from the overarching protection of the trees, Isaac tasted the sting of the wind on his lips and tightened his eyes against the cold. His sight blurred a bit at first, but then it cleared as he gained speed, pressing his blades first in one direction on the surface and then in another in short, jabbing steps. As his strides lengthened, his entire body seemed to relax, and he found a rhythm. His breath now coming more easily, Isaac's mind returned once again to his father, dead now for three weeks, and he recalled Mr. Smith helping him to lower the pine box into the cold November ground. He did not comprehend yet how much he missed his father – even something so simple as his hand guiding him along the ice when he was six – but he knew that his father had loved him, and now at fifteen he set himself the impossible task of earning his father's respect and pride. What Isaac could not know then on that lonely stretch of ice was that he would spend the balance of his days struggling to earn his own self respect. At this moment, however, he recognized the burden on his shoulders: that his mother would be relying on him and him alone and that he would need to provide her -- and himself -- with a living by whatever means possible. School was a distant and fading memory, and he was aware that his childhood was over, that he needed to find employment and quickly.

The sober face of Samuel Smith reappeared in his mind's eye, Mr. Smith who had been his father's friend, who had helped his family throughout his father's illness, who had given him odd jobs to do and paid him well, and who had suggested that he might have some employment for him at the tavern out on Great Island. Yes, Isaac thought, when I see Mr. Smith next, I will thank him for his generosity and ask him for a job.

At that instant, Isaac found himself in the air. As he had been circling the pond and gathering speed, he had not noticed a considerable rut in the ice, created perhaps by the persistent wind; but it was there, nevertheless, and before he could react to it, he was in mid-flight, arms flung wide, feet splayed apart. To an observer he must have looked as if he were making a frantic attempt to levitate, and as he spun in the air, he imagined he heard someone say, "Oh, my dear Lord!"

And at that moment he fell. Then he was lying on the ice staring up at a solemn sky framed by pine trees, his preoccupation with the past and his future having vanished, and he rediscovered one more time the meaning of pain. After a few seconds had passed, he heard a burst of soft laughter amid the pines, and knowing he was not the source of this merriment, he propped himself up on one elbow and looked toward the edge of the pond. There, maybe thirty yards away, was Maria Hallett, still laughing, her blonde hair loose in the breeze, and all alone. She was sitting on a large boulder with a pair of skates in her hand, and at that moment, Isaac realized that it had been Maria -- and not his imagination -- who had cried to the Lord and delivered him to the ice. He winced.

Whether it was the pain deep in his bones or the humiliation of the moment that hurt more, he could not be sure, but he knew that Maria Hallett was the last person in Eastham that he would have chosen to see on that rock at that particular moment. As every boy under eighteen was aware, she was the prettiest girl in the town, but Isaac sensed something else about her, a freshness born of impatience, a resistance to the daily tedium of being young that had brought her to the edge of this pond on a December morning to teach herself to slide on skates.

When they entered church on Sundays, he had regularly tried to direct his mother toward a pew from which he might see Maria across the room. He delighted at the way an angular shaft of light through a window could backlight her blonde hair and make it luminous, and he would have been happy just to look at her undetected, from some secret vantage point. But looking at her from his present angle on the ice, he could only imagine how he appeared to her.

"Isaac Doane, is that you, and what are you doing down there on that ice?"

Isaac reflected for a moment, ignored the question, and responded,

"I was testing the ice," he said, which was, in part, true, "and I found that it is hard enough to skate on. In fact, it is quite hard." He then paused to rub his aching right hip and slowly began to gather his knees beneath him to rise, taking special care not to slip and repeat his humiliation.

By now Maria was laughing again, and she said,

"If that is the case, and it is thick enough to hold the two of us, do you think we could skate together -- that is, if it won't be too painful for you? I am just a beginner, and I admired how well you were doing until your little accident. Perhaps we could hold each other up."

Pleased by the compliment and excited by the chance to be so close to her, Isaac nodded, smiling, and made his way to the rock where she had just finished tying on her skates.

"I would be happy to accompany you," he said, "but you really will need to be careful because the surface is very rough in places." At this, she extended her hand to him, and he took it. It was smooth and warm, and he realized this was the first time he had touched a girl.

As they were standing on the dark ice, a sharp report – an explosion as if from a musket – burst nearby and within seconds echoed in the brittle air. Maria visibly quivered and gasped, "Isaac, someone is shooting out here, and that was very close by. Do you know who it could be?"

Momentarily startled, Isaac then grinned at her and said, "We don't need to worry. As my father used to say, that's only the pond sounding off and warning us to be careful. Actually, as the ice on the pond freezes and contacts at this time of the year, and as pressures build up underneath, the ice does literally explode sometimes, and that is the sound we heard. My father was right, though; the pond is talking to us – he once told me that the sound reminded him of a whale's song -- and we will need to be careful."

Then they were out on the ice, her skates uncertain, her ankles skewed inward, while his were straight and firm. Still holding her hand and with his other arm around her waist, Isaac began to direct their course to the far end of the pond. Before long, and after her confidence had steadied, Maria suddenly pulled away, and with her arms outspread, she sang out, "I'm flying!" And at that instant, Isaac believed that she just might lift off the ice, soar into the sky, and perhaps vanish over the horizon, her bright green scarf trailing behind. But she remained earthbound, and when she returned to him and took his outstretched hand, she asked,

"What has brought you to this lonely pond, Isaac Doane?"

The pond was situated midway between their homes, three miles south of Isaac's cabin in Silver Springs and three miles north of the Freeman home in Eastham, where Maria was living; consequently, the two young people seldom met in their daily travels apart from seeing each other on Sundays in church or at socials.

"I am here for several reasons," Isaac answered. "I thought to try out my new skates on the ice to see how I could do on them alone. This place is special for me because my father taught me how to skate here, and this is my first visit back without him. And last, I have come here to cut out some blocks of ice for Mrs. Smith and take them back to her ice house. She and Mr. Smith have been very kind to me and my mother, and they pay me generously for some of the errands I do for them."

As they reached the far end of the pond, Maria turned her head and looked steadily at him:

"I am truly sorry for your loss, Isaac. You must have suffered a great deal during your father's illness, and I have thought of you often since his death."

For the moment Isaac was somewhere else -- back on this same pond with his father, his small feet wide apart, yet his body secure within the compass of his father's grasp -- learning how to skate. Now in another instant he was gliding next to this lovely girl with blonde hair and a bright green scarf who was telling him that she cared about him. He felt almost dizzy and as if he might fall down again. He quickly recovered, however, and answered:

"Thank you, it has been a hard time for my mother and me, and I have been wondering how we will make out with him gone. I plan to ask Mr. Smith for a job at the tavern on Great Island, but I fear that he may think me too young at fifteen to do a man's work. It is a rough crowd out there across the bay, but there is good money to be made, and the chance to be a whale man someday is exciting to me."

Maria pictured several images of Isaac in her mind's eye -- the shy boy whose eyes would often find her during Mr. Treat's sermons, the earnest young man sharing his past and his hopes for the future with her on this cold December afternoon, and the hopeful apprentice shouldering his way among the hard men at the tavern. She was fourteen, almost fifteen, but she had already begun to look across the years, and as she did so now with Isaac beside her, she felt a transitory gust of sadness pass through her. She wondered whether the years would lead him to the prow of a whale boat, and perhaps away from Eastham, and she questioned whether she would ever do more than care for others' children.

"Yes," she responded somewhat wistfully to him, "Would it not be wonderful to set sail out of Town Cove someday, to watch the church top disappear from view, and head down the wind and into the open sea?"

Isaac paused a moment and then said, "I am not so sure. Right now I'm just interested in getting a job with Mr. Smith and helping my mother make do. If I encounter some whales along the way, that will fill the days to come with plenty of excitement for me."

"You will make some young woman a good husband someday, Isaac," Maria replied, and then as she pulled away from him once again, she laughed, "Perhaps I will be the one!"

At that moment Isaac recognized a familiar sound but one that he had not heard in several years. It was a deep, aching moan, and he knew immediately that they had ventured into an unsafe cove of the pond where the ice was thinner and danger was imminent. He reached quickly for Maria's hand, but she was several feet away by now and had a vaguely quizzical look on her face. When the ice creaked gain, now more threateningly, her puzzlement turned to quiet fear, and she came to a complete stop, ceasing all motion. Standing on the firmer surface, but slowly edging toward her, Isaac said,

"Maria, remove your scarf carefully from your neck and gently swing one end toward me; then I will pull you over here to where the ice is thicker. While you are doing this, imagine that you are as light as a maple leaf."

Maria involuntarily laughed but did as Isaac had instructed and softly swung one end of the long green scarf in his direction. He grabbed it and began to pull her while backing up to where the ice was firmer. Neither said anything during this interval -- he pulling and she gently applying pressure to her skates -- but when they were satisfied that they were no longer in immediate danger and that the ice was firm beneath them, they exhaled in relief, the clouds created by their warm breath mingling together in the December air.

"I think I make a superior maple leaf, don't you, Isaac?" Maria exclaimed lightly.

"I'm just glad that you are safe and that I am not trying to rescue a wet maple leaf from the icy water right now," said Isaac as he slowly pumped his legs up and down on the ice to reassure himself once again that they were on a secure surface. They were.

Their adventure now ended, Isaac and Maria made for the boulder where they had met earlier, she to return to the children in her charge and he to begin cutting ice for the Smiths. As she removed her skates and tightened her scarf around her neck, Maria looked at Isaac, who now appeared to be a dark silhouette outlined by the pewter sky.

"Thank you for the skating lesson, Isaac Doane. Not only did you rescue me from great peril, but you saved me from spending an afternoon alone with my own thoughts. Thank you for sharing yours with me, and I hope to see you again before too long."

Isaac smiled at her, and bowing with a semblance of gallantry, said, "Perhaps before the bruises on my hip have disappeared. I too have enjoyed your company, Maria, and I will look forward especially to Reverend Treat's church service on Sunday. Please wish me luck with Mr. Smith."

"I do, Isaac."

With that she was off, as light as a bird, and the last he saw of her that day was a wisp of green against the whiteness of a birch tree in the darkening woods.

Chapter Four
The Apprentices
May, 1715

As happens so often on Cape Cod, spring took its time to arrive in 1715, and Isaac knew that once it had come, it would not stay long -- at most a month or perhaps only a week -- before the heat of summer set in. But it was here today, May fifteenth, and as Isaac lay in his bed, his hands clasped behind his head and his elbows splayed out, he contemplated the prospects of the day and the season with genuine anticipation. Two quail were conversing outside his open window, soft saffron light was suffusing the sky in the east, the air was warm against his face, and he had a job. Mr. Smith had promised to let him start working at the tavern when he turned fifteen years in May, the month when the whales began to move, and the day had finally arrived.

As these impressions sifted through his mind, others came, uninvited and more insistent: memories of his father's wasting body, the gathering desperation in his mother's eyes, his frustration with last year's failed crops, and the seemingly endless trail of gray days that had intervened between last year's losses and this sunlit May morning. As he had often done of late, he dismissed these images with a perceptible shake of his head and pictured himself once again skating across Great Pond with Maria on that December afternoon; since then he had spoken with her at church a number of times, but that day on the pond was set apart, illumined, in his memory. Then his mind turned again, the lovely recollections dissolved as he called himself to the day at hand, and he threw his legs over the side of his bed.

He moved quickly and quietly to prepare for his sail to the island, trying not to disturb his mother in the next room, and soon he was closing the cabin door before she could fuss over him and kiss him on the cheek. His grandparents had named her well,

Isaac reflected. Mercy: she had lavished her only child with love and grace for his fifteen years, but she had suffered greatly, through several miscarriages, the death of his sister, and now the loss of his father. God had been sparing in his mercies toward her, and Isaac had determined to act on the old proverb: to help himself and her, believing that God might then begin to do likewise and grant her the blessings she deserved.

****

Mr. Smith had given him direct instructions: to leave early, to pick up a passenger at James Neck, to report to Daniel Atwood at the tavern, and to be there an hour after sunrise. As he made his way toward the Bay Road well below his cabin, Isaac noticed that the wind was out of the southeast and that the sand along the shoreline was dark, indicating that the tide was going out. This meant he could slow his pace somewhat and enjoy the morning because the conditions were favorable for a short sail. Ineluctably, then, his eyes were drawn to his destination across Grampus Bay, the massive building high atop the bluff on Great Island. The two-story structure stood twenty feet high, not counting the steeple on top, and extended fifty feet along the rim of the cliff. Adjacent to the tavern rose the lookout tower used to locate pods of whales in Grampus Bay to the east or Barnstable Bay, later known as Cape Cod Bay, to the west. When he was a boy and the wind was out of the northwest, Isaac had believed that he could hear the thrilling cry of the sentinel calling him to action from three miles across the bay. Now, years later, he was answering the call.

Stopping briefly on the Bay Road to survey the landscape, Isaac stamped his feet hard on the ground to shake the early morning dew from his shoes. Below he saw a scattering of homes in Silver Springs and beyond that to the east, a larger cluster at Fresh Brook village. Isaac quickened his pace, and after walking two miles and crossing the rickety bridge over Blackfish Creek, he saw the small sloop that he and his father had sailed in so many times together. The blue boat was resting on the sand due to the receding tide, and Isaac moved quickly to pull it off the sand and walk it down the shallow creek; the air was cool so early in the morning, and the water frigid enough to numb his feet and legs. After raising the single sail, he was headed out of the mouth of the creek and west into Grampus Bay. As he approached the far side of James Neck, he jibed sharply to the north and soon after beached the boat on an empty expanse of sand below the high bank of the Neck. Mr. Smith had asked him to transport a young man from there out to the tavern, and Isaac was glad to oblige him, so he set the anchor in the beach and sat on the sand not expecting to be there long.

As he waited, Isaac watched a school of bluefish in the distance thrashing and snapping as they pursued fleeing mackerel. Above this turmoil he saw graceful gulls with crooked wings circling and plunging into the foaming chaos below, sometimes emerging with a baitfish and sometimes disappearing into the white water not to return. Further off he saw the oblong shape of a fisherman's dory steadily approaching and assuming its part in the gathering carnage. Isaac's stomach grumbled as he watched, and he reflected that all of nature must be hungry, that the mackerel, the bluefish, the gulls, the dorymen, and countless other creatures in the bay and the vast oceans beyond must be driven by the same moment-by-moment effort to keep their stomachs full. For a second time that morning Isaac felt grateful for his new job and recognized the need it filled.

Lost in these thoughts, Isaac started when he turned and discovered a young Indian boy about his age standing no more than ten feet behind him. The boy grinned tentatively at him, his dark eyes glistening, and asked,

"Are you Isaac Doane who is to take me to the tavern on the island?"

Isaac nodded. Although they were roughly the same age and had grown up within a few miles of each other, the boys had never met before. Isaac was aware that the township had recently granted the James Neck area to the Indians and that no white man would be allowed to settle there; but white people and Indians had a close daily relationship on the lower Cape, and he was particularly surprised that he had not seen this boy at one of Reverend Treat's Sunday services. In answer to the boy, Isaac said,

"I am Isaac, and we need to go quickly so we will not be late. Please help me push the boat off the sand and then jump in."

The Indian boy did as he was asked, and when they were underway, he said, "My name is Running Water, and I am the son of the sagamore, Kecan Jones. My father wants me to learn to hunt the great whales. He has arranged with Mr. Smith for me to work with Drifting Goose, who is a member of my tribe and who is in charge of the whale house on the island. I guess by seeing the insides of the whale and smelling it when it burns, I will learn the worst part of hunting him first." Then the boy grinned again. As an afterthought he added with pride, "My father tells me that Drifting Goose knows all there is to know about hunting whales."

Isaac also smiled. He had heard of Kecan Jones and his brother, Tuis, who were the leaders of the Pononakanet tribe, and he knew of their family's powerful influence in the area.

"I have heard Reverend Treat speak well of your family in his Sunday sermons," he said

"Yes, Reverend Treat comes to Tuttomnest often," responded Running Water. "He is a kind and good man, and he is the one who taught me your language."

"Where is Tuttomnest?" Isaac asked.

"Right over my shoulder, where we have just come from," Running Water laughed. "Your people call it James Neck, but to us it has always been Tuttomnest. My family and I have moved there from Great Island only recently because the trees are disappearing, and it has been harder and harder to survive there."

The two fell into a thoughtful silence contemplating the distances that separated them from each other and the rapidly diminishing distance between them and the island, both becoming aware of the great looming tavern that was rising above them. The building had surveyed both Grampus Bay and Barnstable Bay from the time Sam Smith's grandfather, also named Samuel, had built it twenty five years before. Now as they approached the island, Isaac pulled the tiller toward him and let out the sail so he could curl the boat into Smith's Cove, originally named for the prescient and wealthy grandfather. As he did so, the glimmering water in the cove and the eastern side of the island unfolded for both boys, and in the early morning sunlight, both shared the realization that they were turning a page in the story of their lives.

After securing the boat near several others on the beach, they stood for a moment looking for a path through the woods up to the tavern. Shortly, Running Water identified a freshly carved sign with Mr. Smith's name on it, and he gestured to Isaac that he had found the way. As they began walking the path together, they fell to talking, perhaps out of nervousness, anticipation, or even fear, and Isaac said, "I think my work may be less exciting than yours, Running Water. I will be helping Mr. Atwood in the tavern, and I don't know what to expect. I do know, though, that my mother and I can use the money."

Running Water nodded and answered, "I have never been in the tavern, but I have seen the tryworks many times, and I know it will be hard work. Drifting Goose has told me much about it, and when we lived here, I would listen carefully to the stories he would tell about chasing the great whale. Now he is the chief of the workers, and I will be working for him. I hope someday to ride the boats and throw the harpoon."

"I have had the same dream too," Isaac said.

As they were walking, Isaac noticed that they had passed through a copse of white oak and pine trees but that these soon gave way to stumps and a broad expanse of cleared ground surrounding the tavern; in fact, the top of the island was largely devoid of trees and undergrowth. He turned to look at Running Water, but the young Indian was already quickening his pace toward the tavern. At that moment Isaac paused to look at the building from this new angle. The structure had always seemed large to him from across the bay, but standing so near it only reinforced his impression of its massiveness. It had a second story, which made it the tallest building he had ever seen. Adding to its sinister effect was the fact that there was no entrance from this approach because the front door faced south toward the bays, and a spectral tower nearby rose fifty feet into the sky from the top of which the boys could see the back of a dark human figure.

As the boys neared the building, a great black dog turned the corner and came hurtling toward them, its lips laid back from its teeth, its yellow eyes sparking.

"Pilgrim," a voice rang out, "Avast and come here."

The boys, frozen in place, watched as the dog suddenly stopped and a large man with one eye appeared a moment later. More than the dog's bared teeth, the man's single eye commanded their gaze. It protruded from its socket, orbicular and brilliantly blue, and was arresting not so much in itself but by contrast with its mate. In the other socket was the semblance of an eyeball, a dark unmoored object that moved randomly and independent of the man's will. It had long since lost any purpose or luster, and the man had not chosen to conceal its meanderings behind a decorative patch. His good eye quickly encompassed them, held them still, and he said,

"You need not be afraid of Pilgrim, boys. He treats all strangers alike -- scares the hell out of 'em, sometimes knocks them over, but then licks 'em on the face. I inherited him from an old mate of mine from Martha's Vineyard, and he helps me keep order around this place."

With this greeting, he approached them, his hand held out, and said, "You must be the boys Sam told me about. I am Daniel Atwood, and I run this operation. Mr. Smith is the owner, I am the captain, and you two will be members of the crew." In the early days of the eighteenth century, innkeepers often came from highly respected families, and although Daniel Atwood could lay no claim to social rank, he did enjoy the regard and affection of those he served at the tavern. Not only was he an unofficial sheriff of Great Island, but he was a magistrate, a justice of the peace, a go-between for business transactions, a source of local news, and a trusted commentator on that information. In fact, so central were taverns and those who ran them to their communities that almanacs of the time provided distances from tavern to tavern instead of town to town. Atwood's stable eye saw the world very clearly, and others trusted his vision.

After the boys had shaken his outstretched hand and introduced themselves, Atwood said, "Running Water, you will be working down the hill at the tryworks, but I will show you and Isaac around the tavern first because you both will be spending a lot of time here."

When Atwood threw the tavern door open, the boys stepped across the threshold into the shadows of a cavernous room. The interior was dark, and the early morning light played eerily along its surfaces. When Isaac inhaled, he became keenly aware of birch wood smoldering in the massive fireplace, of sooty, smoke-stained walls, of wide pine floors exuding spilled ale, of cod fish served the night before, of the lingering, humid weight of stale pipe smoke and human sweat. Taken separately, these impressions might have been repellent, but combined, they made a sweet aroma that Isaac would relish for the rest of his life.

The large room was, in fact, divided in the middle by an imposing double-sided fireplace and chimney, creating an area for drinking and talking on the left side and on the right a place to eat. The interior walls were plastered, an effect neither Isaac nor Running Water had seen before, and the windows were the shape of diamonds, not rectangles as was common at the time. The furniture was rudimentary and heavy, with tables of various sizes and shapes on the eating side and a long bench with smaller tables on the drinking side. At the far end of each area was a side door with an entrance to separate storage cellars, but on the bar side was a stairway leading to sleeping quarters above.

As his eyes strayed in that direction, Isaac saw a young woman tucking in a wayward wisp of hair as she descended the stairs. Noticing his glance, Atwood said, "For the time being, the stairs are out of bounds for you two. Isaac, you will need to keep your thoughts on your work down here." The only other people in the room were two older Indian women, who were sweeping the floor and placing the ceramic mugs and stemmed glasses on the long bench to dry after they had been washed. Each looked up from her work, smiled briefly, and quickly returned to what she was doing. After nodding hello to the women, Atwood turned to Isaac and said, "You will usually be working outside during the day, sometimes with Running Water, but when things get busier at night, you will be carrying meals and drinks to our patrons." Then he said with a grin, "Just be sure to navigate clear of them when they get too rowdy."

As they emerged from the tavern, Atwood shouted to the shape in the tower, "William, do you see any of 'em moving out there?" to which a young man responded, "Not yet, Mr. Atwood, but it's still early in the morning." Atwood then said to the boys, "Before too long, you two may be up there spotting whales for us. In the meantime, we'll visit the whale house down below. Follow me, and be sure not to fall." Atwood then walked to a rugosa bush, turned toward them with a grin, and disappeared. They quickly followed and peered over the cliff, where they saw a rope ladder snaking down the precipice and leading to the beach at the bottom. Running Water quickly obeyed, but Isaac paused a moment to get his bearings.

Down the shoreline to the left he believed he could make out his home at Silver Springs, and across the bay to the right he could make out Billingsgate Island where he was interested to see men working on a large structure at the island's tip. On the beach below, he could discern several campsites where seasonal whaling crews stayed and the whale house, which was little more than an elevated roof with open walls. His curiosity aroused, he began his descent to the beach for a closer inspection. About half way down the cliff, however, Isaac felt his throat contract and his stomach convulse simultaneously, and he almost let go of the ladder. The heated stench rising from the huge vat in the house engulfed him, made his eyes sting, and stiffened the hairs in his nostrils. He thought of those directly below him and doubled his effort not to fall and not to be sick. By concentrating and dropping as swiftly and surely as possible, he reached the bottom and quickly sprinted behind a large bush so as not to embarrass himself. When he had composed himself and returned to his two companions, Daniel Atwood regarded Isaac seriously and said, "Lost your sea legs, did you, Isaac? I am sorry I did not warn you about the smell, but now you have found out, haven't you? You will get used to it, I promise."

The source of Isaac's misery emanated from a large cauldron mounted above a high, licking fire. Standing on a platform, a thickly muscled Indian and a bearded white man were sliding "Bible leaves," thinly sliced slabs of whale blubber, into the cauldron where they popped, sizzled, and gave up their oil. When the oil was thoroughly rendered from the slabs, the shriveled remainder was thrown into the blaze to maintain the fire. Nearby, another man was preparing to toss a log onto the blaze from one of the immense piles of wood that had been cut from the steadily diminishing island forest.

His skin gleaming in the heat and the early morning light, one of the crew approached and said, "Morning, Daniel. I see you have brought Running Water and a friend."

"Yes," said Atwood, "his friend is Isaac, and they are ready to work for us."

"Well, if they had come a week or two later, they would not have found us here. The whales have been leaving us, and we will soon be moving this house and the camps over there," he said, pointing to Great Beech Hill, the island where Isaac had noticed activity earlier. Drifting Goose continued,

"Very few whales wash onto our shores anymore, so we have to go out after them in long boats. Some brave spirits have even hunted them in the open ocean. As you can see, the hunt is swiftly changing, almost as fast as the tides do, and we have to change with it."

Shifting his tone, Drifting Goose looked at Running Water and said, "And now we must find some work for this young man. He will be chopping and splitting wood today because the fire always needs to be fed, and I know he can handle an ax." Running Water's eyes indicated his pleasure at the compliment, and he stepped next to Drifting Goose.

The introductions finished, Atwood turned to Isaac and said, "You can help by taking the hand cart and collecting some of the wood Running Water cuts. Then you can bring it to the tavern because our fireplace eats a lot of wood itself. The four soon concluded their planning, and after that Isaac's day passed quickly. He gathered and piled wood, ran errands, cleaned the grounds, and set tables for the evening to come.

As the afternoon wore on and the spent sun settled in the west, the lanterns were lit. Isaac paused while gathering kindling and watched as small boats from across the bay began to make their way to the island. These dories, sloops, and skiffs each held two or more people, men and women alike, all drawn to the flickering lights of the tavern on the bluff, all seeking the lightest of human pleasures, escape and a good time.

Isaac's reverie dissolved when he heard Atwood's voice calling to him from the tavern porch. He quickly returned, and Atwood said, "Now your education begins, Isaac. I want you to help Michael by serving the meals tonight, but you will also need to help me at times on the bar side, so you will be a busy young man tonight."

Michael Baker, the tavern's cook, was a survivor. Orphaned as a child, he had gone to sea as a boy and had served with Atwood on a British Man-of-War as a gunnery mate for twenty years. When he later washed ashore on this new continent, he became a cook in Boston where he mastered the art of cooking porridge, goose, wild turkey, and all manner of seafood, including eels with fennel, cod, and lobster, of which twenty-five pounders were common at the time. Deeply cratered, his face bore silent witness to the ravages of small pox, and perhaps as a result of these struggles, he spoke infrequently if at all. Some mistook his quietness for dullness, but he was far from stupid; he had merely translated his sufferings into the language of gesture and implication. So, when Atwood introduced him to Isaac, Michael Baker had simply held out his hand and nodded.

As Isaac soon learned, the two primary rooms of the tavern were defined by those who served in them: the eating area was more subdued according to Baker's terseness, and the drinking area was more raucous according to Atwood's generous spirit as he dispensed drinks from behind the bar. On the wall behind Atwood were bottles arranged in an order apparent only to him: bottles with such common and exotic names as Rum, Cherry Rum, Madeira, Grog, Tod, Rumboozle, Kill-Divil, Switchel, Peachy, Ebulum, Mumm, Sillabub, Stonewall, Calibogus, Blackstrap, Brandy-Sling, and Whistle-belly Vengeance among others.

However, Flip was the house specialty and would remain popular throughout New England for 150 years. This concoction was made of home brewed beer, sweetened with sugar molasses or dried pumpkin, and rendered potent with rum; it was then stirred in a great mug with a red-hot loggerhead or a flip dog which made the liquor foam and gave it a burnt and bitter taste. Atwood's special variation on this favorite was to blend four pounds of sugar, four eggs, and one pint of cream and let it stand for two days. When a mug of flip was ordered, he would fill a quart mug two-thirds full of beer, place in it four large spoonfuls of the mixture and then thrust in the blistering loggerhead while adding a gill of rum to the creamy confection. If a fresh egg were beaten into the flip, the result was called "bellows-top" for the foamy froth that rose over the rim of the mug.

Perhaps the strongest potion of all, though, was the Whistle-Belly Vengeance, made from sour beer simmered in a kettle, sweetened with molasses, filled with brown bread crumbs, and swallowed piping hot. Such were the tastes of those who enjoyed the hospitality of Daniel Atwood at Smith's Tavern.

****

Dusk had turned to darkness, and Isaac was weary. He had watched the tavern steadily fill with men and women, Indians, whalers, and local farmers as well as pipe smoke, the smell of cooking goose, the heat of human bodies, and the sound of rising voices. At nine o'clock Drifting Goose entered the tavern with a large hour glass and planted it conspicuously on the bar; several of his crew were present and nodded knowingly to each other as he quietly withdrew and the sand began to sift down.

By that time Isaac had been serving meals and drinks for several hours when the tavern door flew open, and a large man entered. Something about the man's presence arrested the company's attention. Perhaps it was his massive girth, which was encircled by a sash with a silver buckle that secured his trousers, or maybe it was his arrogant manner signified by a scented gentleman's wig and an elaborately curled beard, but whatever the reason, conversations ceased as this stranger strode toward Daniel Atwood's bar. When he neared the bar, the stranger said,

"Barkeep, may I inquire as to the cost of a meal in this establishment?"

Atwood, who had been washing out a tankard, eyed him over, paused, and then said, "You certainly may, sir, but you will have to wait a moment." Then, reaching beneath the bar he produced a cloth tape measure and emerged from around the bar. With his large eye sparkling and the other one rolling, Atwood extended the tape around the man's waist as an exacting tailor might and said, "For you, sir, for a man of your magnitude and volume, the cost will be four pounds!"

Silence cloaked the room as the large man's eyes flickered and he drew himself up to his full height. Then in a low, resonant voice that everyone in the room could hear, he said, "Daniel, men have died for less than that, as you well know..."

"Of course, I do, Bart, but you have put on a few pounds since I saw you last, and I am only a lowly innkeeper now and no longer one of your mates in the King's service."

"Indeed, you are not, but you are just as much a rogue as you ever were," the stranger said slowly beginning to laugh and clasping his old friend to him. "Nor do I serve the King anymore, and, in fact, I have taken up with a different sort nowadays, but I will speak to you of that in private. For now all I want is a good meal, a good tankard of flip, and a bed to sleep on, and I will not pay more than six pence for your goose nor a penny for your best flip".

Turning suddenly toward Isaac, Atwood said, "Isaac, tell Michael to serve up his best goose for my old friend here, and bring it as soon as it is ready."

Little did Isaac know that evening that he was serving roasted goose and flip to Bartholomew Roberts, a man in his early-thirties who would become one of the most notorious and dangerous pirates along the coasts of the Atlantic Ocean; nor did he know that Roberts had come to recruit Atwood to join him in his escapades and that Atwood would refuse. Little did Isaac know that another adventurer with similar designs would soon enter the tavern but that this second figure would alter the course of his life completely. Nor was Isaac aware that some of the young women climbing the stairs with men they had met that night would not be returning to the mainland until morning. And little did Isaac know when Drifting Goose returned to retrieve his hour-glass that his first day of employment was done. As Drifting Goose picked up the glass, he turned to his men and said, "We work early tomorrow. Follow me," and with that his men rose and followed him -- albeit reluctantly -- out the door.

Atwood then turned to Isaac and said, "Isaac, your day is done too. You need not concern yourself with Running Water tonight because he will be staying at the camp down on the beach. You have worked hard and well today, and you can come in a little later tomorrow, but no later than mid-morning." Patting the boy on the shoulder, Atwood added, "It will be dark on your journey home tonight, so be sure to mount this light on the bow of your skiff." He then handed Isaac a small lantern, which he gratefully accepted.

As Isaac approached his sloop on the beach, he stopped for a few moments to watch the glinting lights of departing boats bobbing on the bay. Just hours before, they had had this tavern, this well-lit place, as their destination, and now they were dispersing like moths into night air that seemed to swallow them. Isaac continued to watch as these lights became indistinguishable from the glistening reflection of stars on the water. Then he placed the lantern in the bow, set his course for home, and became another of the flickering lights in the darkness.

Chapter Five
Tuck-a-Nuck
June, 1715

Isaac loved what the June sunlight did to the left side of Maria Hallett's face. From his position in the third pew behind the Freeman family pew, he could see the curve of her jaw, the gentle slope of her shoulder, and an occasional wisp of blonde hair below her cap, all bathed in the light that filtered through the long window at the side of the church. In the distance he could make out Reverend Treat's voice warning that his soul was caught in a spider's web, that it was suspended over a pit of eternal flames, that it was encrusted with vanity. He could not be exactly sure, however, because his eyes kept returning to Maria's delicate features, and his mind was in no condition to accept, or even entertain, the notion of eternal damnation. Isaac had often wondered how the good minister could be so stern and rigid every Sunday and so affable and sociable on the other days of the week. From the pulpit his trumpet voice was backed by the steel of conviction, yet in the village it was gentler and often punctuated with peals of laughter. But this morning Isaac could barely discern the man's voice -- so delighted was he by the play of light over Maria's face.

Isaac had a plan today that he intended to put into action. Ever since he had encountered Maria on that December afternoon when they had skated together, he had wanted to be with her again, but they lived six miles apart, and their paths seldom crossed except on Sundays. But on this June day he was going to ask her to join him for a picnic on their first day off. Because his mother would be visiting relatives in Chatham for a few days, he was free, and he planned to take advantage of the fact. Mr. Treat's insistent words, which had seemed so far away, finally stopped, the final hymn ended, and the congregation began to file out down the center aisle of the church. Isaac caught Maria's eye as she walked by him, and her lips quickly curled into a smile. As soon as he could, he fell in behind her and kept his eyes trained on the blonde tresses swaying ahead of him.

After exchanging a few words with Mr. Treat, then stepping down the front steps of the church and surveying the crowd that had gathered on this brilliant June morning, Isaac recognized most of the congregation, including Sam Smith, his new friend, Running Water who was standing with an older man Isaac took to be his father, and Mrs. Freeman holding her baby. But no Maria. At the moment he began to believe she had vanished, he saw her with her back turned to him laughing with another working girl from the town. When this girl saw Isaac coming toward them, she seemed to melt away, and as he came closer, Maria turned to him with a half-smile on her face and, seemingly surprised, said, "Why, Isaac Doane, I was just thinking of you. I'm very glad to see you."

Having planned this encounter for the last week, Isaac felt his determination momentarily waver, and he briefly imagined that serving flip to a drunken whaler would be preferable to having to utter the next sentence. But he forged ahead.

"I have been watching you in church, Maria..."

He paused, reconsidered his words, took a nervous breath, and started over again,

"Maria. I was wondering if you would like to sail to Great Beach Island and have a tuck-a-nuck with me there next Sunday after the service." Having committed himself, he quickly continued, "A lot has happened since we last talked and since I started working at the tavern, and I thought you might like to get away from your work for a little time."

Maria's eyes shone, and she said, "Yes, I would like that very much, Isaac. I am glad you asked me. In fact, I am surprised it took you so long," she said with a smile. Throughout the long winter, Maria had felt like a butterfly in a jar, a listless sail awaiting a breeze. She was restless and impatient for her life to assume some form apart from tending to her aunt's children; and so when Isaac approached her with his offer to go on a tuck-a-nuck, she was both charmed and excited. She had thought of Isaac often since they had skated together, and she had often been aware of his eyes lingering upon her face in church. Somehow the distances that separated them -- the pews in church, the miles between their homes, the duties that filled up their days -- seemed to make him more attractive to her. He was unlike other boys because ever since that December morning on the pond, he had maintained a distance from her, as if he were afraid of saying the wrong thing to her, and that reticence only made him more appealing to her.

"But I don't think I can go with you even though Sunday is my day off from the children," she continued. "I can already hear my Aunt Elizabeth, telling me that going to an island by myself with a boy is not only shocking but an impossibility."

Having conquered his early nervousness, Isaac quickly said, "But we have already skated by ourselves, and nothing bad happened to you. In fact, I even saved you from trouble. Don't you remember, Maria?"

"Of course I do," she said, "but I never told Elizabeth of our meeting then, and even if I had, she would never approve of my sailing to the island with you."

"Then don't tell her."

Maria paused for several full seconds after Isaac said this, and she looked at him directly in the eye. Then she glanced around her and saw Elizabeth Freeman impatiently gesturing to her from a distance, indicating that the family was preparing to leave the churchyard and that Maria should hurry. Nodding to her, Maria turned to Isaac and said impulsively, in almost a whisper, "Yes, Isaac, I will go with you to the island. Where shall we meet and when?"

Almost instinctively, Isaac glanced over his shoulder toward the Freemans and their girls; then he turned back to her and said, "By Blackfish Creek. I have a little sloop moored there, and the place is easy to find. Make some excuse to the family, and I will bring all the food we will need. I will meet you an hour after next Sunday's service." Maria lightly and imperceptibly touched his sleeve as she stepped around him and went to catch up with her family. But once she had joined them, she called out gaily and yet conspiratorially, "I will see you next week, Isaac!"

****

Until the next Sunday, the days went by slowly, but the week

41

passed quickly. As Isaac watched a gull circle lazily over Duck Creek with a quahog in its clutches, he wondered if Maria had been able to find some way to free herself from the Freemans and come to him. When he had seen her at the church earlier in the day, she had given little indication that she recognized him; she had never looked in his direction, and following the service, she had not lingered behind with the Freemans in the churchyard but had disappeared without a word.

Lost in these thoughts and with his hopes for the afternoon beginning to fade, Isaac heard a horse's hooves clip-clopping on a path nearby. His first inclination was to conceal himself behind a nearby forsythia bush, but, instead, he simply turned and waited to see who was approaching. There, mounted on a large mare was Maria, dressed in white, her hair falling loose about her shoulders, and her face and neck glistening with perspiration. For a passing instant he imagined she was a queen. From her position high in the saddle, Maria peered down to see Isaac, disconcerted but his eyes bright, struggling to find his feet and stand up. She laughed at this and said, "I guess I am a sinner on the sabbath, Isaac. I told my aunt that I needed Brown Tail here to see Mercy Goodall, the friend you saw me talking with last week. I also told her that we would be away until dark. Mercy is aware of my little plan, and I trust that the Lord will forgive my telling an untruth."

"I hope so too, Maria," Isaac said, reaching up to help her down from the horse. As he lifted her down, he was surprised at how slender and light she was, and he was excited to be so close to her -- closer than he had ever been to a girl. Hurrying to get past the moment, Isaac then said, "I've got the boat all ready, and I thought we could sail out to Great Beach Island."

"Oh, Isaac, "she said with feigned disappointment, "I thought we might go to Provincetown, or maybe Boston across the bay, or even to England, just across the sea." Then upon seeing the basket Isaac had prepared with a neatly wrapped lunch in it, she said, "But then again, Great Beach Island will be very nice, and the day is so lovely."

In fact, it was. The sun was directly overhead, the breeze was out of the southwest, and the temperature was warm for the early days of summer. After they had clambered into the sloop, Isaac set a direct course for the island, keeping his sail close-hauled to the wind. In the distance, they could make out a few other boats -- none of them working crafts, because it was Sunday -- and they were both exhilarated by the freedom and intimacy occasioned by their being alone together in a small boat under the overarching blue sky. As they neared the island, they turned to each other and smiled, aware that they were doing something only they knew about, that others might disapprove of, but that each of them wanted to do. In a strange way they felt they were approaching unmapped land, yet all they were doing was going on a tuck-a-nuck together.

As he turned the skiff into the wind and the boom came trimly about, Isaac momentarily felt in control of events: he was with a beautiful girl on a sun-dappled day nearing a solitary beach on a remote island, and her radiant smile was matched only by his own. His reverie dissolved as quickly as it had crystallized, though, when he discerned a vague figure becoming more distinct each moment and waving to him from the beach.

It was Running Water. Isaac's smile froze, and his first impulse was to continue pressing on the tiller, to bring the sail off and run before the wind right out of the cove. His friend had identified the shape and color of the blue boat from afar, and by the time Isaac had brought it into the wind and the boat had begun to slow, Running Water was up to his knees in the shallows preparing to help him secure the anchor while crying. "Isaac, my friend, let me help you!" As Isaac's hopes for an afternoon alone with Maria vanished, he could not tell what she was thinking or feeling. For her part, when she saw the strange Indian boy wading toward them, her eyes sparkled, and as she turned to Isaac, she asked, "Is he a friend of yours?" When he nodded, she instinctively rose, touched his knee and laughed, "Well, Isaac, our little tuck-a-nuck has become a party, hasn't it!"

Disconcerted, Isaac shifted his weight suddenly in the stern, and as he did so, his knee inadvertently pushed the tiller too far away from himself, causing the boom to slue savagely around and hit Maria hard in the lower back. Before Isaac could reach out to grab her, she had plunged into the shallows head first. Without thinking, Isaac let go of the tiller and mainsheet and dove into the water, yelling,

"I'll save you, Maria!" Before he could reach her, however, Running Water had sliced into the lapping wavelets and was the first to reach the girl in the waist-deep water. The instant before she had entered the water, Maria had instinctively taken a great breath. When she reemerged, eyes momentarily glazed, arms helplessly outstretched, and still holding her breath, she resembled an infant making its first acquaintance with the world at the moment of birth – shocked, swollen, on the verge of screaming. Then, realizing she was now safely cradled in Running Water's arms, she exploded into laughter and said, "This water is freezing. Get me out of here!" With a wide grin and a firm hold on her arm, Running Water helped Maria to her feet and began to lead her as quickly as he could to the shore.

As he stood in the numbing water, inhaling deeply, Isaac realized not only that he had failed to rescue Maria but that he now needed to rescue the skiff before it drifted too far away on the ebbing tide. At once he made a long shallow dive toward the boat, so filled with stinging anger at his own clumsiness that he did not feel the bite of the chilling water. Then, after grabbing the bow line, which was trailing in the water, he redirected the skiff toward land, pulled violently on the line and began to wade slowly to shore, the boat bouncing behind him like an untrained puppy on a leash.

Minutes later the three young people were settled together on the beach, Maria drying her hair with a towel Isaac had brought her from the boat, her cold skin drinking in the warm June air. Running Water, beads of seawater still glistening on his shoulders like crystals, was looking at Maria as if she were some kind of mermaid. And Isaac was finishing laying out the provisions for their lunch, apologetic, resentful, sullen as a frozen pond. Then with an odd, quick glance at the two boys, Maria said to Running Water,

"Well, while we're waiting to dry off, and since I haven't met you before you saved me a few minutes ago, why don't you tell me about yourself and your family, and I will do the same." Then, dropping her eyes, she murmured softly, "Isaac, my friend, I know your story, but maybe Running Water would like to hear some of it."

Responding to her kind tone, Isaac's skin prickled, his lips curled into a smile, and he said, "Yes, I like your idea, Maria. Let's have Running Water start first."

Before he began, the Indian boy paused reflectively, gazing for a few moments down the beach at the bow of a small schooner just rounding the bend from Smith's cove.

"Do you see that schooner coming out of the cove, Isaac? Drifting Goose is on that schooner. He is finishing the job of moving the tryworks from Great Island to Billingsgate Island south of where we are now. Whalers have reported more whale sightings off that island, and the new location will make the whole business easier. Once the new tryworks are done, I will no longer be traveling with you but, instead, will be taking a packet straight from James Neck to Billingsgate Island. Drifting Goose has promised me that in a few months, I will be out on the bay learning how to harpoon the whales. But that will mean we will not see each other very often."

When Running Water paused, Isaac broke in, "But I am sure I will be ferrying customers back and forth between the tavern and the island and you will be among them. We will still remain friends."

"Yes, I hope so," said Running Water as he assembled his thoughts, "But my people are facing so many changes." Then looking up toward Smith's Tavern, which loomed above them on the high bluff, Running Water said, "You see Great Island there, do you not?" When Maria and Isaac both nodded, he said, "I was born on Great Island, yet except for the tavern and a few sheep, it has become like an old man's head – bald. The trees are almost all gone and the planting soil is blowing away. Because of this my tribe now lives on James Neck, as you know, but our numbers are growing smaller, and my mother wonders how long we will be able to stay there. In the last weeks many lots were granted to settlers, and that is just another reason the tryworks and my tribe are moving."

Then, sitting up straighter, Running Water said, "My father's name is Slow Turtle, and he is the sachem of the Pononakanet tribe; he is also known by the English name Kecan Jones. You probably know that the sachem is the leader of the tribe, but to my people a sachem is a small bird with princelike courage and command over greater, larger birds. That is my father. My mother is named Yellow Butterfly; she is as light as the air, but she is a strong woman, and she has seen her family through many illnesses. My mother was from the Nauset tribe, and her people were the first to meet the English near these shores almost one hundred years ago. At that time they were slicing the blubber of a whale, just as I did yesterday!" As he said this, Running Water smiled and looked once again at the schooner that by now had come into full view almost half a mile away.

The schooner seemed to be suspended on the water, a few wispy clouds framing it as it moved toward Billingsgate, and after a short silence, Maria mused, "My father was a landowner and farmer in Yarmouthport, and he died several years ago. He was a wealthy man, but I cannot say that I knew him..." Isaac looked quickly at Maria, wondering whether her eyes were perhaps glistening, so subdued was the tone of her voice and manner. Up to this moment she had simply been a beautiful, young apparition who had come to work for the Freemans two years before, already complete unto herself, an incarnation. He had not conceived of her having parents.

After pausing, Maria continued, "My father and my mother lived in Yarmouthport, but they did not live together, and when I was born in 1700, my mother named me Maria – after her mother." At the thought Maria smiled almost to herself, took a deep breath of the perfumed summer air, and continued, "My father was quite successful, people have said, and my mother was poor. I lived with her when I was a child, and she told me many stories about him. But I seldom saw him. Then three and a half years ago my father died, and he left my mother with no money or land for that matter. The day we heard the news was the saddest day of my life because Mama took it so hard. She began to take walks late at night on the beach in the weeks after his death. She was such a delicate and pretty person, and she would return to tell me that she thought she had heard my father's voice calling to her across the open water. Then her walks became longer; she would walk out into the dark and return to me in the early morning, every time telling me how my father had called to her. Finally one day she did not come back, and after a search one of the town constables found her dead on the beach. He told me that the waves were lapping around her lovely oval face as she lay in the sand...." Here Maria stopped and then added, "and there were large rocks in the pockets of her coat."

A silence followed, and then Maria concluded by asking something she had often wondered during the last two years, "Who knows what sorrows she had stored up in her heart? Nevertheless," she went on, "I would never choose to die the way she did." Then, smiling through watery eyes and diffidently shrugging her shoulders, she said, "Well, I've told you almost all of my short life. Soon after my mother's death I arranged to come here to work for my aunt, Mrs. Freeman. I have taken care of her children for the last two years, and just after I started, a brave young man saved me from drowning while I was skating on a not-so-frozen pond not very far from here. That's all there is to tell..." As she said this, she looked at Isaac out of the corner of her eye, nodded her head, and challenged him in a gently humorous way, "So now it's your turn, Isaac."

Isaac grinned at her, his earlier anger with himself having evaporated and his good spirits returning as he listened to the stories of his friends. By now the schooner had reached Billingsgate Island, and, trying to lift Maria's spirits, he said, "I have an idea: first, I'll tell you about my very humble life and then let's take a sail down to the new tryworks to see how they are coming along. But this time I promise to take better care of Maria." The other two laughed, and after they agreed, Isaac began.

"I'll start with the worst thing that has ever happened to me. As Maria knows, my father died about a year and a half ago; and ever since then, my mother and I have been struggling to make all we can of our small farm. What made it so hard was that he came in from the fields one day, lay down on his bed, and never rose from it again. We nursed him for some time, but it was no use and he died on the day after Christmas in 1713. It has been a lonely life for the two of us, but it has been more lonely for my mother since I took the job at the tavern up there on the bluff. My job has made a difference, however, and thanks to Mr. Smith, we are getting along. Happily, I enjoy working with Daniel Atwood, and I like the excitement of the place. Maybe someday I will even run the tavern."

At this Maria perceptibly quivered and asked, "Isaac, have you no wish to get away from this desolate place, maybe to go out on the sea as Running Water will, or to travel to a city, even one as close as Boston? I would love to do those things and more."

For an instant Isaac was taken aback by Maria's outburst, and then replied, "I really don't know how to answer you, Maria. My duties at the farm and tavern leave me little time to think of such things, but I suppose that in fifty years I will still be sailing my skiff on this bay just as I have today."

When Isaac said this, Running Water broke in and said, "My tribe has lived here for generations, but I doubt if I or my family will still be here at all in fifty years. My mother says our people are like the sand on the beach -- continually moving and shifting -- and I wonder if that is nature's plan for us." Then, changing his mood and grinning brightly, he said, "However, I am happy that I am here on this beach with two new friends today, and I want to teach you something that my father taught me when I was a little boy."

The young Indian then rose from the sand, withdrew a knife from the sash around his waist, and walking back to firmer ground, he began to dig a hole about one foot wide and one to two feet deep. When he finished, he turned to look at Isaac and Maria, who had been watching him intently as he dug, and said, "I have just created a memory hole. My people believe that when an important event has taken place, a member of the tribe should make a hole at the site of the happening so that others coming after will know that history was made in this place. Today I have made this memory hole to mark the friendship of three young people, all born in the same year, and, who knows, maybe we will still find it here and celebrate this day fifty years from now!"

Delighted, Maria turned to Isaac and said, "And now you must keep your promise, Isaac. Let's sail around Billingsgate Island for the rest of our afternoon, but I warn you, now that I have dried out, I will hope to remain so!"

Within minutes the three of them had rounded the point, tacking south down Grampus Bay, and before long were admiring the new tryworks and wharf that had been constructed on Billingsgate Island. The large pots were already visible and in place, which prompted Running Water to muse, "Before long I will be tending to those pots, cutting the blankets of whale into horse pieces and then into Bible leaves before we load the meat into the pots "Then he paused and smiled, "You see I have already learned the language of the trade. But you would never believe how hot it gets standing next to those pots..."

"My bet is that you'll soon be harpooning live ones out in the bay," Isaac quickly responded.

As he continued to look at the island, Running Water said, "My grandfather tells me that the island used to be higher and larger than it is now. There are thirty people living there now, though, and it is becoming a sand dune he tells me."

"Maybe someday it will vanish," Maria suggested, to which the boys shrugged their shoulders. Then, her voice tremulous with delight and surprise, she cried out, "But there is something that won't vanish! Look out there!"

As the boys turned to see what she was pointing to in the bay, they were stunned. Although both had seen many whales before, there no more than two hundred yards away, beyond the western shore of the island, were a mother and her calf rolling and playing in the afternoon sunlight.

"Those are sulfur bottoms," Running Water exhaled excitedly. "Some call them blue whales; they are the largest creatures in the sea, and they can swim as fast as a man can run. I have only seen one once before..."

As he was talking, the whales had submerged, but then, only moments later, they detonated from the water, twisting and arching as they did so, their great forms transforming the water on their bodies into shimmering tinsel that hung for several instants in the warm, equinoctial air. The creatures' blue-gray color blended almost soothingly against the background of the bay's blue water, but their sheer size – the mother was almost eighty feet long and weighed one hundred tons -- and the violence of their play silenced their audience. Then, seemingly heedlessly, the whales began to swim toward the sloop, their massive heads growing ever larger as they approached.

"Will they hit us?" Maria shouted.

"It's quite shallow in here," Running Water cried out almost simultaneously, "Maybe they're beaching themselves!"

Then when they were no further than fifty yards away and as if to demonstrate their indifference to the three friends, the two creatures gradually shifted direction toward the open water, and flaunting their immensity in one last silvery bridge of a leap, they disappeared into the welcoming depths of the bay.

After bearing witness to this display, the three young people giddily looked at each other and then laughed aloud as one.

"For a minute I thought they were coming at us to jump into the boat."

"And we don't even have a harpoon!"

"Have you ever seen creatures so large?"

"Maybe because we were here, we saved them from beaching themselves!"

"As long as I live, I'll never forget those two."

"And someday, Running Water, you'll be hunting them…"

Isaac's last statement shifted their attention from wondering admiration of the whales to a sharpened sense of each other, and the three of them fell silent for several moments. Then, looking steadily at her two companions, Maria asked, "Would it not be wonderful to be as free as those two were? Somehow they seemed so lonely, just the two of them out there, but they were also so liberated – yes, even happy -- and we were able to see them!"

Isaac returned her gaze and asked, "Weren't you even a little afraid when they started toward us. Maria?"

"No, I can truly say that I was not," Maria replied. "What would we have lost except our lives," she added with a laugh, "and can you imagine the stories Mr. Treat would have told of us? We would have been as well known in these parts as Jonah." Little could Maria have known that years later, after fate had twisted and defamed her, that sailors would tell tales of Goody Hallett, the witch of Eastham living with Lucifer in the belly of the "Whistling Whale" and wreaking vengeance on any seaman who might venture too close to the shores of the outer Cape.

Completely enchanted by her, Isaac grinned and said, "Well, I guess we have missed our chance at fame, haven't we, so we should be heading home because people will be wondering what has become of us." As he said this, Isaac pushed the tiller away from himself and swung the bow of the boat back towards Blackfish Creek.

During this exchange Running Water had been far away in his own thoughts and had heard only fragments of his friends' conversation. Then, as the sloop came off the wind and the landscape momentarily swirled and blurred in front of him, he turned to Maria and asked,

"Do you really think that those whales will not vanish, Maria, and, Isaac, do you think that I will be the one to hunt them? I am quite sure one of you is right, but if the lives of my people provide a lesson for the future, one of you is very mistaken." He said no more, and his words hung in the air for several minutes, uncontested and unquestioned.

Then, as they rounded Lieutenant Island and headed directly toward James Neck and the angular teepees that dotted it, Isaac broke the silence, "How free, really, are any of us," he said pensively, "the two of you, me, even the whales out there in the bay? We all do what we have to do, learn what we learn along the way, and we are as tied down as a harpoon is by the rope that connects it to a whaleboat." Then he paused, smiled almost apologetically, and said, "Forgive me, I'm sounding like my father used to."

"Or my father," Running Water laughed, "who I can see walking there on the beach...."

Within minutes Running Water was standing on the beach with his father, waving farewell to Isaac and Maria as they made their way back to Blackfish Creek. Exhilarated by the day's events and at having made a new friend, Maria continued to wave to the two on the shore until the sail swung abruptly around and obscured the two diminishing shapes from her view. The rising wind puffed the sail out, played erratically over the bay, and hovered in her light blonde hair. When she turned her face to Isaac, her eyes were intensely bright.

"Oh, Isaac. What a very special day, and I thank you for it. You and Running Water were so serious when you talked about the whales and the future, but I have not felt freer or more excited in the last two years – and I even had a chance to do some swimming!"

Isaac crimsoned when he recalled his clumsiness with the tiller and the anger he had felt afterwards, but he quickly composed himself and warned her wryly, "Be careful, Maria, because we are coming in to shore again, and this time Running Water is not there waiting for us."

Then he continued, "I am sorry about the accident, and as I hope you know, I would never let any harm come to you if I could help it." Now it was Maria's turn to flush, and she said softly, "Yes, I am aware of that, Isaac, and I appreciate it. Our friendship means a great deal to me." For the rest of the short sail to Blackfish Creek, the two young people settled into a comfortable silence, each recalling stories, words and moments that had just passed and both vaguely wondering what the other was thinking. Then the tuck-a-nuck was over as suddenly as it had begun: Maria was sitting atop Brown Tail, no longer a queen or princess but just a lovely fifteen-year-old waving to her friend as she turned the horse up the path and blowing him a kiss off her fingertips.

At fifteen Isaac could not be sure he knew what love was. His life had been too short and too filled with milking cows, plowing fields, pouring ale and serving beef at the tavern, and tending to his mother's needs for him to give any attention to the boundaries, duties, and complications of something so alien as the notion of love. This spring day's events, however, had subtly rechanneled the stream of his thoughts and tightened the rhythm of his breath. For two years whenever he had thought of Maria, he had pictured her as if from a distance, a lovely exotic mountain creature relocated to the shores of Cape Cod. But from now on he would see her more precisely and recall the sympathy he felt when she described the rocks in her mother's pockets, his excitement at the quaver in her voice when she first called out the whales, his delight in the softness of her voice, even his anger at himself when he saw her emerge cradled in Running Water's arms, holding her breath like a blowfish, her blonde hair sodden and matted, enclosing the lovely features of her face. Now the possibility of love and what it meant was something Isaac began to consider. And as Maria gently tugged on the reins and turned the horse up the path, he hoped that she might be doing the same.

When he pulled the bedcovers up to his neck that night, Isaac tried to picture in his mind where love might take him. At first he dimly envisioned it as a path, a crooked, twisting one, and one that took a long time to traverse -- anything less could not really be called love. He also imagined that he had just made his first steps along this path, and he pictured Maria waiting for him at the end. Oddly, however, he did not see himself walking the path with her, and this last thought not only unsettled him but troubled his dreams that night and many nights that followed.

Chapter Six
The Burying Acre
September, 1715

Some said the tree was as old as the Good Book, that its roots had settled into the soil in the days of creation, that it had heard the crying of Adam and Eve one sad evening, and that its leaves continued to whisper the song of their sorrow on breezy afternoons. Regardless of legend and the natterings of town gossips, in late August and early September, the tree was expansive, sheltering, and crimson with apples that fell around it, much to the delight of neighboring children and bees. Apples spread out in random profusion from the base of the tree, and children brave enough to enter the burial ground would dare each other to race to the outermost limit of the branches' reach, grasp the first firm apple they found, and flee. In their ears they would hear the warning fizz and hum of yellow jackets mingled with the low murmur of the awakened spirits of the place. Before they bit into their prize, they would inspect it first for lurking worms and bees; the taste was always sweet and exciting. Such were the intoxicating dangers the tree had witnessed since the settlers had come and, before them, the Nauset tribesmen.

Maria Hallett loved the apple tree that presided over the Eastham Burying Acre. Having just turned fifteen, Maria was a girl doing a woman's work, and she knew it. The recent years had been hard ones for her: Following the illness and death of her mother, her move from Yarmouth to Eastham, and the contract she had made with her Aunt Elizabeth to take care of the children, Maria knew that her life's prospects were already beginning to dwindle and narrow. As a young woman with no parents on a windswept reach of land in 1715, she was a free agent in the universe, and while her freedom was exhilarating, the reality of her independence haunted her. One asset she knew she could rely on, however, was the effect of her dark brown eyes and her blonde hair; she knew this because she had seen young boys' eyes linger over her face and body in unguarded moments. For several years she had been aware that this gave her a measure of power over them, but she did not know how much power, and she was not sure how or when to exercise it; she only knew that it seemed to be increasing, and it gave her an uneasy sense of confidence.

As she contemplated these matters early one afternoon in 1715, Maria lay on the ground beneath the apple tree, counting the ripening apples among the green leaves and calculating when the first one would fall. Freed for an hour from the whims and needs of the children, she luxuriated in the broad, cool shadow that the tree cast on this warm day. She especially loved the tree for the way it stood alone among the silent gravestones, and she felt as if she had entered a charmed zone where she had nothing more to lose and where she was accountable to no one. The impassivity of the surrounding stones comforted her.

As she sat musing in easy solitude, Maria's thoughts turned to her recent history and to Isaac. Unlike so many boys, he was not bold, and he sometimes seemed so hesitant in her presence. He spoke as if he cared about the effect his words would have on her, and she not only noticed such things but was grateful for them. Their picnic on the island had made her more aware of his feelings for her: he had been so angry with himself when the boom had hit her, and although the blow had hurt at first, she thought her swim in the water a lark. His concern and sullen silence just after had shown her how seriously he had taken the mistake. Yes, she thought, Isaac might actually be falling in love with her. He was so kind, especially in the way he brought his ailing mother to the meeting house every Sunday morning and tended to her comfort while she was there, that Maria found herself wondering if they might marry someday and whether he would treat her in the same gentle way.

Her father had disappeared years before, and after her mother's death, Maria often found herself speculating about journeys she might make and where they might take her. In her loneliness, she pictured herself in a dark and winding cave and wondered whether Isaac would be there in the future to accompany her, to envelop her in his arms. Of course, her obligations to Aunt Elizabeth and the children consumed most of her week's time, yet she sensed that the

Freeman home was a temporary stop for her, a stage, something impermanent like a vanishing wave or dune.

From the prospect of the graveyard, Maria could see across the fields to the few dwellings of the Nauset tribe and to Town Cove, where small boats plied the water. She imagined the thrill of sailing away from this small town, the wind riffling her hair, and she envied the young men who were able to throw everything of value to them into a seabag, simply wave goodbye to those on shore, and disappear over the horizon. From the same prospect she could also see the neighboring meeting house, where every Sunday she and the community would gather for the better part of the day to listen to good Mr. Treat's sermons. While not especially large, the building was imposing in its own way, and it served as a kind of second home for the eight hundred residents of Eastham. With its white clapboards and trim black shutters, it resembled many other New England churches; in the summer it was warm and filled with long shafts of light, but during the long winters it was often dark and so cold that the baptismal waters would sometimes freeze in the bowl next to the altar. Nevertheless, comfortable or not, parishioners would spend countless hours every Sunday at the meeting house -- worshipping, sharing food, gossiping, debating town issues, and planning the coming week's activities.

This world to which Maria had come a year before was not unfamiliar to her, yet she felt alien to it -- as so many teen-agers do with others and within themselves. So much of her young life had seemed to be a vague dying -- something, she thought wryly, that those around her had perfected -- a long procession to a grayer place and time, and at times like the present she found herself longing to be free from destiny's coil, to be anywhere but where she was.

From their pulpits every Sunday the Puritan fathers of the Bay Colony decried human vanity and the vanity of women, in particular, but, as Maria knew, it was easy to be humble in 1715. At a time when people would clean their teeth with cuttle bone, brick-dust, coral, and pumice stone, many women were toothless by the age of eighteen, and vanity was the preserve of those wealthy enough to have artificial teeth engrafted to their gums; this latter solution was only marginally helpful, however, because the new teeth were useful only for display and talking, but not for eating. Maria was grateful for God's blessings: Despite her poverty and the clergy's warnings, her mouth was full of teeth, and she praised the Lord for her good fortune. As she lay in the brittle, late summer grass, she unpinned her hair, shook it loose, and propped her chin on her hands. Then she allowed her gaze to roam freely and randomly to the east, away from the town road behind her and over the bright sails entering the cove.

As her midday hour was drawing to a close, Maria's attention was arrested by a red-tailed hawk hovering high above the trees near the cove. The bird seemed to hang in the air, as if suspended from a cloud, and she marveled at its grace and the tracery of brilliant colors on the underside of its wings. It held itself motionless in the air for at least a minute, seeming not to move a muscle, patient in its inspection of some unsuspecting mouse, mole, or household cat. Maria lost herself in the dangerous story that was unfolding before her eyes.

"It's quite beautiful, is it not?" a low voice behind her said.

Maria started at these words which snapped the thread of her reverie, and she turned quickly on her elbow to see a large, dark silhouette looming above her. The figure was backlit by the noonday sunlight, so his features were indistinct to her, and the heat of the day seemed to be absorbed into his darkened image. She was further unsettled by the angle from which she viewed him -- she lying prone on the ground and he standing in a commanding way above her, his hands on his hips and his elbows bent outwards.

He laughed and spoke again, "The bird, I mean. It's beautiful the way it seems to be the master of the sky and can strike with such speed and ease."

Having yet to say a word while having had her thoughts spoken for her, Maria felt at a considerable disadvantage; so she slowly rose to her feet, brushed some stray blades of grass from her dress, and turned her eyes to survey the stranger's face.

What she saw was pleasing to her. Standing before her was a young gentleman who seemed not to belong to this place and time. He was older than she, almost thirty she guessed, and the way he stood, with his plumed hat in the crook of his arm, suggested his poise and comfort in this strange place with a strange young girl. She was immediately struck by the contrasts in his appearance -- the blackness of his curled beard, his blood-red frock coat, his shining satin neckerchief, the pink plume in his hat -- so different from the darker, grayer men and boys of Cape Cod.

Some inner resource enabled her to speak, some force that overcame her surprise and confusion, and she said,

"Sir, I was thinking how I would like to be as powerful and free of care as the bird, that I .....," and her voice trailed off.

The man laughed again and answered, "First, you need not call me sir because I am not a fine gentleman, and, second, the bird is far from carefree. At this very moment it is hungry and attempting to feed both itself and its greedy young ones."

Like American heroes that would follow -- with names like Alger, Gantry, and Gatsby -- Sam Bellamy, the imposing figure facing Maria this sunny summer day, was a product of his own prodigal imagination. A young man nearing thirty years of age, he had adopted his elaborate style of dress while still a part-time fisherman and seafarer in the West Country of England. In part a deferential bow to the upper classes of his homeland and in part a sly sneer, Sam's dress was one aspect of a grand design. His fantastic and carefully arranged clothing contrasted with his pale blue eyes and quick smile to create the odd impression of a young boy chafing his neck against a starched Sunday collar, a colt learning to adjust to having a bit in its mouth, a snake becoming accustomed to its new skin. But Sam also knew that these clothes -- this costume so alien to the manners and landscape of colonial America and far removed from the London streets of his birth -- were a passport to his future and his freedom. He had also prepared a name for his arrival, Black Bellamy, which was intended as a description and a warning to any who might oppose him. As aware as he was of the impression he made on others, Sam was not a slave to popular trends; consequently, he intentionally refused to wear a wig, then much in fashion among men and even children in the colonies, and instead allowed his glistening black hair to fall loosely about his shoulders and the ringlets of his beard to assert his independence. As he stood face-to-face with this strikingly lovely, yet solitary, young person on this September day, Sam cared nothing about how he might appear in a looking glass and only about satisfying his curiosity concerning this mysterious young woman he had discovered musing alone in a graveyard.

"If you are not a *sir*, then I am at a loss in not knowing your name," Maria responded, "nor how to address you. I am further confused as to your reasons for wandering off the road and into this quiet acre."

At this moment Maria looked directly into the man's eyes, and, amused by her challenge, he returned her gaze with equal intensity.

"To be square with you, my name is Sam Bellamy, and I am here for as long as it takes to gather a crew to sail to the Caribbees where we will make our fortune. As for my reasons for straying off the traveled road, you should know the answer to that question. I saw a lonely girl with long blonde hair staring up at a circling hawk, and I decided I wanted to find out who she was."

Maria was both disarmed by the man's candor and secretly delighted by his interest in her. He had come from a distant land and would soon travel to other ones; he also spoke with an easy grace, acquired over many years with weathered men and worldly women. Yet he had found her beneath her apple tree, and she marveled in private satisfaction at the powers that had drawn him here.

"My name is Maria Hallett," Maria replied, "and I come here at noontime every day while the children I care for are resting. I have found that the residents of this small town," -- smiling, she extended her arm about her -- "are more quiet and grave than my Aunt Elizabeth's young ones, and I enjoy meeting here with them and their neighbors." As she said this, she looked up at the hawk, which had apparently identified its prey and shifted its position lower in the sky.

Sam's eyes followed hers, then quickly returned to her face.

"Maria Hallett, although I am not highborn, I am an unrecognized prince, a free prince, as free as that bird, and I am glad to make your acquaintance. I admire your spirit, and were you not so young and fair, I would ask you to join my crew," he said smiling. "There is treasure to be found and a fortune to be made from Spanish galleons that have sunk in recent months off the Florida coast, and I aim to be the first to find it, come what may."

The man's words both flattered and thrilled Maria, but in the phrase "come what may" she detected tempered steel. His complimentary manner and the pale blue of his eyes attracted her, but the sword-like quality of his tone indicated the vast distance between the decks of his ship and the four walls of the Freeman cottage where the children were presently sleeping. At this thought Maria realized that the sun had moved beyond the steeple of the church, and she knew that she would be late in returning to her duties.

"Mr. Bellamy, I thank you for your kind attentions, and perhaps someday I will be sailing away from this little town; but for now, I must return to the little ones in my charge. Watching the hawk has put them out of my mind, and I will be late in getting back to them. I have enjoyed our interview and meeting with you, nevertheless, and perhaps I will see you again."

"I, too, have enjoyed talking with you, Maria Hallett," Sam said. "I am sorry if I -- and not the hawk -- have detained you from your duties, and I wish you a speedy return. I also hope I will discover you here again by this tree in the days to come." As he said this, Sam's quick grin appeared, and Maria sensed that, indeed, she would see him again. He then bowed, sweeping his pink plume in front of him with the exaggerated flourish of a king's courtier but immediately dispelled the illusion by sauntering away in the manner of a sea captain who still feels the roll of a ship beneath his feet.

He did not turn around to look at her again, but Maria watched for a few moments as his red frock coat and the pink plume grew smaller in the distance and soon vanished around a bend in the dusty road. Before she turned to the path that would take her back to the Freeman house, she reflected that the interview had taken no more than ten minutes, but during that time she felt as if the tide had changed within her, as if the stars would be configured slightly differently when evening fell. She was charmed by the man, and she believed he had been charmed by her -- and she enjoyed the sensation, the surge of pure energy she felt. Yet its strangeness scared her: in her young heart she felt a fear that she had not known since the night her mother had died.

As Sam was making his way back to the Poseidon's Toy and Maria was returning to the children, the red-tailed hawk was rising from the ground with a small rabbit clutched firmly in its talons. As it rose, it saw the two figures moving in different directions, and it subtly adjusted to the same gust of wind that was rustling through the leaves of the solitary apple tree in the graveyard below.

Chapter Seven
The Poseidon's Toy
October, 1715

After that first meeting Sam returned to find Maria again lying under the tree, but on the days that followed, she was waiting for him, sitting on the rise with her hands clasped about her bent knees. Her smile was quick when she saw him coming into view on the dusty road, and she typically waited until he had mounted the small rise to the tree before she stood to meet him and take his hands in hers. By now the formalities of their earlier words and conduct had dissolved, and both were less attentive to how they appeared to each other than to how they might be regarded by an idle townsman who could be passing by. The differences between them were great and, at the same time, exciting: Maria knew only of Cape Cod dunes and tending to children while Sam knew English ports and the circumscribed world of a ship; her eyes were brown and her soft hair blonde, his eyes were blue and his curled beard black; she was fifteen and he was twenty-eight; she wanted to escape her home and he would never return to his. But they were both impatient -- she to begin her life and he to give his form -- and this impatience lent each of them a certain electric quality in the eyes of the other.

On this day, a Friday afternoon, Maria was anxious with anticipation. Sam had not arrived yet, and she would have to return to the children before too long. Then in the distance she saw a flash of pink, and as Sam sauntered into view, she recognized there was something almost laughable about the man -- the extravagant pink plume, the carmine coat, the satin neckerchief -- yet the qualities that made him so strange and alien to her also made her want to touch him. As he neared, she realized he was singing in a minor key a tune she had never heard before.

"Oh, I'd ninety bars of gold as I sailed, as I sailed

Oh, I'd ninety bars of gold as I sailed.
I'd ninety bars of gold, and dollars manifold
With riches uncontrolled as I sailed, as I sailed,
With riches uncontrolled as I sailed."

As she rose to meet him, instead of taking the hands he offered, she laughed spontaneously, tangled her fingers in his beard and gently pulled him to her, saying, "Mr. Bellamy, you are late for our meeting, and where did you learn that rousing song you were singing?"

Ignoring her chiding, he instead answered her question, "I've known it for many years now, Maria, ever since I was a boy. It's about the famous Captain Kidd; I'm sure you have heard of him, and I can assure you that I'll never forget him. You know, when I was a boy I saw what they did to him – they tarred him after they put him to death and then hung his body at Tilbury Point on the Thames to scare pirates and outlaws. I saw him there. He didn't scare the gulls, however, because they pecked out his eyes." Sam looked steadily at her. "I saw him hanging there in that cage, and I will never forget him – or his song. Do you want to hear how it ends?"

Taken aback, Maria hesitantly nodded, and in a lusty voice he began,

"Oh, Take warning now by me, for I must die, I must die,
Oh, take warning now by me, for I must die,
Take warning now by me, and shun bad company,
Lest you come to hell with me, for I must die, for I must die,
Lest you come to hell with me, for I must die."

When Sam had concluded, Maria's eyes began to glisten with tears, and she turned her face away from him,

"Are you crying, Maria?" he asked.

"Yes."

"But why? It's just a song...."

"Oh," she said, "it's just so sad, about warnings and dying and going to hell, and I would hate for that to happen to you."

"But why should it?" Sam answered.

"I don't know, but I don't want to go there, and I don't want you to either."

Sam looked at this girl with tears shimmering in her eyes and softly touched her blonde hair. As he did, he sensed that her tears had taken them across a subtle boundary.

Then his tone shifted. "The only people who should go to hell are those that hanged old Captain Kidd. Did you know that they did it to him twice? He was so heavy with grief and grog that the rope broke the first time, and he fell into the mud under Execution Dock. So they did it again. They should have been ashamed before God for the way they treated him. A crazy parson even climbed up on the scaffold next to him trying to get the old drunken man to repent his sins -- and in his confusion, he did! -- and then he was dead."

Maria looked at Sam, who by now had fallen silent, and she wondered at the depths of his anger. As if reading her mind, he said, "Kidd was a man of the sea who did what he had to do on the sea, and when he came ashore, the governors betrayed him.

I too am a man of the sea, and I aim to make my fortune by my own wits, just as the old captain did. But you won't find me dangling from a yardarm at the end of my days."

For a second time Maria was moved by Sam's words, but this time she felt a thrill pulse through her.

"You speak of making your fortune, Mr. Bellamy, but I thought you already had, dressed in such fine clothes as you are."

Sam watched her for a moment, and then he laughed,

"Maria, I believe you are mocking me, but I am what I am. At present I am a captain without a crew, but I have a sloop, and when I have men enough men to sail her, I plan to go to the Caribbees. I have read journal accounts of ships that have foundered on the shoals in the West Indies, and I intend to salvage as much treasure there as my small boat will hold. I have all the charts and maps. Now all I need is a small crew of willing men."

"Then I would like to go with you," she said quietly, almost solemnly, and turned her eyes upward to his face.

This girl fascinated him – the defiant curve of her jaw, her soft hair, her knowing eyes; somewhere in his past he had heard the phrase "born from the foam of the sea," and he recalled it at this moment, so elemental, free, almost wind-driven did she seem to him.

"Maria, life on a ship is no place for you. It is full of danger from the weather and from other men. It's a man's world on the decks of a vessel, and as a matter of truth, I will not even recruit married men for my crew; there are too many chances for women to lose the ones they love on the sea." As he said this, Sam suddenly realized that he was thinking about this girl in ways he had never considered another woman before. He felt an impulse to protect her, and the sensation was strange to him.

Though still a young man, Sam Bellamy had known many women. From the time he was a very young habitué of the port towns of England, women had seemed to find him, and he was accustomed to taking from them what he wanted. This girl looking up at him, however, was a different sort of creature, and he found himself choosing his words very carefully with her.

For her part, and for the first time in her life, Maria sensed that she had found someone to fill the space in her heart created by those who had been taken from her. This dark man now holding her hands and looming above her – so courteous yet vaguely dangerous – seemed to be a passport to the future, and she already knew she would gladly travel with him to tropical islands on the next tide. Like him, she was a free agent in the cosmos, and this knowledge was exhilarating to her.

Gently releasing her hands, Sam said with a flickering smile, "Come with me, Maria. I have something to show you, but it is some distance from here." Without hesitation, or any thought for the children who would be waiting for her, Maria nodded in assent, and together they made their way through the tall grasses and around the gravestones to the road. As she struggled to control her quickening breath, she reflexively took Sam's hand and wondered at the revelation waiting for her, what mystery he would reveal to her.

The afternoon sun had by now lost its power, and the long shadows the couple cast were linked yet solitary as they followed a westward path. After a mile or so, Maria playfully spun around, walking backward, and with her eyes flashing, she said, "Tell me, my captain, where you are taking me." But he only answered her with a grin. Before long, they turned onto a road very familiar to Maria, one that led directly to Rock Harbor, whereupon she burst out, "We're going to see your ship, aren't we? I should have known!"

Sam smiled broadly and said, "Yes, indeed we are…"

Now they both moved more quickly, and before long they rounded a gentle turn and smelled the distinctive aroma of a working harbor – salt rising from drying eel grass, the pungency of discarded fish guts, the miasma left by a retreating tide.

"There she is," Sam said, "The Poseidon's Toy. What do you think of her?"

Anchored in the cove was a sleek two-masted sloop with several cannons protruding from its topdeck. Under full sail, a large, square mainsail and a topsail would extend from the mast, along with a foresail and a spritsail, which was set on the bowsprit. The vessel rode high in the water, and although it was not large by the standards of the day, it was trim and seaworthy.

"It's a lovely ship," Maria murmured, and she believed it was. The shadow created by the sun setting in the west extended on the golden water toward her, seeming to beckon to her, and she was momentarily entranced by the vision.

"To be exact, she is a sloop and not a ship," Sam said, "but she's fast and can out-sail many larger ships she might encounter." Then he paused. "Would you like to walk on her decks? My only mate at the moment will be singing and dancing at the Smith Tavern on Great Island tonight, and there is no one aboard her now. Then again, perhaps you would prefer to remain here on land."

In a few words Sam had said a great deal, and Maria appreciated both his delicacy and the obvious pleasure he felt in his small vessel. As he looked at the sloop, and not at her, she said, "I would very much like to walk on her decks, my captain," and her voice caught as she added, "I can think of nothing I would rather do."

Then they were in a small rowboat, Sam pulling steadily on the oars and Maria gazing intently at the sloop and beyond it. There in the distance to her right in a small skiff that she had seen many times, Maria recognized a familiar figure: it was Isaac who was most likely returning home with some fish he had purchased for his mother's dinner, Isaac the good son, Isaac her friend. She doubted that he had seen her, and was grateful for that, but she knew it was he and impulsively turned to Sam and said, "Captain Bellamy, I may have discovered one of your first recruits! That young man in the distance, Isaac Doane, is a good friend of mine, and he may be just the kind of hand you are looking for. He even works at the Smith Tavern, where your companion is tonight, and I am sure you would be able to find him there tomorrow evening! As a matter of fact, that might be a good place to start recruiting your crew!" There was a breathless quality about this girl, a generosity that delighted Sam, and he responded with a laugh, "If you say he is a good man, Maria, I will travel to the island and talk to him tomorrow. In fact, I need an extra mate to help me sail Poseidon's Toy around to Town Cove in a day or two, and he may be just the man. Maybe I will find some others to boot."

There was also a breathless quality about this evening, so still yet intensely shimmering, and the two soon fell silent as each contemplated the other: to Sam, Maria seemed an exotic petal newly born of cold New England soil, fresh and lovely, and to Maria, he was his own master, a maker of designs that emanated as easily as those curling from the ends of his oars. She longed to touch him, so she did, placing her hand on his knee. He smiled at her and said in a husky voice, "We're just about there." And they were. Over his left shoulder, Maria saw the stern of the vessel obtruding above them, and she became acutely aware that she was no longer land-bound, that she was alone with this man she had only known for a matter of days. She could barely control the tightening in her throat and voice as Sam held her waist and she ascended the ladder leading to the topdeck,

"Thank you, Captain Bellamy," she managed with an attempt at irony as she said his name.

And then they were standing together on the foredeck of the sloop in the penumbral light of the evening. As a young boy might, he had shown her the helm, the galley below deck, the guns, large and ominous. All she recognized, however, was the excitement and pride in his eyes; all the rest had just seemed to loom around her, unhoused and ill-defined. Loosed from all ties to the land, they had entered another zone of space and time on the boat. She had lost all memory of the children. Sam gently placed his hand around her waist, and looking at the horizon, said almost to himself, "The flaming gold out there in the sky is the color of the gold that will make me rich. Maria. Do you like the color?"

"Yes, I do," she said. "I do, yes."

On this uncommonly serene evening with a tracery moon beginning to appear on the horizon, Maria closed her eyes, leaned her back against the mainmast, and allowed the mingling, reds, yellows, and golds of the sunset to blend in her mind's eye with the faces and images of the day: the drunken and disgraced Captain Kidd, his hollowed eyes, the lonely figure of Isaac framed by the setting sun, the piercing gaze of the man standing next to her, and finally, the vision of this sloop which she imagined could transport her out of this harbor, over the tranquil bay, and beyond the farthest reaches of the luminous horizon.

As they stood on the deck of the sloop in the gathering darkness, they spoke in low voices, and Sam slowly began to unfasten the buttons on the front of her dress. Unlike so many young girls in later years whose imaginations would have rehearsed the scene to follow and would know its outcome, Maria, with few preconceptions, gave herself to the allure of this man, to this place, to the unborn future – and then she felt the curls of his black beard upon her face.

Chapter Eight
Hail and Farewell
Early Spring, 1716

True to his word, the following evening Sam entered the front door of the tavern looking for Isaac. What he found was a miasma of smoke, loud voices, the smell of spilt ale, laughter, and the mixture of male and female heat. His eyes took an instant to adjust to the low, flickering light in the room, and when they had, he saw maybe fifty people. At that moment, caught by a late summer gust of wind, the great tavern door slammed behind him, as if to announce his entrance, and the pulse of conversation in the room ebbed and then ceased.

As he was carrying food to a waiting couple, Isaac looked at the door and saw an extravagant dandy with a black beard and a big smile, and he wondered what tide had washed this fellow ashore. Although he had been working in the tavern for several months, Isaac had never seen anyone quite like the feathered bird framed in the doorway, and his first inclination was to laugh out loud. He stifled the temptation, however, and simply nodded in Sam's direction. Another of the patrons, Elias Newcomb who had been drinking for an hour and wore the scars from earlier brawls on his face and knuckles, was not so restrained. At the same table with Newcomb were two men in their early twenties, evidently identical twin brothers, although they could be quite easily distinguished from each other. William Cole, a reserved habitué of the tavern, had a crimson birthmark that spread in a warped triangle from his left ear across to his nostril, swooped around his mouth and disappeared under his jaw; whereas his brother, Aaron, had a distinct limp, the result of a childhood injury which left him with one leg shorter than the other. As Newcomb began to stagger to his feet, William reached instinctively across the table to stop him. Failing in the effort, however, he simply rested his scarlet jaw on his hand, exchanged an amused look with his brother, and watched events unfold in what had become a predictable scenario. Aaron was especially intrigued by this recent arrival whose silken cummerbund matched the color of his brother's face.

"Well, what have we here," Newcomb shouted from across the room, "some popinjay fresh out of the King's navy? What brings you to our little outpost here in the middle of the bay, my fine looking fellow?" As he said this, Newcomb angled unsteadily from the table while staring across the room at Sam.

Sam had encountered the likes of Newcomb all his life and, his smile gone, he calmly responded for all to hear, "My name is Black Bellamy, and I have come here from the shores of England by way of the colony of Maine. I am now looking for able bodied men to travel further with me to the West Indies. If a man is interested in finding sunken treasure and is willing to work hard for it, I am making an offer that will be hard for him to refuse."

"You don't impress me with your fine clothes and grand ideas, Black Bellamy -- Did you really say Black?" Newcomb retorted as he slowly moved toward Sam while tightening and untightening his right fist. Isaac had always disliked Newcomb, and knew that a fight would follow shortly; so, when Newcomb brushed by him, Isaac instinctively and as if by accident, extended his foot in front of the red-faced whaler. The man fell awkwardly to the floor, and within the instant, Sam had pulled a knife from the inside of his boot and had its point pressed under Newcomb's jawbone. In almost a whisper that only those nearest them could hear, Sam said,

"You are fortunate, indeed, that you tripped, my foolish friend. Else, I should have had to kill you and feed your entrails to that large dog lying outside the door. I knew you for a fool the moment you opened your mouth, and, true to form, you made the error of misjudging me."

As he spoke, Sam pressed the tip of the dagger harder against Newcomb's skin making a firm indentation from which a thread of blood slowly curled around the man's Adam's apple and found its way under his shirt. Newcomb's widened eyes were fixed on the hand poised beneath his jaw, and he seemed not to breathe for fear the blade would penetrate deeper.

Nodding briefly toward Isaac, Sam went on, "That young pup

over there has more courage than you, friend, and I would sooner have him as a mate on my sloop. My advice to you is to mend your tongue in the future and not return to this tavern until you know I have set sail. If you ignore my warning, it will be at your peril." With that, Sam lifted the hulking man by the back of his shirt, and now holding the knife at the base of his skull, ushered him to the door, where he placed his foot on the man's buttocks and shoved him through the opening. After making sure Newcomb had stumbled off into the darkness, Sam turned to the company and with a broad smile on his face said, "My name is Black Bellamy, and if any of you wish to join me on my voyage, I can make you an offer that will be difficult to refuse. But for now I could use a flagon of Mr. Smith's famous flip."

The crowd laughed in approval and seemed to exhale corporately, relieved that the scene was over and no mayhem had followed. Noticed by only a few, the man with the face of scarlet silently rose from his table, paused for an instant to fix the scene and the image of Bellamy in his mind, and slipped into the night to minister to his defeated companion. His brother remained behind in hopes that the extravagant interloper might provide him additional entertainment.

Order now restored, conversations soon returned to normal, and Sam gestured to Isaac that he wanted to speak with him. Maria had instructed Sam not to reveal her part in arranging this meeting, and having easily identified the boy from her description of him, Sam only said,

"I saw you trip that fellow just now, and I thank you for it. It took courage and quick-thinking to do that, and I was not jesting when I said I would like a person like you to be one of my crew. What is your name, my young friend?"

Flattered, Isaac responded, "I am Isaac Doane, and I have never liked Elias Newcomb. He has always been a bully, and I am glad you made him look like a fool. You handle that knife very well."

"I have to," Sam replied, gently rubbing his thumb along the glinting blade. "If I don't, it may mean my life – as it could have just a few moments ago. Now, my good fellow, I would like a large mug of that flip I spoke of."

When Isaac returned with the drink, Sam said, "Isaac, I have been thinking. I know you are a young man, and I suspect you have not been working here too long, but I wonder whether you would be willing to make a short voyage with me from Rock Harbor around Provincetown and back down to Town Cove on the other side of Eastham. It would take only a day, and you could get a taste of the salt air aboard my sloop. I need to find a better port for Poseidon's Toy, and I could use your help for the day."

Surprised, Isaac was intrigued by the offer, and he paused briefly to consider it. From the way he carried himself, to his easy grin, to his skill with a knife, Sam Bellamy had impressed him, and on an impulse Isaac answered, "Tomorrow is Sunday, and I won't be working, so I could go with you then." Isaac had risked nothing by assenting to the proposal, and the prospect of sailing with such a man would be an exciting way to spend the Sabbath. .

"Then it's a pact," Sam said quickly. "We'll set sail at early light tomorrow," and shaking Isaac's hand, he added, "I'm pleased to make your acquaintance, Mr. Doane."

****

A chop was on the water the next morning, and the bay was flecked with white caps. Because the tide was in, Sam had little difficulty maneuvering Poseidon's Toy out through the shoals of the harbor and into Barnstable Bay. But the brisk wind out of the southwest was another matter. On nearby Billingsgate Island, now off their starboard bow, they could even see the sand being blown into the early morning air from the ghostly dunes. Due to the stiff winds, they put a reef in the mainsail, and with the wind now at their backs, Poseidon's Toy rode easily on the waves.

As the last of the morning stars flickered out, Isaac looked at Sam Bellamy. Isaac knew the ways of the wind, but he had never been on a boat as large as Sam's. Somehow he felt larger himself as he sat there on this lovely June morning. Sam's hands seemed so sure at the wheel, his body balanced and erect in the morning air. Sam's hand was relaxed at the helm as he directed Poseidon's Toy down the wind, and Isaac admired his easy grace. As he pointed the ship up the bay, Sam's eyes coolly assessed the way the wind played on the water's surface, and he said to Isaac, "When I sailed here from England, I noticed how difficult the shoals around this land are. They are legendary. Many men have died along this cape, and I suspect there will be many more. The tides are especially treacherous, and in a few hours when we reach Provincetown, you will see how fast they move, which is why they call the area Race Point."

As the mast creaked, the wind whispered in the sails, and water curled silently from the rudder at the stern, Isaac gazed intently at the shore, and after a few moments, he said to Sam, pointing in toward shore, "There it is, there is the farm where I live, the place with the large field in front."

Sam squinted for a moment in the rising light, and following the direction of Isaac's outstretched finger, he said, "I see it." Nestled in the trees, a smudge on the shoreline with a neatly planted field spread out before it, was the Doane cottage. a solitary outpost with no other cottages nearby. In an instant Sam grasped how essentially isolated Isaac and his mother were, how simply they lived, and how proud the boy was to be maintaining the small farm largely on his own and without the help of a father.

"How long have you worked at the tavern?"

"Not very long," Isaac replied, "only a few months now."

"And do you like it? Are you paid well?"

"I suppose so," Isaac said. "The money helps me support my mother and the farm too, and Mr. Smith and Dan Atwood have been very good to me. I will probably be there for a while."

To this Sam responded pensively, "I don't know that I could ever work for long in one place, maybe because the air never changes. In a tavern, for example, it's always the smell of ale and smoke and people's talk, not like out here where the wind always changes direction, you're free, and you have to have your wits about you. A man's free to be who he wants to be out here, that's what I say." Sam stopped suddenly, almost abashed at having made such a personal statement to someone he had known for such a short while. But then he continued in a slightly altered tone,

"When I have gathered my crew, we are going to travel far. We are going to hunt for gold, and we will return home wealthy men. Mark my words, we will."

Isaac then broke in, "Where will you find it – the gold -- and whose gold is it?"

Sam laughed at this and answered, "Thirteen Spanish ships have foundered off the Florida coast, and the treasure is there for the taking. As for whose gold it is, it will be ours if we get to it first. Have no doubt about that! The English and the Spanish have no love for each other, and although I have left his Majesty's service, I am an Englishman who is only too willing to become rich on Spanish gold." Isaac nodded and laughed, and for the time being, discussion of their respective futures subsided.

An hour into their voyage Isaac spied the flag of a British frigate in the distance and started to comment on the number of British seamen who would visit the tavern, when Sam cut him off:

"Never again will I serve aboard one of the King's ships. I count myself a good and loyal British subject -- as good as the next man -- but life in the King's navy is hard, Isaac, often cruel, and it's no wonder that so many men have gone upon the account."

"Upon the account?" Isaac inquired.

"Taken up pirating," Sam explained. "Jumped ship and made their way as private businessmen, if you will," he added with a smile. "I would never turn against the King, mind you, but I can understand a man wanting to live his life on his own terms and not be beholden to any other man, be he the King or some highborn scoundrel sitting on his bags of gold back in London. On the decks of a sloop like this one a man feels free and owes nothing to any man," Sam muttered fiercely and almost to himself.

Shortly after, broad expanses of beach were sliding into view, and the Poseidon's Toy was nearing the outermost extension of the Cape, Provincetown. Dunes like camel humps rode the shoreline, and the sand seemed to turn almost silver in the late morning sunlight.

"They call it Helltown," Isaac murmured, and Sam said, "I know. In my travels, I've heard sailors say if you make it past the shoals of the Cape in a storm, you're grateful to arrive in Hell, and there it is. It is a beautiful sight, though, isn't it?"

"I've heard men in the tavern describe it," Isaac answered, "but I've never traveled there. It's more than twenty miles as the gulls fly, you know."

For an instant Sam looked appraisingly at Isaac and then said, "We'll have traveled further than that in this sloop by the end of this day, my lad......

"In fact, I suspect Provincetown is not much different from the isle of Jamaica in the Caribbees, that I hope to see someday. There, almost fifty years ago, Henry Morgan was as great as a king. Have you heard of him? He was an Englishman, a rogue and a scoundrel, but he walked on both sides of the law, and, by god, he could command men by land or sea!

"One story had him joining up with French pirates before making an attack on a Spanish port at Cartegena in the Gulf of Darien. The story goes that when he, his men, and the French made their alliance aboard Morgan's ship, they sealed their bargain with rum, ale, and women. Well, as you might guess, strong drink, music and wild men and women often lead to explosions, and before you knew it, someone set off a powder keg on board blowing the ship and two hundred men into the clouds. Morgan survived – he always did – and his mates who lived dived into the blood-red sea after those blasted overboard. But they didn't do it to save them! No, they went in after the gold on their carcasses, and when they couldn't remove the rings and such, they cut off their arms or hands to make it easier."

Isaac's winced, and he laughed nervously as he imagined severed and swollen hands and torsos still clinging to lustrous gold as they floated on the crimson water.

"I tell you this story, Isaac," Sam continued, "not to appall you but to suggest that men are not so different anywhere you find them. At the end of Morgan's life as a freebooter, a marauder, an unscrupulous but brilliant general, and a scoundrel, King Charles II appointed him the governor of Jamaica, an island he had pillaged for years. The distance between the virtuous and the evil, the powerful and the weak, is sometimes as narrow as that between the gunwales of this ship and the sands of Helltown over there, and I wonder how many with the spirit of Henry Morgan have anchored their ships in that protected harbor."

Just as he finished, Sam gazed over Isaac's shoulder and said excitedly, "Look, Isaac, look to the port. Do you see them? I never get tired of the sight."

There, no more than one hundred yards away, was a pod of humpbacked whales. Isaac had lived all his life on the bay and had seen countless whales in his short life, but he was now about to witness something new and profoundly affecting, one of the most memorable images of his life, the kind that reappears in the mind's eye at odd moments. There, so close to the ship, swirling the water into a glistening meringue, were no fewer than nine whales. As he watched them, Isaac became ever more fascinated, wondering if one might meander toward the sloop and shoulder it over. When Sam said, "Watch how they perform together," Isaac perceptibly leaned forward, training his eyes on the area so as not to miss an instant of the show to follow.

As he watched, amazed, the whales formed in a wide circle, perhaps thirty yards in diameter. There was a purpose in their movement, but they were likewise playful. In their midst Isaac could perceive a white, bubbly froth, and on top of this froth were thousands of maddened herring – spinning, flipping, flying, trapped and left with nowhere to go by the circling gaping whales. As the circle rapidly tightened, the whales disappeared as one from view, their tails waving on the surface like the wings of birds mingling with the hordes of terns, and gulls flying just above the roiling surface that seemed to be a moving, knotted white carpet of bubbles. At the exit of the whales, which seemed so finely choreographed, Sam said to Isaac, "Now just keep watching. Don't be impatient...." Perhaps two to three seconds later, the whales came bursting through what had been the center of the circle they had created, like a great blossoming flower, mouths agape, the frantic herring being consumed in the cavernous mouths of the towering whales. The whales' mouths had become small cataracts, filled with brine and fish. Then the whales disappeared and reappeared again, and then again a third time, and a fourth, exploding through the surface each time consuming all they could see. And each time they rose, they fell back with a great thunderous clap, joyfully filled with food and luxuriating in their power.

As the whales exited the stage, Isaac turned and looked at Sam, his eyes flashing with delight as if the whales were still leaping in them, and would continue to do so.

"Sam, did you see that?" he asked nonsensically. "Did you see them jumping? Did you see the one whale swallow the gull and then the bird flew out of his jaws?"

With the resounding explosions echoing in his ears, Isaac seemed almost fearful, and Sam laughed ever more loudly at his response. When the show was over, the whales dissipated, no longer interested, like exhausted Olympians, debauched royalty of the sea, satisfied children who knew they would play again before long.

"I knew a woman who hoped to ride a whale someday," Sam mused almost to himself. When I was your age, I would row her out into the sound off our English shores; then she would remove her clothes, jump into the cold waters, and call to them as they were swimming nearby. She was older than I was, but I think I loved her..."

"Whatever happened to her?" Isaac asked.

"I don't know if she ever made her dream come true because after that summer I was off to sea. That was when I was about your age, Isaac." Then after a pause, Sam asked, "Have you ever loved a girl, Isaac?"

Isaac paused for a moment and then said, "I... I don't know. I have been so busy with my mother and our farm since my father died that I haven't thought much about such things. But there might be a girl." His voice started to trail off, but then he began again, "Yes, I know a girl, but I suspect you have known more...."

Sam replied, "I've been to many ports, Isaac, and I know I'll go to many more," but then in a more serious tone he said, "Yes, there is a girl I have been thinking about a great deal recently..." As they passed the time together, neither one of them was aware that the same girl's face was lingering in their thoughts, and both quietly let the subject die.

Sam pulled a pipe from his pocket, pinched come curls of tobacco into its bowl, and deftly using a flint, lit it. Then he blew a puff of smoke that vaguely resembled the shape of a whale.

"Isaac," he said, "I have an offer for you. It would mean that you would have to be away from that girl and your mother for a few months, but when you returned to them, you would be a rich man. I can almost promise it. You would have the money to make farming that small plot of land a much easier task. Then Sam continued, "I aim to be a rich man, Isaac, and you could be too. I have already enlisted some men to accompany me, a few last night at the tavern, and in a month's time, we will set sail from Eastham bound for the Florida coast and further south. As I have told you, I have read of thirteen galleons that have run aground in those seas, and their treasure lies along the shoals for any man who has the spirit to seek and salvage it. I am not greedy, but I pursue my own advantage, and there will be equal shares for all the men who travel with me."

To Isaac this man seemed to be what he said he was, as free as the gulls dipping for baitfish off the port bow, unaccountable to the pull of the tides that directed the lives of so many men with less courage and more limited dreams. Filled with a sense of anticipation, even joy at the romance of it all, Isaac grinned and said, "I would like to join you, Captain. It will be different from serving ale at the tavern, but it should be a grand adventure, even if I am gone for only a few months, and, God knows, I can use the money." Even as he said this, though, Isaac recalled his mother waiting for him back in the cabin, and the image of Maria flickered briefly in his consciousness. But Sam Bellamy had charmed Isaac in a way that only a boy of fifteen can be charmed. In less than a day's time, Isaac had come to love this man for the stories he told: for the places he had been and the far-off ones he was planning to see; he wanted to live in the older man's skin, to walk around in his shoes, and his decision to ship aboard Poseidon's Toy made him tremble to his core.

As the sunlight dwindled through the late afternoon, the two new friends tacked their way down the outer side of the Cape, finally arriving in Town Cove when the twilight had deepened into darkness. In the lowered light Isaac felt even closer to Sam -- as if they were somehow in cahoots together and plotting something underhanded. Isaac felt this strangeness even more sharply when he saw the ghostly outline of Reverend Treat's home looming before him at the head of the cove. He welcomed the feeling, though, and its promise of something new and dangerous. After they had parted some time later – Sam to remain with Poseidon's Toy and Isaac to return to Silver Springs – Isaac lingered for a moment on the beach to gaze at the lantern hanging from the stern of Sam's boat; it seemed to be a beacon of sorts, emblazoning his future and offering possibilities of enchantment he had never conceived of before. When he turned back to the path leading to his home, the moonlight seemed to have silvered the way, and he suddenly felt the impulse to run – so he did.

****

Time passed, and several weeks later as a thin, misty film enveloped Town Cove early one morning, Isaac knew he would not be traveling south after sunken treasure. The Poseidon's Toy was fitted out, stocked, and manned with six crewmembers, and Isaac had come to watch her young captain direct her out into the open sea. The sun had not yet risen in the east, and Isaac hung back in the dewy shadows so as not to be seen by those shipping on last minute provisions or, in particular, by Sam Bellamy. At some elemental level his spirit was ashamed that he was not going, that he had informed Sam of his decision a few days before, that his sense of obligation to his mother and the memory of his father was holding him back. At some deeper level, though, he sensed an inadequacy in himself, an unwillingness to depart from the familiarity of the tavern, to leave the solidity of the land for the open ocean. He was too young to understand his motives – or to want to – but he was sorrowful and envious of the strong men in the distance carrying out their appointed tasks.

Then not more than one hundred yards away, Isaac saw Sam approaching with a woman on his arm. As they came into view, he realized the woman was not a woman at all but, instead, Maria, from whose neck hung a glinting golden necklace, which contrasted sharply with the desolate expression on her face. As they drew nearer and approached the dock, Isaac slipped deeper into the shadows. Although he could not hear their voices, he could read a natural intimacy in their gestures, especially in the attentive way Maria tilted her chin up toward Sam when he said something or in the way he quickly and gently brushed her cheek with the back of his fingers. On looking more closely, Isaac realized that she was crying and that Sam was attempting to dry her glistening cheeks. Suddenly Isaac felt very young, too young to be watching these two people who were obviously in love and whom he loved in very different ways; yet, though shaken, he continued to gaze at them in guilty fascination.

What Isaac could not hear were the heated words that passed between the two lovers. At the moment Sam touched her cheek, Maria threw her hair back defiantly and looked searchingly at him from the corner of her eye.

"I've shown you that I love you, Sam, and now you need to do the same for me. I know you've said from the first that you don't want me to come with you, but I don't understand why. How can life on your sloop be any worse for me than the life I am leading now and will continue to lead while you are gone?"

Unable at first to respond to her desperation, Sam looked at her ravaged, angry eyes for a long moment. Then he sighed, and, smiling sorrowfully, said, "I have no answer for you, Maria, except that you know how I feel -- that I cannot and will not take you on this voyage." After a pause and in a lower, more tender voice, he added, "I promise you, however, that I will return for you. Whether I am rich with pockets full of gold or still a poor dreaming sailor, I will come back and take you away from here."

"I can't settle for that, Sam Bellamy. I want you to know that I love you and curse you," she said, her voice trembling imperceptibly. "Know that I will curse you until I see you set your anchor down again in this cove; then, perhaps again, I will love you as much as I love you at this moment."

As she said this, the light of the early morning sun had sifted down through the trees and shone directly in her glistening eyes, causing her to blink and turn her head away from him. Patiently yet firmly, he took her face between his hands and kissed her softly on the lips. Then, looking at her steadily, he said, "I vow to return to you, Maria. I have never said that to another woman, but I say it to you. I will come back, and I will come back a rich man. Until then, remember the words on the coins we have exchanged."

With that, Sam spun on his heel and without looking back, walked the short distance to his sloop and boarded the vessel. As Maria watched him, she slowly unclasped the necklace he had given her and held it to her lips. Its odd scent evoked a wave of nausea in her, a sensation she had known more than once recently, and she wondered whether the advancing tide of loneliness she was feeling had filled her entire body. Attempting to banish the thought from her consciousness, she dropped the necklace with its pendant coin, and with the toe of her shoe she slowly ground it into the soil until the words on the coin – Death if we be parted – were indistinguishable in the dirt. Then, as if wearied by a long illness, the young girl made her solitary way away from the dock and disappeared beyond a hedgerow.

Isaac did not know what to make of the scene he had witnessed. Until a few days before, he had hoped to ship aboard the sloop of Captain Sam Bellamy, a man he admired perhaps more than any man he knew; and until a few minutes before, he had harbored the secret ambition to marry Maria Hallett someday. Now, derided by his own vanity, Isaac knew himself to be a fool, yet his anger at this knowledge was deep and inadmissible. He was still fifteen, still too young and unacquainted with his own failings to be able to accept them; so he directed his quiet yet considerable fury not at the lovely young woman who had just disappeared from view but at the flamboyant figure of a man who was standing at the helm of the sloop that was just turning into the wind and sailing toward the now golden sun.

Chapter Nine
Letters
Fall, 1716

A free-thinking schoolmaster once told Maria about Penelope, Odysseus's loyal wife who waited twenty years for the return of her wayfaring husband. Although Maria felt a kinship with that patient woman now that Sam had left her, she was much more aware of the differences between them: Whereas Penelope was a married mother and wife to a wealthy king, Maria was a single young woman of no means who, as she would soon discover, was to become a mother without a husband. Lacking the security of Penelope's rank and social power, Maria was terrified.

Within days of Sam's departure, the feelings of loss and discomfort that Maria had felt on that fateful morning transmuted into something more defined and physical. Frequently when she awoke, the smells of baking bread and frying eggs permeating the Freeman household would churn her stomach and make her ill. In the weeks that followed, she recognized her condition; she had helped Mrs. Freeman through a recent pregnancy, and well aware of the symptoms, she gradually began to reconcile herself to facing the prospect of motherhood alone.

At first, myriad fears swirled in her consciousness – fears of being discovered, of illness, of estrangement; in Boston unmarried mothers had been whipped and even stoned. Especially at night when she was alone with her thoughts, Maria's mind turned in upon itself. She knew intuitively that silence was the only ally of a young girl in her situation, yet she also knew that concealment of her condition was ultimately impossible. At such times in the deep expanse of night or at unshielded moments during the day, she would think of Sam. After he had given her the engraved coin on their last night together, he had said he would write to her as soon as he could. In her darkest moments she recalled that promise, the tender tone of his voice as he made it, and in her heart she held him to it. Every day that passed without the promised letter attenuated her memories of him, her best and truest companions, and increased the desperation she felt.

****

Raw weather arrived sooner than usual in September, 1716, and its shafts of wind seemed to deliver up Jack Rudd to the Freemans' door one cold evening. The Freemans and the children had already retired leaving Maria alone with her thoughts by a dwindling fire. Sam had told Maria that he would communicate with her through Rudd, a cousin from Nantucket, so when the man appeared at the door and announced his name, Maria knew at once that he had news from Sam. They spoke in low voices. A man of few words, Rudd simply said, "I am traveling by packet up to Boston, and I told my cousin that I would deliver these to you." As he said this, he held out two letters to her, then continued, "I haven't read 'em because I can't read, but I promised Sam to help him when I could. If I return this way and if you have anything to send to him, I'll do what I can to get it to him. He's a good man, Sam is, and that's why I am here."

Maria stared for a moment at the paunchy, weathered man and could hardly restrain herself from embracing him. Instead, she took the letters, saying, "Thank you, Mr. Rudd. Mr. Bellamy _is_ a good friend of mine, and I am grateful to you for bringing his letters to me." Hesitantly, she added, "Have you heard anything about him and how his voyage is progressing? He has been gone now for almost six months."

Rudd merely shrugged and said, "No, ma'am. A vessel arrived in our harbor a few weeks ago with these letters, and the only news you'll get about Sam will be what you read in them." With that Rudd began to edge away from her, his craggy face seeming almost to dissolve in the gathered darkness.

As he receded from her, Maria called out to him, saying, "Mr. Rudd, I hope you will return. If you do, I will have a letter for you to send off to Mr. Bellamy." But he was no longer visible as she uttered these words, and she almost questioned whether he had heard them. Maria wondered at the diffident and shy nature of the mysterious

Mr. Rudd but only for a passing moment because in her hands she had two letters from Sam.

As she slowly returned to her place by the fire, her fingers trembled as she opened the first envelope.

May 2, 1716

My dearest Maria,

The seas are calm today, and I am grateful to have the opportunity to write to you. After I left you, I put in at Newport for a few days where I met Paulsgrave Williams, a goldsmith, a good man, and a boon companion. I was there when he bade farewell to his wife and children, and I marveled that a wealthy man like him would sign in with my small crew. But we have nevertheless made a pact, and he has joined me on my voyage.

We have found no gold so far – not a farthing after a number of weeks of searching -- and the men are beginning to grow restless. And so am I. Spanish divers have been here already and taken as many as 600 chests that were lying in the shallows, leaving only those in the deeper, more dangerous waters. They had returned to Spain before we arrived. Thirteen vessels along these shores, and we have found nothing! Some say that as many as 700 chests of gold still remain offshore, but we have no way of securing it, and our patience is gone. Our weeks here have been long, hot, and empty, and maintaining order among the men has become more difficult as our hopes of finding gold have vanished.

I think of you often, my queen, and hold you in my thoughts as I did on our last night together. The memory of our hours together bears me up in these difficult days, and I am cheered by the thought that you are happier than I am. I send you this letter in hopes that someday you will read it and recall my pledge to return to you.

With all my faith,

Sam

P.S. Paul and I have met a man named Hornigold, a desperado but an able captain who knows the waters and the cays in this area. He may have much to teach us. We have discussed joining forces with him, and perhaps our prospects will improve.

Before opening the second envelope, Maria read the first letter a second time and then a third. She imagined the blue water of the West Indies, she heard the timbre of Sam's voice in the words on the page, she examined the sweeping curves in the letters he had made with his pen. Of all the events he had recounted, however, one phrase transfixed her – that he believed her to be happier than he was. As she read that line again and then again, she felt a great, dark chasm open within her, and she felt herself the most miserable person in a very lonely place. How could he imagine her happy? How could he not know that she was carrying his child? All of a sudden the great distance separating them seemed vaster than the spaces among the autumnal stars, and she wondered if his promises to return were as empty as his dreams of gold. As she stared at the letters in her hands, she sensed what a fragile thing hope is.

Deeply shaken, she inhaled, opened the second envelope, and began to read a letter that had evidently been written several months after the first.

July 4, 1716

My Dearest Maria,

So much has happened in the last few months. After I last wrote you, I sold Poseidon's Toy, and Paul and I joined with Benjamin Hornigold and Louis LeBous. Until recently Hornigold has been the leader of our band, made up of two sloops and a combined crew of 140 men. Three months ago, I had given up all hopes of riches, and, in fact, if I had continued to seek the galleon gold, I would still be there and have nothing to show for my time. Instead, Paul and I decided to go on the account and make our money where we could find it. With Hornigold and LeBous we were very successful. We took a number of prize ships with the expense of only a few shots, and now we have their wealth in our holds.

For a month now I have been captain of our small fleet. Hornigold and the crew had a falling out over whether we should attack English vessels. Hornigold resisted. The old man, who taught Teach how to sail, would not cross the line and take a ship manned or owned by an Englishman, so he has been deposed, and I have been elected captain in his place – such is the sweet trade of the pirate. I no longer feel a bond to my homeland or my king but, instead, only to my men and to you. I do feel a debt to my mentor, Hornigold, however. We supplied him with a sloop and twenty-six willing men, and when he sailed away from us, I saluted him with a cannonade from our guns. He taught the mad drunkard Teach, known as Blackbeard, the ways of the sea, and he taught me as well. I am grateful to the old man, and parting from him was one of the saddest days of my life. But now that I am outside the British law, I intend to pursue my own advantage and that of my comrades, the best of men.

We have overtaken many vessels in recent weeks, and our crew of men has increased with men who have joined us of their own will and a few who have not. We are men of all sorts –runaways, adventurers, Englishmen, Irishmen, Frenchmen, Negroes, and men who have left the King's and merchant service – but we are all free, and I am their prince, not their king.

Maria, I have gained substantial treasure, and when I return to you, I will have more. Paul, LeBous, and I are looking for a ship of force, one that will dominate the seas hereabouts, and when we conquer it, we will be in a position to become very wealthy men indeed.

You cannot imagine the beauty of these islands and of the blue water surrounding them. The breezes are so warm and steady. Here a man can live by his own rules and wits, and I vow to return here with you after we are together again. Of necessity, my men and I must move in secrecy now, so I will be unable to write you for some time. Know, however, that you are always in my thoughts, my future queen, and I look forward to the day I will once again hold you in my arms. Until that time, wish me well.

Faithfully,
Sam

When Maria finished reading, she stared fixedly into the embers of the fire for several minutes; then her fingers tightened slowly around the pages, and she threw them onto the smoldering coals, where they momentarily flared gold, blackened, and then curled into wisps of smoke. As she watched the letters blacken, curl, and wisp up the chimney, she knew that she had crossed a terrifying boundary: Sam would not be returning to her, and if he did, it would be as a fugitive who must die violently; the child growing inside her would never have a father, and she would forever live outside the approval of everyone she knew, even the small children sleeping quietly in the next room. In these moments as she sat by the dying coals, she recognized the shame ahead of her, but stronger were the surges of anger she felt: anger that he had not taken her with him, anger that his reckless quest for gold had destroyed any promise of a future together, anger at herself that she still loved him so wildly. In a room barely lit by the dying fire, Maria bowed her head, and her body silently pulsed with great sobs of frustration and grief.

Although Maria was unaware of the fact, at the time she was reading these letters in late September, Captain Sam Bellamy was fulfilling his promise and becoming one of the most successful pirates of the era. Having won the loyalty of a fierce band of seadogs within only a few weeks of meeting them, and having deposed the legendary pirate, Hornigold, in that short time, he and his men cut a path of terror through the Windward Islands and the Virgin Islands. By 1716, the reputation of pirate crews for unrestrained violence had become so widespread that many merchant ships would lower their flags without a fight when they saw a vessel flying the skull and bones pursuing them. In many such cases the pirate crews outnumbered them by ten to one making resistance pointless. For all his conquests -- more than fifty in all – no record exists of Sam Bellamy exercising violence against those he overcame; in fact, most often he would take what he was after and allow the victimized captain to keep his vessel. One exception occurred toward the end of his pirating career when Bellamy planned to return the ship of Captain Beer to him but was outvoted by his crew. This account, however, must await a later chapter.

When she awoke from restless dreams two hours later, Maria raised her head stiffly from the table. The room was still the same – tomb-like in the pre-dawn darkness – and she felt illimitably alone in the silence. Her anger was still smoldering, however, and she moved quickly to restart the fire that was now almost cold in the hearth. Once she had done this, she impulsively located a quill, ink, and some paper. Sam Bellamy would not have the last word in this exchange, and she intended to scald his heart with white-hot words and the news of their coming child:

September 22, 1716

Dear Sam,

   You call me your queen, yet on this lonely night I am far from exalted. I have received your letters from the hands of your cousin, Mr. Rudd, and they have made me the most miserable and deject of creatures. By turning against the law and your country, you have forsaken me and left me the loneliest of women. Tonight as the morning light nears, I curse you for leaving me, for leaving me to face being a mother alone, and for leaving your child. Yes, Sam, in a few short months you will be a father, and from what you have told me, you are now an outlaw. I wonder if you will ever see your child….

   If you can recall yourself to your rightful mind, if you give up your present adventures, and if you return to the woman you call your queen, I will welcome you joyfully, but if you do not, I will whisper your name as a curse until I die.

Maria

   When she finished the letter, Maria held it before her in the wavering light and read it twice. Then she looked at the hearth, in which the fire had rekindled and sinuous flames were curling upward. Her mind was ariot with wild thoughts and questions:

   "Hornigold? LeBous? Edward Teach? (She had heard the name Blackbeard before), On the account? How would she care for the child? And what would become of the two of them? What are love and hatred, or are they just different words for desire and fear? Where should she send the letter and how should she send it?" She did not know the answers to these questions, but she did know that her belly was growing larger and that she longed to see Sam Bellamy's face once again in spite of what she had written.

   Then she looked again at the fire. The yellows of the flame moved and blurred through the tears in her eyes, and for an instant she imagined the eternal embers of hell. In her hand was the letter she had written, and she considered its contents long and hard. The words were so harsh and final, and she pictured her lover reading them: his hurt would be deep and the scar would last. She recoiled, and for this moment, at least, she was unwilling to add more to the pain either of them was facing. He *was* her lover, and honoring that memory, she cast a crumpled letter into the flame and watched it decompose as the others had before it.

****

In the weeks that followed, Maria gradually lost weight in her face and arms and became rounder with her child. By October, no longer able to disguise her condition, she had begun the seventh month of her pregnancy when Mrs. Freeman looked directly into her eyes one morning and said, "You have something to tell me, don't you, child?"

Maria had sensed Mrs. Freeman's suspicions for several weeks yet she was still unprepared for this question when it came, so she remained silent. Mrs. Freeman persisted, not unkindly, "Maria, your uncle and I have been aware of the changes in your manner and appearance for some time, and we believe that you are to have a child. Is that so?"

"Yes, ma'am."

"If that is the case," Mrs. Freeman continued, "we will allow you to stay with us until the child is born, but you must find a new home for yourself after that time. We are thinking of our children and of your interests too. Perhaps the father of the child will take you in."

Maria inhaled deeply. She had known this moment had to come – an unmarried young mother could never be permitted to tend to the care of young children – yet she had only imagined the reality, not confronted the shock of the consequence as she did now. Her aunt had defined her immediate future for her, and tears began well up in her eyes. Formless panic threatened her unanchored soul, but as quickly as it took her breath, she struggled to master it. Looking steadily at Mrs. Freeman and speaking as evenly as she could, she said,

"The father of my child is away at sea and does not even know of his child's existence." Then more loudly and fiercely, she said, "Aunt Elizabeth, I have served you faithfully and well for the last two years, but if I am to be sent out of your home, it will be now rather than later. If you do not wish to have me here in two months, then I will begin to make my way on my own as soon as tomorrow!"

"How can you mean that, Maria? Who will take you in?"

"I don't know as yet, but I will find my way. My life has not been an easy one, it never has, and although you have been very kind to me and taken me under your roof, I will not live where I am not wanted."

The words had been said, and Maria was unwilling to take them back -- nor did she want to. As Elizabeth Freeman regarded this young woman, she felt a great wave of regret pass through her. Her sister's child was lovely and willful but so vulnerable, solitary, and young. Poised between sorrow and guilt, she dropped her gaze from the girl's pooling eyes and murmured, "Then so be it."

Chapter Ten
Outcast
October - December, 1716

After a fitful night and a tearful morning farewell with the Freeman children, Maria was on the road to Silver Springs. In the depths of the night, she had considered the full extremity of her situation: she had been living in Eastham for just two years, and as a young girl in a desolate place, she had few people she could call on for help. The women of the church would shun her, the men would be afraid of her, and her friends would be told not to associate with her. In this world the community regarded single people as a moral threat: in some towns unmarried men were fined, and until recently some unmarried women with babies had even been whipped. As these thoughts filled her mind, she summoned the faces of those she might turn to in her distress, and only one kept reappearing: Isaac's. Isaac was gentle, caring, and quiet, and he was her friend. She knew he would help her if he could, and she could not say that about many of the people she knew. Isaac had lived in the area his entire life, and he might even know someone who would assist her when the child was to be born. As these thoughts tumbled and blended in her mind, she finally gave herself up to sleep, and her last thought was, "Tomorrow I will find Isaac."

The road to Silver Springs was narrow and dusty in October, and the gusty morning air promised an early onset of winter. Maria hardly noticed the pine needles whispering in the wind, and when she stood on the large, flat rock slab at Isaac's door, she rehearsed for a final time what she planned to say to him. Then the door opened, she was looking directly into the young man's face, and despite all her preparation, she was momentarily surprised.

When Isaac opened the door and found Maria standing there, he saw a fawn-like expression of mingled fear and surprise on her face that made her seem immensely beautiful to him, more lovely than he had ever imagined her before. He had seen her infrequently and only from a distance following the day Sam Bellamy had sailed out of Town Cove, and although he had often thought of her, he had doubted he would ever speak to her again, so distant had she seemed to him that morning. As they both stood on the threshold of the cottage, disconcerted and surprised, they seemed rooted in the doorway, moving neither inside nor outside.

Maria breathed in deeply and began, "Isaac, I have no place to live, and I need your help. Can you and your mother take me in or help me to find a place?"

Staring at her in disbelief, Isaac could think of nothing to say at first, so she took another breath and quickly continued,

"In two months I will have a child, Sam Bellamy's child, and I have decided to leave the home of my aunt and uncle. They said I could stay until the baby came, but I refused to remain knowing they did not want me there." As she said this, small tears formed in the corners of her eyes, but she managed to control her voice and keep her gaze fixed on Isaac, as if losing this hold on him would plunge her over some deep abyss. "I have come to you, Isaac, because you are one of the few people I can count as a true friend."

Isaac vividly recalled the morning when he had last seen Maria and Sam together – how alien and young he had felt standing in the shadows – and he particularly remembered the bitterness he felt toward Sam Bellamy, which had not subsided. Now, seeing her so altered and solitary before him, he felt another wave of anger wash through him. He paused for a moment to gather his thoughts; then, focusing his attention solely on her plight to the exclusion of all other competing feelings, he said, "Thank you for coming here, Maria, and perhaps I *can* help you." He was pensive for another moment or two, then took her hand, directed her away from the house, where his mother was still sleeping, and led her past a well tended garden to the nearby bluff overlooking the bay.

"Do you see the tavern there on Great Island across the bay? I look at it every day, and, as you know, more than a year ago Mr. Smith gave me a job working there. I know him well – he is a good man – and I am sure he would do the same for you." Isaac paused to let her absorb the idea and then continued. "It is not a place for you to live because it is a rough crowd out there at the inn, but the pay is adequate, and the food is better than that." As Isaac was speaking, Maria removed her hand from his, and looked tentatively out to the bay and then back at him. Isaac soon began to think and speak more excitedly. "It would not be fitting for you to live in my cottage. My ill mother would not allow it, but let me think..." and he paused again. After a long interval and while still looking at the bay, he said, "My uncle, Colonel John Knowles, lives near Salt Pond, four or five miles from here, and his wife, my Aunt Mary, broke her hip in a fall recently. She has been confined to her bed for a couple of weeks, and I'm sure they could use the help of a young woman around the house – even if it is for a short time. There are children everywhere in that family, seven of them young and old, and I know my cousins will make you feel welcome in the house." From the corner of his eye, Isaac then looked at Maria.

As he had been speaking, images welled in Maria's mind -- living in the same house with two strangers and seven children, serving ale to the rough sailors on the island, Isaac tending to her while Sam was so distant, the child growing within her, its approaching birth -- and a tremor passed through her. Isaac was a sweet young man, a friend, but his plan was so dangerous for a girl like her. It was all she had, however, and she whispered, "I hope so. I hope we will be safe" In almost every way the plan was uncertain and frightening to her, yet she had few choices, so she said with an optimism she did not feel,

"Isaac, would you speak with Mr. Smith and your uncle for me? It would be a great favor, and I am very grateful to you." Then, barely audibly, she began to cry, at first quietly and then, her throat contracting spasmodically, she inhaled deeply and large tears made their way down her face. She was helpless to control them so she did not try.

As she looked up at him, her eyes glistening in the early morning light, Isaac's first impulse was to kiss her tears dry, to place his thumbs gently on her cheeks and softly press away her sadness. Instead, aware that he had no rights in the matter, he embraced her somewhat awkwardly, as he might have held his ailing mother, as if she might break at his touch. Then, taking her by the shoulders in each hand, he slowly pressed her away from him, and smiling, he said, "You will be safe, you and your child, and I will be here to help you. We need to pay a visit to my uncle."

****

At the age of forty-two, John Knowles was a colonel and commander of the local Barnstable Regiment, a juryman, the town coroner, a respected farmer and planter, and the father of six sons and a daughter ranging from twenty to seven years old. At an early age, before he could remember, he and his sister, Isaac's mother, had been orphaned and subsequently raised by their uncle, Joshua Bangs. Disciplined, efficient, and practical, a man of the land and his time, Colonel Knowles had also had his sympathies enlarged by the absence of his unremembered parents, which was perhaps the reason he had surrounded himself with a small flock of children; in fact, he was so grateful to his uncle for becoming a surrogate father that he named his first son, Joshua, after him; furthermore, his younger sister had always been dear to him, and his nephew was a good boy. Having lost his parents as an infant, Knowles had a deeper sense of the loss they had endured when Isaac's father had wasted away in front of their eyes two years before, and the sympathy he felt for them was one of the firm threads that moored him to the earth.

As a consequence, when Isaac appeared at his door that October morning accompanied by a pretty young slip of a girl, Knowles was glad to see him. Isaac had always been willing to help him with the crops, and although the young man's life had been attended by misfortune already, Knowles admired his resilience and his devotion to his mother. He was a good boy. The girl was another matter altogether. As the two young people stood in front of him, her eyes seemed to assess him in a glance and then wandered over his shoulder into his house and from there to his nearby barn. In her eyes the Colonel read willfulness, even defiance – as if she were well acquainted with disappointment and was prepared to confront it on her own terms the next time she encountered it. Although the girl stood somewhat behind Isaac as he addressed his uncle, her silence and the intensity of her gaze forced Knowles to revise his initial impression. This was no slip of a girl but quite a lovely young woman, and he involuntarily wondered what fate had yoked these two young people together.

At the time his wife, Mary, was recuperating from having broken her hip in a fall two weeks earlier, and Knowles knew that they could use the help of a young woman with meals and cleaning the house. After all, the Knowleses had six hungry boys and a seven year old daughter to feed, and with his wife temporarily incapacitated, he needed all the help he could get. After inviting Isaac and Maria into the dwelling and listening to Isaac relate the girl's story, Knowles felt conflicting currents of emotion: he was a good Christian farmer and the girl was in need; furthermore, while he was a good Christian, he was also a town official. He wanted to help his nephew but he wondered if this young woman would complicate the life of an already large family; and he questioned whether his wife would allow her into the house in the first place. Finally, how was he, a vital man with many jobs to do, to be responsible for this vulnerable young woman?

When he posed this last concern to the two of them, Maria said, "If it would be agreeable to you. Mr. Knowles, I could sleep in your barn until the weather turns colder." Then, running her eyes around the interior of the room, she added, "I am an able cook and a good housekeeper, and I could provide you with a small rent from the wages I hope to make at the tavern across the bay." Then more quietly, she added, "I am also good at taking care of myself."

As he pictured this pregnant girl tending the tables at Samuel Smith's tavern, Knowles's misgivings dissolved, his sympathies widened, and he began to smile. "Child, you needn't pay me any rent, but if you would be more comfortable sleeping on the hay in the barn for now, you are welcome to do so. You have a long road ahead of you, and if we can make the journey any easier for you and your child, it will be our pleasure. Of course, I will have to speak with my wife about your living with us, but your being a good cook and a help around the house should win her over."

And so a bargain was struck: In exchange for Maria's cooking the family's meals and keeping the house in order, the Knowles family would provide her with shelter, a place to sleep, food, and, perhaps most important, as much privacy as possible under the circumstances. Having had seven children in the span of fourteen years, and temporarily hobbled by her injured hip, Mary Knowles was delighted to have some extra help with the household duties, even if the young woman was single, uncommonly pretty, and pregnant. With her husband associated with the military and her father, Paul Sears, a noted sea captain, Mary was as suited to regimentation and discipline as a Canada goose flying south in October or November. She was also as partial to babies as her husband was to orphans, and she agreed with him that so long as the girl was willing, she could sleep in the barn until she could find better arrangements. At this time in their lives, these two parents sensed that the arrival of this girl would somehow substantially affect their family; yet they were both too entangled in the demands of their children and work to fret about the consequences. And so Maria settled into the barn adjacent to the Knowles home and awaited the arrival of her child.

Despite having had some doubts about hiring a young woman who had left the employ of a good church family, Samuel Smith acquiesced to Isaac's request and hired Maria to do odd jobs around the tavern. In the weeks that followed, Isaac and Maria would meet every morning at Blackfish Creek and sail together to the island and then return in darkness after the tavern closed.

On one such evening, as they were making their way home in Isaac's skiff and the moon was playing lightly over the bay, Maria, who by now was well round with her child, looked across at Isaac and said, "Isaac, the time has come for me to plan for the delivery of my child. I have been thinking a great deal about this, and while I am quite afraid, I have some thoughts I would like to share with you."

These evening boat rides had been both a delight and torture for Isaac. He loved the way the low lapping of waves on the boat's hull mingled with the lilt of Maria's voice, the way the moon provided just enough light to illumine the features of her face; and he reveled in the silences that seemed to softly encircle them, encapsulating them in this boat as if they were guided by a fairy's wings instead of his firm hand on the tiller. His torture was that he could never share these sensations with the girl. For Isaac, the presence of Sam Bellamy prevailed everywhere, his name in her idle comments, his face in Isaac's mind, his voice in the wind, his life in her rounding shape. Although he was in far distant waters, Bellamy constricted Isaac's voice as surely as if he had his hands on this throat in this skiff, and Isaac hated him for that.

Preoccupied with these impressions, Isaac paused for a few moments to assemble his thoughts before responding, and then he asked slowly, "What are your plans, Maria?"

"Well," she said, "Sam knows nothing of this child and will not return for some time – if at all.... I have no intention of returning to my own family members, especially since your uncle and aunt have been so kind to me. I cannot thank you enough for introducing me to them. Your aunt has been wonderfully helpful to me, and she has told me of a Nauset tribeswoman, Solosanna, who has helped her with the birth of each of her children. As you may know, Solosanna is a healer and mid-wife, and she has attended to a number of the girls in her tribe and others like me." After a pause, Maria added in a lower tone, "In fact, I have already spoken with her and she has said she will help me when my time comes." Then her words tumbled forth, "Oh Isaac, my time will be coming so soon, within two weeks, Solosanna tells me, and I am afraid of being alone when it happens. I have no family of my own to call on, and I have only known your people for such a short time. When my time comes, would you be willing to come and be with me? One of the Knowles children, maybe John or Seth, could fetch you, and it would mean so much to me to have you there. Have I told you that I intend to name the child Samuel if he is a boy?"

She had not told him the name, and Isaac felt Bellamy's presence even more keenly now with this reminder. Though inclined to speak bitterly, Isaac restrained the impulse and measured his tones:

"Running Water knows of Solosanna and has told me she is a wise and capable woman. She should be a great help to you, and, of course, I will be happy to attend you. Is there really no chance that the father will not return in time to see his child?

"No, no chance," Maria murmured softly, "Perhaps someday..." Then she added quickly, "Thank you, Isaac, for being my friend. I have been so alone, and were it not for you and your family, I should be totally lost."

Isaac considered telling her how her hair seemed to flow like gold around her shoulders in the low moonlight, but carefully eying the shape of his sail, he simply said, "Yes, my family are good people," as he turned the skiff up into the wind and expertly directed it ashore.

✶✶✶✶✶✶✶✶✶✶✶✶✶✶✶✶✶✶✶✶✶✶✶✶✶✶

Samuel had fine, black hair, dark eyes, long fingers with oval shaped nails, and small, softly creased lips, but those witnessing his birth saw the infant in very different ways: To John and Mary Knowles, he was a vulnerable little wayfarer, a nestling that had fallen from its nest, a newborn that would need all the protection it could find. To Isaac, the infant was Sam Bellamy's son, a wailing reminder of the distance separating him from Maria, a representation of the obligation he felt to the girl he still loved.

To Maria, he was a memento mori, the image of her lover who she feared would never return to her, an insistent presence that separated her from friends, family, a quickly receding past, yet a soul connected her to the pulsations of human experience. Only Solosanna, who was accustomed to ushering tender creatures into crude and often hostile conditions and whose vision transcended that of the others, saw the child for what it was: a wondrous creation requiring human care and attention, a butterfly in transition, a breathing miracle bathed and cleansed in the blood of life.

Yes, the child had been born healthy and strong. As Maria had planned, Isaac was there when she sent for him, the Knowles family tended generously to her needs while the Nauset mid-wife presided gently yet firmly over the scene, and in the early morning, with a soulful cry, the child was born. When she was alone in the hours that followed, Maria stared frequently at the infant's features, trying to locate her lover in them Then – and she could not tell why – her breath would catch, her vision would swim, and she would crumble into helpless, chest-constricting sobs. When her tears had subsided, she would lie awake, unable to sleep, feeling as if the stranger cradled next to her were still living within her, as if she were a massive, ruined, old mansion. These sensations and the tasks lying ahead of her, even the effort required to rise from her bed, exhausted her. Nevertheless, although the cellar of her despair was dark, she found the strength each morning to tend to her duties as a new mother.

When she had knocked on Isaac's door seeking help, Maria had also been looking for a measure of privacy, of relief from the judgments that she knew would follow her; and in the weeks that followed, the Knowles family, large as it was, respected her condition as they would that of a family cat, allowing Maria a zone of separation and a distance that was both comforting and painful to the young girl. After the birth of the baby, however, as birds randomly disperse seeds about a region, so townspeople spread rumors about Maria living in John Knowles's barn north of Town Cove and west of Salt Pond. Maria was too absorbed in her fears for her child and their uncertain future to be aware of these undercurrents; if she had known of them, though, they would have only added to the sense of isolation she already felt.

As a consequence, three days after she had given birth to the child, when she saw three darkly clad men approaching the Knowles farm by the path leading up from the Cove, their breath making ghosts in the cold December air, her first panicked response was to conceal the child. Before considering what might ensue, she pulled the child from its cradle by the fire, clasped it tightly in her arms, alerted John Knowles that some men were coming up the path, slipped through the back door of the Knowles dwelling, and stealthily ran to the barn, fearing only that she might be seen. After she had gently placed her baby boy on the stiff straw, she purposefully turned back to the house, vaguely hopeful that the men, tithing officers charged with enforcing church attendance and upright behavior in the congregation, might have veered from their path and disappeared.

Her hopes were futile. Upon returning from the barn, Maria saw three dark shapes outlined in the doorway, with a fourth, a concerned John Knowles, facing them.

Of the three, Maria knew only one, the Reverend Samuel Treat, but she had seen the other two men, Daniel Smith and Hesekiah Doane, in church and recognized them as tithingmen for the congregation. As she approached them, Mr. Knowles turned to her and said, "Maria, these good men would like to have some words with you."

Before he could go any further, Maria said, "Gentlemen," and as she said this, she looked directly at Reverend Treat, who she knew would listen to her, "I have been without family for over two months now, and Mr. Knowles and his family have been kind enough to employ me to cook their meals and clean their house. For these services, they have provided me with room and board. As you may know, I have no parents, and because I have left the home of my kinfolk, the Freemans, I have had to take care of myself. Thanks to the help of the Knowleses I have been able to do so. My question to you is simply why you have come here and what you want from me."

Somewhat taken aback by Maria's challenging tone, Mr. Treat spoke first among the men, "Miss Hallett, you are, indeed, the subject of our visit, and our concerns have to do with the many rumors surrounding your behavior as a young woman in our community. I have not seen you at church services for some months, you have left the care and employ of the Freeman family -- that family has provided no reasons for your departure -- and now we have heard that you have had a child by an unknown man. If, in fact, you have had a child, we ask of you the name of the father. Furthermore, we would like to see the child and ascertain your plans for baptizing the infant."

Any illusions she might have had that the existence of her child was unknown to the community dissipated into the crisp morning air. Her privacy gone like an evanescent soap bubble, she began to tour an interior emotional landscape in a matter of instants. At first, she quailed before the razor-like visages of these men, so stern and intimidating to a young girl. Then, as she thought of revealing Sam's identity, she felt simultaneously an upwelling of resentment at his abandonment of her and loyalty to her love for him. Then, as she examined the faces of these men, she instinctively knew she would resist their intrusiveness yet also wondered at the necessity to baptize the young child lying so quietly in the barn outside. What, after all, did baptism mean? Then, having traveled a great distance, she returned to Mr. Treat's importunate face, tired and feeling more isolated not just from these men but from the God they spoke for. Finally, she rediscovered her earlier sense of fear; now, however, she knew that she wanted to be rid of these men as soon as possible, to banish them to the outer edges of the heavens.

"Miss Hallett," the good reverend persisted, "did you hear me?"

"Yes, of course I did, sir," Maria said. "You are right that I have not been in church recently, but the reason is that I have been... somewhat out of sorts." Then, taking a breath she said, "The rumors you have heard are correct. I have had a child. At present he is sleeping in the barn where I have been living, on and off, for the last two months. The Knowleses have been kind to me, but I have also worked hard for them and for Mr. Smith at his tavern on the island.

"As far as the identity of my child's father is concerned, that is my business alone, but if it will ease the minds of the local matrons, he is not one of their husbands. In fact, he is presently sailing on the high seas and is no longer in our colony." Then, after a long pause, she added, "I do not know when, or if, he will return..." Maria's eyes flashed momentarily as she concluded, but she immediately dropped her gaze to the floor, aware that her provocative defense may have stirred the good Mr. Treat to anger.

For his part, Mr. Treat, who would die the following year after completing forty-five years of pastoral service, first looked at his two companions and then wearily regarded Maria with a measure of sympathy. He admired the spirit and energy of this girl, yet he felt a duty to her and to his congregation; he was the shepherd of a flock, after all, and that involved traveling to the far reaches of his parish to call them in. He was conscious, too, as he looked at this beautiful, young girl, of the chasm of years that separated them – she just beginning a lifetime and he was concluding one. This awareness softened him: she was a puzzle that he was, for the moment, unwilling to piece together.

After a brief pause, Treat said, "Maria, we have not come to judge you. We have come simply out of regard for your reputation, your spiritual condition, and the welfare of your child. You have spoken strongly here this morning, and I will take your passion for what it is – the voice of youth -- without holding it against you. We would, however, like to see the child and to be satisfied that you will bring it to the community of the Lord by baptizing him. Will you bring him to us so we can see him, child?"

Not wishing to enflame the minister, whose softened tone of voice had eased her anxiety, Maria decided not to contest the question of baptism or explore its meaning with him. Instead, quietly assenting to his request with a nod and a demure, perfectly performed curtsey, she went to retrieve the infant from the barn. Throughout the interview she had worried that wails or cries from the barn might interrupt them, but the child had been quiet and had not disturbed them. As she parted from the men, she moved toward the barn with the quick, nervous energy of a hummingbird; she knew that she would be exhausted once this interview was over, but she was also proud of her baby, and she was excited about showing him to others, even these dark-clad and forbidding old men.

The barn was silent, and she was vaguely surprised that she detected no movement anywhere. Then, as her eyes adjusted to the darkened interior, she sought the nook where she had nestled the child. Still there was no noise or movement, and Maria began to sense an amorphous terror in the shadows of the dilapidated building. To her left, where she had placed the child earlier, Maria saw the small shape, like an unrisen loaf of bread, immobile and silent. At that moment, a barn owl hooted softly from the rafters. Startled, she reflexively looked upward into the felt-like darkness for the source of the noise, and finding a pair of golden disks peering back at her, she quickly averted her gaze.

When she turned her eyes back to the child, she already knew what she would find. By now her pupils had widened, her eyes were accustomed to the dark, and she approached the baby on tiptoe. The child lay face-away from her on its stomach, and in his hands she saw stiff strands of hay. Immediately she rushed to right the child, to look it in the face. At first touch the child was cold, and its skin had already developed a blue tinge, as pale as a robin's egg.

Then she looked at his purple lips. In his mouth were yellow, broken strands of straw, straw that had stifled his cries and choked off his life. She immediately extracted all that she could, and when the child failed to respond, she thrust him above her head into the darkness as if he were an offering. Then she began to shake his limp torso, at first slowly and then more violently. And then she began to scream.

Her repeated cries were filled with exhaustion, terror, impotence, failure, and sorrow, and they carried up into the dark hayloft, out to the adjacent house where the church officers were waiting for her, down the path they had come by, and far into the neighboring bay. No sooner had she accepted the reality of the child, its fleshly existence, than it was dead, and now events would inexorably snap together and chain her to this moment for the rest of her natural life. The shapeless, almost inhuman cries emanating from the barn filled Mr. Knowles with foreboding and simultaneously caused the four men first to look at each other and then move as one to the barn.

Moments later four sober men were poised at the threshold of the barn disbelieving what their eyes revealed to them. Standing in the half-light, and inhaling the sweet smell of the hay, they saw the beautiful Maria Hallett, her face twisted and wet with despair, holding her child high above her head, staring at the lifeless corpse of her young boy as her body heaved with throbbing, but now silent, sobs. As she stood there in her solitary pose, a great bird with piercing eyes swept down out of the rafters, looped once around the mother and child, and oared its way over the heads of the four bedazzled men and out into the pewter sunlight of the early winter morning.

Mrs. Knowles, having been startled awake from restful dreams, arrived late to the scene limping on her mending hip, and with wondering eyes surveyed the devastation.

****

Two of Eastham's leading town fathers were Samuel Smith and Samuel Treat, both of whom figure significantly in this narrative. If Reverend Treat ministered to the souls of the township's settlers, then Mr. Smith tended to their wallets as the area's leading landholder, merchant, employer, and politician. Not surprisingly the two men controlled the township's two largest structures: Reverend Treat, the meeting house near Fort Hill and Mr. Smith, the expansive tavern on Great Island. The former was the official hub of the town at which farmers, merchants, Indian converts, and upright maids and matrons would gather in times of trouble and, assuredly, every Sunday. The latter was a no less important political center, a demi-monde where whalers, oystermen, Indians, laborers, wayfarers from afar, and stray women would gather every night of the week except Sunday. Treat and Smith each straddled the social conditions, classes, and problems of the time in his own way, but they shared a common impulse, to include the white and Indian populations in the same vision, to weave the differing threads into the same social cloth and thereby frame a thriving Christian community.

To this end, Treat traveled into their villages, taught their children to read and write, learned to speak to them in their own language, engaged in foot races and javelin throws with them, and nursed them when they were sick. If Mr. Treat was zealous and congenial with his flock -- white and Indian -- during the week, he was cautionary and forbidding in his sermons on Sunday, plunging them into the flames and torments of hell and not releasing them until several hours had passed. His congregation never adapted completely to his braying voice nor the odd spasms of laughter that would often punctuate his sermons. But the Indians loved him. The louder his voice, the more they esteemed him; the longer his tenure as pastor, the more they revered him, the man they came to know as "little father." Not only did he recruit and train them to teach the word of the Lord in English, but he established schools for their children to learn their own language. His missionary vision was to provide the Indian people with the tools, the knowledge, and the Christian word so they could lead better lives, and he pursued this dream for forty-five years. When the end finally came in the winter of 1717, it happened amid the great snowstorm of that year. With his second wife and many of his fourteen children gathered around him, his great abrasive voice fell silent, but outside his Fort Hill home, now encircled by snow, more than one thousand of the Cape's "Praying Indians" had come to stand watch. In their preternatural way their sagamores had prophesied weeks earlier the death of "little father," and now they intended to pay their respect to the man.

Through the night and the next day following his death, church officials, townspeople, and Indians tunneled and shoveled a passage from the Reverend's small home to the Burying Acre. The snow had melted and then refrozen for the day of the funeral and interment, and when the time came to convey his stiffened body to its grave, alternating teams of Indian converts carried Reverend Treat the considerable distance to his final rest. The snow, piled high on each side *and glistening in the midday sun resembled a crystalline cathedral as the somber yet colorful pallbearers bore their burden to the graveyard. Only fifteen years later, the Indian population of Eastham amounted to one hundred and six residents.*

Chapter Eleven
The Outermost Dwelling
December, 1716

The Eastham jail was small, damp, barred, and constructed of unforgiving stone, and as is so often the case with jails, it embodied two radically opposed perspectives. From inside the jail cell looking through its single grated window, an inmate became aware that the hourglass had been inverted, the cylinder of the kaleidoscope had been twisted, the roulette wheel was spinning and the silver ball preparing to click and settle into a new slot. For Maria, captivity reconfigured time, events, and fate, and as a fifteen year old young woman charged with fornication and murder, she felt that all she could rely on were her wits. Her loss of freedom gave those outside the jailhouse walls the freedom to judge her, but in the silence of her cell, she felt that burden slowly slip from her shoulders. She had always felt herself a free agent, and now that the town fathers had confirmed this as fact, she gradually began to consider what she might do with that knowledge.

An observer walking past the Eastham jail in December, 1716, would have seen the structure and the inmate it housed in a very different light. The good people of Eastham believed that God's moral law flowed in a continuing stream from the Almighty through the scriptures to nourish the roots of human law; following from this proposition, the family was both a beneficiary of God's goodness and the ultimate expression and foundation of the community's moral stability. For these pious people, then, any unmarried person posed a threat to the communal order, and Maria was the emblem of this danger. Not only was she a beautiful and single young woman who had committed "carnal copulation," considered a crime at the time, but she had had a bastard child, which she had then reportedly murdered. The young woman stood outside the pale of forgiveness and inside the Eastham jail, and that was where she belonged.

****

The child's mottled blue face haunted Maria's dreams. Out of the velvet darkness the little boy's glassy eyes would gaze down at her as she held him above her head trying to wish breath back into him. Then she would see the four spectral figures magnified in the doorway of the barn, their mouths agape, judgment inscribed in their faces, and she would wake up terrified and quivering, as if she had just emerged from a bath in chasms of the frigid sea. In calmer moments she would recall the events that followed that horror: how Mr. Treat's face had transformed to granite, his voice rising an octave, cawing at her like a wounded bird; how Mr. Knowles had tenderly and sorrowfully placed his hand on her shoulder and taken the child from her; how the three churchmen had escorted her from the barn to the town jail, one on each side with Mr. Treat leading the procession more than a mile south, past the Burying Acre to the jailhouse on the west side of Town Cove; how random acquaintances and strangers they met along the way had stared in wonderment at them; and how dark the interior of the jail cell had seemed when she entered it that winter day.

The two young jailers assigned to guard Maria, Jeremiah Smith and Caleb Crowell, did not know what to make of her. In their early twenties, neither was accustomed to having a woman in the jail, much less a teenaged girl accused of murder. In fact, Maria fascinated them. For more than two years local boys had spoken of how pretty she was, and they were right -- her blonde hair, the curve of her lips, the slope of her eyebrows above the intelligent eyes, the lashes that curled lightly up. But now her story added to her allure: she was the lover of a mysterious man with whom she had sinned, she had killed her own child, and, lonely as she was, she was also available. In the early hours of her captivity, then, she was a temptation to the young men, and each of them took every opportunity to look in on her, to make his presence known to her.

Maria's mind, however, was elsewhere, traveling to other planets, unaware of the young men's glances and attentions. In the early morning light and then at the last moments of twilight, she would fold her arms on the ledge of the cell window, rest her chin on them, and watch the stars alternately recede or loom into view. At first dawn she watched the stars vanish like small children tiptoeing beyond the verge of sight, and in the gathering evening light she imagined them to be the lanterns of heavenly sentries assigned to protect her through the night.

After several nights in the Eastham jail, however, she knew that these sentries were empty phantasms of her mind. She had not been permitted to witness the burial of her baby in the Burial Acre, and that night, after being startled awake by the vacant eyes of her dead child, she rose quickly from her cot and went once again to sit by the window. There, in the upper corner of the embrasure she saw a spider's web stretching from the wall to the grated window, shimmering in the moonlight. She had not noticed it earlier in the day – perhaps it had been constructed while she was sleeping -- but now, seeking any relief she could find from the terror of her dreams, she began to contemplate it. She was drawn not to the motes of dust and moisture frosting on its strands nor to the small fly, which had already given up any attempts to extricate itself. Instead, she noticed the high degree of order at the center of the web and the increasing levels of disorder as the rectangles of the structure radiated to their outer limits. What interested her most, however, was the way the web was secured to the wall and bars of the jail. How hard the cement walls of the jail were, how rigid, and how delicate were the threads attached to it, and she questioned what random impulse had moved the spider to anchor its creation there.

Then her eyes moved beyond the web to the stars glinting like hard gems in the winter distance. What were the larger forces, she wondered, that encompassed their delicate, silver light and held them in their places? Were they ordained of God, or were they as adamant and hard as the darkened walls of this cell? Was God as harsh as the men who had accused her and brought her to this jail? This thought, more than the chilling dampness of the cell, made her shiver. Tangled in these musings were other questions: Where was Sam Bellamy? Would he someday return to her? Why had he not allowed her to sail with him? Would he ever find out about little Sam? How difficult had it been on this December morning to dig the hole for the small body of his son – how hard the ground? As these thoughts mingled together, she turned her head slightly, resting it in the crook of her arm and, exhausted, fell asleep returning to violent dreams filled with anger, sorrow, and regret.

Despite Maria's degradation and shame, her beauty gained an added dimension, her eyes no longer seeming to see as a girl but as a woman might, expressing a melancholy born not of youthful boredom with the present, but of regret for actions already taken. At some level that they could not fully comprehend, Jeremiah Smith and Caleb Crowell came to recognize this after a few days. When they would replace each other on duty, they would shrug their shoulders, smile ruefully, and beyond Maria's hearing, whisper to each other about her midnight cries and her long silences as she sat by the window. They were young men with no experience or knowledge of the depths Maria was plumbing, yet they were decent boys, and they felt those most basic of emotions toward her: curiosity and human sympathy. Although she was as beautiful as a hothouse flower seeming to demand that they look at her, to each of them her cell resembled a death bed scene, and they were the unwilling witnesses. The girl was younger than they were, and whether it was the bond of their shared youth or her appealing vulnerability, they wanted to help her, to somehow release her from her pain.

Intermingled with these dark, nighttime thoughts were the feelings stirred by the events of her first days in the jail, stirred as if by a poker rearranging smoldering logs and embers in a hearth. At mid-morning of her first day in the jail, Mr. Treat and John Snow, the town constable, appeared outside the door of Maria's cell, and waited silently while Jeremiah Smith swung the bars open for them. As they entered the cell, Maria noticed that Jeremiah had placed himself in the adjoining room so he could hear the conversation that occurred within.

By nature a jovial man, John Snow was the first to speak, but the gravity of his words belied the impression created by his kindly eyes and the pendulous red nose that seemed to hang from the bridge of his thick glasses: "Miss Hallett, we are here to inform you of the charges facing you and the date that has been set for your trial. As of now the judge is considering the charge of carnal copulation because you clearly gave birth to a child outside of wedlock. In addition, you will be charged with murder for negligently contributing to the death of your child. Your trial will take place in Barnstable township, and the authorities in Boston will be contacted about these proceedings. Mr. Samuel Knowles, who is the uncle of John Knowles, your recent protector, will be the judge in your case, and he plans to begin your trial within the next two weeks."

Maria could only stare stonily at the two men, unable to reconcile in her mind how her passion for Sam Bellamy had brought her at such a young age to this cell and to the accusations that had just been made against her. Her silence unsettled the two men, and they wondered whether the girl had heard what Snow had said; in fact, in light of the infamous trials held in Salem a generation earlier, Mr. Treat fleetingly questioned whether the girl might be possessed, due to her distracted expression. With this in mind and attempting to arouse her from her apparent torpor, the Reverend said,

"Maria, do you realize the severity of these charges? We wish to deal fairly with you. However, you need to know that in Boston women have been whipped and even hanged for such offenses. In some cases, suspects have even been made to touch the faces of those they are suspected of murdering – this is called the ordeal by touch – and if blood rises in the face of the dead one, the suspect is hanged. We recognize that the facts of your case are tempered by your youth, but you have committed serious offenses, and you need to know that the law of the church and state is clear in such cases."

Images of having to touch the face of her dead son again, of being whipped and perhaps hanged, eddied in Maria's mind, and after a brief pause, she cried out, "Do I realize the severity of the charges? Do I want to touch my dead child's face? Do I want to be hanged? What do you want me to say, gentlemen? What choices do I have, and who is to defend me? My only offenses are loving the wrong man too well, trying to protect my newborn child from the likes of you, and being too young to take care of myself ... But I am learning, gentlemen, I *will* learn!"

As she finished, Maria saw from the corner of her eye Jeremiah Smith's alarmed face peering through the doorway, and realizing how loudly and disrespectfully she had spoken to these officers of the court and the church, she quickly dropped her eyes to the floor and fell silent. Disconcerted by her outburst, Mr. Treat responded,

"I am sorry our words have upset you so, Maria, but we must do everything in our power to align your soul – and your son's soul – with the will of God. Mr. Snow and I will leave for now, but when I return, I will bring with me an officer of the court who can help defend you in your trial. May God be with you and may you live by His commandments."

After the two men left the building, Maria's face twisted into a knot of rage, and she whispered to herself, "I *am* learning, and I must save my soul by getting out of this God-forsaken place." As she said this, she once again became aware of Jeremiah Smith's silent presence, and she turned her moist eyes to meet his gaze.

****

On the following day, late in the afternoon, Isaac appeared in the doorway of the prison holding a bag containing needles, cloth, many colored threads, and some stitch work that Maria had begun during the weeks she and Mrs. Knowles had spent together prior to her baby's arrival. Nervous and uncomfortable at seeing Maria sitting alone in the cell, he said, "My aunt asked me to bring you your sewing, Maria. She said you had been working on this before…before you were taken away, and that you might want to have something to do while you are here." Maria was an adept seamstress, and she had designed a dress for herself adorned with a spreading apple tree and a girl sitting beneath it. Although the dress was not finished as yet, bright red apples were already stitched into the collar. Mrs. Knowles had wondered at the time why the girl was not making clothes for her child, but she had restrained herself from seeking the reason. Then when she witnessed the girl's agony in the barn and the abandoned look in her eyes as Mr. Treat led her away from that scene, the kind lady knew that she would never judge her. Sending Maria her stitch work was the least she could do for the poor girl.

As he surveyed the brick walls, touched the cool bars, and felt the December air chilling the cell, Isaac had trouble imagining Maria spending a night in this place, much less more than one night, and as much as he wanted to flee the place, he wanted even more to help her leave. Twisting the fabric of the unfinished dress slowly in his hands,

Isaac said, "Maria, this is no place for you, and no matter the charges against you, I wish to help you in any way I can."

As she took the dress and the bag from him, Maria coolly looked at Isaac and said. "Perhaps you can someday, Isaac, but first you need to hear what I have to say, and then you can judge whether you still want to help me or not." Maria then described the events of her life with the Knowles family, the scene in the barn and its aftermath, including the visit from Mr. Treat and the constable the previous day. When she finished, Maria said tremulously, almost as if she did not want to be heard, "And so, as you can see, helping me could be dangerous business for you, Isaac. I did not kill my child, but I will have to pay for his death."

"Maria," Isaac said, "I have been your friend before, and I always will be your friend. Things have changed so much since you came to my door several months ago, and I hate to even think of you in this place." Isaac paused and measured his words. Then he said, "If we can ever get you out of here, I know a place that Jeremiah – at this Isaac nodded in the direction of Jeremiah Smith who was sitting outside – that Jeremiah and I have used as a fishing shack in the spring and fall. It is near the beach in Hither Billingsgate, and it might meet your needs. It is a very simple place, but it is some distance from the people and troubles you face now. It is also a place where all you hear in the morning when you wake up is the sound of the waves on the shore and the calls of the wild birds." Isaac paused again and then added, "But perhaps I have said too much. When you are free from these charges, which I hope you will be soon, we can talk about my little house by the sea.

"I'll leave you now, Maria. I've delivered your stitch work, but you should know that I will always be ready to help you – despite any dangers…" With these words the young man moved quickly to the cell door, slipped through it, and was gone as unobtrusively as a deer eluding danger by gracefully becoming a part of a surrounding forest. After Isaac had left, Maria lay down on her cot, closed her blue eyes, and carefully listened again to the voices she had heard during the last two days. As she considered what she would do next, the voices began to blend into a low hum, and she fell into a deep, complete sleep that she had not known for days.

****

After several days passed and another visit from the constable, Maria awoke early and through hooded eyes realized that Jeremiah Smith was watching her from the other side of the bars. Before she opened her eyes completely and let him know that she was aware of him, she considered what she would say to him. Then as she rose from her cot, she smiled and said in a husky, still-sleeping voice, "Why, Jeremiah, what has brought you here before the sunlight has even come through my window?"

Seemingly surprised by her question, Jeremiah swallowed, met her gaze squarely, and began, "I have overheard what others have been saying to you, Miss Hallett, and I feel sorry for you. You are so pretty, and you are in so much trouble…"

Before he could say anything more, Maria interrupted him, her voice now quite changed, low and coiled in anticipation, "Then why don't you help me to escape? Why not unlock the door, Jeremiah, and let me go. You could make it look like a mistake, an oversight. Or if you wish, you could say I cast a spell over you!" The two laughed in youthful complicity at this, but as they did, Maria assessed the young man and smiled at him as if they were conspirators, the best of friends. Jeremiah swallowed again, hard, and grinned back at her.

****

And then she was off. During the evening Jeremiah had inadvertently left the door to her cell unlocked and fallen asleep on duty, and by the time he awoke, Maria had vanished. Within hours, she had visited with Isaac and secured the directions to the dune shack in Hither Billingsgate. While Maria was making her way through the desolate, darkened by-ways of the township, Jeremiah was alerting John Snow that she had escaped, and telling others that, for the life of him, he could not figure out how it had happened: he had simply dozed off and she had disappeared.

As events unfolded, Maria was back in her cell by the afternoon of the following day. At daybreak as she was nearing a rise on the King's Highway no more than a mile from the shack by the sea, she heard a protesting whinny of a horse and the irritable creaking of an old buckboard wagon coming toward her from the other side of the rise. Then, before she could conceal herself behind some low scrub pines nearby, the horse, the wagon, and its driver were upon her. The instant she saw the face of the driver, she knew her brief flight was over because, seated in the front of the wagon was John Knowles, and in the back, almost out of view, were two of his sons, Joshua and Seth, the three of them returning from having purchased provisions in Provincetown the day before.

The moment he recognized Maria in the early light, John Knowles understood what had happened and called out to her, "Maria, you must come back to town with us. Child, it will only go harder with you if you run away, and the countryside is wild this far from town and at this time of the year.

"Come back with us. I have been told that my uncle, Samuel, will be judging your case in Barnstable, and I will do everything in my power to intervene with him in your behalf because, as you know so well, I was there that morning in the barn."

After he had spoken, Knowles silently nodded to his sons to bring the girl to the wagon and to do so quickly. They need not have worried that she would run from them, however, because Maria had already resigned herself to returning with them. Plodding along rural paths and fretfully anticipating her place of exile by the sea had worn her nerves threadbare, and she was simply unwilling to contend with two young farm boys, much less the sons of a man whom she greatly respected. Her shoulders seemed to sag as the paper skin of a kite does when it momentarily billows then loses its fitful, upwelling air, and settles abruptly to the ground. Averting her eyes from the two young men, she allowed herself to be led back to the wagon. Within an hour Maria was sitting once again on the cot in her cell, but Jeremiah Smith was gone and Caleb Crowell was sitting in attendance outside her cell.

****

At the age of sixty-five years old and having seen virtually every permutation of human behavior, Judge Samuel Knowles was at his wits' end. The Hallett girl had now escaped not once but twice from the Eastham jail prior to her case coming to trial, and he was not at all confident that she would not flee a third time. The young jailers he had assigned to guard her seemed incapable of resisting her obvious charms, which she was only too willing to employ in the service of her freedom. As he pondered her case one late-December night, however, he realized that the problem ran much deeper. Existence here on the edge of a continent was not like living in the more settled inland cities and towns. Somehow here both the elements and the people seemed more extreme, wilder, than in civilized Boston, and the weathervane atop his house, which moaned when the winds grew violent, seemed to reinforce the point on this silver-cold winter night.

Justice, Knowles believed, was difficult to administer in such places and under such conditions. Not only had Jeremiah Smith and Caleb Crowell been duped by this willful young woman, but his nephew, John, had spoken on her behalf, telling him how alone she was in the world, how terrifying the scene in the barn had been. John was not a soft-minded man, but something he witnessed that terrible morning had subtly changed him. "Plate sin with gold and the strong lance of justice hurtless breaks," so said an old, wronged king, but Knowles knew that this girl had no gold, no family, and now no child. In Boston women had been whipped, humiliated with scarlet letters, placed in stocks, and worse – Knowles knew all this – but Eastham was not Boston; the rigor of the law, the fist of justice, might relent somewhat in this untamed place by the sea, especially in the case of a young girl like Maria Hallett who had meant no harm to anyone and kept escaping, just as the flame of a candle curls away to evade a gusting wind.

Samuel Knowles was aware of his obligations. He had carried out his duties to his community and to the court for many years, and he would continue to do so for another twenty-one years until he died at the overripe age of eighty-six. However, on this night in late December, he felt Father Time was looking over his shoulder and was anxious to close accounts on events of the passing year. As he peered through the window of his study into the moon-glitter of the night, Knowles imagined the face of the young girl as it must have appeared to those who apprehended her in that dilapidated shack by the dunes – caged, strangely impassive, exotic like a catamount.

Knowles exhaled a time-worn sigh as he dismissed these images from his mind and decided that should she flee again, he would allow Maria Hallett to remain in that God-forsaken dwelling so far from town.

****

On that same December night, an inhospitable time for planting, Maria was carefully nurturing the seeds of her freedom. She had chosen her destination, a remote hovel high atop the dunes of Hither Billingsgate, in its own way a different kind of prison, she knew, from the one that presently housed her, but it was there, not here, and that thought had upheld her ever since Isaac had mentioned its existence almost three weeks earlier. In the cavernous despair she felt at having failed twice to elude capture, she had also become aware that on this oceanside frontier, justice might be tempered by sympathy for a young girl like her, and she intended to play as skillfully as she could on the heartstrings of her captors – Samuel Knowles, John Snow, Mr. Treat, Jeremiah Smith, Caleb Crowell, and who knows how many other good citizens lurking outside the prison's walls.

If she was inclined to rebel against the town fathers and sons, Maria was more contrite toward her Heavenly Father, and on this December night her moods gusted as wildly as the wind-driven leaves outside her cell window. As she contemplated once again the shimmering stars spread out against the sky, she recalled Mr. Treat's parting wish that God be with her and that she live according to His commandments. Then she began to wonder not whether God was with her but whether she was with God. If, as seemed to be the case, she was unacceptable to those here on earth, could she possibly be acceptable to God? And if she was, how could she understand his ways? How was she a part of his blessed order?

As these questions swirled in her mind, Maria decided to take Mr. Treat at his word and ask herself how well she had attended to her Lord's commandments. Maria had learned her commandments by heart, all ten of them, and she began her inventory with the first ones:

"Thou shalt have no other Gods before me. Thou shalt not make unto thee any graven images. Thou shalt not bow down to them or serve them." She was on firm ground with these. She knew of no gods other than the one she prayed to in church, she was not idolatrous, and she worshipped only at the cross. Somewhat more confident, she moved on.

"Thou shalt not take the name of the Lord thy God in vain." She never swore, and despite her recent ordeals, she had not spoken out against the Lord; she had of late begun to question the ways of her God, however, and these doubts had begun to unsettle her.

"Remember the Sabbath day and keep it holy." Maria exhaled softly as she reviewed the Sabbaths of the last few months: her unwillingness to enter the church, the shame she felt, the days of her incarceration. She honored God in her heart but had clearly failed to honor His house with her presence. As she considered this injunction further, she realized that she was exhausted in spirit, that she had not truly rested for one day in the last three months, much less one day in the last seven. She recalled the fifth commandment.

"Honor thy father and thy mother." Soft tears formed in her eyes as she tried to recall the faces and voices of her parents, now slowly but inexorably dimming in her memory. All she had that remained of them were fading images, and honoring a memory was not the same as respecting a parent.

"Thou shalt not kill." This one was too painful, and she dismissed it quickly from her mind.

"Thou shalt not commit adultery." A current of anger seized her. This town considered her relationship with Sam Bellamy to be adulterous because they were not married, and they had had a child. Neither of them had deceived anyone, and all they were guilty of was loving each other; yet one of the reasons she was sitting in this cell was that she had broken this commandment. With tightened lips and fists she considered the eighth.

"Thou shalt not steal." Maria smiled with relief and almost laughed: she had never stolen a thing in her life, and although she might have to in the future, her record for the moment was clear on this score. Not guilty.

"Thou shalt not bear false witness against thy neighbor." She sighed. Her sins, great as they were, were driven by youth and desire – they were honest sins, and although she was not proud of them, she could not truthfully say that she would, or could, have acted any differently. However, she had not and would not lie to protect herself or to hurt others, and she hoped to remain true to this code throughout her life.

"Thou shalt not covet thy neighbor's house nor anything that is thy neighbor's." She paused a moment to struggle with the meaning of covet. If it meant envy, then she was guilty as charged. She envied the settled solidarity of the Knowles and Freeman families, the spiritual certitude of Mr. Treat, the good sense of her friend Isaac. In fact, on this dark night in this dark jail, she realized that she enjoyed none of the constants that anchored the lives of those outside these walls -- no parents, no family, no child, no home, no Sam Bellamy -- and suddenly she realized that she envied the entire exterior world.

By any measure Maria recognized that she had sins on her head, but, suddenly and strangely, she felt a throb of exhilaration pulse through her. If the laws of man and God were arrayed against her, then she would attempt once again to flee them, and the next time she would succeed. Yes, she said to herself as her eyes surveyed the four walls of the cell that had become her home, she would commit any sin short of killing if it meant that she could be out of this place.

****

It was one thing, Isaac thought, to direct Maria to the shack on the dunes, but it was quite another to steal the key to her cell from under his friend Jeremiah's nose and to slip it to her. However, he had done it, and he was not sorry. On one hand, he knew that Jeremiah was sympathetic to her – he had told Isaac as much – and on the other, rumors in town had it that the town's authorities wanted simply to be rid of the young girl and the problems she posed, to forget the moral complications of her case, to erase all memory of the mysterious lover, the dead child, and the beautiful young girl from their minds.

Isaac hoped this was the case, and because he loved the girl, he waited for her astride his workhorse at midnight in the woods north of the jail. From there they made their way along winding paths toward the outermost dwelling, the horse's footsteps being muffled and covered over by gossamer snowflakes that had begun to fall swiftly the moment Maria emerged from the jail. As he gathered wood and helped her start a fire in the chilled air of the shack, Isaac promised to visit her often and to bring supplies when he came, but her silences had grown longer as the night had lengthened, and by now, as Isaac was preparing to leave, Maria had said nothing for some time while her eyes seemed to search the dwelling for something that was not there and that she knew she would not find.

Uneasy at leaving her alone, Isaac, nevertheless, walked back through the feathery snow to his horse, and as he mounted it, he turned to look at Maria who was standing in the doorway of the cabin, a flickering candle in one hand and a thin shawl clutched firmly around her shoulders in the other. Then he recognized something he had not noticed earlier:

"I see you have finished the dress I brought to you in the cell, Maria. It's very pretty, and the apples you've sewn into the collar are beautiful"

Although Isaac could not detect it in the dim light, Maria's lower lip quivered slightly and she reflexively pulled the shawl more tightly to her; then she beamed and said, "Thank you, Isaac. The designs in the dress hold happy memories for me, but ones that seem to have happened ages ago. " Then, after a brief pause, she added, "I will never forget your kindnesses to me, Isaac, and the risks you have taken for me. You need not worry about me because I can take care of myself, but I will always look forward to your visits."

Isaac only smiled and swept his hat from his head in a gallant, half-moon flourish, powdery snow rising from its brim as he did so. Then he slowly turned his horse away from the cabin and back toward the town. As he did so, however, he could not resist casting a last look over his shoulder at the lovely girl who now appeared to him as a dark angel framed in the doorway and whose face was illumined by the candle that might be extinguished any moment by the falling snow or the gently gusting wind.

For her part, Maria somehow already knew that the sorrow of women waiting for lovers who would never return swirls endlessly in the winds of the Cape: heard in low moans from the south, felt in the sharp bite from the northwest, tasted in the spume of angry waves borne in by nor'easters – a sorrow mingling the salt of waves with the salt of women's tears. Years later a man of letters would ask whether the sadness of Londoners caused the fog or whether the fog caused the sadness. Maria would have had no trouble answering the question: she knew that the tapestry of a landscape was intricately stitched by the fate of its people and was colored by women's tears. Hers fell this night as silently and secretly as starlight.

Chapter Twelve
On the Account
1716-1717

Fifty-three ships, twenty-thousand pounds sterling (from the sale of slaves), jewelry, gold beads and pendants, rivers of gold dust, gold ingots, and gold nuggets; twenty-eight cannons, swivel guns, grenades, muskets and ramrods, elegant pistols with ribbons tied to their handles, leg irons, thousands of pounds of shot, swords; a large ship's bell, anchors, keel spikes, and handwrought nails; hogsheads of rum and ale, the skeletal remains of fish and birds, and the devotion of a ten-year old boy, the youngest pirate in recorded history. These were the measures of Sam Bellamy's success as a pirate, the bounty the sea offered up to him and that he was delighted to take whenever and wherever he could. In 1717 an honest sailor could expect to earn between one and two pounds sterling per month, but on April 25, the day prior to the Whydah's destruction, 180 fifty pound bags of gold and silver, at least one for each man on board, were hanging unguarded between decks waiting for the men when they landed -- and the men were free to look at them whenever they wished. Captain Bellamy and his men won these prizes between November, 1716, when he raised his Skull and Bones aboard the Mary Ann, and April, 1717, when the Whydah ran aground in a chaos of wind, sand, and salt water ending his short and flamboyant career as a sea captain.

****

In the short interval of three months, Sam had come to love the boy. Perhaps it was the spirit the lad had shown when he had threatened to kill his mother if she would not allow him to accompany Sam and his men after they had finished plundering the Bonetta. Perhaps it was the boy's hero-worship or his admiration of the pirates' freedom. Perhaps it was Sam's own desire to protect the lad better than his widowed mother could from people like himself. Or perhaps he saw himself as a ten-year-old mirrored in the boy's reckless spirit. Whatever the reason, in his own fashion Sam adopted the lad on the decks of the Bonetta and promised the stricken mother that her child would come to no harm aboard the Mary Anne; in fact, he sealed the oath by telling her the boy could bunk in Sam's own cabin, a covenant that seemed to give her no solace.

The scene at the end had been almost comical. For the two weeks it took the crew to move goods from the Bonetta to the Mary Anne, the boy had followed the men around like a spaniel, pestering them with questions, offering to help with a variety of jobs, clambering back and forth between the two ships, standing as tall as he could at the helm of the anchored Mary Anne, even sauntering in the manner of the ship's captain. Sam and the men had laughed at young John King, whom they called Puppy, but after fifteen days, when they were preparing to depart the now barren Bonetta, the boy acted on a plan that he had been conceiving for days. As Sam had bowed with a flourish to the captain of the ship and the young, widowed mother, the boy produced a dagger with a fine scrimshaw handle, touched it close to his throat, and turning to his mother, said, "I will do myself in if you make me stay on this ship. I want to travel with Captain Bellamy and his men, or I will die."

At first Mrs. King, a finely boned woman with pale blue eyes, laughed as if to dismiss the boy's grandiose gesture, but when she put out her hand for the knife, the boy quickly thrust it toward her, narrowly missing her outstretched fingers, and hissed, "Mother, if you try to stop me, I will kill you before I kill myself." The woman's eyes seemed to pale further as she gasped, "John, what are you saying? What would your father say? Is it not bad enough that we have been robbed by pirates, that you have lost a loving father, but now that you also wish to leave me?" As she spoke, a wisp of hair came loose from under her tightly drawn blue bonnet, subtly adding to her look of desperation and fear. Then her tears completed the portrait.

Noticing this, Sam grinned at the boy and said, "Young Pup, before you go threatening your mother, you should talk with the Captain of the ship to determine if he would want you in his crew.

Behavior such as yours is unbecoming even a pirate." As the boy slowly lowered the knife, Sam pressed his advantage. "Having watched you for the last two weeks, I like your daring, but you come a few years short of being old enough to ride the seas with me and my crew."

Completely ignoring his mother's anguish and with the dagger still clasped tightly in his fist, the boy strode determinedly toward Sam, and looking up at him, he said evenly, "Captain, find a place for me. My father is gone, I am too young to be of any use to my mother, and I can do odd jobs for you and your men just as I have for the last two weeks. You will have no truer mate than John King, and maybe I can learn to be a captain just like you," Upon finishing his appeal, the boy grandly waved the dagger over his head and slid it into the sash at his waist.

At this, Sam burst into laughter, then paused for a moment. After assembling his thoughts, he turned to Mrs. King, who was now staring fixedly at her son, and said, "Madam, I well know the dangers of sailing these seas – as do you, don't you? – and I will make you a promise: I admire your young son – there's fire in the lad – and I will watch over him as carefully as his departed father might have. The life I lead is a dangerous one, I know, but most of our prizes surrender before a cannon is fired, and I believe I can return your boy to you safely. What is more, perhaps he will be well on his way to becoming a man by the time you see him next."

The young mother would never forget the face of Sam Bellamy at this moment. Somehow he inspired belief with his clear eyes, the sheen of his black beard, his easy smile. But as she peered at him through tear-filled eyes and at all the other men surrounding her – including her own bedazzled son – she dropped her head in seeming defeat. Then after a few seconds she raised her eyes, and encompassing the man and the boy in the same steady glare, she spoke fiercely yet at just above a whisper, "Mr. Bellamy, you have enchanted my boy, and I lack the power to undo your hold on him. I choose to believe that you are a decent man although everything you represent as you stand on this deck suggests that you are not. As I look at my boy standing there with you, I believe that I have lost him for now, just as I lost my husband within the past year, but if you or your men hurt him…" At this thought she paused to control the upwelling emotion in her heart, "If you allow any harm to come to his innocent soul, I will follow you into Hell and torment you there for eternity…"

Sam had taken a bold step when he acceded to the boy's plea, and although he was abashed by the woman's despair, he would not back down before her anger. After all, crewmembers had been observing the scene, along with his counterpart on the Bonetta. Instead, as he took the boy's hand to lead him away, he looked at the mother with kindly eyes, yet there was something almost haunted in his expression, as if he were a prisoner coming to terms with a judge's death sentence. As he turned to depart, he said, "I repeat my promise that you will see him again, Mrs. King, and when you do, he will no longer be a boy but a young man. I will house him in my own quarters to ensure his safety, and on the day he returns to you he will have gold in his pockets. "

Without saying a word, she moved quickly to the boy, knelt down, and before he could recoil, she embraced him. Tilting her head up to look at Sam, she said, "Gold that belongs to someone else, I fear." Then in a soft voice, she said to the boy, "You are too young for the path you have chosen, my dear, but until you return to me – if you ever do --remember that your mother loves you, and she always will. Please remember always what I've just said to you."

If the boy felt any twinge of affection at this instant, he did not show it but, instead, grasped the dagger at his sash and said, "I will, I will, Mother, but now I am off to become a pirate. When I come back to you, I will have gold in my pockets!" And with these grand words, he stepped from the deck onto the gangplank that would lead him to the Mary Anne.

In the hours that followed, Sam must have wondered how he could have accepted a ten-year-old boy's challenge and allowed the child to join his crew when only months before he had refused to permit the girl he loved above all else to do the very same thing.

****

Although the ten-year-old John King was the youngest of all known pirates, the random manner of his recruitment was not especially extraordinary. In fact, pirate crews were among the most accepting and democratic societies of the time, or any time for that matter. Unlike the Puritan colonies taking root in the north, which firmly valued right and wrong over freedom and liberty, pirate societies functioned in just the opposite manner: the unfettered liberty that was so alluring to the young John King must have been similarly intoxicating to runaway slaves, deserters from the Royal Navy, soldiers of fortune, escaped convicts, young adventurers, expatriates, and any other early-eighteenth century males weary of routine, hierarchy, and social obligation.

However, the devil's bargain they made required them to forsake the certainties of right and wrong in exchange for the freedom to elect their own leaders, to share equally in the profits of their labors, and to walk on a deck where social status had nothing to do with birth or wealth. In no sense were these men revolutionaries interested in spearheading a new social order; instead, they were young men seeking the wispy possibilities of justice and equality that privilege and power denied them. In this sense, they were the precursors of those later in the century who would fire their muskets in Lexington or storm the Bastille in Paris. Of course, the wages of this contract were frequently violence, alienation, intimidation, and injury; and in this regard pirates of the time were simply the harbingers of the more dangerous terrorists wearing swastikas, white hoods, or turbans who would follow them in ensuing centuries. Sam Bellamy's crew must not have lost their moral compass entirely, though, because they referred to themselves as "Robin Hood's Men," the critical difference being that their moral generosity was never truly tested: Having taken fabulous wealth from the rich --slave traders among them – Bellamy's pirates never had the opportunity to return any of it to the poor before the Whydah's wealth was buried in the swirling sands along the shores of Cape Cod.

****

Maria. Eleven months, almost a year, had passed since he had left her, and here it was already February. How much had changed in his life. No longer was he a salvager or even Hornigold's faithful lieutenant, but now he was a captain in his own right. Legitimate might not be the right word to describe his status because he and his men had now been operating outside the law for five months; but the crew had elected him their leader as a mark of their respect for him, and he aimed to continue to deserve that respect. Yet the thought of Maria kept intruding at moments like this one – late one night as he sat in his cabin watching the candle tremble fitfully over his charts and the Sultana rolled gently with the waves. Suspended in a hammock, the boy was sleeping in a corner of the small cabin, and as Sam watched his small chest rise and fall like the sea waves outside, thoughts of the boy and Maria intermingled. The boy delighted him just as Maria had; they were both so young, so full of hope, and at twenty-nine Sam was beginning to feel old. He had last written her in August, yet not a day passed when her face did not flicker in his mind like the flame of the candle in front of him.

With these thoughts becoming confused in his mind, Sam pulled out the single drawer of the chart table, reached into it, and carefully lifted a volume from the drawer, placing it gingerly on top of the assorted maps. Then he began to peruse the contents. This book was his testament to the future, as detailed a record as he could compile of his life on the sea. He knew that communication with Maria was difficult, if not impossible, while he sailed under his present flag, but he hoped that someday she would read what he had written in these pages and give him the credit that was his due. As the boy, John King rocked slowly back and forth in the corner of the room, and as the sea appeared and disappeared, rising and falling intermittently in the cabin's porthole, Sam reviewed the recent past.

October, 1716

Paul has been with me since the beginning, and I could not hope to have a better friend and quartermaster. But why did he come with me? What possessed him, he with the fabulous gold earring that he himself had made, he with a fine wife and two children, he who is almost forty years old and willing to ship with men so much younger, he with wealth of his own already? His father was one of the most powerful men in Rhode Island, after all, his mother a descendant of English kings, and his family one of the wealthiest in the colonies. Despite all this, Paul was willing to stand behind me when Hornigold refused to attack ships under the Union Jack, and when it came to a vote, Paul was the first to stand up and shout, "Sam Bellamy is the man for us! We've come this far and gained precious little for our efforts. Those of you who sailed in the Royal Navy know you were paid two pounds sterling per month, and that is a pittance when you think of what we can make if we are not bound by unprofitable allegiances to the Crown. Benjamin Hornigold is a good man and an able captain, but I cast my lot with Sam!" Almost the entire crew, including Quintor, Noland, Brown, Van Vorst, and Ferguson, sided with him, and so I was elected captain. As I stood on the deck that misty morning and raised our flag with the death's head, I told the men that at that very moment they had been resurrected as free men and that I planned to lead them to greater wealth than they could imagine.

Sam Bellamy's questions pose mysteries with no answers. In fact, Paulsgrave Williams was thirty-nine years old when he agreed to join and financially support Bellamy's small band in Rhode Island prior to departing for the promise of Caribbean treasure, and he would remain with him almost to the end. In the two years that followed he became his most trusted officer and quartermaster. He was a large man, almost six feet tall when the average size of pirates, who were generally from the lower classes and therefore smaller in stature, was five feet four inches; but his hands were delicate, capable of fashioning fine works out of gold including a glistening mermaid that hung from his ear and a large pearl embedded in a shell on his ring finger. Adding to the impression he created was the pomaded wig he typically sported when on the attack; as Williams stood tall on the decks of his various ships, beleaguered merchant captains must have wondered, as they peered through their spyglasses, at the figure of a magistrate of the court pursuing them while a Jolly Roger undulated above his head.

His motives for leaving his family must have been complicated, however, because the day he set foot aboard the Poseidon's Toy, he said farewell to a wife, two young children, and a successful career; furthermore, his father, a wealthy merchant, had once served as attorney general of Rhode Island, so Paul, the son, was forsaking family, financial security, and ultimately the rule of law when he set sail with Bellamy from Newport. His two years with Sam Bellamy must have been intoxicating, however, because after retiring briefly from the "sweet trade," following the Whydah's ruin, he reentered it and continued to plunder Atlantic vessels until he finally retired at the old age, for a pirate, of forty-five.

Pursuing Bellamy's musings further, perhaps Williams was a latter day Ulysses, whose hungry heart grew impatient at not shining in use and longed to pulse again in the delight of battling with his peers. Whatever the case, when he finally returned to his presumably faithful wife early in 1718, even as he promised he would not leave her again, he must have known he was lying because he was gone again within the year. When he ultimately retired from the trade in 1723, he made a final transformation from Ulyssean adventurer to early American icon: Upon returning home, he gave up the pirate's life, assumed a new name, remarried a lovely younger woman, began a new family, and died at peace with himself and the world. In so doing and in the tradition of so many American figures who would follow him -- business successes, celebrities, politicians, heroes and rascals alike – he demonstrated the resilience and vision to remake himself over again and again, and perhaps this is the quality that Sam Bellamy so admired in his best friend as he thought about him one February evening by candlelight.

December 10, 1716

We've done well by any measure. Now that we have taken The Sultana, we have a well-armed ship with fourteen cannon that can do battle with most ships. It is one thing to encounter small merchant ships, to raise our black flag, and to have their captains surrender without a shot being fired. It is another thing altogether to be able to go after richer vessels and overcome them by force and the pluck of our men. My men are ready for larger prizes now, and, damn me, so am I. Aboard this ship every man thinks himself a captain, a prince, or a king, and let them think so long as I am their leader and can maintain their trust. Our crew amounts to one hundred and eighty men now, and when these merchant ships spy my black flag with the death's head and bones on it, they know they are outgunned and outmanned. The crew has not demanded that we fly the red flag, which means death to our victims, and I never intend to. We are in this for all the money we can take as long as we have the freedom to take it, and now we will be on the watch for larger prey.

December 20, 1716

Damn Thomas Davis! Every ship needs a carpenter, and by all accounts he is a good one. When we took the Saint Michael, we were twice blessed that we gained both her goods and her carpenter –Davis – and who could blame us because a ship cannot remain under sail without such a man. Then the sniveling cur comes crawling to me telling me how he was an honest man who wanted to be released at our next port o' call, and I, damn my eyes, told him I would let him go. I choose to do no harm to anyone unless it is to my advantage, yet the crew forced my hand, and I had to call a vote on him against my will. The men, after all, have the final say so, and they have voted against the puling blackguard. Many would sooner shoot the young man or whip him at the masthead than let him go, so he is bound to the ship until hell swashes over our gunwales.

Almost all of my men are volunteers, and though they will claim to the death that they were forced into my service – if it ever comes to that – they have signed on of their own free will. God knows, the hell they have known at the hands of the rascals who have robbed and cheated and enslaved them has been hotter than the decks of The Sultana ever will be.

But this cursed Davis is another story: he will help us along the way, I am sure, but he is also our prisoner, and he will be with us to the end....

Sam's index finger turned some more pages in the log until he came to an entry written only a few weeks before.

January 25, 1717

The girl continues to haunt me. When we were together, I told her once that I would make her a princess of the Spanish Main, that when I returned to her I would bring her gold and rubies and sapphires. My men and I have taken goods from many merchants' ships – rum and ale, tobacco, spices, fabrics, and the like – and while we inspire fear, we have neither intended nor carried out violence on any of those we have plundered. But my pockets are only half full, and I will not be satisfied until they are brimming with coins and my fingers can place a tiara on Maria's head.

But why do I love her so? Did it start that night we talked of gold to be had beyond the horizon? She loves me for the freedom she thinks I have, and I love her for her willingness to forsake the safety of her Cape Cod home to come with me. Damn, she is a lovely girl – so willing to cast her lot with the likes of me – and I swear I will never leave her again once I have fulfilled my promise to her – and to myself.

The hour was growing late, and the words on the pages had begun blur and swim in front of Sam's eyes. As his chin slowly dropped to his chest, he then almost mechanically bent his arm on the table and slid his head into its crook. Before he had given over completely to the gently swelling waves and a deeper sleep, however, he was startled awake by a sharp rapping on his cabin door, a knocking that also caused the young John King to sit bolt upright in his hammock and hit his head on the ceiling.

"Captain," a voice called loudly, "Come quickly. We have spied a ship, a very large one, off the starboard bow. Mr. Williams says it may be our greatest prize yet!"

Chapter Thirteen
Ouidah
April, 1717

Ouidah, Whidah, Whida, Whydow, Whidaw, Widow, Whido, Whydah. By any spelling or representation, the word stood for slavery during the seventeenth and eighteenth centuries. Located on the western coast of Africa in what is now called Benin, Ouidah was a thriving French-operated seaport whose primary export was human flesh and labor, a very lucrative trade at the time. The ship to which the town gave its name was no less intimately involved in the slave trade, and its inordinate size was a proportional reflection of the profit to be made in the business of selling human beings to other human beings.

At about the same time that Maria Hallett and Sam Bellamy were conversing under the apple tree in 1715, the Whydah Gally was setting forth on its maiden voyage from London bound for Africa and then the West Indies. Laden with cloth, liquor, and other trading goods, it was beginning to trace a triangle among three continents that connected them in the commodification of African tribespeople through barter, trade, and coercion. The ship's captain, Lawrence Prince, must have inflated with pride as he maneuvered down the Thames on that day because his three-master was large by any standard of the day: one hundred feet long, three hundred tons, capable of making thirteen knots, wide enough of beam to contain seven hundred prospective slaves beneath her decks, and sporting eighteen cannons to seal any and all business transactions.

In return for its breathing cargo, the ship's owners would accrue great wealth in the form of gold, silver, sugar, indigo, and cinchona, all of which Captain Prince was charged with bringing back to them from the Spanish-held West Indies. The horizon that spread out before him that day must have seemed to glimmer with gold dust. Unfortunately for the vessel's avid British investors, however,

Captain Prince's career as the skipper of the Whydah would end before he could complete his second voyage when the erratic travels of the piratical Sam Bellamy intersected the vicious trading triangle and ultimately brought the entire venture to a crashing halt on a dark Cape Cod beach on the night of April 26, 1717. Curiously, of Sam Bellamy's 145 pirates who died that night, approximately one quarter were black men – many of them former slaves -- fighting in their own desperate way for freedom, equality, and wealth.

****

Lawrence Prince, deflated, looked across the table in Sam Bellamy's small cabin and quailed. He had heard of these freebooters and their practices – of hanging their victims by their testicles; of cramming their captives' mouths with oakum and then detonating it; of cutting off lips, noses, hands, and heads, of attaching an iron ring to the victim's tongue and burning it with a red-hot poker so it would swell up, thus preventing the victim from cursing his captors. As Captain Prince looked into the dark, steady eyes of Sam Bellamy, he questioned his own fate and that of his men. The chase from the Windward Passage to Long Island in the Bahamas had lasted three days, and he had only defended his command by firing two chase guns of the eighteen cannons he had aboard. Prince cringed at the thought that the vessel's owners might discover his cowardice: however, two boats had been in pursuit, both flying black flags rather than red, "bloody" ones, which suggested that mercy might be a possibility. In addition, his crew was hopelessly outnumbered (one hundred and eighty against fifty as it turned out), and Prince was simply terrified. He was a merchant sailor, after all, not a fighter.

Vain, overweight, and habitually nervous, Prince was, nevertheless, a shrewd judge of human behavior, and as he sat in Bellamy's uncomfortably warm cabin, he searched his captor's eyes and his lips for signs of the fate in store for him. If he had known Bellamy, however, he would have looked more carefully at his long fingers, uncommonly delicate ones for a large man, which were then gently rubbing the ridges of a gold coin and running along the chain attached to it as they had many times before. As it was, Prince's attention was distracted by his captor's dress: the black satin breeches adorned with bright silver studs along the outer seams, the flowing crimson cape and matching sash, both secured by gold pins as large as pocket watches, the gold earring ending in a massive pearl which hung from his left ear. And the black hair! It flowed down over his shoulders, tufted from the opening in his white damask shirt, and punctuated the features of his black eyes and brows in a narrow mustache that curled above his upper lip. He even referred to himself as Black Bellamy as if to make the impression complete. In short, the man was out of the question: a poseur, a mannequin, a laughingstock who would be hooted out of London's salons, off the city's wharves, and into the Thames. Yet as the defeated captain measured his counterpart, he knew he was facing the most perilous moment of his life, and he accurately sensed that the apparition he was looking at embodied in both manner and dress a powerful and terrifying rejection of everything that he, Lawrence Prince, merchant ship captain, represented.

For his part, having overcome fifty ships in the open sea already, Sam Bellamy knew well the type of man he was facing, and his lip quivered into an ambiguous smile. He had seen the same face so often, the eyes dancing with fear, the tell-tale twitch in the well-fed cheeks, the rhythmic movement of the jaw revealing the grinding molars, the perspiration causing the man to glisten like a freshly caught cod fish. Prince seemed to be doing all of these at once, and for an instant Sam thought he would laugh out loud. He quickly controlled the impulse, however, and, instead, began to speak in a carefully modulated way,

"Mr. Prince, "I regret to inform you that you have lost command of your present ship, and that I and my crew are demoting you. We are not, however, taking away your rank – just your ship, the Whydah Gally, which will now serve as the flagship for my growing fleet. In fact, as we speak, my men are transferring cannons, swivel guns, and the considerable wealth we have collected in our travels from the Sultana to the holds of the Whydah.

"So where does that leave you, you might wonder. Well, it is your good fortune that we will no longer be requiring the use of my present ship, the Sultana, so I have decided to give it to you. Under the circumstances, you will grant that this is a most generous gift, will you not? In addition, we will be supplying you with provisions that will meet your needs for some time to come, and I want you to have sufficient gold and silver from my own hand as a token of remembrance of this meeting."

As he said this, Sam cupped his hands into a chest beneath the table and cascaded more than twenty pounds of gold and silver in front of Prince's wondering eyes.

"I want you to know," Sam continued, "that the gifts of the Sultana and the money have nothing to do with you, scurvy fellow, but they are a consequence of my success and that of my men. Do not flatter yourself in any way that we approve of you or that we are taking mercy on you; but know, instead, that every breath you and your men take from this day forward is a gift from Sam Bellamy and his rebel crew. If you have any honor at all, you will pass my words on to those respectable curs you are accountable to."

Having finished, Bellamy abruptly stood up, but as he did so, he was startled by a sharp rapping on his cabin door and the jubilant voice of Richard Noland calling to him from outside. Noland, the quartermaster in charge of securing, assessing, and distributing the wealth of captured ships had just returned from his inspection of the Whydah, and he could not wait for the door to open before he shouted for all to hear,

"Captain, we are made men! There is more gold than you can imagine on the new ship. I have just come from the holds of the ship, and there must be 20,000 pounds of gold and silver down there, maybe more...."

As Sam opened the door for Noland, he turned back to Prince and smiling widely, he said, "Well, Captain, it seems that you have been holding out on us, haven't you? What do you have to say for yourself?"

Prince was mute. The movement of his eyes, which had slowed when Sam had poured the gold pieces on the table, now quickened again. Unsure whether to thank him for his generosity, apologize for not revealing the treasure on board, congratulate him on his conquest, or upbraid him for his arrogance, he simply dropped his eyes to the coins, supported his head with his two hands, and darkly contemplated the days to come.

Satisfied with the man's silence and now anxious to be rid of him, Sam concluded the interview by saying with a shade of sympathy in his voice, "When my men have finished making the arrangements I have ordered, you may assume your new command, Captain Prince." Then, spinning toward Noland and clapping him joyfully on the back, he said, "Now, Mr. Noland, show me the way to our new fortune!"

****

From the time he had contemplated the night sky as an English farm boy, stars had captivated Sam. Two centuries later scientists would assert that humans are composed of stardust, but as Sam stood at the taffrail of the Whydah gazing up at the sky, the stars seemed so close that he thought he could touch them with his fingertips. He had no way of knowing as he stood on the deck in the early April night that those stars were masses of swirling gasses, hydrogen, nitrogen, oxygen, and that they were constantly altering light years away. Even at the age of sixteen Sam's mind had been filled with thoughts that took him beyond the stars, somewhere beyond the seas, but this night with the stars so close that he believed he might hear them moving across the sky, he thought of Maria. Sam had lived his life according to the stars: as a young boy, he had learned the constellations – Orion, Cassiopeia, the Pleiades, the Northern Cross, the Great Square – and he had learned to chart his way across the sea using them as his guides. He knew how to measure their longitudes, the distances that kept him from his goals. As he had grown older, he had come in some way to measure himself against those stars. He had no way of knowing then that we are all constructed of stardust, but he sensed the identification that evening as he stood with his elbows propped on the rail that connected him with those dots in space and with the face of a young girl, his own Polaris, to whom he was returning.

Captain Sam Bellamy loved walking the decks of the Whydah. He loved its roll under his arches, he loved the curl of its sails when the wind filled them, he loved the twenty-eight cannons fitted in their ports, he loved the vast gold ballast beneath his feet, and he loved that he was heading north toward Cape Cod. On this mid-March afternoon as he scanned the horizon and saw the Marianne to his stern, he felt an upwelling of pride at what he, Paul, and their men had achieved in the last year. They were richer than they had ever dreamed of being, and they had plans. A pirate's life was a short one - they knew that - but they were well-armed, wealthy to a man, and free to sail wherever they pleased.

Studying the sky behind the Marianne more carefully, Sam did not, however, like the clouds quickly piling up in the west, massive, quilted, dark as the flag flying from his mainmast. He knew the waters off the Virginia colony well, and he sensed immediately that the two ships would not be able to outrun what was coming at them. Few knew better than he the dangers aboard a ship: that the chances of being hurt attacking a merchant ship paled in comparison to climbing a mast and falling into the sea or, worse, plummeting to the deck of the ship. He admired his men for the risks they took every day, and he knew they would be facing the greatest risks within the next few hours. Yes, a pirate's life was a short one. Then he shouted,

'Avast there, Mr. Quintor, look to the west and north and you'll see we're in for a heavy blow. Mr. Noland, order the men to take down the staysails, the topgallants, and topsails. When we need to, have the men ready to reef the mainsail and mizzen. We'll sail ourselves by the goose wings if we have to, and we need to be ready to look into the pit of hell. Mr. Rivers, find the boy, and make sure he is safe in my cabin. Mr. Fitzgerald, whatever you do at the helm, when the winds and waves come, keep her head to the sea! If we broach to, we will be finished!"

Within minutes, like hummingbirds, young men were in the rigging, teetering on the bowsprit, nosing along the yardarms, swinging on halyards, readying for what was to come. Within the hour the storm was upon them, and Sam was right: it lasted for four days and three nights, the seas towering and cavernous, and when it had finished crawling over the decks, the masts were bare or broken, the hull shipping water, and the men exhausted. At its height, with lightning webbing the sky overhead, Sam cursed the gods for being drunk and swore that if he could fire his cannons, he would salute their thunder with his own.

Ultimately the winds shifted, as they always do, and a northerly breeze calmed the seas. In the end, however, Sam was grateful that two of his pilots who had been washed over were saved by the stern netting, and he even brought himself to praise Davis, the captive carpenter, for locating and tending to a sizable leak in the hull. Perhaps the trouble of keeping him had been worth the cost. Apart from losing a mainsail, the Marianne had suffered no significant damage, but the men needed time and a place to careen the ships, to take stock, and to rest. Ocracoke, off the Carolinas, seemed the best solution, but when the winds turned once again, now coming from the south, they aimed the yardarms north toward Block Island and Cape Cod. The plan was for Paul to lay over in Rhode Island for a time to see his family, and then the two ships would skirt the coast to Maine where they would make necessary repairs before they set out to sea again for more treasure.

In The Freebooters of the New World, one of the earliest and most illuminating memoirs of pirate culture, Alexandre-Olivier Esquemelin (known popularly as Oexmelin), chronicled his ten year career as a 17th century surgeon aboard Henry Morgan's ships in the Caribbean. Among his most incisive observations is that "The pirates observe the most perfect order among themselves... There are some who are very courteous and very charitable to the point that if one has need of a thing that is possessed by another, he offers it to him with generosity." Such civility was the rule aboard ship, but not on the land, where morality and temptations were more confusing to those accustomed to the expectations, the regulations, and the duties required to survive on the sea.

Ambrose Fairweather was an Englishman whose mental candles, when they oscillated at all, flickered dimly, but what he lacked in intellect he made up for in the capacity of his heart. He was as trustworthy as the sunrise, as loyal as the family dog, and as helpful as a penitent husband; a lilting song from his homeland could move him to tears, and the influence of strong ale would only increase their flow down his cheeks. Fairweather was also large; in fact, his torso closely resembled some of the casks of rum he would roll on planks from captive ships into the holds of the Whydah, and his fists seemed the size of the cannonballs he would fire upon occasion at the gunwales and masts of merchant ships. When moved to anger, especially when his sense of justice had been violated – either by intention or by accident - Ambrose could also become violent, and among human nature's most dangerous personality types is the aggressive ignoramus. On April 2, 1717, Ambrose had been drinking rum punch, and he had just discovered he did not like Alexander the Great.

The storm now past, the spring coming on, and the ships pointed toward a safe haven in the north, the crew exhaled and sought entertainment where they could find it, be it in a mug of rum or putting on a dramatic production. On the morning of April 2, Jack Spinckes looked at Simon Van Vorst, and said, "Let's put on a show, and I know just the one, 'The Royal Pirate.' All we'll need are some togas, some sandals, and some men willing to act." By that evening the stage was set, and Ambrose Fairweather was confused not only by the amount of rum he had consumed but also by the complexity of the play he was watching. A man named Alexander, wrapped in a sheet and looking like someone familiar, had won Fairweather's devotion, so that the poor soul laughed when the great man laughed and cried when the great man cried. But then the besheeted Alexander raised his hand against Fairweather's best friend, Jack Spinckes, and threatened to hang him in the morning. At that instant, Fairchild, the world spinning uncontrollably before him, drew the line. From the far end of the deck, with a marlin spike in his left hand and a grenade in his right, Ambrose Fairweather charged the makeshift stage on the poop deck yelling to his equally sodden companions, "They are going to hang sweet Jack Spinckes, kind Jack Spinckes, true Jack Spinckes, and if you cowards allow it, you should all swing from the high arm." With this declaration, he fired the fuse of the grenade and heaved it among the players, where it burst in a blinding gust of smoke and sound.

Not to be outdone by this heroic gesture, several in the crew, with their cutlasses drawn and flashing, also rushed the stage to rescue young Spinckes, who by now was curled in a ball laughing oddly, wide-eyed, as he stared at his left leg just broken by the blast. Alexander did not fare so well, losing his arm to an attacker but answering him with a decisive pistol shot to the chest. For Fairweather dramatic illusion and reality fused, and when he reached his injured friend now rolling on the stage in pain, he embraced him, crying out, "Oh, Jack, look what they have done to you. I tried to save you, and I'll get him that did this to you!"

The next sounds anyone heard were the sharp crack of a musket and Bellamy's voice rising above the miasma of smoke, bloodied swords, and vaporous rum. Standing at the door of his cabin with young John King at his side, Bellamy rested his smoking musket in the crook of his arm and shouted, his voice crackling, "This play is over, and it will never be shown on the decks of the Whydah again. Punishments will be decided tomorrow. In the meantime, all crewmembers are ordered to their quarters.... now!"

The boy reflexively clasped Bellamy's hand. Although these men had treated him kindly since he had left his mother, they seemed so big to him now, and he could not take his eyes off Alexander's arm still lying on the deck, hairy fingers gripping a knife, strawberry-colored tendons snaking from the severed end.

****

For their exertions, the combatants, including Fairweather, earned a day in irons, but as tempers cooled, the seas calmed and the early days of April grew balmy off the Virginia coast. During these days the Whydah would replenish its holds, no longer with human cargo but with loot from the steadily increasing number of merchant ships making their way north and south, east and west. Now that the spring was unlocking the coastal harbors, Pirate season was beginning again, and Sam Bellamy and his crew intended to make it a season to remember. With southeasterly winds abetting their plans, among their first victims was Captain Beer out of Newport.

Captain Beer was clearly a man of the sea; perhaps this is the quality that earned him Sam Bellamy's respect. With his forty men, Paul Williams and the crew of the Marianne had easily subdued Beer's vessel in the waters off Long Island, and when they rowed their captive up to the Whydah, Sam admired the man's proud posture as he sat at the stern of the boat.

As he set a heavy foot on the Whydah, Beer surveyed the scene -- the impressive size of the ship; the men, black and white, clad in gold cufflinks, high silk hats, white waistcoats, and ruffed collars that they had stripped from passengers they had captured. Then he coolly regarded the emplacements of cannon that would have splintered his smaller ship. It was the largest pirate ship he, or perhaps anyone, had ever seen before. Directly in front of him, he saw a large man wearing a red cape and, beside him, a young boy with a similar cape. Upon seeing the boy standing there, Beer impulsively knelt on one knee and placing his hands on the boy's shoulders, he asked, "What is your name, young man?" When the boy responded, "John King, sir," Beer laughed softly and said, "Well, John King, I have a son who is just about your age, but he has not become a pirate yet. Perhaps he will some day..." Then turning his eyes to Bellamy, he said in a more serious, even sorrowful, tone, "And, indeed, captain, you have certainly taken my measure.... Mr. Bellamy, I am traveling from Newport to Charleston, and for all I care, you may take every grain of cargo aboard, but I ask you to spare the lives of my men and allow me to return to my family."

As simple in dress as Bellamy was elaborate, Beer was only a few years Sam's senior, and when he spoke, he asked no mercy, nor did he appear to expect any. Quickly Bellamy warmed to his easy manner, his quick, gray eyes, and the rusty beard that curled down to his chest. His body was large, almost ungainly, but he carried himself gracefully, and the set of his lips indicated that he had already accepted his misfortune. From the man's words and manner, Sam sensed that their lives had not been much different, that they shared a kinship with the sea, and before long he invited him to share a mug of rum in his cabin.

Moments later, Captain Sam Bellamy took a long swallow of rum and looked appraisingly over the rim of his glass at Captain Josiah Beer. He liked the man. He intended to return his ship to him, but the decision belonged to the crew.

"Captain Beer," Sam began, "your loss is our good luck. But my intention is to return your ship to you once we have removed all the goods that will be useful to us. Captain Williams tells me that you handle your ship well..." Then, almost surprising himself, Bellamy said, "Captain, what would you say to sailing with me and my men. As our fleet grows, you could command one of the ships,

144

and you will certainly gain more wealth than you would working for Newport merchants"

Beer paused for a long moment, his eyes slowly inspecting the cabin and finally settling on Bellamy. Then he said, "Captain, I have a home, a wife and children in Newport, I have a...... and for what it is worth, I have a reputation. Your offer is tempting to me -- I will not deny it -- but at bottom, I cannot sail against the King's ships and break with the laws of God and man. I will not imperil the futures of my family..." Before Beer could finish, Bellamy clenched his fist tightly and slammed it on the table that separated them.

"May God damn you, you are a groveling dog like all those who accept being governed by the laws that the rich have made for their own security; for those cowardly little dogs do not have the courage to defend in any other way what they have won by their mischief. But, may you be damned altogether: they, as a pile of clever scoundrels, and you, who serve them, as a brainless packet with the heart of a chicken. They revile us, those rogues, although there is only one difference between us and them: they steal from the poor under cover of law, yes, my God, while we pillage the rich under the sole protection of our courage. Would you not do better to become one of us instead of crawling after the asses of those blackguards for a job?

"You are a devil of a conscientious rascal, damn ye," he continued. "As for me, I am a free prince and I have as much authority to make war in the whole world as if I had one hundred vessels on the sea or one hundred thousand men in the field. And *this* my conscience tells me. But there is no arguing with such sniveling pups who allow their superiors to kick them all about the deck, to their heart's content, and who pin their faith on a pimp of a Parson, a squab who neither believes nor practices anything he tells of the chuckle-headed fools he preaches to."

Bellamy's voice had risen as he had gone on, but by the time he finished, it had fallen almost to a whisper, and when he stopped, the blood slid slowly from Beer's face, leaving it a pale mask. Then the man stood up suddenly, momentarily lost his balance, and after righting himself, said, "As you are aware, Mr. Bellamy, the sea has not made me a wealthy man. My clothes are homespun, and I live in a modest home in Newport. But I still remain loyal to the King and to those whose vessels I command. I ask for no favors from you other than the security of my men and my safe passage back to my home, which is not far from here."

From the days he had broken with Hornigold, and even earlier, Sam had battled with his better angels, but now, many months later, he realized that he could no longer discern the good angels from the bad. There was something hopeful about the man, as if the loss of a ship, maybe even his life, would not affect him too deeply. This man, Beer, was a decent man, one who made Sam think once again about his own motives, why he was taking gold from others and whose gold he was taking. Then he said, "I took ye for a better man, Beer, but I will do what I can to return your ship to you..." Then he suddenly stopped, stared down at the table, and looking up at Beer, he muttered, "Come with me. We'll settle this matter now."

Within minutes he and Beer were standing before the assembled crew of roughly 150 men, on a softly rolling deck with the evening sun glinting gently off the sea surface and causing them both to squint at the men.

"Mates," Bellamy began, "Captain Beer, who is standing here with me, is a good man, and Paul Williams tells me he is a very good sailor. The two of us, the Captain and I, have had a long talk, and though we do not see eye to eye on some things," as he said this, he took a sidelong look at Beer, "I want to offer him the courtesy of having you vote on his fate and the fate of his ship. To make the matter short, we have emptied the holds of his ship, and I believe we have enough. In fact, we have taken more than we need. His ship is of no use to us, and we are heading north for some rest. Therefore, I vote that we return the man's ship to him, and let him find his way home to his soft bed in Newport."

Perhaps it was the rum, perhaps the cut of the man's beard, his ungainliness, or the fact that he was coming out of Newport, but most likely it was the rum. In any event, as the crew stood on the deck looking at the two squinting figures on the upper deck, they were not in a charitable mood.

"To hell with him, and to hell with his ship," yelled Thomas Baker from the back of the crowd. "No, I take that back, Captain. If you like him, let him go, but burn his ship to hell. That's my vote." Before Baker could finish, another voice coming down from the rigging above echoed the same sentiment, and then another, and within a minute the verdict was in: Beer would have his life – as would the men of his crew – but his ship was doomed. With the decision clear, Bellamy turned to Beer and said, "Damn my blood, I am sorry they won't let you have your sloop again, for I scorn to do anyone a mischief when it is not for my advantage.... Damn the sloop, we must sink her, and she might have been use to you."

Within the hour Beer was once again sitting erect in the stern of the rowboat. A small explosion burst in the distance, and to the starboard Beer saw his ship stream into flame and then begin the inevitable process of sliding to the bottom of the sea. After contemplating this for a moment, he turned back to Bellamy, who was still standing there on the deck, and making a graceful wave of farewell, he called to him, "So long, Mister Bellamy. Y'are a better man than you think you are, and I thank you for your considerations".

Sam stared stonily at the ramrod figure in the stern of the small boat pulling steadily away in the distance. Then, with a half-smile, he turned to the men gathered around him and said, as if he already knew, "Mates, someday that man will join us as we walk lightly over the hottest stones in hell." With that, they laughed together and soon after turned to the work seamen do.

****

Seen from the long perspective of time, Sam Bellamy embodied a peculiarly American paradox: On one hand, he thirsted and dreamed of wealth, and he was willing to go to great lengths to achieve it, even if it meant crossing oceans, skirting coastlines and braving storms, or transgressing laws to gain it. At the same time he pursued justice. As he presided over an expanding crew, he recognized his men for what they were – young men who had made the same decisions as he: the products of the class they had been born into, of the color of their skin, of the circumstances that had led them to the decks of a pirate ship. To Sam, the fates had tilted these decks against these men. As he looked in toward the continent, he was aware that justice would assume the shape of a noose for his men if they ever hoped to walk on the land again. He felt responsible for this. He also knew that the justice they would find on a pirate ship was the most limited kind, that on the Whydah it embraced all the men, from the most weathered seafarers to a ten-year-old boy – and he, at least for the time being, was the one the crew expected to measure and dispense it. These thoughts tumbled in his mind for a time, and as they did, he gripped the rail of the ship so tightly that the tips of his fingers slowly whitened, and he released them only when he became aware of the pain in his knuckles.

He was on the account – he knew that – He was a pirate, and he knew he would have to pay the price for that, but he also sensed that if there was a God, he was willing to wager that he would come out on the side of the angels: he was a captain, elected by his men, and he knew that for them and himself, he wanted a fair deal. His spirit smoldered when he thought of the rich merchants in London, the armies, the nations so willing to pursue their own interests by any means possible and call it justice. In some recess of his brain, in some deep chamber of his heart, Sam wondered if that was why he wanted wealth so badly – so he would not have to administer justice but could, perhaps, buy it.

Beneath his feet, in the holds of what was now his ship, were the ill-gotten gains of slave traders, and now by his own good fortune and the hands of his fine crew, a number of whom were former slaves, those gains were his to control. At what bar should he and his men be arraigned? Who would be the justicer? Who dare call him to account as an outlaw? He wanted the best for himself and his men: that was as far as the compass of Sam Bellamy's sense of justice extended.

On a ship, the elements are an immediate reality -- the movement of the clouds, the waves, the stars, the temperature, the horizon on which ships and people could appear and disappear. Among the many ironies of a pirate's life is the central fact that stability exists only in movement -- in the headlong clouds, in the flashing sunlight, in the changing colors of the sea, in the roll beneath his very feet, in the shifting horizon's edge as sharp as a dagger's blade. If the stars were not aligned against Sam Bellamy in the months before his ruin, vast meteorological forces were. Beginning in January, when

Samuel Treat died, and extending through March and April, when Bellamy and his crew were making their way up the Atlantic coast, massive warm and cold fronts were colliding, creating the kind of snow storms in the winter months and rain and wind storms in the early spring that white men had seldom seen before. As Sam and his small fleet made their way up the Atlantic coast, atoms, molecules, dust motes, and droplets of water swirled, gathered, massed, and after joining with the jet stream, began an inexorable sweep across as yet uncharted territory, burying the land in snow and buffeting the ships of the sea, including Sam Bellamy's small fleet that was making its way up the coast..

****

Within weeks of their conversation, Beer was asleep in his own bed in Newport while Sam was making his way up the seaboard toward Cape Cod with his spyglass trained on the horizon searching for the masts of the Marianne and Paulsgrave Williams, who had vanished in a dense fog. The monotone of the Whydah's bell had reverberated throughout the night, but when the fog lifted the following morning, Paul and his ship were gone. Now, two days later, as the sun was beginning to set over the Virginia coastline, Sam assessed his options: Paul had vanished, and if he did not find him and the Marianne safely anchored at Block Island a few days hence, he would direct the Whydah up the coast to Maine. He and Paul had agreed that the Marianne sorely needed to be careened and refitted and that Damariscove Island off the Maine coast was the place to do it. Now that the Indians and the French had burned most of the settlements for miles up that rocky coastline, this Maine island would be as safe as the sands of the Bahamas had been for them. Slowly placing the glass in his pocket, Sam comforted himself with the thought that he would find Paul for sure any time now. He also knew that Paul was peering as carefully at the horizon as he was – the gold in the Whydah's holds guaranteed that. On this cool April evening, Sam wanted a respite from worrying about his missing friend, so he turned toward his cabin and the welcoming promise of restful sleep.

As his muscles relaxed and his eyelids closed, Sam briefly

recognized that the measureless darkness of sleep contained no horizon. Then, seemingly an instant later, Maria's face was before him, appearing as it had so many times recently. But on this occasion the face he saw before him was neither fresh and laughing as he liked to recall it nor tear-washed and angry as it had been at their last meeting. Instead, her eyes were wide with fear, as if they knew something he did not, perhaps of the past or events to come. She was dressed all in crimson, with a glimmering red bow in her blonde hair; then rising in his mind's eye was her lovely face as it had many times before. Instinctively, he reached toward her with both hands to touch her pale cheeks, but as he did, the vision dissolved into fragments– and he was wide-eyed in his dark cabin

Across the cabin, staring at Sam from his berth was young John King. The boy was wearing a crimson sash about his waist, and his legs were dangling over the side of his bed. For an instant the two gazed at each other, and then the boy said, "You woke me when you cried out the Virgin Mary's name, captain, and I was afraid when you spread out your arms to her."

Shaking himself fully awake and composing himself quickly, Sam looked at the boy, "Sometimes I have bad dreams, boy." Then, smiling broadly and reaching over to touch the boy, he said, "Don't you worry yourself about me and my dreams, John. We still have some more pirating to do, don't we, and like Robin Hood's men, we will!"

In the days that followed, the Whydah attacked the Tanner, the Agnes, the Endeavor, the Lieth, and the Anne, and the pickings were easy. Between April 7 and Tuesday the 9th, the crew looted four of these ships, freed their crews aboard the Endeavor and the Lieth, sunk the leaking Agnes, and commandeered the Anne, a one hundred ton, two-masted snow. With these conquests Sam's plans gelled: With Noland now commanding the Anne, they would cruise for the rest of the month in Delaware Bay and then off Long Island while making their way toward Maine via Cape Cod.

As they worked their way north, they would take as much loot as they could from ships coming to and from the ports of Philadelphia

and New York, and all the while they would be looking for Williams and the Marianne.

For his part Paulsgrave Williams was nervous. Since losing sight of the Whydah, his crew aboard the Marianne had grown increasingly restive as they feared their sacks of gold hanging in the holds of a flagship might now be lost to them. To make matters worse, without the cannon power of the Whydah to back it up, the Marianne was unable to intimidate merchant ships as it had before, so it had to choose its quarries very carefully. In fact, at the time the two captains were harrowing the horizon for some sign of the other, they were only a few miles apart but drifting further apart: Bellamy cruising the Chesapeake and Delaware Bays and Williams moving steadily toward Block Island and his family there. Ultimately, they were confident of meeting again in Maine, but the intervening weeks without their mutual support were difficult -- especially for Williams as he tried to reassure his twenty-eight men that their newly-found wealth was secure.

For his part Paulsgrave Williams is one of the truly fascinating figures in the history of American piracy. Akin to land-bound pirates of later years, who would commandeer boardrooms, loot companies, and scuttle others with unfriendly takeovers, creating fleets of businesses known as monopolies, Williams and his bosom friend Bellamy were simply more forthright in their methods and more joyful in the way they executed them. They enjoyed practicing terror on the high seas in the service of gaining wealth, and nowhere are they reported to have killed a captive during their two years of sailing together. Unquestionably the two were more physical and brazen in their methods than their later brethren, and the contrast of Williams's curling, pomaded white wig against his walnut-brown seafarer's skin must have disconcerted the merchant captains he subdued during his travels. Perhaps even more unsettling to these honest sailors were his manners, his locutions, the natural poise evolved from class status and inherited wealth. If asked, he could trace his roots through the halls of power in the colonies and even to English royalty: through his father, to the statehouse in Rhode Island, and through his mother, to Harvard University and the Plantagenet kings of Britain.

The early death of his father and his mother's remarriage led to his *family's resettling on Block Island, a desolate outpost in Narragansett Bay. There, as a young boy, he met the likes of Scottish rebels against the crown, smugglers, black marketeers, and Captain William Kidd, whose close associate, Edward Sands, married Williams's sister and helped to cache some of Kidd's stolen treasure when that notorious figure was eluding the authorities. With footholds in both civilized society and the colonial underworld, Paulsgrave Williams had the money and maturity to complement Bellamy's seamanship and daring, qualities that knotted an extraordinary friendship. The unraveling of this knot in the April fog and during the two weeks that followed was equally painful to both men, but as much as each man wanted to see the other's masts on the horizon's edge, neither could know that they would never again lay eyes on the other. And so the final act was set.*

****

April 26, 1717, 2:00 p.m. – Gardiner's Island, N.Y.

The winds are picking up quickly, and the whitecaps are everywhere. We are in for it, and we need to find safe harbor soon. Where could Sam be now?

- P. Williams

April 26, 1717, 3:00 p.m. – Approaching Cape Cod

This morning we boarded the Mary Anne out of Boston. It was loaded with wine, and the men are happy. A fog as thick as chowder has set in, the winds seem to be shifting, and I suspect a storm may be in the offing. Still no sign of Paul.

- S.Bellamy

April 26, 1717 5:00 p.m.

Andrew Mackconachy was terrified. A stranger had a knife to his throat, and his well-rounded stomach was quaking uncontrollably. Folds of wrinkled, grizzled skin layered Mackconagchy's throat so thickly that the press of Simon Van Vorst's cold blade against it was an almost distant sensation; yet the fifty-five year old cook had no doubt that the knife was there and that it was very sharp.

By any estimation Captain Crumpstey's pink, the Mary Anne out of Dublin bound from Boston for New York, was not a great prize:

it leaked, was sluggish in the water, and held no gold or silver. But to a boarding crew of young pirates who had been at sea for months and had recently survived a grinding storm, the boat was a floating tavern. Since the crew had taken the boat earlier in the day, rumors had spread that she was carrying stocks of Medeira, port, rum, and every other variety of Caribbean potable, so Van Vorst had decided to find out for himself if the rumors were true. From the moment Van Vorst and his cohorts had entered the galley, laughing and loud, Mackconachy sensed their comfort with the easy cruelties of youth, and he was afraid. Van Vorst's first words to him, "Old man, tell us where the rum and wine are, or I'm going to let the air out of you," had only revealed to the old man what he already knew.

April 26, 1717, 6:00 p.m.

All Robert Ingols could do as he stood on the deck of the Whydah with a rag-tag helmsman was stare back at Sam Bellamy, who was hollering at him through the rising wind. Earlier that day, a boarding crew of seven had commandeered his sloop, The Fisher, and now Bellamy, this upstart crow, was calling on him to assist in navigating the small fleet through the shoals off the outer Cape in high winds. Not likely.

Ingols knew these waters and could read their winds as well as any, and he knew the situation was doubtful at best; at worst, this man, Bellamy, was blindly leading them all to their deaths in the brewing nor'easter. In the rising wind Ingols looked at the small, gaily dressed black helmsman next to him, with a cutlass in one hand, a pistol in the other, and a bottle of his own best rum tucked under his arm, and he muttered softly to himself, "Well, Captain Bellamy, if you want me to navigate for you and your men, I'll be glad to usher you right up to the gates of hell."

April 26, 7:00 p.m.

Nineteen-year-old Thomas Fitzgerald was no pirate nor had he ever intended to be one. A skilled seaman, he did what he was told without asking questions, and he enjoyed the comfortable order of a merchant ship. As he stood at the helm of the Mary Ann and contemplated recent events, young Fitzgerald sadly recognized several facts: one hundred and forty-five armed pirates can subdue ten merchant sailors without so much as a fight. He was now in the service of outlaws, and he was following a bobbing light ahead of him that was leading him to almost certain destruction.

Not a shot had been fired, and Fitzgerald was glad of it. Only the previous morning, the Whydah had loomed to the stern of the Mary Anne, guns at the ready and two other ships in the distance. Captain Crumpstey had given up without a fight, and just that fast, Thomas Fitzgerald had become a part of a pirate fleet. Now his eyes were straining to discern a lantern, elusive as a firefly and attached to the stern of the Whydah ahead of him. Added to that difficulty was his knowledge that the small fleet was sailing directly into the jaws of a gathering northeaster.

The young man hoped to command his own ship someday -- or perhaps a fleet of ships-- but now as his chilled fingers whitened on the wheel, he knew he must not lose sight of the lantern skittering above the surface in the distance.

April 26, 9:00 p.m.

Thomas Baker was drunk, as drunk as he had ever been in his life, and he had good reason to be. Working back through time, Baker recalled the sickening moan as the flat bottomed pink had lurched heavily onto the shoal and then turned slightly, delving deeper into the roiling sands. He recalled feverishly cutting the rigging and hewing the foremast and mizzen masts. He recalled hearing the terrible and constant roar of the surf on the beach and the small crew's attempts to steer the boat into the wind and away from danger. He recalled thinking there was a chance the fleet would avoid the full fury of the storm. He recalled feeling safe. Then his mind leaped forward, and he contemplated the company surrounding him at this moment. On the periphery of consciousness, Baker dimly recalled that today, April 26, 1717, was his birthday-- number twenty-five if he was not mistaken -- and raising the bottle he had clutched firmly in his fist, he turned to the others huddled in the close compartment. "It is my birthday, mates, and so today, April 26, will mark the day I was born into this world and the day I went out of it."

They looked like a clutch of unhoused kittens, six of them -- abandoned, wet, cold, fur plastered to their skin. As the boat swayed gently under them and the wind howled outside the thin hull that protected them, they had moved beyond drunkenness to despair, all except young Fitzgerald sitting in the corner holding a book in his lap.

Baker surveyed the bodies of his mates huddled in the small cabin: Brown, Van Vorst, Hoof, Quintor, Shuan, South, and Davis, the carpenter. His eyes dismissed Mackconachy, the fat cook, and settled on young Fitzgerald clutching a worn gilt-edged book that resembled a Bible. Baker's eyes raked the boy, and finding little he could respect, finally said, "Well, boy, since we are going to die anyway, read us a story from your book there."

April 26, 1717, 10:00 p.m.

Aboard the Anne, Richard Noland peered into darkness through the stinging rain and tried to collect thoughts now addled by the wild pulsations of the relentless, bone-freezing wind. He had lost sight of the Whydah hours before, and while he could still see the lights of the Fisher nearby, his complete attention was riveted on the anchor lines that extended from his stern. His best hope was that the Anne, light and seaworthy, would not overburden the anchors and dislodge them from the saving sands below.

In the distance he could hear the arhythmic sounds of the waves grinding and pounding as the surf met the shore no more than three hundred yards away. As he watched the anchor lines sporadically grow taut and then release – yet still hold – he wondered how the Whydah, much larger and less manageable than the Anne, could possibly survive. Then as the ship jolted once again and the cable held, he realized he and his men were still safe for the moment.

April 26, 1717 11:00 p.m.

Maria's mind often returned to thoughts of that disastrous morning in the barn when she first saw the child, straw in its mouth, blue and cold, and she had heard the sound of her own voice echoing throughout the building. This night the wind's howling so insistently outside brought back to her that day many months earlier when she felt as if she were tumbling down a deep, endless well, her screams echoing back to her over and over again as they had for the last two years. This night recalled that experience so vividly. Then she rolled over and tried once again to return to sleep as the night roared furiously about her small home by the dunes.

April 26, 1717 11:00 p.m.

The wind alternately moaned and crackled through the rigging like a mother bereft of her child. Momentarily confused and distracted by the sound, Sam gazed up at the full, straining sails that were driving the ship steadily to the west and inevitably toward land. Then above the sound of the wind, he heard a deeper more foreboding roar, one that he recognized at the core of his being, the relentless pounding of waves on a beach. The din growing steadily more massive, his thoughts snapped quickly into place, and he hollered to all the men within earshot, "To the capstans, men. We're going to lay down the anchors." None of the men questioned the order. They sprang to their jobs, and with their feet spread wide on the wet, frozen deck, they gripped the handles of the great machines and began to turn them. Then increasingly faster, the great one thousand pound anchors with their massive cables descended into the roiling waters and the rolling sands. For an instant the great ship shuddered, and when it did, the men and their captain cheered. In the next moment, however, they felt the cables relent and slowly begin to drag. Turning to stare at the Billingsgate cliffs that awaited them, Sam shouted again to the men,

"There's no time to waste, mates. Our last hope is to bring the bow around to ease the impact when we run aground. Mr. Julian, take the helm, and at the moment you feel the cables release, swing the wheel hard to face the ship to the shore." Then looking stonily toward the bow, he hollered above the wind, "Now, men, cut the cables fast and pray that we come about. This is our last chance, so hop to it!"

Within minutes, the anchor cables were loose, but the 300 ton Whydah failed to turn. Julian pulled mightily on the wheel but to no effect, and the ship, like a great elephantine dancer plunged stern-first toward the shore. When it met the land, the small world of the pirates exploded into fragments:

Below him he heard the final terrible roar, then felt a ripping jolt as the hull of the ship met the sand. At this meeting, to those who would never live to describe what happened next, young James Gaskill seemed to rise out of the crow's nest and inscribe an almost perfect swan dive against the murky, wind-lashed sky before his face met the wildly tilted deck below. Cannons careened across the ship crushing anyone in the way. Barrels and casks of goods became bombs rising and then exploding when they landed on the deck surfaces. Following the initial impact, the mainmast shrieked, then bent, and finally admitted defeat falling almost majestically, trailing its tattered sails into the roiling surf.

****

The boy?... the Pup?.... Where was the lad? No sooner had he thought of the boy than after scanning the deck and not seeing him, Sam was running to his quarters hoping the child might be there – perhaps by some miracle still asleep. As he ran down the passageway, he recalled his promise to the boy's mother, and he felt his dream slipping away ever faster. When he threw open the door to his cabin, Sam heard a great crashing sound, as if the unoiled gates of hell were creaking open, and he knew that the ship was breaking apart. Above the pounding wind and rain, he heard Julian's voice rallying the last of the crew to save their lives by leaping into the churning surf. Momentarily deafened by the cacophony, Sam stepped into his compartment and closed the door behind him. The cabin's enclosing quiet provided him sudden and unexpected comfort. In the low light, he made out the shape of the boy sitting on his bunk next to a stern porthole. The boy had been watching transfixed as the waves rose to the level of his enclosure, and when he heard the cracking of the ship's spine and the door closing behind him, he turned to fix his gaze on Sam.

As Sam regarded the boy, a wave of sorrow and regret washed over him. The child's skin, soft in the dim light, glistened with tears; his customary spirit had been quelled. As the door closed, the boy said, "We're not going to make it, are we, Captain? I can see the men going under in the waves." Then after a brief pause, he murmured, "And I do not know how to swim."

Sam looked steadily at the boy, and then he said, "Nonsense, Pup.

If you follow me, we will make it ashore. That I promise you. But first I have some business to attend to before we are on our way."

As the boy watched, Sam made his way deliberately to the chest in the corner. The dream was over -- the boy's face had told him so – and Sam now acknowledged the fact. Consumed by this realization, he resolved to save his own wet skin, perhaps the boy's, and whatever remnants of a future that might still be available to him. Falling to one knee and steadying himself by placing a hand on the chest, he slid the necklace with the key to the chest over his head and fit it into the lock. The sound was pleasing to him as the hasp clicked open, and when he lifted the lid to the chest, he was once again dazzled by the varying and brilliant shades of gold in the box. Almost mechanically, he undid the large sash around his waist, spread it out on the cabin floor, placed as many coins on it as it would hold, and after knotting it tightly in several places, secured it again around his waist. The heft of the belt was considerable, but Sam was strong, and he knew the small fortune resting on his hips was worth any risk he might have to take. Then without so much as a backward glance at the treasure remaining in the chest, he approached the boy, and extending both hands to him, said. "The time is now, Pup. Come with me." The boy's eyes explored Sam's face as he slid uncertainly from the bunk and clasped his left hand. Then they moved as one quickly to the door where Sam opened it to the wind and rain and slammed it shut behind them.

The scene that confronted them back on the deck had altered since Sam had left it minutes before. Although the elements continued to scream in the riggings and around the contours of the ruined hulk, only two or three men remained at the ship's railing, and those who were there were silent, peering into the churning waves breaking thirty feet below them. At that moment each was determining his own fate, and for an instant Sam felt like an intruder, unwilling to compel them to action, knowing he would be making the same decision a few moments hence. Rivers, Ferguson, Hoff, and finally Julian had made this decision within the last ten minutes, and now were battling the crushing waves below.

With this last thought in mind and with the biting wind directly in his face, he forced himself to look down at the boy. Rain and the spume of the sea had by now replaced the tears on his soft skin, but something else had also appeared there. In the creases of his squinting eyes and his tremulous lips, fear had taken hold of the child -- fear and the defiance that sometimes accompanies it. As he returned Sam's gaze, the boy violently pulled away from him, his small, wet hand slipping easily from the older man's, and he screamed above the wind, "I'm not going with you, and you can't make me, Captain! You don't have a chance in those waves, nor do I, and I would rather drown aboard the ship than down there." As if to save Sam the trouble of argument, the boy leaped beyond his reach and fled back in the direction of the cabin, avoiding a wayward boom, skipping over a fallen crewman, and deftly eluding a cannon sliding slowly in front of him on his way.

His patience with the boy at an end, Sam watched him disappear and turned wearily to the taffrail. The few who had been there moments earlier had apparently made their decisions because Sam now stood alone on the deck, the most solitary of sea captains. As he stood on the heaving surface, images overwhelmed him – the furious waters below, the trembling features of the boy, and finally the face of Maria, who by his calculations must have been within a few miles as the crow flies of this God-forsaken place. This last thought filled him with anger and sharpened his mind: he would survive by whatever means possible.

With new energy, Sam gripped the rail in front of him with both hands, and charted his course of action. Floating fast toward the stern was a large spar that he instinctively calculated he could reach if he jumped at that instant. And so he did. As he entered the breath-taking water, his body went temporarily limp, yet the image of the floating spar was fixed in his mind as he fought his way to the surface. There it was, a boom from the foredeck, and he grabbed for the tangled lines lazily trailing in its wake. His fingers had already begun to numb, however, and the adrenaline that had enabled him to push up following his leap into the water had begun to ebb. Nevertheless, he continued to pull on the trailing lines until at last he was able to touch the spar. As he attempted to throw his arm over the boom and rest his weight upon it, however, it rolled toward him, and he was unable to gain a purchase on it. At this point the insistent weight around his waist and the sodden burden of his clothes became more relentless, and he could feel their pull. Now with a frantic effort, he began to tug as hard as he could on one of the lines still connecting him to the spar, but to no avail. At that moment Sam's body began to describe an arc beneath the water's surface, and when his feet reached their downmost point, his face suddenly disappeared from view. Whether young John King, by now once again ensconced in his bunk by the porthole, witnessed this disappearance, only he knows.

As Sam's head submerged beneath an oncoming wave, the roar of the wind and the waves instantly transmuted into an eerie silence, one that many sailors have encountered. Above him the water's surface was inexorably vanishing in a swirl of sand and fast-fading light, but his benumbed, strangely alien fingers were now fumbling desperately with the knots around his waist. He had been a sailor too long, however, the knots were tied too well, and his fingers could not solve their riddles that bound him so intimately to his gold. As his mouth and throat and lungs began to fill with saltwater, Sam's fate finally became clear to him. In that instant his body relaxed, as all bodies ultimately do, and his mind fixed on the face of Maria with such intensity that his muscles tightened and he reached out to touch it. Then the vision dissolved and slid back into darkness.

Chapter Fourteen
On the Beach
April, 1717

A scintilla of evidence crucial to the continuation of our tale nevertheless exists that may yet persuade a doubter -- the lone soul sitting at the far end of the jury box --that received wisdom is mistaken, that the historical record may be flawed. Historians generally subscribe to the account of Sam Bellamy's death that concludes the previous chapter. But then the doubter, the skeptical jury member, raises his hand and asks, "But they never identified Sam's body, the corpus delicti? What about the skull? The tavern? Aren't there details we haven't considered?" At the intersection of history and fiction, boundaries often blur, and where ambiguities persist, imagination necessarily steps in to provide the illusion of certainty; perhaps, even better, imagination can offer us a facsimile of truth that raises dull facts to a higher romantic power and makes sense of nature's chaos -- for such is the dream of mankind. In this spirit, the remaining chapters of this narrative will unfold some answers to the aforementioned questions. At the end of the tale, the jury member may still be dissatisfied with the verdict, but he will know that his concerns have at least been addressed.

****

The wind was wild in her hair, and she wondered if her mind had deceived her. Maria could not tell whether she had heard cries of anguish in the distance or merely fragments of the wind. Amid the tumult of the storm she even believed she had heard the clanging of a church bell. The sounds had come sporadically to her, borne in from the beach on freezing sheets of rain and uneven, slashing waves. For some time she had resisted the urge to seek their source, but finally she gathered her cloak about her, unlatched the door to her shack, and stepped out into a dark world of wind and rain.

The sheer immediacy of the elements -- the rain in her eyes, the din in her ears -- overwhelmed her senses, and she had difficulty distinguishing among her thoughts. Some will beyond her own had drawn her from the warmth of her small home, but now that she was out on the dark dunes, she knew only enough to move toward the shoreline. As she made her way through the long grasses and down the declivity of sand, she saw two ill-defined shapes a little more than two hundred yards down the beach -- one crushed on the shore and a larger one further out, aground on a shoal and slowly swaying in syncopation with the beating waves. As she drew nearer, she realized that she was looking at two ships, a smaller one now thoroughly demolished and a massive sailing ship that had turned stern-first to the beach and foundered in the storm.

The bell she thought she had heard in her hut was no longer being rung by a human hand but now was clanging intermittently from the distant ship's helm at the pleasure of the wind and the waves. However, the muted cries she believed she had imagined before were now more distinct and horrifying. Beyond the spray and fume of the cresting waves she could hear men's voices crying out to their god, to their mothers, to any distant stranger for help and mercy. And in the curl of the now mammoth breakers, she saw still figures rolled in a watery quilt and delivered to the shore.

In the darkness and in her fixation on the scene beyond the breakers, Maria was unaware of the silent population that had gradually gathered on the beach until she stumbled and fell over a sodden young man lying in her way. His hair was matted over his eyes, and his torso was bare to the buckle that cinched his breeches. His mouth seemed to gurgle a response as she fell, but when she rose and realized he was dead and then saw other bodies lying nearby, she screamed. For all the noise of the scene, the beach seemed eerily solemn. If there were survivors, they had quietly crept away, and the voracious salvagers had yet to discover their good fortune.

At this moment Maria made out a living figure some fifty yards distant grappling to maintain his hold on the sand before an ebbing wave dragged him back and under an oncoming breaker. Shouting,

"I'm coming," to him, she started running in his direction, the frigid sand firm beneath her feet. As she neared him, the man righted himself and slowly rose from his hands and knees. In the low light, with the icy water numbing their ankles and feet, Sam recognized Maria before he could discern the outline of her face. Her silhouette, the way she carried herself, perhaps the sound of her voice in the distance had unmistakably revealed her to him, and he said softly to her, "Maria, I came back for you."

The words electrified her. Uttered by this ghost-like figure, a dark Jonah returned from the sea, this sentence seemed to emanate from the ocean's depths -- or perhaps from her own dissembling imagination. But standing here in the biting salt air and the lashing sands, Maria stared at this shadow of a man and tried to locate the features she had loved and reviled. His voice and the carriage of his body were twisted by fatigue and pain, and she felt an overwhelming impulse to take all his wounds into her soul and heal them there.

This pity would pass away slowly, but the fear that accompanied it would not. As she reached to take his hand and pull him to her, she instantly thought of the salvagers who would be appearing soon, the light of their torches curling back in the wind, and she knew that certain danger awaited them both -- no longer from the sea but from those on land. As these thoughts streamed through her mind, Maria heard herself saying, "Can it be you, Sam? It has been so long, and so much has happened..." She was surprised that her words sounded so forgiving because her suffering had been so severe; yet she found herself embracing him and kissing the dark hair on his neck as the black water swirled around their legs. They clung to each other for only a few brief seconds before she said, "Come, we must leave here quickly. Men will be here soon."

"No," he said, "My men are dying in the sea."

"They are already gone," she replied. "Come, we must go."

At these words he pulled free from her and began to make his halting way up the beach, looking first toward the hulk of his flagship and then upon the beach where he saw countless solitary shapes impeding the water from returning to the sea. His interlude with Maria had congealed his clothes to his skin, and his body quivered from the cold and the desolation of failure. None of these men would rise from their sandy rest, and none of those who might be delivered from these furious waves would ever again look to him as their captain.

"Maria, you are right. We must leave here now, but we must also part. I have tales to tell you, tales that will thrill you, but they do me no credit, and I fear that my name -- that any association with me -- will bring you pain. I know we must leave, but I must leave alone."

Maria then laughed more bitterly than any woman had ever laughed before. Amid the drops of stinging rain and the random sweep of the wind, she screamed above it all, "You, Sam Bellamy, master of the seas, you presume to speak to me of suffering -- you who know so much and so little. Yes, make your way from the beach alone. But do so knowing that I have loved you, that I still love you, and that I have suffered the greatest pain because of you."

As Maria's venom was subsumed into the storm's fury, three torches appeared over a dune no more than one hundred yards away. Sam noticed them first and pulled Maria to the ground, stifling her words against his chest. Those with the torches took no notice of the two lovers and, instead, moved with great speed toward the massive forms that loomed on the shoreline.

The voices belonging to the flickering lights were muffled by the wind and soon receded as the salvagers made their way down to the ships. Sam knew that more would follow soon and that he would be summarily hanged if he were discovered on this beach; he also shuddered for Maria whose breath was warming his face as they watched the torch flames bob along the sand. Unconsciously and reflexively, his right hand reached for the thick sash encircling his waist.

"I must go," he said, "but I will find a way to see you again very soon. Where are you living now?"

Her anger having now subsided somewhat, Maria silently pointed in the direction of her small dwelling. Then she whispered in his ear, "You may find me on these dunes. Some people in the town say that I haunt them anyway, and as you will discover, I have become quite well known since you left me. Should you wish to find me, however, I will be living no more than a few hundred yards from this very place upon that bluff in the distance." Then, aware of his chattering teeth and blue lips, she said, "Yes, I know you are right. You must find shelter – and warmth-- away from here. First, go north to the Pierce Tavern in Yonder Billingsgate; it is not too far away, and you can find a room there. Here you are too close to Fresh Brook, and my cabin is known to everyone."

Unsettled by the undertone in her voice, Sam, nevertheless, looked in the direction she was indicating, rose stiffly from the sand, and gently helped her to stand. As he did so, he said, "I will go to the tavern, and then I will find a safer, more remote place. After I am settled, I will return to you again -- and it will be soon." In the dim light he held her face between his hands as if to fix its lineaments in his mind forever and pulled her to him in a convulsive embrace; then he buried his face in her windblown hair and repeated, "Soon."

Swept by intermingled feelings of fury, sorrow, love -- and, finally, fear when she saw perhaps ten more torches approaching in the distance -- Maria pushed Sam from her, barely restraining herself from screaming, but keeping her voice low and controlled,

"I will be here, waiting, as I have for two years.... and I will be alone."

Upon hearing this bitter promise, Sam took one last look at her, turned his back to the onshore wind, and made his way up the beach, bent over and solitary. For her part, Maria had turned to stone. Her gaze followed her lover's outline to the skyline where it paused for the slightest moment atop a dune and then vanished. To her fevered imagination the particles of his being had seemed to disperse into the swallowing darkness and merged with the unrelenting drops of rain. And in that instant of time she felt a sense of foreboding that the delicate thread connecting them had been stretched to the point of breaking.

****

When he gained the last dune before leaving the beach, Sam paused to take a final look at Maria and what was left of his ruined flagship. In the rising light, and struggling to maintain his balance in the unforgiving wind, Sam witnessed an age-old scene of change, survival, and transition: friends he knew were breathing their last in the choking and frigid waves, and strangers were coming to salvage what the sea would yield up to them. And seeming to preside over the scene was the young woman who at first seemed transfixed in the wild elements but then turned away and began to kneel over the sea-washed bodies and look for any signs of life in them.

Strangely for the moment, Sam felt supremely safe: the new arrivals hurrying beachward from over the dunes were interested only in the goods they could retrieve, and the wave-driven souls from the ship were in no condition to give up any secrets about themselves or their leader. For the next day or two, time was his to do with as he was able. An assessment of his condition was encouraging; apart from some bruises, stray cuts, and stiffening muscles, his body was sound, and he could walk with no difficulty. Then, as he had a number of times since landing on the beach, he felt for the bulging sash at his waist. The gold was still there, and he recalled how it had almost pulled him under when he first leaped into the snow-white water. Had he not been able to grab a fractured spar that had floated his way, he would have been tumbling along the ocean bottom, weighed down by the gold, the sorry victim of a dream, food for lobsters.

But he was here, he was alive, and he was cold, and as he watched the sinuous movement of torches now snaking down the beach, he knew that he must find Pierce's Tavern soon if for no other reason than to stop the irritating chatter of his teeth.

****

The wind had been blowing relentlessly out of the northeast for two days, and the bay was full of white caps, large sea curls that could swamp a small boat in an instant. As Isaac surveyed the distance separating Silver Springs from Great Island in the early morning light, he knew that he would not be making the trip from Blackfish Creek to the tavern in his skiff today. Yesterday's rain had subsided somewhat, but the bay was still perilous, and because northeasters generally lasted three days or more, Isaac knew that tomorrow would pose the same dangers. He had promised Mr. Smith and Daniel Atwood that he would repair some winter damage to the tavern before the busy season began, however, and he did not want to lose any time to the bad weather. A larger boat was what he needed, and the best person to help was Sam Harding, who at thirty was like an older brother to him. Sam had a wide-beamed work boat moored next to his in Blackfish Creek, and he had often loaned it to him in the past when the winds were up.

Sam Harding's crooked grin seemed to curve down his long face and disappear into a cavern created by several missing teeth at the corner of his mouth. His face sat atop a similarly long, bony, and weather-tested body, but his eyes were his most arresting feature because they seemed to look in two directions at once. If the eyes are the window to the soul, then Sam's bifurcated brown ones revealed a man who was simultaneously true to his friends and the friends of his friends but who was also intent on finding and saving gold. In fact, someone peering into Sam's eyes saw a heart of gold through one eye and a vault to hold it in through the other.

For a man who had lived so close to the land and sea for a lifetime, Sam's voice was surprisingly soft and gentle; consequently, Isaac was surprised when as he approached the Harding home in the Solley's Hollow part of Fresh Brook Village, he heard Sam calling sharply to him, "Isaac, I'm glad you've come. You're here just in time to help me out. There is no time to be lost!" While he was saying this, Sam was leaping onto his wagon, his eyes gleaming. As Isaac drew nearer, he was also surprised to see a man sitting quietly with his legs dangling off the back of the wagon. Without looking at him or acknowledging him, Harding cried, "The storm has blown a ship ashore just east of here, a huge one, and our companion here tells me that there is gold and silver to be had, lots of it..."

Thoughts of sailing to Mr. Smith's island, tavern repairs, and contending with churning whitecaps dissolved in Isaac's mind, and he quickly jumped into the seat next to Sam. Conversation was difficult because the wind was sporadically driving stinging pellets of rain into their faces, the storm rush in the trees overhead was constant, and the wheels of the old wagon complained loudly over the rutted cart path. Amid the confusion, Sam looked at Isaac and then rolled his eyes toward the man in the rear.

"That one back there came to my door no more than half an hour ago, telling me that he was no pirate but that a large ship had foundered off the Billingsgate dunes. He was as nervous as a spaniel, and he told me that the vessel – the Whydah, he called it -- is part of a pirate fleet and that many are dead. I told him he had come to the right man and that I would not turn him in, but I want him along to show me just where the ship is. He swears he is not a pirate, but that will be up to the judges in Boston to figure out." Here Harding paused to catch his breath in the wind, then continued, "Soon people from all over the Cape will be on that beach to salvage what they can, and I aim to be among the first. Are you ready for some adventure and some treasure, Isaac?" As he said this, Harding grinned, and Isaac laughed and nodded. Then he slapped Sam on the knee, and said, "Can't your old horse go any faster, Sam? We've got some work ahead of us."

When they rounded the dunes guarding the top of the beach, Thomas Davis shouted from the back and pointed to the south, "The wreck is down there," but Isaac and Sam needed no further directions. Peering into the rising light, they fell speechless at the scene spread out before them. Massive snow-white waves were rolling in and criss-crossing with each other, the spume of their crests lingering in the air like spent gunpowder. The sand was dark from the rain and the tidal reach of the waves, but darker still were the dozens of inert figures that seemed to be steadily burrowing into the sand as the sea washed the beach over and around them. Moving between them and stepping over them were men with bags slung over their shoulders and carrying torches while seeking anything of value that the sea might cast their way. But towering over all in the background was the great ghost of a ship, now stern-first to the shoreline, partially capsized, and having lost its bow to the sea. As they drew nearer, the wagon moving more easily on the firm, wet sand, Harding pulled out his glass and inspected the ship in the distance.

"Isaac, I see someone moving at the stern of that vessel, and he seems to be waving to us. No, he is standing on the starboard railing of the ship and is about to dive into the surf... My God, that's just what he has done.... I can no longer see him in the waves."

As Isaac peered in the direction Harding was indicating, he saw a shape reappear atop one of the icy waves and then catapult forward, only to be ground down as the wave caught up with him and forced his torso into the chaotic, twisting surf and swirling sand. By instinct Isaac began to run down the beach to help but stopped at the water line when Harding shouted, "Isaac, stop. He needs to come in closer, or you'll be swept out in the undertow with him. You can't handle him by yourself. Wait and I'll help you." At this warning, Isaac paused and saw a young dark-skinned man rise in the chest-deep water, perhaps twenty-five yards away, and like a punch-drunk fighter attempt to avoid the next punishing blow that swept over him. This last wave, however, cut his feet from under him and delivered him to the beach, quivering and contorted, the way a spent fish flashes its gills and finally curls, exhausted, into a fisherman's net. As the man lay gasping, his body warped on the beach, Isaac and Harding ran to pull him quickly from the receding surf before another wave could crash over him.

Against the dark water and the rising light in the east, Isaac realized that the dark-skinned man was not a man but, instead, an Indian boy no older than himself. He also felt as if they had met before. Through chattering teeth, the boy said, "I am not a pirate, sir, and I should not hang for what I have not done!" Still gasping and having difficulty rising from his hands and knees, he continued, "I was forced to serve with the dead men, the outlaws, now lying on this beach, and by your leave, I ask you to let me go. I waited until the last minute, until I was truly free of them, and then I leapt from the ship. You saw me, didn't you?"

"Yes, we did," Harding said, "and we never thought you'd make it."

"The man you are looking for," muttered the boy, "is our captain – Bellamy, Sam Bellamy – he is the one responsible for running this ship aground."

Almost simultaneously Harding and Isaac reacted, Harding saying, "We're not after anyone today. All we want are any goods or riches that we might rescue from the sea." But Isaac, as if electrified by the name, murmured, "Bellamy? Did you say the captain's name was Bellamy?"

"Yes," said the dark young man, "and if anyone should hang, he is the one. My name is John Julian, and the captain forced me to help him sail these waters.

Isaac then repeated, "Are you sure the captain was named Bellamy?" whereupon Thomas Davis, now standing directly behind them, almost shouted, "That was his name indeed. He took me off the St. Michael last year because he needed a shipwright and I was a good one, but he and his crew wouldn't let me go, and I tell you again that neither one of us is a pirate."

Sam Harding listened to this exchange and responded, "We have no side to take in this, and, in fact, I have an offer for the two of you. Once you have recovered a bit, and if you help us load my wagon with some of the cargo here, I will provide you with some food, a place to bed down, and I will protect your interests before the authorities to the extent that I am able. So let's put our backs to it and grab what we can...."

Of particular note is the story of John Julian; Julian was one of Sam Bellamy's earliest and most trusted comrades, and his story traces a familiar arc in the annals of the early American colonies. He was a Native American Indian, hailing, some say, from the Mosquito Coast of Nicaragua and Honduras. The path of his life would lead him from the sands of Central America to those of Cape Cod in New England. He walked the decks of merchant ships and pirate ships, and he paddled periaguas, small ocean-going canoes on piratical forays in the Caribbean. He was standing at the helm of the Whydah when it met its end, and he would be one of only a few to survive the wreck on the beach. In the weeks that followed April 26, 1717, he would be apprehended, accused, tried, and then released by the authorities only to be sold into slavery to the Quincy family, the illustrious forbears of two American presidents. He would then flee that service, be apprehended, flee again, and ultimately die at the point of a knife while attempting to elude his captors. John Julian was with Sam Bellamy almost from the beginning; in the bow of the Periagua Sam commanded at the outset of his pirate career, and at the helm of the Whydah when that same career ended.

For his part, Thomas Davis, the reader may recall, was coerced into service by Bellamy's crew because he was a shipwright and " a Single man"; and despite his frequent and loud protestations, he remained the ship's carpenter for four tumultuous months until the Whydah met its end. Davis, a twenty-two year old Welshman, was an honorable young man, who had no desire to be a part of Bellamy's crew. However, in the mind of Sam Harding at least, he was entitled to a portion of the Whydah's bounty, and ironically, Harding would ultimately make Davis heir to the loot that they would claim on the morning of April 27ᵗʰ and the days that followed. As we shall see, Davis would never collect his unwanted inheritance.

During that morning and in the ensuing days, the beach was awash with shadowy, ghostlike figures mingling with friends, strangers, people coming and going and returning; with wagons and wheelbarrows; with horses, mules, and beasts of burden; with terns, gulls, and hovering ospreys; and with lovers meeting and departing. And all the while – and for days to follow – the sea winds blew ceaselessly, driving the sand on the beaches indiscriminately, lashing the skin of those busy at their work and burying those who could no longer feel the sting.

Chapter Fifteen
The Fugitive
April-May, 1717

Located in Yonder Billingsgate at the southeast corner of the junction of King's Highway, in later years called Gull Pond Road, was Pierce's Tavern. The tavern was a substantial structure with a low ceilinged yet sprawling saloon on the first floor and six rooms for travelers on the second. It sat atop a rise that overlooked treeless farmland and provided a glimpse of the Atlantic Ocean to the east and Barnstable Bay to the west. King's Highway, the thoroughfare running north and south, was a slowly deepening dent in the landscape, a hard-packed thread of dirt and sand that sunk a little deeper with every cycle of spring rain. By latter day standards, it was a quiet country road, but on April 28, 1717, it was the locus of a prosperous local business, and – so he hoped – a haven of safety for Sam Bellamy.

As he contemplated crossing the road and entering the inn, the events of the last thirty-six hours flooded back upon him. Recalling the shock of seeing and then parting again from Maria so quickly, he instinctively rubbed his chin, which was smooth to the touch. He smiled at having found an abandoned fishing shack not far from the dunes where he had begun the process of transforming himself. As he stumbled in the absent light of the cabin, he had felt like a dark lobster scavenging the depths of a bay for any source of protection or sustenance, and in the tangle of gear, old poles, rusted hooks and line, he had been rewarded with a blade to shave himself with and dull scissors to cut his hair. Hanging on a hook on the wall was a frayed jacket, a size or two too small, but he took it nonetheless, and in a small cabinet he found some hardtack and stale biscuits. He avidly ate several and stuffed the remaining ones in the pockets of his new-found jacket.

The man who emerged from the shack the next morning after

fitful dreams was different from the one who had entered. He had left the long, black curls of his beard behind him on the floor of the shack, and he had decorated the hook on the wall with his still sodden red silk captain's coat. He grinned at the thought of some Cape Cod hunter or fisherman walking through the woods or traversing the dunes in Sam Bellamy's bright red trademark. Drawing his fingers slowly across his now-smooth face, Sam had stepped out into a world where distant sounds and movements caused his muscles to tighten involuntarily and set his teeth on edge. As he rubbed his face, his other hand rested on the bulge at his waist, the belt of gold, an umbilical cord of sorts. Setting his course northward, he hoped to put the beach and the dunes far behind him as quickly as he could. The silence of the surroundings unsettled him as he came out of the cabin, accustomed as he was to life aboard a ship with one hundred and fifty men.

Little seemed to have changed during the two years he had been away, and he recalled that King's Highway, which extended north and south up the Cape, would lead him toward Provincetown, a place where he could possibly disappear from the world he knew and the world that knew him, where he might hire on as a mate, where he might begin anew, where he might find some news of Paul, who knows?, where he might find a ship on which to sail off the end of the earth. Provincetown was at the very tip of this new, unfolding continent, but to get there he first needed to make his way north, safely and undetected, up the King's Highway.

A mile or two up the road Sam was forced to stand aside as a large wagon filled with four large men and a boy came rumbling toward him. They were laughing and armed with shovels, bags, axes, and ropes. Grinning broadly, two of them lifted bottles of what Sam took to be ale and said,

"Stranger, you're heading in the wrong direction. There's treasure to be had for those who get there first, and if you're a wise man, you'll join our party!"

When he had first spied the men in the distance, Sam's inclination had been to slip off the road and blend into the woods until they had passed, but now he knew he was safe behind the veil of his new appearance and the hum of their alcohol.

"Thank you for the offer, mates, but I have business north of here more important even than pirate treasure – yes, I have heard of the wreck on the beach – but I must tell you that you are in a race, and my wager is that more than half of Cape Cod will be out on that beach before the sun goes down tonight."

"You're right about that, my good man!" shouted one of the drunkards in the wagon, but there will be plenty for us all thanks to the generosity of the good Captain Bellamy, and you can be sure that we will not forget to thank him when we meet him on the beach!" With that the men and the boy moved past Sam on the road, and as they did, he stood and watched them for several moments. As their wagon disappeared around a bend, the sound of their laughter jingled lightly in the distance like the sound of coins, golden ones, sifting through the men's fingers.

For the moment he was safe, and with wolfish delight he resumed his walk up the rutted road. His name was on every man's lips, and he knew that soon his gold would be in their pockets. The thought filled him with quiet fury. Then as he gazed at a wispy, ramrod pine tree some twenty yards ahead, he pictured hanging from its branches a cage, like the one that had held the bird-pecked body of William Kidd years before and which he had seen on the dock of Tilbury Town; he quivered and quickly dismissed the thought, but the confidence of a few minutes before, the camaraderie of the treasure hunters, the comforting sense of anonymity he had felt was gone, and once again, he was the lonely wolf, hungry and alert to the dangers of any baying hound that might happen upon him.

As he stood in the middle of the road, looking down and then up, he recalled that Pierce's Tavern lay perhaps two miles ahead and decided he would test again his new identity in that country tavern. The readiness was all, and he knew that he needed a good night's sleep in a soft bed.

As he approached the building, Sam noticed several horses grazing in a paddock across the road from the tavern. Two wagons, their traces empty, had been left next to the paddock. Reflexively fingering the sash at his waist, Sam gazed down the sandy pathway, and, seeing no one, crossed the road and entered the tavern.

The interior of the building was dark. One man was seated at the bar, which stretched across the north end of the room, and two others were talking quietly at a table in the corner. A shaft of light extended diagonally through the room from a large window on the western side and ended on the floor where Sam now stood. Motes of dust seemed to play lazily in the early evening light. After taking a seat at the far end of the bar, away from the lone man and the bartender, Sam waited quietly to be served. To the best of his knowledge, he had never seen any of the men in the room before, but he had been away from the area for two years, and he could not be sure. Yet for the moment he felt safe.

Minutes later, having arranged for a room for the night and feeling the cool relief of his first several sips of ale, he heard the tavern door open and then close. He peered over the rim of his glass and saw three men entering the room. Two were unfamiliar to him, one of them with waxen blond hair that cascaded down his shoulders and the other whose nose challenged the limits of disfigurement, its tip extending the nostrils so high that he appeared to have four eyes instead of two, giving him a porcine look that reminded Sam of a pig he had once had to slaughter when he was a boy back on his parents' farm. But Sam knew he recognized the third man. The man was somewhat smaller than his companions, but prominent on the left side of his face was a triangular birthmark that curled circuitously through his cheek to his jaw. Unaware that this mark set him apart in any way, the man wore an air of authority about him as easily as he wore a crimson cape and held a wide cocked hat in the crook of his arm. As he led the other two into the room, he seemed to be inspecting everyone there, as if he were a regular in the establishment and were looking for old acquaintances, his eyes darting from person to person. When his gaze came to Sam, whose face was still partially obscured by the glass of ale, he paused for a long instant seemingly puzzled then moved quickly on.

For his part, Sam continued to sip slowly from the raised glass. Then as he lowered it to the bar, his eyes continued to follow the three men as they proceeded through the shaft of light and sat at a table by the large window not far away and within earshot. As Sam inspected the pattern of foam atop his ale, the bartender, a man with few teeth and even less hair, addressed the newcomers across the room.

"Hello, Mr. Cole… I see sand on the shoes of you and your friends. Have you been down to the beach today, perhaps cussing the moon? Across the room William Cole looked sharply at the man, and then he laughed.

"Who could blame us for seeking our fortune down there, Mr. McPherson? In fact, there were hundreds of men, women, and children combing around the wreck. There are riches to be had there, and people were loading their wagons full. But the saddest thing I saw there on the beach was the body of a little boy dressed up like a pirate with a big sash around his waist. I won't forget that little man soon."

A momentary silence settled over the room. Then, to lighten the mood, the bartender asked, "And did you see the famous pirate captain, Sam Bellamy, the one we have been reading about in the Boston paper?"

Cole chuckled softly. Then he said, "I don't think that's likely. My wager is that the good captain is tumbling around somewhere at the bottom of the sea or swimming with the fishes." Then as if a thought had just occurred to him, Cole's attention shifted quickly to Sam who had been sitting motionless at the bar delicately tracing the rim of his glass with his index finger.

"And you, stranger, have you heard of the great wreck that happened two nights ago on the beach not far from here?

At this Angus McPherson, the bartender, broke in and said, "And that's not the only one, Mr. Cole. Several miles south of the big ship's wreck on Pochet Island a smaller ship went aground, the Mary Anne they call it. We hear they've caught all the men from that boat, six of them, I think." At this McPherson paused, toweled a glass dry behind the bar and continued. "Sam Harding was in here only yesterday – you know him, I'm sure. He told me only two had survived the wreck of the big ship and that he had caught them. He is as full of wind as a bellows or one that blows in from the east, but I believe the man."

As McPherson was talking, Cole had been examining the man at the end of the bar carefully. He had seen something familiar about him when he had first entered the room; perhaps it was the shape of his face, or something about his eyes, or the sheen of his closely cropped black hair. Whatever it was, the impassive stranger had caught his eye.

"My fine fellow," Cole said looking appraisingly at Sam, "You seem somehow familiar to me. Still holding his ale and looking over his shoulder toward Cole, Sam said, "If you are addressing me, sir, I doubt if we have met before. I come to these windblown parts only seldom, and I am just passing through on my way from Boston to Provincetown, where I have some business to transact."

"Then you have not heard of the excitement around here," broke in one of Cole's companions, a bovine, befreckled young man with long hanks of yellow hair hugging his shoulders. "You haven't heard of the witch lady, Maria Hallett, who walks these shores every night and who called Captain Bellamy to his ruin two nights ago."

Sam turned quickly to face this young man, perhaps too quickly. In that instant Cole seemed to nod to himself as if he had just recognized an old friend. Sam recovered quickly.

"I have heard of the pirate," he said, "but not of the girl, who is a witch, you say?"

"To tell the truth," Cole broke in, "She is no longer a girl, but a young woman, who is a harlot, a mother, and a murderess."

"What are you speaking of?" Sam asked intently. And then more slowly he inquired, "What has she done?"

Cole's flushed companion, by now having quaffed a mug of ale, laughed aloud and said, "Don't you mean what hasn't she done, mate? She's had a child without the benefit of a god-fearing husband, she's murdered the child in a country barn, she's broken free from the jail that held her, and now she lives alone on the outer beaches calling men to their deaths just as she did two nights ago; and the strangest thing of all, the reason I am laughing, is that rumors tell us that Sam Bellamy is the father of the murdered child."

So unprepared was Sam for this revelation that he turned quickly and silently back to the tankard of ale on the bar as if to calm his seething mind with its contents. For several minutes now, Cole had been watching Sam with a jeweler's eye, and Sam was aware of this. As he stared once again at the circle of foam in his tankard, he could still feel the man's eyes trained on the back of his head. But what of the truth of the story? Had Maria done all those things the man had claimed? Had she murdered his child? She had given no hint of these tragedies that night on the beach, but with all the danger and chaos about, there had been so little time to talk about the past. He must see her. But, first, he must get out of this place and away from these people.

No sooner had he resolved to do this than he was startled out of his reverie by Cole's voice once again.

"In your travels back and forth to Boston, my good man, have you ever made a stop at Sam Smith's tavern? It is well known in these parts and popular with all sorts – sailors, whalers, merchants, and even pirates," he added with a laugh.

Sam was more prepared now for such probing questions, and he responded with a mirthless laugh, "Noooo, I seldom travel this far east, and when I do," he paused and caught himself; he had been about to say, "I travel only by land," but if he had, Cole would have caught him in the lie. The question was, of course, a test, and Cole's asking it as he had, was a challenge of a sort. Cole had discerned his identity -- of that Sam was certain. "No," Sam repeated again, "My travels usually take me to Mr. Williams's colony in the south or to the woods of the west. I seldom travel this way and when I do, I am not one to consort with sailors and pirates," he concluded with a dismissive laugh. "And now I must leave you, gentlemen. I have miles to go in the early morning, the journey from Boston has been a long one today, and my tankard is now dry."

With that, Sam rose slowly from his seat at the bar and made his way across the tavern floor toward the door and his room upstairs. The flinty-eyed man below had recognized him – of that he was sure. But where had he seen him before? Where had they met? Who was this man who could present such a danger to him?

The windows of the room on the second floor looked out on the King's Highway and across the road to the paddock where the travelers' horses were tethered. As he sat musing fitfully, darkness swallowed up the spent light of the sun. Then in the gathered shadows, Sam could discern a figure emerging from the front of the tavern, making its way as rapidly as it could to the paddock across the road. The silhouette was distinct, and in the briefest second the links in the chain connecting the past and present snapped together: Of course, the scarlet birthmark. The man's name was Cole. They had last encountered each other two years before when he was recruiting his crew for the Poseidon's Toy; that was the reason for his question minutes before. The man had recognized him – all doubts vanished. The man was on his way to alert the authorities, and at that instant Sam knew what he had to do.

The stairway down to the first floor was steep and the steps were narrow; but Sam negotiated them quickly and silently. Within moments he was through the door unseen by those in the adjoining barroom. The night air was moist and sharply cold against his face, and he quivered involuntarily as his eyes adjusted to the darkness. For an instant ghosts seemed to be looming up at him, so blurred and indistinct were the shapes he struggled to make out. The shapes tightened and defined themselves, but he could see no more than twenty yards into the gathered gloom. Sam made his way quickly across the road toward the paddock. When he reached the enclosure, he stopped at its entrance. Standing there, he looked up at Cole who by now was seated in his carriage and seemed surprised to see him.

"Where are your friends, Mr. Cole, and where might you be going at this time of the evening?" Sam asked as if the response was of little significance to him.

"Why should my travels around the countryside be of any interest to you, stranger? Cole replied.

"It's dark," Sam answered, "and this country may be dangerous with desperadoes and pirate ships so nearby. What could take you out so late in the evening with such dangers lurking about?"

"My business is none of yours, sir, and now I will be on my way." With that Cole raised the small whip in his hand, snapped it above the horse's head, and attempted to move forward. As he did so, his patience at an end, Cole spat out, "I know you for who you are, Sam Bellamy," and dropping the whip, he turned away from the oncoming form and reached quickly into his right hand pocket. Before he could pull his small flintlock pistol out, before he could cry loud enough for help, before he could raise his arm to protect his neck, Sam was upon him, his knife doing its work, Cole's cries lost in the bubbles of blood that flowed from his throat.

As they had been talking, Sam had been planning his next

movement, so at the utterance of his name, Sam leaped up at Cole to pull him from the carriage. When Cole fumbled to find his pistol, Sam gained enough time to subdue the smaller man, secure his body with his left arm and draw his knife across the man's throat swiftly and surely. With one stroke, Sam became a murderer. He had ordered other men to do violence; he had taken other men's goods; he had disciplined and punished other men; he had terrorized other men. But never had he killed one with his own hands; nor had he ever harmed another with less justification.

As he looked up and down the lonely road and back at the tavern, Sam felt Cole's blood already becoming adhesive on his fingers, and he knew he must flee this place and dispose of the body along the way. He assumed Cole had told his friends of his plans to alert the authorities of his whereabouts, so he calculated he had an hour or two at the most before this barren outpost began to stir with questions about what had happened to him. Darkness seemed to whisper through the trees, and as it came to breathe about him, Sam hastily took the reins from Cole, shoved the body to the back of the wagon, and stirred the horse into motion. Cole's blood seemed everywhere – on his hands, on his clothes, on the carriage seat – and Sam's first wish was to be rid of the body curled up behind him.

Every sound offended him. He knew that if he were to find safety, he must flee at once, but where could he go? Within an hour, at the most two, this small inn would be roiling with activity. When Cole did not return, his companions would certainly assume the worst, and Sam was certain that his name would be on their lips and in their thoughts. Maria's cottage was not possible because he did not want to attract attention to her, and that would be the first place they would look for him. What had Cole spoken of that evening? The island, Great Island. Sam Smith's tavern. Given the ebb and flow of people who passed through those doors, he might blend in for a time, long enough at least to recapture the old confidence, to plot a course. If they were still there, his old friends, Daniel Atwood and Isaac Doane, might even help him.

As his thoughts eddied, Sam turned and looked over his shoulder at the body of Cole lying curled in the back of the carriage, his eyes staring accusingly at him as if to say, "I didn't think I was going to die just yet." His throat was scarlet, and a pool of blood had collected under his head. The birthmark on his face had faded to a splotchy pink that Sam would never forget.

Trying to rid himself of the vision, he turned away, roughly shook the reins to quicken the mare's pace, and found his thoughts involuntarily recalling his days as a boy on his parents' farm in Wessex. That time seemed so distant now: then he had been transporting slowly yellowing bales of hay, and now the steadily stiffening body of a man he hardly knew, a man he had killed on the suspicion that he might harm him. Sam shivered in the moist coolness of the night air and pulled the collar of his coat more tightly around his neck. How far he had traveled and how different this outcome was from the dreams he had had as a boy. The dark, sandy road rose up to meet him, and he shuddered at the prospects that lay ahead. His fingers still binding with Cole's blood, he gripped the reins more tightly. He resolutely cast aside thoughts of the past and began to plot his new course: first, to Great Island and then, in the days to come, to see Maria and settle their accounts.

The darkened road rose up to meet him, and the east wind was at his back as he made his way toward Billingsgate harbor. After having traveled a mile or two, and now even more anxious to rid himself of Cole's eyes and the faded birthmark, he discerned a small interval beside the road with a path leading into the woods. Quickly he wrestled Cole's body to the ground and trundled it up the path into the woods. Cole's gaze seemed to inspect every step he made, and before he left him, Sam used his thumb and index finger to seal the man's eyelids firmly for the last time. After completing this task, he felt not safe but safer. Somewhat further down the road, perhaps two miles from the harbor, he reined in the mare, unharnessed it, and shooed it back in the direction they had been traveling. Then he pushed the wagon down an abandoned byway into some nearby undergrowth and made the rest of his journey to the water by foot.

One hour later, Sam was standing on the beach at the mouth of Duck Creek contemplating the lights of Sam Smith's tavern, which were floating like fireflies in the distance across the bay. When he thought of the vast circle his life had traced since he had last stood here two years before, he marveled that he was still alive and shivered perceptibly when he thought of those who had paid too great a price for following him.

Chapter Sixteen
A Prince Deposed
May, 1717

For Sam Bellamy, life on the run was different on land than it was on the sea. On a pirate ship he had a crew of like-minded men, all of whom were willing to die for him and for each other. They could direct their ships to deserted little islands dotted with empty coves along shore if need be; they could choose their foes, fleeing from larger ships and overcoming smaller ones they encountered along the way. Within the scope of a spyglass, they could separate their friends from their enemies. On dry land, however, Sam was alone, his crew lost to him, and at every turn in the road he might come face to face with a constable or some looming figure from his past who would do him harm. This was an alien land to him: while not densely settled, it held dangers at every turn.

As it had for so many years, the tavern stood like a sentry watching over the bay, surveying the comings and goings of the whalers and merchant ships, overseeing the sun rising in the morning and setting in the evening. But on this evening there was something more foreboding about the structure, as if the building itself could be an agent of danger. Sam pushed through the now familiar oaken door, reflexively letting his hand rest on the bulge at his waist inside his homespun coat. As he stepped across the threshold, he became immediately aware of a change in the air.

Having shaved off his curling beard, cut his hair short, and assumed the dress of a common whaler, Sam Bellamy was a very different man from the one who had entered Mr. Smith's tavern two years earlier. Gone were the crimson sash, the silk shirt, the feather in the hat, and, most significantly, the name Black Bellamy. In sharp contrast, the man who entered the tavern in May, 1717, hoped only for anonymity and to find asylum in this outpost as far from the law as he could travel. As he pushed through the tavern's massive door, however, he had no idea that the cast of characters would be so similar to those who had walked the wide pine floorboards two years before: Daniel Atwood was still behind the bar; young Isaac Doane was in the back of the large room serving drinks; some of the same slatterns were still making their way up and down the tavern stairs; even the drunkard Elias Newcomb was present although his friend with the scarlet birthmark was significantly missing.

Unlike his first entrance when the room had hushed in anticipation of what the extravagant interloper, Black Sam Bellamy, was going to say and do, this time the regulars of the tavern, numbering some fifty or sixty, barely acknowledged the presence of a stranger who might have just shipped in on the last packet boat. The large room was aboil in conversation, and only a few paused to assess the new arrival. One of those who took more than a passing interest in Sam's appearance was Aaron Cole, who immediately became attentive when Sam sat down to order a flagon of flip. Unknown to Cole, his brother had made a similar assessment only a day earlier, and also unknown to him at the moment was the fact that his brother was dead. Perhaps it was the shade of the hair, the contours of the face, or simply the stranger's manner of walking, but Cole vaguely sensed he had seen him in this place at some earlier time, and something within him demanded confirmation of the fact.

For his part, Sam was much changed not just in his appearance but in what his nondescript exterior concealed. In particular, under his loose-fitting shirt, and encircling his waist, was a belt filled with gold of incalculable value to him. The belt represented all he could show for the last two years of his life. Although it amounted to far less than he had hoped, it *was* something, and he had paid a high price for it. When he was ready, he would share it with Maria, but until then, he would reveal its existence to no one and would guard it as he would his dearest possession, his own child if he had one. In his deep heart's core, Sam concealed something else from others and perhaps even from himself. Gone was the old bravado, the optimism, the confidence that he could outface any weather and prevail. During the last two weeks, the midnight wreck, his encounter with Maria, the need to erase his identity, and his land-bound life as a murderer and an outlaw, all had altered and humbled him. Necessity, in fact, now governed his actions, and he deeply resented his impotence. Like a tide-washed clam, dependent on random events for his safety, he hated the fact.

One antidote for this sense of dependency was a final item he had hidden from general view. Strapped inside his leather boot, smooth against his calf, was the same long bladed knife that he had pressed so convincingly against Elias Newcomb's throat two years earlier. If anything, Sam was now more skilled in its use, and while on his voyage, he had carved an inscription into its whalebone handle, "Death when we be parted." The discrepancy between this injunction and the one on the coin necklace he had given Maria was not unintended, and he had ruefully grinned at the irony when he etched the line into the bone. Perhaps at that moment "we" no longer stood for a pair of lovers but for the violent path he had chosen for his life.

When Sam nodded in his direction and ordered a pint of flip, Isaac immediately knew who he was. He had no doubt because he had admired the man so intensely, wanted to be just like him so much, and hated him with such pleasure for two long years that the lineaments of Sam Bellamy's face were burned into the cortex of his young brain. Yet the unobtrusive man gesturing toward him was so altered that Isaac made an unspoken compact with him not to reveal his identity. Word of the Whydah's destruction and of its storm-strewn fatalities had spread through the area as if carried on the same wind that had destroyed the two ships; and while most assumed Sam Bellamy had drowned with his crew that evening, his celebrity was such that any man in Samuel Smith's tavern that evening would have been delighted to shake his hand and then turn him over to the authorities for the reward that was certain to be offered. Isaac knew all this, yet despite the conflicting currents swirling within him, he honored the man's obvious desire to remain unknown.

After briefly surveying the room, Sam took a seat at a table outside the halo of flickering candlelight. When Isaac came to serve him, the boy's eyes kindled acknowledgment, but in response Sam looked quickly down, discouraging any conversation. As he did, he said, "I'll have a tankard of flip, young man and perhaps a room for the night if one is available." Isaac understood, and nodding, turned to retrieve the drink for his old friend. After being served, Sam settled in and surveyed the room.

Within a few moments, a roar burst forth from a nearby table, one voice rising above the others, "I tell you she's a witch, she is! She uses her charms to destroy men and ships."

In a more sober tone, another voice added, "She walks with ghosts out there on the dunes, the ghost of her child, the ghosts of Bellamy and his men, and who knows how many more to come."

In a darkened corner of this outpost above the bay, Sam Bellamy peered deeply at the white foam still remaining at the bottom of his mug. Then with an air of decision, he placed it slowly on the table and rising to his full height, he walked over to the table of strangers and stopped. Then in a low and steady voice, he said, "You were right, mates. The young woman has charms, many charms, but not the ones you speak of." Sam then spun on his heel, without so much as casting a glance at Isaac who was standing at a nearby table and had heard every word Sam had said, and walked rapidly to the door, opened it, and was gone.

The three men, surprised, looked at each other and then at Isaac. After a brief pause and looking directly at the boy, one of them asked, "Who was that man? Have you ever seen him before, boy? Lost momentarily in his own thoughts, Isaac shrugged, shook his head no, and then turned quickly away. And so the scene ended as quickly as it had begun. Isaac turned abruptly away, responding to a whaler's call for another mug of flip; and for his part, Aaron Cole, who had observed the incident carefully, rose from his seat and left the tavern to seek his brother who might be able to help him recall the stranger's identity.

Chapter Seventeen
A Parting of the Ways
May, 1717

For Maria life on the dunes was solitary but not lonely. During the warm, breezy days of summer, she would fish the ponds, clam the flat beds, cut wood for the winter, put up berries, and, with gulls as her partners, she would scavenge the shoreline for any treasures she might find there. The tasks were simple but so were her needs. She only had one person to care for, herself. Now that she was free from the Eastham prison, she was free to walk the dunes and the nearby fields, free to rise early to tend her garden, free to sit in the evenings and watch the moonlight dapple the waves or gaze at a patient hawk hovering above the beach for minutes on end, free of caring for other people's children, free to direct the course of her own days, free of all human entanglements. She was, nevertheless, a prisoner, a prisoner of mind and memory. In idle moments when she was mending a dress, heating water for tea, sweeping out her small home, her child's face would loom once again in her mind – blue, as tight as a fist, eyes soldered down the way they had been that now distant morning in the barn.

Wounds to the body are painful at first: the blood flows, the skin ulcerates, but over time the flesh comes together, mends, and ultimately whitens into the familiar form of a scar; such wounds are memories, the body's map, landmarks. Wounds to the mind and heart are different. For some, these wounds heal quickly whether due to ignorance, an unwillingness to revisit the past, or simply human resilience. For others, such wounds take much longer, perhaps a lifetime to heal. These wounds never scar over and turn white as the body's do. No, these wounds continue to seep life's blood and remind the victim at odd moments that the past never dies, that it pulses in the soul unto death. Maria's wound was the latter kind. Ironically, however, the specific instants of her pain were surrounded in a glow, a series of golden moments that occurred during one summer when she had fallen in love for the first and last time of her life.

Whereas the face of her dead child woke her at unshielded moments of the night, the face of Sam Bellamy hovered in her mind's eye by day. And so as she sat on the Billingsgate dunes one evening, she realized that a natural compass – North, South, East, and West --no longer guided her; now her compass points were regret, yearning, necessity, and persistence. She could not know that the image others had of her was also mutating, nor would she have particularly cared.

Living on the outermost edge of a society was difficult for a young girl, especially one like Maria, who was used to taking care of children and enjoying the attention of others. But life was so different now: a girl of seventeen needs friends, and Maria had very few. The baby, dead now for two years, would be walking and talking had it lived, demanding her attention and all the power of her love. In the years since the death of the child, Maria's solitude had changed her. Her eyes, always her most outstanding feature, had assumed a more distant quality; the natural pulse of her vitality had been diverted as a violent storm may divert a stream from its natural bed, leaving the original one dry, and cutting new paths into the landscape.

In the two years of Sam's absence, Maria had become a nomad of the dunes, an explorer. Having established her abode on the beach as a mooring, she ventured out like a spider, finding points of contact, traveling to Provincetown, the outermost reach, connecting once again with Solosanna and Running Water, trading needlework for much-needed provisions, reconstructing a life from what was within her. Her interior world, much like the wind-blown, shape-shifting world outside of her, grew more wild. Her eyes, a deep blue, became quick – like a bird's – ever vigilant and alert. Her hair fell long and loose about her shoulders. When seen from a distance, she seemed to walk lightly along the sand and across the tops of the dunes. Perhaps these qualities contributed to the stories that had begun to swirl about her.

To those who knew her story, she seemed always an object seen from afar: at twilight, a shadow; at dawn, as she raked the beach for clams, a distant figure. To boatmen who might see her seated on the sand, hands clasped about her knees on a cool evening, she seemed a temptress who called ships to their ruin. But she was still just a young girl.

Isaac had seen Maria only seldom in the two years since he had left her alone at the cottage in the light snow. He had thought of her often, though, and when the pull became too great, he would take her food from his garden or other provisions that he and his mother might afford her. As the poet would say many years later, horses have gone lame traveling the distance between two people, and that was certainly the case with Isaac and Maria. From the morning he saw her and Sam standing on the dock that fateful day, Isaac had felt a veil of regret descend and separate him from her; for Sam he felt anger born of his own impotence – Sam so much older and knowing, more daring and sure of himself.

As he rounded Great Pond, early one sunny May morning, Isaac saw a slim, dark figure silhouetted in the morning sunlight. He knew immediately that it was Maria sitting alone on a small promontory that extended into the pond. She was fishing. He had not seen her for some time, yet he knew immediately that it was she. As he drew closer to her, he saw her blonde hair swing loose in the breeze. From some distance away, he called, "Hello, Maria! Any luck?"

Momentarily startled, she turned toward him with a smile, having recognized him by the intonation and timbre of his voice. "Hello yourself, Isaac, Yes, I've caught a few. Keep it a secret, though, because this is a good place," she called back to him.

Isaac wondered for a moment what it was about this girl that set her apart from all the others. Despite the shame, the loss of the child, her affair with Bellamy, her flight from the jail, her isolation, and the rumors that continued to swirl around her, there was something playful about her, and he loved her for it. He would continue to work at the tavern, or some such job, until the day he died – he knew that – and he hated himself for it. But she, no matter what she was doing – tending a garden, fishing for bass, threading a needle, hanging laundry to dry in the spring air, or walking on the beach – would wear the moment lightly, and he loved her for that also.

"So, Isaac, have you come out to visit with the wicked witch of Billingsgate, the dragon of the dunes, the she-devil of the seacoast?"

she laughed as he drew nearer. "Those are the names they give me, aren't they, the men in your tavern, the ladies about town?" She was young, and her eyes sparkled, bright as the sunlight on the pond water.

Isaac laughed with her and, nodding, said, "Yes, I've heard those names." The morning sun shone warm upon the faces of the two young people As he looked at her, Isaac noticed the changes in her face: at seventeen she was no longer a young girl; her hair was no longer neatly pinned as it had been when she worked for the Freemans but now hung loose about her shoulders. The seeming calmness of her voice and manner was belied by something frantic in her eyes. Creases crawled from their corners, and Isaac suspected those creases had felt many tears. Isaac also noticed that her hands were fine and light on the pole, twitching it periodically, practiced and sure. He thought to himself that this was as it had to be; her expertise was a result of necessity: she was alone with no one to catch the fish for her. As this occurred to him, those fine hands tightened around the pole.

Maria felt a strong pull at the end of her line. Her bait, a small herring, had sunk to the depths of the pond and had been well below the surface when the fish took it, so no detectable ripple appeared in the water, yet Maria gave a perfectly timed tug, even as she was looking at Isaac, and the fish was secure. Her face was stippled by sunlight, and Isaac watched her skillfully play it to the shore, laughing as she did so. Then she unhooked the bass and in a deft motion flipped the silvery fish onto the rocks behind her.

"It's a nice one."

"I should be out with the men on the ships, shouldn't I?" she said as she smiled back at Isaac. "I can catch fish with the best of them!"

Isaac laughed and said, "I don't know if I can see you as a whaler, Maria, but I do wonder what your future holds."

Maria looked at him steadily, and after a moment had passed, she said, "Nowadays I have fewer hopes for the future than I do for the past."

"What do you mean?" he said.

Shifting her position on the cool rock, she said, "I have memories and dreams that visit me in the night, the same memories and dreams, and I cannot rid myself of them. You have heard about them, but I lived through them. My baby's still blue face rises up to me at night, I can still see the walls of that jail, and I often see Sam Bellamy gazing at me as if through a cloud of sadness. I am seventeen years old, and before I dream of the future, I need to cast off my past. It hasn't been easy for me to do these last two years, Isaac,…" Then, almost shyly, she made a half-shrug and, laughing softly, said, "But listen to me, I am talking too much."

Silvery glimmerings danced on the pond's surface, and Isaac squinted as he looked at her in the brightness of the morning light. He could not believe that the two of them were the same age, and in his heart he knew they were not. She had traveled distances he never would, and he knew that, just as he had known years before that he could not travel with Sam Bellamy on the sea. His was a smaller life.

Maria looked appraisingly at Isaac. What had brought the boy to this lonely place? What could he possibly want from her? What did she have to offer?

Isaac walked over to the rock where she was sitting, sat down a foot or two away from her, and then looking not at her but at the sheen of white light on the pond, he said, "I've been wondering, Maria, if you would like some company out on the dunes, or, for that matter, would you care to live on my farm with me? You might not be aware of it, but my mother died last winter so I'm running the place by myself, and I could always use some help."

Maria's eyes ran up the fishing pole and down the line to where it vanished into the pond. For several moments she was as silent as the fish below the surface. When she turned her face to him, Isaac saw first the curling lashes of her eyes and then her eyes themselves, warm with tears. She smiled at him, and said, "Oh, Isaac, I have had difficulty learning to live with myself on those dunes, and I fear I am no fit companion for someone else, much less someone as kind as you." Then after a pause, she murmured, "I have bad dreams, and I don't want to visit them on you.

The pond was a screen of light, and in a moment of confusion and bedazzlement, Isaac heard himself asking, "Do you think of him often, Maria?"

"Whom do you mean?" she responded, "my dead child or my lover? If you are speaking of my child, yes: he is one of my constant companions out here on the dunes. If you are speaking of Sam Bellamy, I have nothing to say. Some feelings cannot be expressed, so perhaps it's best to say nothing at all about them." Then, after a few seconds had passed, her voice tightened, and she said, "No, some feelings need to be spoken. I still see his face: I still love him, yet I still want him dead. I want to erase him from my mind, but I am not able to. The townspeople, and the people in your tavern, and people I have yet to meet will not let me erase him either."

Isaac surprised himself when he found himself saying, "You know that he's back, don't you? You've spoken with him, haven't you?"

Glancing quickly at Isaac and then slowly looking away, Maria murmured, "Yes, yes I have."

"So have I. He was at the tavern two nights ago, but he wouldn't say anything to me. He did start people talking, though. He no longer wears a beard as you may know. Some of the drunkards at the tavern have begun to ask questions. And if there is a reward for him, they will surely seek it."

Maria looked down at the fish that was still curling and convulsing fitfully at her feet, her evening dinner,

"Do you know where he is?" Isaac asked.

She looked again at him with a quick turn of her head, and in measured tones she said, "I have seen him only once since his return, and that was on the night of the great storm. I suspect he fears attracting attention to himself or to me, but in any case, you have seen him more recently than I have. No, Isaac, Sam Bellamy can burn in Reverend Treat's hell for all I care. I am done with him… except when he appears in my dreams."

As her voice trailed off, Isaac saw the tip of her pole suddenly dip, and he cried excitedly, "You've got another one, Maria!"

"Then we'll have dinner for two!"

As if they were still children, Isaac extended his hand to help her up, and smiling, she took it. Within a minute she had brought the fish ashore, and they admired it. It was a large one, and they smiled at each other. They did so, however, knowing that Maria would never live under the roof of Isaac's small home and that he would never sleep under the stars of the Billingsgate dunes with Maria.

𝒩ew 𝔈ngland   𝒩umber 682

Boston News-Letter.

Published by Authority.

From 𝒪onday May 6. to 𝒪onday May 13. 1717

𝒪assachusetts 𝔅ay 𝔏and.

By His EXCELLENCY, Samuel Shute, Esq.; Captain General and Governour in Chief, in and over the said Province (Mass. Bay), and Vice-Admiral of the same, A PROCLAMATION.

Whereas a Ship of The Burthen of about three hundred Tons, Mounted with Twenty eight Guns, Manned with One hundred & thirty Men, Commanded by Samuel Bellame, said to be an English man, a Reputed Pyrate, has lately Infested and Annoyed the Coast. And on Friday the 26th of April last past in the Night time the said Ship was cast on Shore in a storm on the back side of Cape Codd, against the middle of the Table Land, and broken to pieces, the most of her Men drown'd: on Board of which Ship there was Money, Bullion, Goods and Merchandize of considerable value, much of which has been taken up before Information thereof was given to any in Authority; And it is very probable that much more may be recovered.

I do therefore with the Advice of His Majesty's Council strictly charge, command and require all Justices of the Peace, Sheriffs, Constables, and other His Majesty's Officers and Subjects within this Province, to use their utmost Endeavors and Diligence to Seize and Apprehend, or cause to be seized and apprehended, any Person or Persons belonging to the said Pirate Ship, their Accomplices and Confederates, with the Money, Bullion, Treasure, Goods and Merchandizes taken out of said Ship, or any of her Apparel, that shall be found with them, or any of them, or in the possession of any others; and to carry such Person or Persons before One or more of the Members of the Council or other of His Majesty's Justices of the Peace to be imprisoned and Proceeded against as the Law directs. And all persons whomsoever are hereby strictly forbidden to Countenance, Harbour, Entertain, Comfort, Conceal, or any of their Money, Treasure, Goods or Merchandize, as they will answer the same at their utmost Peril.

Given at the Council Chamber in Boston the Fourth of May, 1717, in the Third Year of the Reign of Our Sovereign Lord George, by the Grace of GOD of Great Britain, France & Ireland, KING, Defender of the Faith &c. by the Order of the Governour, by and with the advice of the Council, Joseph Marion, Dep. Secr.

S. SHUTE

GOD SAVE THE KING

As the poet would say many years later of a New England spring, "Nature's first green is gold her hardest hue to hold," but on this bright May morning Maria had learned the truth of these words already. She had found it in the brilliant yellow of the forsythia bush whose blossoms flashed gold for such a short time and then receded to the more durable green of summer. She loved to be surprised by these bushes on rounding a corner, on topping a rise in a path, upon encountering a splash of yellow in the woods, or on her way along the dunes. Today Maria was seventeen years old, yet she had lived much longer than that. Living outside the laws and daily customs of the town as she had for so long, she felt free to go where she wished and to travel when and where she desired. She smiled to herself when she considered that her status as a witch permitted her a privacy that others could not enjoy. And on a gusty May morning like this one, she was determined to be as free as she could as she sauntered past the now familiar ruin of the Whydah, laughing at the highjinks of the small dog ten yards ahead of her and shaking her hair dry following her recent plunge into the frigid ocean water.

Cyprian Southack was a ramrod. He was a man of straight edges, whose back was as stiff as a ship's mast, his resolve as firm as its keel, and his gaze as fine as that of a spyglass. He was no man's fool, and he did not like being played for one. In the rising wind of this early May morning he felt another bulbous tick on the back of his neck: he found these creatures almost as irksome as their brethren Cape Codders, and he derived a special satisfaction in securing it between his fingers and then driving his thumbnail into its small carapace, severing it, and then flicking it away. In the last few days he had become especially adept at this motion as he and his men had made their way through the high reeds, the rushes, and cordgrass at Boatmeadow Creek and Jeremiah's Gutter on their way across the outer limits of the Cape.

Cyprian Southack was a man of considerable accomplishments. By the age of fifty five he had mapped vast reaches of the New England, Newfoundland, and Nova Scotia for which he had received a gold chain from King William III. He had fought against the French and Indians in Maine, served aboard ships for twenty-five years, and commanded his own for a number more; he enjoyed the trust of those highest in the colonial government, and in years to come, he would explore and map English holdings along the Mississippi River from its mouth to the St. Lawrence River. Most recently, he had traveled from Boston across the roiling waters of Barnstable Bay to the harbor inside the curl of Long Point off Provincetown, the very place Sam Bellamy had hoped to reach during the storm. From there he had traveled down the more protected western coast of the Cape to Boatmeadow Creek, a place he remembered from earlier mapping explorations of the area. Then with his contingent of nine men, he had paddled, slogged, and portaged his way across the outer Cape retracing slim veins of water that at the time connected Barnstable Bay with the Atlantic Ocean. He had done this in a matter of only a few days. To arrive at his destination and find the Whydah bottom up and its entrails spread across miles of shoreline, its men and the treasure it held now mute and vanished, he

*had been stunned. And then he had been angry. And now he wanted
answers.*

Captain Cyprian Southack wanted nothing more to do with
Cape Codders, with the raw bite of salty air, or the ephemeral notion
of finding pirate treasure. He had had his fill of Governor Shute's
expectations, and if he never again heard the name Sam Bellamy, it
would be too soon. A reminder of the recent storm, a stinging spring
wind was blowing hard from the south across the dunes and out
to sea as Captain Southack stood firmly in the sand, legs outspread
inspecting what was left to inspect strewn along the beach. There
was not much. Samuel Shute, the governor in Boston, had given him
specific instructions to return to the city with all the treasure he
could salvage from the wreck of the Whydah, yet all reports had it
that within twenty four hours of the wreck, residents from all over
the Cape had spread as far as twenty miles up and down the beach
scavenging for remains. As if that were not enough, the wind and
seas refused to relent so his men in their whale boat had no chance
to inspect the hulk offshore. The final outrage was the bill for 83
pounds he had received from the local coroner demanding payment
for burying the dead pirates – the bloody insolence of the man.

"These damnable maggots, these festering carbuncles, these
barnacles, these damnable Cape Codders," he muttered angrily to
himself. "They've taken everything they could find, and then when
I ask them where I might track it down, they look me straight in the
eye and plead ignorance. Damn their eyes. Damn them all!"

As he continued his inspection along the beach on this May
morning, Southack discerned two figures in the distance, one large
and one much smaller outlined against the gray background. As they
drew closer, he realized the smaller shape was a dog, its hair matted
and shining in the early light; it had obviously been swimming in
the frigid surf. As the gap between them closed, the hair on the dog's
back rose, and it began to run toward the man. Trailing the dog, the
shape of a young woman came into view.

Southack was a mapmaker, a seaman, and a stern leader of
men, but he also knew beauty when he saw it, and the young girl
approaching him walked as if to her own music with a gentle,

lingering sway. She was unlike anyone he had seen before: she wore no shoes, and her muslin dress seemed to cascade from her shoulders, loose yet curving about her hips; the features of her face were fine and delicate, her upper lip curled into two half moons. But her hair was what caused his eyes to linger over her; she must have been swimming only minutes before because her hair took on a sheen in the early light, falling in a silken stream past her shoulders. She was young – there was no question about that – but she did not meet him with the same practiced, timid smile of so many young girls her age. Instead, as she approached him, she gazed at him directly, almost boldly, in no way committing herself to words but shrewdly assessing him with her eyes.

Cyprian Southack was fifty-five years old, yet before a word had passed between them, he felt himself challenged by this girl standing before him, her hair and face glistening with seawater, in a dry dress. Her eyes were luminous, and she laughed freely when her dog began to sniff around Southack's boots and pantlegs.

"Stop that now, Wizard," she said in a lilting way. "You're bothering the gentleman."

Her easy manner engaged Southack's attention. Then, shaking the dog from his leg, he said, "Wizard, that's an interesting name."

Maria laughed, and swinging her hair to dry it, she said, "Well, since everyone calls me a witch already, I might as well live with a Wizard. So when my little friend here came to my door one day, I knew just what to name him. We're both strays, you see."

For a moment Southack was captivated by this young girl. "Tell me more about your witchery," he said, "because you are unlike any witch I have ever seen."

Maria gazed at him carefully, then murmured, "Ask any of the townspeople you meet about Maria Hallett, and they will be more than glad to speak with you about my witchcraft."

Southack returned her gaze, then said after a pause, "I have heard your name before, but you do not strike me as being a witch. I have also heard of your connection to Sam Bellamy, whose misadventure is the reason I am here. Is it his presence that brings you also to this place this morning?"

Maria laughed lightly, and, her eyes alight, she said, "For all I know, Sam Bellamy could be swimming with the whales, he could be riding the wind, he could be throwing back a mug of ale at Sam Smith's tavern, he could be .... He could be hanging from a yardarm." By the time she had finished, Maria was no longer smiling, and Southack was interested in her change of mood.

"Then you have not seen the man?" he asked.

"I just told you," she responded quickly, "I have no idea where he is, and I can assure you that I do not care."

Still gazing intently at her, Southack reached into his pocket and pulled out a heavy piece of paper that appeared to be a map. "For the last few days," he said, "as I've been traveling across this territory, I have been speaking with people and mapping the landscape. You know these people well and the places where they live. I'm here by the governor's order to salvage what I can from this sorry business, and perhaps you can help me. Mr. Bellamy and his treasure seem to have vanished, but maybe you can direct me to those who might help me recover it."

Almost before he finished, Maria had begun to laugh softly, barely disguising the scorn she felt for the man, and said. "Sir, I do not even know your name, but I will tell you that I live maybe a half a mile from here, just over those dunes to the north. I live in a small shack all year round, and I can assure you that if I found some of Mr. Bellamy's treasure -- to which I have some claim -- I would keep it, as would anyone else in this area I am sure. Would you not do the same if you were in my circumstances? If you have found no treasure by now, you will find none," she added. "Of that I can assure you."

As she was talking, Southack was considering small waves breaking firmly on the shore. Then he suddenly began to laugh himself; he was a man comfortable with carrying out tasks given to him, a mapmaker accustomed to ordering the shape of the landscape, but when he saw Maria's dog race into the frigid water and attempt to ride one of the small waves, he had to laugh. Freed for a moment from the spell of this lovely girl and the disappointing prospects for his mission, he smiled in his crooked way at the dog, now belly up, being propelled to the shore on its back.

Following Southack's gaze, the corners of Maria's eyes crinkled in amusement, then turning back to him, she said, "Sir, I know this beach, and I know these people all too well – perhaps better than anyone – and the chances of your finding any gold on these sands are about as good as Wizard's turning around and swimming from here to Boston Harbor."

In the fixity of his gaze upon her, Maria saw the same look of determination that she had seen in the face of Sam Bellamy two years before when he had said goodbye to her aboard the Poseidon's Toy, and she knew this man would not be easily deterred from pursuing his mission. So with a sigh of indifference, she said to him, "If you still plan to continue your treasure hunt, you may wish to talk with two people: one is Sam Harding, and the other is Isaac Doane, an old friend of mine. Mr. Harding knows this land and its people as well as any man, and if anyone can sniff out salvage, he is the one if you know what I mean. My friend, Isaac Doane, is a barkeep at the Smith tavern on Great Island, and ale not only loosens men's lips but eases the passing on of many rumors.

"Those paths are short ones and will not take you very far, I fear, because Cape Codders are a funny lot. For better or worse, I have learned their ways well, and I can tell you truly, were my little shack beyond the dunes brimful of Captain Bellamy's gold, which I can assure you it is not," she said with a brilliant smile, "I would not tell you one way or the other. And I suspect you will have the same answer from anyone you speak to out here."

Cyprian Southack was a skeptic by nature; he prided himself on his ability to mine truth from the nuggets of people's conversation, and as he talked with this glistening young woman on this uncommonly blustery May morning, he believed her. He was not given to smiling easily or often, but when she finished, the corner of his mouth curled upward, and a small unused dimple appeared in his cheek. "If I am to be disappointed in my mission," he responded to her, "at the least I want to speak with those who might know about this matter, those who may have been here in the days following the wreck or would know those who were."

"You are not suggesting, are you," Maria asked with a lilt in her voice, "that I was a party in a crime or would reveal the names of those who were?"

"No, I am making no such accusation," Southack quickly added.

"I wish only to complete this mission and complete it as thoroughly as I can. From my inspection of these beaches, I have found little that is salvageable, and I suspect I will find little in the days to come. Mr. Bellamy's gold seems to have sunk into the depths of the sand or vanished into the air. But perhaps the people you have mentioned can confirm the facts and help me close the book on this sorry affair."

Maria brushed aside a wisp of hair that had dried while they were talking, and she stared intently at him. In another time and place, his proposition might have posed a problem for her, freighted as it was with the power of the law and the government, of inquisition, of potential difficulties to those she had named or might name. Unmoored as she was from any devotion to those laws, however, she simply grinned and repeated the names, "Sam Harding and Isaac Doane. You will find them at Sam Smith's tavern across the bay. Isaac is there every day, and Sam drinks his ale there when he is not farming his land. But as I have told you, they will tell you no more than I have about this sorry affair," she said echoing Southack's phrase.

Were he a younger man, Cyprian Southack might have wished to continue his conversation with this girl who seemed to have emerged from the sea free as a mermaid and accompanied by a dog named Wizard. But up the beach his men would be waiting for him, and he knew he must be on his way. Accustomed as she was to a solitary life, Maria smiled to herself as she watched Southack making his way back up the shoreline, navigating around small tidal pools, walking on the firm sand darkened by the receding tide, attempting to keep the sand out of his thick colonial shoes. Meanwhile, Wizard tugged at the hem of her dress as if to ask her to return to the swirling water and swim with him for awhile.

****

Southack had seen the gold dust vaulted in Sam Harding's unbalanced eyes. The man was a weathered Cape Codder, the type whose family tree had sent down roots two generations before, and whose branches would still be bearing fruit ten or fifteen generations into the future. His sons and grandsons might not troll the shores for what they cast up, as Sam did when he was not farming his land, but they would be just as shrewd, wary, and opportunistic as he. His thumb was on the pulse of this place, and he knew well the limits of colonial authority. Southack also suspected that the man's barn was filled to the top with the wealth and the remains of the Whydah. In fact, the man had confidently told him as much:

"Mr. Southack, on the night of the wreck, Thomas Davis woke me from a sound sleep, and when he told me what had happened, we went back to the beach to see what we could see. He was a sorry sight, that one, and we later added another one by the name of Julian, a mongrel pup if I ever saw one, who washed up on the shore right in front of Isaac's and my eyes."

"Isaac?" Southack had asked.

"Yes, Isaac Doane, a local boy who was with me that morning. As I am sure you know, the constables have taken in the other two, but the four of us managed to save all we could from what washed up on the beach in the night. To tell you the truth, I promised the boys that I would guard their share of what we found in a safe place, and that's just what I am going to do until their cases have been tried in Boston. It's the least I can do for the boys. My heart goes out to them because they're no pirates as anyone can see. I am sure you would do the same, Mr. Southack, would you not?" As he concluded, Harding's eyes glinted separately.

Unnerved by the undisguised glee the man felt in his own hypocrisy, Southack shot back, "Harding, you are as guilty as the pirates you have saved. You are no better than they, and I daresay even worse."

The sanguine vulture had infuriated all that was military in his being, but Southack refused to give the man any additional satisfaction of scorning his authority, and he ended the interview by issuing a threat through gritted teeth: "If you see me again, Harding, I will have in my hand a warrant for your arrest signed by the governor."

As Southack spun on his heel and turned his back on him, Sam Harding shrugged and smiled, innocently revealing a tooth that appeared to be gold among the few others in his mouth.

✳✳✳✳✳✳✳✳✳✳✳✳✳✳✳✳✳✳✳✳✳✳✳✳

There was a staccato knocking at the tavern door, but no one appeared. Then moments later Cyprian Southack threw open the door of the Sam Smith's tavern and entered, fully aware that he was at the end of his investigation. Talking with Harding had been like falling into a dark, bottomless pit, and his last hope before returning to Boston was this boy, Isaac Doane, who might provide him with some useful threads of information to which he would be willing to testify in court. The customary hum of conversation had diminished with the insistent rapping on the door, and the congregation fell silent as the door swung open and then closed behind the man. Perhaps some of the denizens recognized Southack's face, or perhaps the area's spiderweb of information had warned them to be ready for his imminent arrival at the tavern; nonetheless, an air of expectation pervaded the room, and his unique way of announcing himself had only heightened the bated anticipation in the room.

In fact, the knocking had resulted from Southack's nailing the following announcement to the outside of the door, a notice he had posted in countless public places but none perhaps so public as this one.

Advertisement

Whereas there is lately Stranded on the back of Cape Cod a Pirate Ship & His Excellency the Governor hath Authorized and impower'd me the Subscriber, to discover and take care of S. Wreck and to Impress men & whatsoever Else necessary to discover and Secure what may be part of her, ... With Orders to go into any house, Shop, Cellar, Warehouse, room or other place, & in case of resistance to break open any doors, Chests, trunks & other package there to Seize and from thence to bring away any of the goods, Merchandize, Effects belonging to S. Wreck, as also to Seize any of her men. And all his Majesty's officers and other his loving Subjects are Hereby Commanded to be aiding and assisting to me, my Deputy or Deputies In the due Execution of S. warrant or they will answer if Contrary at their utmost peril. These are therefore to notify all persons that have found or taken up any thing of S. Wreck on what was belonging to or taken out of S. Wreck vessel that they make discovery thereof and bring in the Same to me at Mr. Wm. Brown's In Eastham or where else I Shall order Or they will

Answer the Same at their Utmost peril, and then all officers and other persons will give information of any thing of S. Wreck taken up by any person or Suspicion thereof, that they may be proceeded with and a Discovery made Pursuant to my powers and Instructions.
Eastham May, 1717

Cyprian Southack

Southack's eye quickly assessed the room's inhabitants and soon settled on a lad standing behind the bar studiously drying ale glasses. Then he resolutely made his way toward the young man past a number of men staring at him over the rims of their glasses.

For his part, Isaac's life had altered the night the Whydah ran aground. Isaac was now seventeen years old and had become a fixture at Sam Smith's tavern, tending the bar, stocking supplies, serving customers food and ale, even opening the doors for business in the early afternoon and locking them at night when the day's drinking was done. Isaac was a known quantity, like a familiar flagon of flip. He was comfortable at the tavern, his world a small one, but the night of April 26, 1717, changed all that. Gold was to be had on the beaches, Sam Bellamy was back on Cape Cod, and Isaac's small hive on Great Island was abuzz with the news.

When he returned from the beach that first night with Sam Harding, his wagon was overtopped with pirate gear; the lives and possessions of a pirate crew had been spread along the beach that night and in the few days that followed. As he had turned over sodden bodies on the sand, Isaac had expected to meet again the face of Sam Bellamy, his old friend, but that had not happened nor had the two hundred or so men scavenging along the beach found the pots of gold rumored to be on board the fated ship. After they had transported several wagonloads of what treasure there was and after tending to the dead in their own way, Sam, Isaac, and their two shadowy friends stood on the shore like disappointed birds of prey looking over the dismasted Whydah -- forlorn and dark against the evening sky, but still holding a trove of gold in her depths as a swirling skirt of water spread darkly around her ruined hull. In the twilight the men had been happy at their day's work and profits, but the promise of glimmering gold had not been fulfilled as it so seldom is.

Like breath given to smoldering embers, that night had revived many memories for Isaac. With Maria's shanty so close to the scene and with Sam Bellamy's name on everyone's lips, he had vaguely expected the two figures to loom up at him while he and his friends were working throughout the day and the early evening. But they had not, and now eleven days later, having heard of a man from the colonial government who was asking questions about that night, about missing gold, and about Sam Bellamy, he realized this was the man walking toward him.

From behind the bar Isaac measured the man. He had a military air about him, dark eyes, quick and direct, and Isaac's chest tightened as the man approached. Isaac reassured himself that he had seen Sam Bellamy with his own eyes – he knew that. The men in the tavern had already begun to joke about the ghost of Bellamy, but Isaac did not smile when he heard this foolishness: he had seen Sam Bellamy – there was no doubt of it – and he was no ghost. He knew he could not betray his old friend, but beyond that he did not know what he would say to this man who was by now regarding him as if he knew who he was.

After quickly identifying himself, Southack placed his hand on the bar and said, "If you please, I would like some ale and some information, young man. I am here on the governor's business, and as you may know, I have been speaking with people about the wreck of the Whydah on the outer beach and the treasure that apparently has disappeared out there. If you can tell me anything about that or the fate of Captain Bellamy, the governor and I would be grateful." When he entered the room, Southack had noticed how the voices had lowered, and by the time he had finished speaking, he was aware that the room was virtually silent.

Isaac, too, sensed the sets of eyes trained upon him, and as his glance skittered quickly about the room, his voice involuntarily rose, and he began, "People came from everywhere during those two or three days. There must have been two hundred at least, searching along the beach for goods and gold. But I don't think any of the men in this room were there," he added with a half smile as he scanned the room.

From the back of the room, a voice called out, "No, I don't see anyone either, Isaac," which provoked a ripple of laughter among those in the crowd. Ignoring them, Isaac continued, "But for all our work, we found very little gold, Mister Southack. Those men on that ship that night were more concerned with saving their skins than with saving their gold, but if some of them had gold on their bodies, you'll never find it now. Our wager that night and now in the days that have followed is that any fortune in gold that Mr. Bellamy stole from the Spanish is buried in the hulk out there. But we can't reach it, and I suspect that you and the governor won't be able to either."

At these words several of the men in the tavern stamped their heels on the floor and coughed, "Here, here. Here, here."

Paying them no attention, Southack continued to gaze steadily at Isaac and said, "I fear that you are right – that Bellamy's treasure is either buried in the sand or in the pockets of your friends. Whatever the case may be, though, I suspect that I will not be finding it. It is a pity, however," he added after a pause, "that Bellamy should have gotten away after doing so much damage and destroying the lives of his men."

Isaac caught his breath at this and asked, "What do you mean when you say he got away?"

Southack noticed the edginess in Isaac's question, and he continued, "Which brings me to the point of my visit: Have you seen Sam Bellamy since the night of the wreck?"

Isaac was immediately on his guard, "No, no I haven't," he murmured almost to himself. "The last time I saw him was several years ago when he sailed out of Town Cove on his hunt for gold."

Eying the boy intently, Southack persisted, "The scavengers on the beach apparently found no evidence of Bellamy, and perhaps his remains are still in the hold of the hulk or have sunk to the bottom of the sea. But my estimation is that he is a survivor, that he would find a way to save his own scurvy skin, and that his face might likely turn up in a place like this. You should know, young man," Southack continued in a more confidential tone, "that if Bellamy is walking these shores, he has abandoned his men. At present, eight will hang for joining up with him; your friend, Sam Harding, tells me that the two of you have already met two of them. Bellamy is a destroyer, and the law will go hard with him and those who might help him. Look to it, boy. If you know anything of him at all, you can tell me now or when you're of a mind to.

Then, raising his voice, he turned to face those who had been listening so intently behind him, and addressing them, he said with a discernible edge in his voice, "Yes, good men and women of Cape Cod, if you know aught of the captain, Black Bellamy, or his ill-gotten gold, I advise you to tell me of it – either now or later. Soon eight men will hang for their association with the man, and it will go hard with those who help him if, in fact, he is still alive and not swimming with the fishes off your shores."

Cyprian Southack was not a man given to grand gestures. Like so many men, he took small, certain steps, building his life on a foundation of hard-won daily accomplishments. As he assessed the young man standing behind the bar, a thought came to him, and he asked in a lower tone, "Isaac Doane, how long have you known Sam Bellamy?"

"A little over two years."

"And have you ever had reason to distrust him or his motives?"

Isaac paused remembering the last time he had seen Bellamy steering his way out of Town Cove at the helm of Poseidon's Toy, Maria's tear-stained face, his own sense of impotence and shame.

Southack read Isaac's pause as doubt, and he quickly continued, "If you have doubts about the man and perhaps about those who joined up with him, I have a proposition for you, one that I urge you to consider very carefully, young man. In short, I ask you to attend the trial sessions in Boston and share with the judges there your observations about the pirate Bellamy and the two of his men you met on the night of the wreck. Even if you cannot help me recover the gold he has stolen and brought here to Cape Cod," Southack said with a crooked smile, "perhaps you can restore a measure of justice and help bring those who aided him to the justice they deserve."

After another pause, Isaac responded, "I have no love for Sam Bellamy. He has hurt many, even some close to me, and I will think over your offer, Mr. Southack. I wonder, though," he added, "what I can tell the judges in Boston that will be of any help to them. I am only a boy, and what can I say that will make any difference in the trial of Sam Bellamy or his men?"

Southack looked at the young man with a kindly eye. "Isaac, I can sense that you know more than you are telling me at this time and in this place, and – the Lord knows – I have spoken with many on this spit of land who have told me nothing at all. But any God-fearing, reasonable man who recognizes the full extent of what Bellamy and his men have done will want to bring them to face the law.

Then Southack asked, "Do you by chance know a young man named John Julian who has been known to frequent these parts and was an associate of Bellamy's? He is a young man, not much older than yourself, and if the governor has his way, he will be hanged before long. Some have said he was at the helm of the Whydah when it ran aground. I have little good to say about your neighbor, Sam Harding, but he did tell me that he saw Julian on the beach the night after the wreck and that you were with him at the time. Your testimony about what you saw that night could be very helpful in Boston."

Isaac's lips twitched into a rueful smile, but Southack did not notice, and he continued, "As you must know from what you saw that night, grievous wrongs have been done to many," he said quietly. "I hope to do everything in my power to set them right, and I urge you to do the same."

When Southack finished, Isaac nodded slowly, and then said, "I will come to Boston to testify for you at the trial, Mr. Southack. I have private reasons for doing this, and I will tell you all I know about John Julian, his crewmember Davis, and Sam Bellamy, a man who was once a friend of mine. I cannot say I will do this happily, but I will do it. I have my own reasons."

Southack stared steadily at Isaac for a moment, his lips thinning into a brief military smile, and then, his mission completed, he said, "So be it. I will contact you when the time of the trial draws near."

As Southack turned and walked to the tavern door, the sound of his boot heels on the wide pine floor was audible, so quiet had the room become. Then, stopping suddenly, as if to punctuate his departure, he faced the tavern's congregation and said, "Before I came in here today, I nailed an announcement on the door of this establishment. When you leave tonight , I think every man jack of you here would be wise to read it, and to heed its warning."

As he turned around to reach for the door, the compressed verbal energy exploded into conversation, questions, laughter, and a few catcalls, and, quickly, he was gone. For his part, Isaac watched the man slide gracefully through the broad door and then began meticulously to rub a stain from the glass in his hand, at no time looking up or acknowledging the delighted confusion that prevailed for some time in the room.

Chapter Nineteen
Bewitched
June, 1717

Weeks had passed since the night of the wreck, and much had happened: Sam had managed to elude escape thus far; eight of his men had been apprehended and were awaiting trial; he had had no contact with Paul, and he had heard countless rumors about Maria. He knew he must leave this area and perhaps find Paul again, but before he did, he had to see Maria once again. Yes, he must see Maria. Witch, murderess, demon child -- these words swirled about her whenever he heard her name, and he needed to know the reasons for them. He also knew he needed to explain his last two years to her: what he had done, why he had gone on the account, and the resonating fact that he had never forgotten her, that in his own way he still loved her.

Sam came up the beach from behind her, and he stopped within twenty yards of her to observe her at her work. She was still as lovely as he remembered. Light loved every feature of her face, and the slender shadows of an early June evening seemed to rub across her skin and make it glow. Two years, a child, imprisonment, and exile to a shack by the sea had not faded her natural beauty. Her hair, cut straight across the back at her shoulders, was drawn back almost severely and tied with a faded blue ribbon; like her skin, it assumed a sheen imparted by the light. On this late afternoon day Maria was kneeling at the water's edge digging for clams, her dog close by daring the small wavelets to overtop him and bear him out to sea. Wizard was the first to see him, and when he did, he ran toward the man shaking his fur dry as he did and then circling the stranger while oscillating his tail in welcome.

At first as she looked over her shoulder at him, Maria didn't recognize the figure coming towards her: the man was thin, clean-shaven, and wearing a seaman's cap. Gone was the luxuriant beard, gone the flowing red sash, and approaching her was a man in his mid-thirties, dark with close-cropped black hair and a tentative air about him. Then she knew who he was.

As he neared her, she called to his mind the figure of a mermaid, an alien creature washed up on the shore, its fanned tail curled beneath her and out of sight. But Maria was no lost mermaid, and as Sam came closer, she had time to compose herself, rinsing her hands free of the sand in the seawash, drying them on her skirt, and running her slender fingers through her hair as she rose slowly to meet him.

"I've been waiting for this day for a long time, Captain Bellamy," she said. "I have often wondered when and if I would see you again," she began slowly and with great dignity. "I am speaking not of the last two weeks but of the last two years." Then with a half-smile she said, "You seem much changed to me, Sam. Times have been hard for the two of us, haven't they?" she continued almost shyly.

"Yes, they have, Maria, and I have missed you greatly over the weeks and months," he answered. "I have stories to tell you, Maria, some thrilling and to my credit, and some terrible as you already know. But since I've returned, I've heard stories of you also, strange and sad ones, and they have brought me here to this beach to see you."

Somewhere deep in her being, a heart muscle tightened, a neuron ignited, and her eyes flashed starfire. "Any stories you have heard about me, Sam Bellamy, should begin with your name. My life in this place began over two years ago when I met you at the burying ground. I still remember the day so well – the great plume in the hat you held, the sails in the distance, the scent of the apple tree -- and everything that has followed has unraveled from that day." Her voice caught as she finished.

In a softer register, Sam said, "Tell me of what has happened, Maria, for I want to know."

Each of them had pictured this moment from the day that Sam had sailed out of Town Cove, but neither could have pictured then the two care-worn faces looking at each other on this desolate beach more than two years later. As he stood there, Sam's gaze extended beyond the curve of her shoulder to a balding dune nearby tufted with seagrass, and beyond that to a shack in the distance that he knew must be hers. In that vision, he sensed the full range of her loneliness, and so when she spoke next, he was not surprised at the depth of her feeling. She had been looking down at the sand as if examining the contours of some whorled periwinkle.

"I had your child, Sam, and I lost it. It was a boy and a lovely one. It had your nose and your eyes."

In a neutral tone Sam mused aloud, "A boy?" and then after a brief pause, "Some at the tavern have said you killed the child."

The young woman's eyes widened at this because she had known the question was coming but was nevertheless unprepared for the horror of it. After a moment had passed, she spoke, "That you, of all people, should question me about how the child died – you who sailed out of Town Cove while I stood on shore crying with your child in my womb. You who left me behind... I did my best by the child," she cried. "I gave it the home of my body for nine months, and then the churchmen, the Fates, God -- call them what you will – they came and took him away from me. Then they put me in jail, and I fled. And they did it again, and I fled again. And now they leave me alone. And I'm damned glad of it," she said smiling determinedly. "That shack you were looking at over the dunes is now my home, and it has been for the last year and a half.

"His eyes were your eyes, Sam, and now they are closed. I saw them for such a short while, and you never will. But don't you dare blame me as others have for I will have none of it. I loved the child, just as I loved you. The child's death was an accident, a terrible accident, and I was unable to stop it from happening. That was my sin, my only sin, and I have paid dearly for it for the last two years."

Maria's entire being seemed to convulse, and tears had begun to form in her eyes and find their way down her face. As her shoulders rose and fell, Sam took her in his arms.

"I have much to answer for, Maria, and my story begins with you," he said as his eyes blankly beheld the point where the sky meets the sea. "When I left you standing on the shore, I was certain I would come back to you with gold in my pockets and that we would then live my dream together. But dreams are fragile, and they can change like the shapes of those clouds out there. My men were good men, you see, and I came to owe them a great deal. At first we faced great hardships; we had no success, and we were hungry. Even the threat of hunger can make men do things they would not normally do.

"And then we crossed the boundary of the law, and we found many others who were willing to cross it with us…. and we weren't sorry for it either. Through it all, Maria, I did not forget you, and that is why I came back along these shores to find you and show you the treasure we had gained."

As Maria looked up at him through tear-washed eyes, Sam continued, borne on by the momentum of his words and the memory of the gold. By now the two seemed circled round by the lambent light of the evening air, for the moment indivisible, holding hands and lost in a dream of the past that they both shared. "I didn't know about you and the baby, but you couldn't know about the gold and the adventure. We took many ships, my men and I, and at the end we had more gold than you can imagine.

"We didn't steal the gold either as some have said. My ship, the Whydah, was a slaver, and its treasure came from the sale of men just like my own. We were just taking back what was already ours. At times we even called ourselves Robin Hood's men. I will be damned for it, but I loved those men and that life." Then after a pause he said, "We would be richer than you can dream of, you and I, were it not for the damned fates above that ran us aground that night."

As he finished, Sam reached inside his jacket for the black sash at his waist, untied several knots in it, and poured its contents on the sand now water-darkened by the receding tide. The gold pieces shone like embers in the low light of the evening, and for several instants the two of them seemed mesmerized by them. "They are lovely, aren't they, Maria? And there was so much more than this."

As she looked at the coins and listened to him, Maria's mind eddied with images of the past and the present. She recalled Sam's shadowed face, his wet matted hair when she had last seen him on the night of the wreck here on this beach. She recalled the silent, dark shapes of Sam's men on the shore, and her mind hearkened back to the small blue shape she had cradled so frantically in her arms two years before. As if to clear her mind, she shook her head; then her eyes focused on the hulking wreck in the distance far down the beach. Sam's gaze followed hers, and for a few moments they stood silently contemplating the waters swirling inexorably around and through the broken timbers of the wreck.

Shivering noticeably in the sharpening evening air, Maria ended the silence by asking, "Sam, what will become of us?"

The question had been hovering around the two of them like an errant seabird throughout their encounter, but now that it had been asked, neither seemed to have an answer. Each of them had thought of it many times prior to this meeting, but for the moment they both seemed dumbfounded by the prospect. Sam's vision of the future had telescoped with the destruction of the Whydah's hull on that fateful night. Never again would his gaze be fixed so firmly and defiantly on the years ahead nor – he seemed to know already – would those years include Maria.

"There is a death writ on my life, Maria, and if the price of my lost gold is not already high enough, I fear it will be much higher. Some of my men have been taken, and I am powerless to do anything for them. Their only hope is Paulsgrave Williams, a man you may meet someday. But to tell you God's truth, I fear for you if you are associated further with me."

"You need not concern yourself further on that score, Sam Bellamy, because the law no longer has any hold on me nor do I harbor any obligation to it. In no way do I any longer fear what men may do to me."

"I can no longer offer you the promise of wealth or independence, Maria," Sam continued tentatively, "and life with me will only be putting off the day until I must pay for my past." He had resisted telling her the truth of his most recent crime, but in the face of her defiance and apparent devotion, he slowly bit off the following admission,

"I must also tell you, Maria, that since my return, I have killed a man, a man who recognized me and was going to tell the constable of my whereabouts." When he had finished, she looked at him levelly.

"As a pirate, you must have killed many," she responded tersely, and sensing where his admission was leading them, she continued, "so why should this one make a big difference to you?"

"In the eyes of the law it doesn't matter because I am already a doomed man. However, the man I killed, Cole by name, is a local man – you may even know him -- and I am sure his friends and others are looking for me even at this moment. For these reasons you will be in great danger if you travel with me."

Maria thought for moment and then said, "No, I have not met the man, but I have heard of him, and I know that he is well known in the area."

"Maria, with the best of intentions," Sam persisted, "I have only done you great injury, and I cannot assume the burden of hurting you even more deeply. I cannot live here – that is clear – and for the rest of my life, I will be a fugitive. I cannot ask you to share that fate.

"The only reasons I have remained here this long and have not fled to Provincetown where I might encounter my friend, Paul, again are that I wanted to see you once again, and I want to discover the fate of my men who have been captured. I owe them that much." With these words, Sam's voice trailed off.

"And so our tale repeats itself!" Maria burst out when he finished. "You will leave me once again, this time fleeing the law, and I will wait here alone until doomsday for you to return or for the gold in that ship of yours to wash ashore piece by piece." Maria could feel her loneliness returning with every word she spoke, with every small wave that broke on the sand, and the pain of looking at Sam in the face was too great for her.

As the soft waves of the turning tide curled about his feet, Sam bent over to retrieve a sodden wooden plank that had bobbed ashore, most likely splintered from the nearby wreck. He held it in his hand for a moment inspecting it and then, without a word, flung it as far as he could back out to sea. The small dog, thinking this was a part of a game and unnoticed by the two on shore, swam obediently to bring the remnant back.

Turning to Maria, Sam then said, "I am a seaman, Maria. I am no landsman who can travel the road west, build a cabin, raise a barn, tend to sheep or cows, and run a farm. I did that as a lad, and I am no good at it. So I know now that I will return to the sea, and, perchance, I will avoid the hangman's noose. I must do that alone, as a fugitive, knowing that in every port there will be someone who knows me or knows my name. It will be a dangerous business, and I cannot take you on that journey."

As Maria stared at him, Sam continued, "I love you, Maria – I will say it. The picture of your face, the presence of your spirit, these have been with me ever since we met, and they will stay with me. Apart from you and the debt I owe you, I must remain here until I know the fate of my men , and then I will disappear—I will join a crew, I will be gone, and you must think no more of me.

The interview was over. Maria knew that words would not change Sam's mind, and with this knowledge, she stepped close to him, then closer, and arched her body hard into his. Then holding his face between her two hands, she brought it to hers and kissed him softly and generously on the lips as if she would never kiss another man again and wanted to remember the sensation. Then she said, "Let that remain with you on your travels, Captain Bellamy. They call me a witch and a demon, and maybe they are not far wrong. But let the memory of this moment haunt you. I curse you to remember me."

Unwilling to watch him walk away down the beach, and aware that his eyes were fixed on her, she turned her back to him, called, "Come, Wizard, come," and began to make her way, barefoot, back to her solitary cottage in the distance. As she did so, her hips swayed almost imperceptibly in a rhythmic motion from side to side. Wizard soon caught up with her, happily carrying the small piece of wood in his mouth.

Tracing his lips with his tongue as if to sense again the pressure and taste of her mouth on his, Sam Bellamy watched Maria move liquidly down the beach, stopping only to take the piece of wood from the dog's mouth and throw it further ahead.

For that instant Sam's field of sight contained the images of the promise and destruction of his life and his dreams: the ruined hulk of the Whydah, the forbiddingly lonely cabin in the distance, and the sinuous young woman who connected them. Then with great sadness he shook himself free of the vision, carefully gathered up his sash of gold, and wearily made his way back across the dunes.

Chapter Twenty
The Trial
October-November, 1717

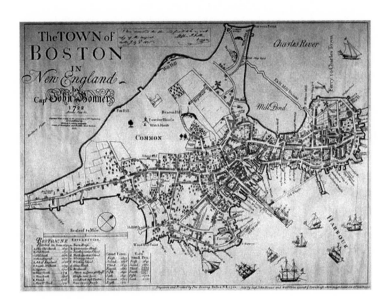

The southwest wind blew cool and fresh through his hair as Isaac stood gazing back toward the Cape from the deck of Captain Yates's merchant sloop, the Mary. At this early hour on this sun-dappled October morning, he felt a riot of feelings. In his hand he was holding the letter from Mr. Southack ordering his presence at the trial of eight pirates, and on this day he was traveling to Boston to obey the order and testify, just as he had promised. Never before had he spoken before a judge, much less traveled more than a few miles away from his home by the bay, and he was exhilarated and nervous at the prospect. But his feelings were more complicated. This day had begun for him as so many had: with the walk to Blackfish Creek and his short sail up Billingsgate Bay; but today, instead of going to the tavern on Great Island, he had headed north to the main dock at Duck Creek where Moses Yates had been waiting for him. As he sailed past Great Beach Hill, he recalled the day when he, Maria, and his old friend Running Water had shared their stories during the tuck-a-nuck, and now as he viewed the shoreline that constituted his home, he contemplated how much had changed in the last three years.

He could still picture her face that Sunday when the three of them had sat on Great Beach Island and how the future had seemed to spread out before them. He loved Maria then, and he had from the day almost three years before when he had skated with her on the frozen pond. Yes, he loved her – there was no question about that – but he had not known how to love her or how to make her love him. These thoughts were occupying him as he considered his motives for traveling to Boston. Any plans Isaac had for a future with Maria had ended on the day she met Sam Bellamy, and ever since, the man had been a persistent figure in his life, appearing at odd moments in memory and most recently in the tavern and in the conversations of its habitués.

As he watched the water slide smoothly beneath the hull of the Mary, Isaac inspected the shoreline more closely, and his eyes settled on James Neck, which led him to recall his brief conversation earlier that morning with Running Water. His friend had called to him from the shore asking where he was going; when he told him Boston, Running Water had inquired, "To the trial?" When Isaac nodded, Running Water had laughed and shouted, "Ask Mr. Southack if he has found any gold yet!" His voice then faded out of earshot, and Isaac had just smiled broadly and waved back.

Now, alone with his thoughts, Isaac could see the Indian village on the Neck receding in the distance, and he realized that it was, in fact, smaller, that the number of "Praying Indians" had diminished due to illness and to many relocating closer to the whaling operations on Great Island. Sensing this inevitable passage of time, something he was becoming accustomed to, Isaac sighed softly and wondered if a single wetu would still be standing on the Neck in fifty years. His premonition would prove true, and he would live to see the day when almost all the tribe's dwellings had disappeared.

As he had so many times in Isaac's life, Sam Smith had helped the boy, this time by making the arrangements with Captain Yates for Isaac's journey. The good captain regularly transported whale oil and massive numbers of oysters from Great Island to Boston, and he told Smith that adding a young passenger would be no trouble. On this day he was to pick up seventy-five barrels of oil from the tryworks and transport them to Boston Harbor, where he would deposit the cargo on the wharf along with the boy.

Several hours later, as the Mary made its way among the outer islands in the bay – Deer Island to the starboard and Long Island, Spectacle Island, and Thompson's Island to the port, he made out Castle Island at the head of the harbor and Governor's Island just to its north. Named for William III of Orange and armed with seventy-two cannons, Castle William, which stood on the island, dominated the entrance to the harbor and would stand there until 1775 when the British destroyed the fort's walls and artillery as they evacuated the city. By that year Isaac would be a very old man when a young patriot, Lieutenant Colonel Paul Revere, and his men would repair the fortifications of the island, which would be known soon thereafter as Fort Independence. But on this day Isaac was unconcerned with the future; instead, he was entranced by the seemingly exotic world unfolding in the distance and especially the sheer size, number, and majesty of the ships scudding before his eyes in the wind.

As Isaac walked along Long Wharf, he was overwhelmed by its size, over a quarter of a mile long, stretching out into Boston Harbor like a great tentacle. A local stevedore had bragged to Isaac that it was twice as long as its name, and as Isaac stared at thirty large sea-going ships tied up at the wharf, he was inclined to believe the man. The planks in the wharf were virtually new having been laid four years before, and the city seemed as new as its dock. Warehouses, taverns, and counting houses had grown up around Long Wharf and the sixty other docks that extended into the harbor creating the impression of a great industrial garden. Isaac was elated. Boston Harbor was full of sailing vessels, maybe one hundred snows, schooners, brigs, and sloops, and he had never seen so much going on at once. He had never traveled as far away as Boston, and the sights and smells engulfed him.

As he walked off Long Wharf, he saw Samuel Wethered's Tavern on the corner of King and Kilby Streets and further down the street the Crown Tavern. To his left, as he walked past Bartlett's wharf, was the Dog and Pot Tavern, and beyond the Dog and Pot was the Widow Day's Crown Tavern at the foot of Clarke's wharf. He had heard all of these names from the men who ordered flip from him at Mr. Smith's tavern, but now he was seeing the places for himself. In his imagination he already knew their interiors -- the aroma of stale beer, the guttering light, and the staccato sound of tavern laughter -- before he opened the doors to enter, and for an instant he felt like a man of the world.

By the time he turned up King Street to find his boarding house, the city had assumed a fresh mantle of light, and the people he passed seemed prosperous and confident, flushed with the optimism that comes from sharing in the extravagant growth of a new city. As Ramblin' Jack Cremer, a local captain, would reflect on the city in those days, "I never saw a beggar or a poor man" although he did admit to having seen a number of "well-rigged women." In the years that followed, the mood and reality would change, however, and by the 1740's, as one wag would note, after shaking hands with a Bostonian, a man would be wise to count his fingers to make sure all five still remained. But to Isaac Doane, seventeen years old and freshly arrived from the edge of the continent, the city was a wondrous place. Its streets and buildings seemed so clean and fine to him, as if they inhaled sunlight throughout the day and exhaled it at night in the sparkling light that played like fireflies on the water.

****

The Courthouse

The Boston Court House in 1717 was a modest structure, in no way extravagant and in every way a reflection of the stern and religious men who had constructed it. Most often it was a place where grievances between landowners were settled, where boundary disputes, damages caused by straying cattle, or rights of inheritance were adjudicated. But on October 17, 1717, the small establishment on Court Street was alive with anticipation: Nine men – Sam Bellamy's pirates – were to be tried for their lives. The town was known as a hanging town: if these men were found guilty, they could well be hanging from a yardarm within ten days to a month from this very day. Because he was a potential witness, Isaac was permitted to enter the courthouse and observe the proceedings.

After informing Mr. Smith, the prosecuting attorney, of his presence, he took a seat on a hard bench at the back of the room and avidly waited for the scene to unfold before him. As he was settling in, a loud voice from the front of the room startled him. It bellowed, "All rise," and a moment later three men, bewigged and solemn, filed in through a door at the right of the room. No sooner had the men seated themselves than the voice cried out again, "Let the sergeant-at-arms lead in the prisoners." Were it not that their situation was so dire, the ultimate penalty so great, the seven men who entered the room might have seemed to be a traveling comedy act. Tall and short, fat and lean, flint-eyed and bovine, dressed in all-colored rags, and speaking a variety of languages, the men could have been mistaken for a band of nomadic clowns, gypsies, jesters. What united them, however, was their fear: Whether evidenced in Brown's bravado, Baker's occasional facial tics, or Quintor's downcast stare, the men's uneasiness was clear for all to see. They had failed to prepare faces to meet those that were staring back at them, and they looked in wonderment at the hostile wave of curiosity that met them.

Isaac felt differently. He knew these kinds of men. He had served ale to them for almost three years, and he knew them to be simple in their needs and strong in their passions. They came from all countries, and they were pledged to the dangerous camaraderie of the sea. They had taken the same oath that he had been unwilling to make three years before aboard the Poseidon's Toy, and at some level he respected them for that.

As he watched them shuffle in and take their seats in the dock, Isaac was startled. Two of the men he was expecting to see were missing, Julian and Davis, the two he had encountered on the night of the wreck on the beach, the two who had helped him and Sam Harding fill Sam's wagon time and again with the treasures that had washed ashore. Julian and Davis were the reasons he was sitting in this courtroom, and if they were not to be tried, he would not be testifying; more important, he would not have to reveal the whereabouts of the loot they had taken that night. So some secrets could remain secret. Cyprian Southack would be unhappy, but as he settled himself on the hard bench, Isaac smiled and sighed softly.

Thomas Baker, Hendrick Quintor, John Shuan, Peter Hoof, John Brown, Simon Van Voorst, and Thomas South. They had all led simple, well-defined lives aboard the ships Sam Bellamy commanded; they were aware of their jobs and their rights, and the promise of great wealth contained in the depths of their last ship only magnified the pleasure that goes with being pirate. But the laws and customs of the landsmen were different, more confusing, to the men now facing the Boston judges. Isaac had trouble pulling his eyes away from the cast of characters before him – the men in wigs, the seven pirates, the large audience swirling before him – but when he did, his eye was attracted by a figure sitting at the back of the room near the entryway, a man wearing a black woolen seaman's cap pulled low on his forehead and which seemed as one with the man's sideburns, A thin black mustache completed the portrait of the man's face. At first glance Isaac believed he had seen the man before, but he was not sure where, and the movement of the crowd hindered him from seeing the man directly. In the next instant, a low, resonant voice absorbed Isaac's attention. It was the voice of Samuel Shute, the governor of the colony and the chief judge in charge of the proceedings. The trial was underway.

An hour later Peter Hoof was on the stand reciting in a heavily stressed Swedish accent the same complaint his fellow prisoners would echo when they followed him.

"It was the captain, Samuel Bellamy. He forced me into piracy," Hoof declaimed. When Hoof repeated the statement, placing an additional stress on the word forced, Isaac's eye involuntarily sought the reaction of the dark figure seated by the entryway, but the man was no longer there.

Moments later, Thomas Baker was saying, "The fault lies with Captain Bellamy. Were it not for him, I'd not be sitting here now. After Baker came Quintor who said the same and, finally Van Voorst who reduced his testimony to one word: "Bellamy." At this, a wave of laughter rippled through the room, causing the Governor to rap his gavel sternly for silence. During this litany of denial, Thomas South seemed lost in the gloom of his own thoughts, but when he was called to enter his plea, he rose slowly and said softly,

"Respected judges, I have listened to these men, and I have little more to add than the following: My mate, the carpenter Thomas Davis, and I were taken forcibly from the St. Michael in December of 1716. This crew of rascals that you have been listening to refused to honor the wishes of the pirate Bellamy and, instead, voted against liberating Thomas when the issue was called. I have no love for Bellamy, but these men here are certainly no better than he, and maybe worse. As for myself, I made an oath with Thomas to escape from these men at our earliest chance, and during my months in captivity I have refused to take up arms against the ships we have accosted. On the fateful night of our wreck I even told one of your witnesses, a mate on the Mary Anne, Thomas Fitzgerald by name, of our intentions. Apart from the truth of this statement, I throw myself on your mercy."

Of the seven defendants, the one who attracted Isaac's particular notice was John Shuan, a Frenchman who spoke no English and was sitting at the end of the long prisoners' bench. Next to Shuan was a kindly Boston tradesman who had been appointed the man's translator. A delicate mustache curled from under Shuan's nose and around his finely shaped lips, and his hands seemed to be perpetually in motion. A young crewman from the Mary Anne, Thomas Fitzgerald, was testifying that on the day of their capture, Shuan had used the crewmembers poorly and that he and Baker had been especially aggressive in trying to discover where they might find liquor. As Fitzgerald spoke, Isaac could see the lips of the translator moving silently. Shuan's eyes widened and his hands moved faster as the man next to him half-whispered into his ear. Shuan was a ruffian, indeed – there was no doubt about that -- but even while Isaac rejected the man's motives and deeds, at this very moment he was watching a man discover that he was soon to die, and Isaac felt sorry for him.

Moments later Thomas Fitzgerald's voice drew Isaac out of his reverie. "That man over there in the red shirt, Thomas South by name, he was not one of the pack. He hung back from the others, and they had little to do with him. That night when the winds were whirling and the others were drunk with fear and ale, he told me he had been forced to join the crew, that he had refused to bear arms, and that he had suffered for it. That night he also told me he planned to leave the scoundrels as soon as the fates would let him."

At this, South suddenly stood up and shouted, "Aye, what the man says is true, Judge, every word of it!" to which Governor Shute responded, "Ye'll sit yourself down now, Mr. South, and we'll deal with your fate as we see fit." This admonition silenced South for the moment, and the trial wore on.

Andrew Mackconachy had lost some weight since his terrifying night aboard the Mary Anne eight months earlier, but his face was still doughy, a yeasty failure, and as he looked across the courtroom and met again the menacing half-smile of Thomas Baker, he quivered slightly and quickly looked away from the man. Unaware of this exchange, the Admiralty lawyer, Mr. Smith, began to question his witness:

"Mr. Mackconachy, would you tell the court what happened to you on the night of February 26th of this year?"

"That was the worst night of my life," Mackconachy said. "Those men over there, they swore to kill me. That I am alive today is only by God's will. The storm, it was fearsome: they drank, and we prayed, and we prayed some more, and only by the grace of God am I here to tell you about it today."

"Mr. Mackconachy, in my opening remarks, I said that piracy was treason, oppression, murder, assassination, robbery and theft carried out in remote and solitary places where the weak and defenseless can expect no assistance or relief and where these ravenous beasts of prey may ravage undisturbed. By this definition, can you tell me whether any or all of these men committed acts of piracy in your presence?"

"Why they all did," Mackconachy burst forth loudly, "if by piracy you mean boardin' a ship with their guns raised, knives in their teeth, and promisin' to kill all on board who don't surrender, then drinkin' themselves to the edge of Satan's shores while

the winds of hell are poundin' in their ears outside the ship." Mackconachy's face grew redder and his voice louder as he continued to speak, and when he finished, his hands reached suddenly to his heart.

"Are you ailing, sir?" asked Smith with real concern.

The witness smiled weakly at him, and then eying the defendants across the room, he said,

"I thank you for asking, sir. I shall survive. It's just that every time I think of that night, it scares me to my core. That man Baker there, he swore to kill me if I didn't tell him where the liquor was. They swore most rudely that they were commissioned by the King, but their only commission was from Satan."

After a pause, Mr. Smith said, "I thank you, sir. You may step down now."

As Mackconachy did so, he looked at the prisoners one more time, but now, to a man, they were much more subdued as if each had suddenly recognized the seriousness of the business at hand.

And so the day wore on. The witnesses spoke and then sat down. After them the defendants spoke and returned to their bench, and this process continued into the late afternoon when the low November sun cast a soft golden light through the windows of the courthouse, cloaking the seven prisoners in its light and causing one of them to wake up, shaking his head, squinting his eyes, and inadvertently smiling until he recognized once again where he was. And then he heard his name,

"Simon Van Voorst, will you come to the stand please?"

Isaac was intrigued by the young man. Van Voorst's hair fell in curling blond ringlets about his shoulders, and he wore a bright red bandanna knotted at his throat. Having just opened from a doze, his eyes moved like a fawn's in the late afternoon light, yet the young man moved gracefully, almost sinuously to the witness stand. By now fully awake and seated, he focused his pale blue eyes on his questioner, and at that instant, Isaac realized how beautiful the young man was. The power of this beauty arrested his attention, and he listened more intently to the tale that followed.

"Yes, my name is Simon Van Voorst…"

Van Voorst was young, about Isaac's age, and as he spoke, he reminded Isaac of himself. By now fully awake, Van Voorst smiled disarmingly, as if he were in another place and time, about to take a quaff of ale with his friends far from this Boston courtroom where he was being tried for his life.

"Yes, Captain Bellamy was a charmer, he was. He stood tall, and he could be fearsome. And I was a young boy two years ago when he took over my ship. He was a devilish charmer, he was. He told us we were on a King's commission to take what we could. He made us believe that that commission covered all the seas and all the world." As he said this, Van Voorst looked down at his hands, which were folded in his lap, and he began to cry softly.

"Yes, the cook from the Mary Anne was right. Those were the words I said the night we took her over – that we were commissioned by the King, that we were Robin's men. Those were the words Sam Bellamy had us believing, and we did believe them, and now look where we are."

As Isaac considered the young man on the stand, he thought once again of the lives Sam Bellamy had touched and ruined, strangers like this young boy - so much like himself - and of Maria, sifting away the days of her youth on a lonely Cape Cod beach. At that moment, although he did not know it, Isaac's heart turned finally and irrevocably away from Sam, the hero and rival of his youth. His soul simply turned a page imprinted with the memory of the boy crying in the courtroom; it was a page he would turn back to and read again.

And so they came and went, the witnesses and defendants. And when the trial was done at the end of the day, six of the seven men knew they would hang. The seventh Thomas South was set free. When that man heard of his good fortune, he fell to his knees before the judges and thanked them saying justice had been done.

But the others, among them Simon Van Voorst, his tears now dried, were led from the prisoners' bench back toward the city jail. Strangely, a silence settled over the room as the men rose to leave, and just as he would remember the sight of the young man's tears, Isaac would recall during the days and months that followed the low metallic sound of their leg irons sliding heavily on the courtroom floor. Unlike many who witnessed the trial that day, Isaac took no pleasure in the judges' decision; instead, he continued to gaze at the door through which the prisoners had exited and did so for several minutes after the last one had departed. The trial was over, the verdict rendered, and the sentence given: six men would die, to be hanged by their necks until dead. But justice in this case was not blind: it had made distinctions among the guilty and the innocent: Van Voorst, Quintor, Hoof, Baker, Brown, and Shuan would go to their deaths; but Thomas South, Thomas Davis, and John Julian, all of whom survived that dark night, would live and travel very different paths.

****

The small but growing city of Boston loomed large for Isaac. He reveled in its sights and sounds. The first lungful of salt air in the morning delivered on a southeasterly breeze, the raucous calls of sailors from yardarms to those below, the wayward gulls curling above them and seeming to answer, the constant movement of people and birds and ships and cargo, a place of captains and shipowners and mates, a place where the strange languages of sailors rose and mixed with the calls of the birds above them, a place where churchmen and farmers and merchants met and transacted business: it was a hub, and it was growing larger. Isaac was beginning to love the place, and so he decided to remain for a few weeks following the trial until the sentence was carried out and the prisoners were hanged -- the end of a chapter, he thought.

In the interim he continued to work, loading goods on and off ships and tending bar at night at the nearby Dog and Pot Tavern. All the while he questioned whether or not he should return to his home by the bay on Cape Cod. Now that his mother was gone, the world was a strange and lonely place to him, and there was little that tied him to the small outpost where he had grown up. But he knew this was not the reason he continued to linger on the Boston docks: it was the picture etched in his mind of the six men being led from the courtroom. He wanted to see the story through to its end. In his youthful heart, he hoped to see them somehow free, to see them liberated at the very last by some miraculous hand, and so he intended to remain in the city to the very end. Until the fate of these men was confirmed, he would be among the crowd that roared as they swung from the yardarm or roared in wonderment as they were set free. But for now, for the next few weeks at least, Isaac would make his home in Boston.

The Hanging

In 1726, nine years after the hangings of Bellamy's men in Boston, William Fly would mount the same gallows to suffer the same punishment. In doing so, however, he created something of a sensation when, upon inspecting the noose that was to encircle his neck, he stopped the proceedings. As if insulted, he gently placed the small nosegay of flowers he was holding at his feet, took the knot in his hands, and declared disgustedly to the hangman, "Can no one here tie a knot properly, especially for a sailor about to die?" Then, to everyone's astonishment, he set about undoing the knot and retying it as a seaman would. However, as he carefully arranged the improved noose about his neck and shoulders, he continued to address those who had assembled as witnesses: "I am not afraid to die here, and I have done wrong to no man or woman." Refusing to acknowledge the legitimacy of the courts or to warn the audience against a pirate's wicked life as his crewmembers had done previously, he went on to address the sailors and ship captains interspersed in the crowd: "All ye masters of vessels take warning of the fate of Captain Green who I and my mates rightfully and righteously put to death. Pay your men their wages when they are due, and treat them better, like the good men they are. For listen to me hard: It is the barbarity of men like Green that makes so many turn to piracy. Damme, but use the men as you would use your own families. I warn you that bad usage will only bring mutiny and your ruin."

Before the hangman could reach to tighten the noose around his neck, Fly did the office for him. Then staring defiantly straight ahead, he awaited his fate. Later, Cotton Mather would attest that he saw the man's hands quiver and his knees begin to fail him, but Fly's voice was firm, and even Mather, who would join other clerics in ordering the corpse to be hung in chains at the head of the harbor, even Mather called him a brave man. In that ultimate moment as he stood in silence, a sailor's voice rang out from the back of the crowd, "I, for one, am with you, Mister Fly." Then, and only then, did Fly's exterior crack, and his lips curl into a broad smile.

In 1726 William Fly was speaking out defiantly yet also somewhat wistfully at the twilight of piracy's heyday, but nine years earlier, as Isaac stood among another Boston crowd at Scarlett's Wharf anticipating the hanging of Sam Bellamy's men, he knew he was witnessing a holiday, a spectacle. The undercurrents in the crowd were very different from those at Fly's execution: some feeling anger at economic losses, many fearing sea terrorists lingering just outside of the harbor, still others envying the success of these marauders, and perhaps all speculating about the amount of gold the six men standing on the scaffold had amassed with such seeming ease and then lost. It was an American story, one of the first such narratives, and Isaac was thrilled and appalled by it at the same time.

****

As the day of the hanging dawned, wisps of fog hung over the harbor and extended up the river, gray and sun-splotched like an old man's beard. Indeed, on this day an old story would be retold of robbery and outrage, of justice for some and injustice for others, of punishment and death. On this day Isaac Doane was drawn like a filing to a magnet to Copp's Hill where six men would hang.

The ten survivors who had emerged on a strange coast on the morning of April 27, 1717, from the Mary Anne were a sorry lot, but the fate of six of them was sorrier yet when they emerged from the old prison house in Boston. In April their minds were still blurred by the aftershocks of alcohol, the previous night's terror, and physical exhaustion, but in November, as their eyes accustomed themselves to daylight and the masses of people awaiting them, they were acutely aware of where they were and the journey that lay ahead of them that day. The rusted ironwork of the prison's oaken door was the same that had cawed the arrival of Hester Prynne on the scene, the same that one observer had noted, "seemed never to have known a youthful era." On this day the men who were to walk from the prison to their execution at Copp's Hill already knew that whatever whisper of youth remained in them would die that day.

Isaac's first awareness of the prisoners was the rolling roar of the crowd several hundred yards up the road and around a corner. As the parade drew nearer, the cries of the crowd intensified, and soon he could see the six men walking together chained at the hands and the legs, and escorted by forty musketeers. A man dressed in red led the procession carrying an oar painted silver to signify the authority of the Admiralty Court.

As he would nine years later at the execution of William Fly, Cotton Mather was leading a vanguard of officials, bewigged and walking stiffly, as if he were habitually uncomfortable in his own pasty skin, staring directly ahead at the gallows that loomed in front of him. At fifty-four Mather had attended executions of men and women by hanging for twenty-five years, dating back to Salem in 1692. At every such event, he appeared to care more than others about the welfare of the miscreants' souls, struggling with the "spectral influences" that beset them. Whether standing by the stake or near the scaffold, he was the one attempting to bring soiled souls to God, and, perhaps equally important, to contrition in the presence of the attending multitudes. His concern must have been shallow, however, because he was not known to object when recently hanged pirates were buried face down at the low water mark in the harbor so their souls might be eternally bound to the earth, never to rise above the high water mark to any level of spiritual rest. Not surprisingly, the pirates of New England at the time were well aware of Mather's sentiments because they were known to force their hostages to curse his name as a part of any punishment they might mete out on board their ships.

In preparation for the arrival of the six, a gibbet had been erected between the high and low water marks just off a point below Copp's Hill. As they stepped carefully into the small boat that was to carry them to the gibbet, each of the men marveled at the numbers of citizens who had come to watch them hang. There were hordes in boats, on the shore, clamoring along the wharves, peering down from Copp's Hill above, and for a time the six fell silent. Then, eying the countless sailing crafts surrounding them, Simon Van Vorst glanced at his compatriots and then said ruefully to Thomas Baker sitting next to him, "Robin Hood's men need him to come to the rescue, don't we? I have been looking, but I've seen no sign of Paul, or Sam for that matter." Delicately rubbing his neck, Baker only nodded and stared ahead; but John Brown, by now having downed several tankards of rum handed to him during the procession through Boston's streets, burst forth, "I'll be damned, but we don't deserve to be saved, and by tonight, I warrant, we'll be jumping on the hot coals of hell."

"Shut your mouth, John," muttered Baker, turning to look at him. "We've got enough to think about without your drunken imaginings." With that the three of them ebbed back into their own thoughts but not before their eyes had fixed almost as one on the six nooses that were awaiting them and looming high off the port bow of the boat.

****

Like a ghost, or more appropriately, a wispy fog, the aura of Paul Williams hovered along the coastal towns of New England during the spring and summer of 1717, and his presence was especially alive in the minds of the surviving members of Sam Bellamy's crew. Rumor had it that he had subdued the Swan, a sloop in the service of Cyprian Southack's mission, and later a ship commanded by Thomas Fox. Williams told Fox that "if the Prisoners in Boston suffered, he and his men would kill everybody they took belonging to New England." Bellamy's men hoped Williams would be true to his word but, more to the point, that he would liberate them from their chains and the dangers they faced. The fraternity of pirates, and the ethos that bound them together, was a strong one, and in the months that followed the trial in Boston, Sam Bellamy's old sailing mate, Blackbeard, would exact a vicious revenge on merchant ships from Boston for the city's treatment of the Whydah crewmembers who had been taken prisoner.

****

Isaac craned his neck to view the gallows and the six men now arranged in a row on the scaffold along with a churchman he did not recognize who was weaving his way among them and occasionally gesticulating. As the men stood above them on the platform, the crowd grew quiet recognizing for the moment the seriousness of what was about to happen. In the gathering silence, Isaac began to inspect those standing with him in the crowd. The full range of Boston society was present: formally dressed politicians, dozens of armed musketeers, wide-chested stevedores, matrons and maidens, merchants taking an hour off for the event, and even a few scattered children. Unknown to Isaac, the presence hovering above them all on the scaffold and speaking with each of the manacled men was Cotton Mather urging them to repent and to do so for the benefit of the crowd who had come to watch them meet their maker.

At the outermost periphery of the crowd, Isaac's s wandering eyes stopped suddenly at a familiar form leaning casually at the corner of a building and discreetly beyond the view of the prisoners. The man stood about six feet tall, and while his head was topped with a common sailor's cap, his features were dark and distinctive; the man was clean-shaven, slim, and in his mid-thirties. Isaac wondered if he was the same man he had seen earlier at the courthouse, and if he could be Sam Bellamy. He had no time to consider this more deeply or to edge his way out of the crowd and approach the man because at that moment, an official of the court began to address the crowd.

"Citizens of Boston, we are gathered here today to bring evil doers to justice and to show, once again, the terrible lessons of piracy on the high seas. By order of the King's court, the six men standing before you are to be hanged by the neck, and may their miserable fate be a lesson unto all who are assembled here today. If any of these men have anything to say before their sentence is carried out, they may speak now or hold their peace."

What followed was brief. When asked to speak, Thomas Baker and Peter Hoof simply hung their heads, and when Simon Van Vorst began to sing an old Dutch psalm, Hoof joined him. John Brown was not moved by their piety, and still feeling the effects of the rum he had drunk along the way, he cried out so all could hear, "I am John Brown of Jamaica, and I warn the seamen among you to beware of wickedness like my own, and I warn you not to fall into the hands of pirates like myself. But if you do and you are forced into their service, then take care which captives you keep and which you set free. But above all, beware of the countries you come into because someday you may arrive in a damned hanging port like this one and end your cursed life as I am about to!"

Brown's voice carried out to the most distant of the surrounding boats, and for a moment, the attending crowd fell completely silent.

232

Then, as if without warning, the floor beneath the men fell away. For several moments their arms and legs seemed to eddy mid-air in a primitive dance as the men turned to face one another and then turned away, alternately regarding their partners with fast dimming eyes as the light wind determined the tempo of their movements. The grotesqueness of the scene hushed those nearest to the scaffold, but some of the women released pent-up high pitched wails that were said to echo a mile away, and those in the surrounding boats and at the furthest limits of the crowd let out a relieved cheer that seemed to unfurl across the harbor and up the Charles River.

Not to be outdone or forgotten in the excitement, Cotton Mather stepped forth, and as his black robes swirled about him in the November gusts, pronounced so that all could hear, "Brethren, God's will has been done, and these miscreants will continue to hang here as a reminder to all of us of the fruits of evil. These agents of terror now have their reward, and we are all witnessing the end of piracy as we know it." Mather would have to admit nine years later that this confident assertion was premature, but for Isaac Doane it combined with all the other sensations of the moment to raise tears to his eyes and a small throb of nausea in his throat. The now glazed eyes of the dead men, the unfettered reactions of the mob, the claustrophobic density of people pressing against him to see the corpses better, the lingering odors of whale oil, tobacco, salt air, the stark masts of the anchored ships looming out of the harbor into the leaden sky – all of these deeply offended the young man, and almost as if in reaction, he glanced back to see if the figure leaning against the building at the corner was still there. To his disappointment, it had vanished.

A dull feeling of resentment began to take hold in Isaac's heart. Perhaps it was seeing the lives of these six men – all still strong -- cut off so soon; perhaps it was the loneliness he felt amid this mob of strangers; or perhaps it was an impending sense of loss, but Isaac knew he wanted to return to Cape Cod and be reminded that some things in his world were certain and true, not fleeting and evanescent like the lives of young men.

Isaac did not remain in Boston long enough to see the same men still hanging weeks later at the head of the harbor – a common warning against the terrors of piracy -- but if he had, the sight would have sickened him.

****

Isaac was going home. He wanted nothing more to do with the ways of the city, with pirates, with robed judges, with Cyprian Southack, with the sad fortunes of young men, and – yes – with Sam Bellamy and his dreams. During the weeks he had worked along the docks, Isaac had come to know the names and destinations of many of the ships that plied the waters of the harbor and the outlying bay. He could tell them by their masts, by the shape of their hulls, their bowsprits, the flags they flew, by their length, their width, by the way they rode in the water. But perhaps the one he knew the best was Captain Yates's Mary: it was the one that had brought him to the city, and, and as he had known from the day he arrived, it was the one that would take him home.

On this date, November 17, 1717, in the early morning light, Isaac was standing on the dock where the easternmost reach of State Street ended at the water, craning his neck and looking for Captain Yates's ship. As he did so, he became aware of a young man's presence nearby. The man's face was familiar to him, and then in an instant he recognized him. The man was Thomas Davis, recently freed by the Court standing no more than ten feet away from him and shivering.

"We have met before," Isaac began, almost surprising himself that he was speaking at all. "I was there that night on the beach when we loaded the loot from the ship onto Sam Harding's wagon. And then I heard your story again two days ago when they set you free at the Courthouse."

"I'm no pirate," the young man mumbled. "I never was." He continued staring out at the mist-shrouded harbor.

Isaac was intrigued by this young man whose story was so intertwined with his own. "I once knew Sam Bellamy," he said. "Was he a good captain?"

"A good captain," breathed Davis, still looking out at the harbor. Then staring directly at Isaac, he said, "That man's men held me for four months of my life, and I won't forgive him for it. I am grateful to the judges of Boston for my freedom, but I aim to get as far from this place as I am able and as soon as I can. That's why I am standing here at this moment talking with you."

"Then you and I are of a like mind," murmured Isaac, "because I am doing the same thing. In fact, there, that boat rounding the point – the Mary is her name – will be taking me back to my home on Cape Cod." At the helm of the small ship Isaac could discern the tall, spare shape of Captain Yates, and having come to know him during his months of working on the docks, he waved to him, his arm arcing in the same long path that a clock takes between nine o'clock and three o'clock.

For a few moments Davis watched in silence as the Mary made its way toward them, and then he said, "You'll be traveling home, and I'll be traveling the high seas, and I wonder if either of us will return again to this place or to this dock for that matter."

"I doubt it," Isaac said, "and I wish you well on your journey."

"And I wish you the same."

And so Thomas Davis, the young twenty-two year old Welshman, disappeared that day from recorded history. For more than a year he had lived in captivity, be it on a pirate ship or in a Boston jail. In that time family had written letters to the Court from across the Atlantic; his minister had attested to his good character; and in open court, hardened but honorable seamen had sworn that he was not one of them. Despite the fact that young Davis might well have shared in the spoils suspended in the Whydah's belly had she survived that night, and despite the fact that Sam Harding may have been a safe harbor for the gold collected on the night of April 26, the Court had set Thomas Davis free. And so he simply vanished into the mists as he intended, perhaps back to the warm embrace of his family, but never again, to anyone's knowledge, to walk the decks under the flag of a pirate crew.

For his part, Isaac happily greeted Captain Yates, trundled his sailor's bag aboard the Mary, and said good-by to Boston forever.

Chapter Twenty One
Reckonings
November, 1717

W hy would a man return to the scene of his greatest horror and regret? Why would a warrior come back to the battleground, the felon to the crime scene? In Sam Bellamy's case, why would he risk his liberty, his one free and precious life, to revisit the place of his greatest failure and humiliation? Perhaps it was a stubborn resistance to accepting the end of a tantalizing dream and the loss of an insistent passion, His men were dead either by drowning or by hanging – he had been their witness—yet on this bright November afternoon he was back on a rutted Cape Cod road, making his way toward the Billingsgate dunes. Summer was past, autumn was upon him, and winter was coming on fast, and he knew he must be off; yet he found himself drawn back to the shores where his gold had settled into the sand and his lover lived alone.

As he walked, Sam was sifting these and other thoughts. He had heard rumors that Paul Williams might be cruising off the outer shores, and he vaguely hoped they might meet again in Provincetown; if not, he would hire aboard on an outbound ship. But for tonight he would bed down at Smith's tavern on the island and the next day make a last trip to gaze one final time at the Whydah. Perhaps he might glimpse Maria once again in the distance, but after their last parting, somehow the words were over between them; the rest was love and anguish.

Yes, he would be returning one last time to Smith's tavern tonight. Just that morning he had encountered young Isaac Doane near the wharf in Barnstable. The meeting had been awkward, both uneasy about others who might be watching them and about what each might reveal to the other. Isaac, subdued and nervous, at first seemed uncomfortable talking with him, but as they walked a short way out onto the wharf, his manner relaxed somewhat. Nevertheless,

Sam had been accustomed to the boy's natural reserve and deference to his age and experience. In the past the lad had always looked him directly in the eye, as if seeking his approval there; but on this day, as they scanned the boats entering and exiting the harbor, their eyes met only seldom, and Isaac had seemed preoccupied. Their discussion had been short because they did not want to call attention to themselves, but in that time Isaac had issued Sam an invitation. He indicated that because the season at the tavern was drawing to a close due to the colder weather, very few people frequented the place now, and Sam might find a safe night's lodging in an upstairs room. Since he would be staying for only one night, he would be undisturbed there and could be off, undetected, in the morning. The prospect was pleasing to Sam, and, the compact made, they shook hands and parted until they would see each other again that evening.

****

When Sam entered the main room of the tavern, a floorboard rasped loudly in complaint, but he did not hear it. Isaac did, however. Along with everyone else in the room he had been waiting for Sam in a charged silence like that in a theater before the curtain rises on the last act of a tragedy and the audience awaits the entrance of the key players once again onto the stage. Absent this night was the pleasant hum of people enjoying themselves, and there were fewer people present than normal -- at this late hour of the evening only ten or fifteen, all men, whose eyes were hooded, wolfish. A sullen ferocity seemed to shroud the room.

Sam recognized the atmosphere because he had experienced it before. He knew the tension that pervades a group about to commit mayhem; he had known it when his own men would attack ships at sea. But these were men of the land, these men sitting in this tavern, and they were no less excited than a band of pirates, no less nervous anticipating the moments that were about to unfold.

The room was as quiet as a grave. As Sam scanned its occupants, his eyes suddenly stopped short and stared intently at the face of Aaron Cole. He knew the face intimately -- he had sealed the eyes shut himself -- but the birthmark was gone, and these eyes were wide open and staring back at him. Appearing to dare him from across the room, Cole's expression seemed to say, "Well, you've finally arrived, haven't you? I've been waiting for you." A wave of horror washed through Sam, but he managed to stifle it and force himself to survey the rest of those in the room. When he did, he saw Isaac behind the bar, at seventeen still a boy; in the middle of the room, Daniel Atwood, his friend of many years, looking nervous, his eyes jumpy like waterbugs; and by the window close to Cole, Newcomb, the aggressive ignoramus he had literally booted out the door two years before. The two men who had accompanied William Cole into Pierce's Tavern were at Cole's table, and the one with long, glistening hair nodded in a knowing way to his companions.

Turning his head to those at his table, Cole said without looking at him, "Come in, Mr. Bellamy. Young Isaac here told us you would be paying us a visit tonight." For an instant, Sam went cold, any pretense of hiding his identity now gone, but he quickly recovered, slowly closed the door, and stepped forward into the room.

"I see I've been found out," he said with a rueful grin on his lips. "What have we here, an execution squad? Are you planning to make me walk the plank?" Sam did not know the name of the man who had addressed him. But he recalled the name of the man he took to be this man's brother … Cole. Then, adopting a more casual tone, he looked at Isaac who was standing behind the bar, studiously washing a glass, doing the best he could to avoid becoming engaged in the scene that was unfolding before him. As he stared at the glass, wiping stray droplets from its rim, the boy's mind was a swarm of hornets – these men who intended violence, his anger over the wronged Maria, his jealousy, his shrunken image of a friend, his fury at his own insignificance.

Shamed and angry, Isaac looked up at Sam.

"Don't you have anything to say, pup? Has the pirate cut out your tongue?" Sam said to him.

At these words, Isaac's temper flared. Then he blurted out, "You're a killer, Sam. You've killed men on the sea, you've ruined Maria, and now you've killed William Cole. Men have been hanged in Boston in your name and for your deeds, Sam. These men here have come to call you to account. I saw your men hanging there at the dock. What do you have to say about that? Six of them. You led them and more than one hundred others to their deaths."

"I've done what I have had to do, Isaac, and I don't regret it," Sam said softly. "For a time we were wealthy men, myself and my crew. Were it not for that terrible storm, we would be sailing free today. We all took our chances. Every man aboard knew the risks. As I recall, you were all too well aware of those risks, and that is why you did not choose to come with me when I asked you."

"They seemed to stand tiptoe on the air as they hung from the gibbet," Isaac continued. "I will never forget them. They were your men, they followed you," and then more angrily, he added, "and look what happened to Maria. You left her too, didn't you? And that is why I told these men here that you would be here tonight."

Sam stared at the young boy long and piercingly. And then something seemed to give way in him. If personality is a shield erected like a sand castle against a tide of troubles, Sam's last defense seemed to ebb away at that moment. No longer was he the cool captain ordering his men over the sides of the Whydah to plunder a merchant ship; now he was one of the men, leaping headlong over the bar at the young boy while reaching for the knife in his sash. The blade of Sam's knife glinted for the briefest moment in the silver light, flashed upward, and made a fine skillfully drawn red line reaching from the curve of Isaac's jaw up to the socket of his eye. As he saw the apple-red blood instantly appear and pulse down Isaac's jaw, Sam looked at the boy levelly and said, "Let God hold you in the hollow of his hand, Isaac. I fear that every time you touch the scar that will appear on your face, you will recall this night. Every time you look in a mirror, you will remember this night and me."

Isaac quickly turned away and reached for a towel to stanch the blood that had begun to flow profusely. By now the other men in the room had moved quickly to pinion Sam's arms behind his back, two at each side, and a third holding a hank of his black hair in his hand, pulling it back and forcing his gaze to the rafters of the room.

Aaron Cole, who had been contemplating the patterns made by the foam in his ale during the altercation, now stood up, turned, and looked directly at Sam. "You and I have another account to settle, Mr. Bellamy, and I am here to collect on the debt." Having had no personal contact with Bellamy other than the hatred he bore him for the murder of his brother, Cole was not constrained by any questions of propriety or honor. Limping slowly across the room while clutching a guttering candle in his hand, Cole brought it slowly up to Sam's face and began to peruse his features carefully.

"So you are the pirate, Bellamy," he said easily, and then after a pause, "And the killer of my brother. You have many deaths on your head, Mr. Bellamy, haven't you?"

"I have never sought the death of any man," Sam replied between clenched teeth, "especially not those of my own men. For them all I wanted was wealth and a measure of justice. Well, now you have me," Sam muttered. "What will you do with me? See to it that your justice is as fair as that you would find aboard a pirate's ship....."

"Well, I guess," Cole said with a smile, "that's why we're here tonight, isn't it? If your men did not know the meaning of justice, at least you will."

Sam realized that court was in session, but he knew as he looked around the room that the verdict had already been decided. With a sudden and dismissive gesture, Cole pointed to the door that led to the cellar of the tavern. Looking to the other men, he said, "Let's take him downstairs, out of sight. We can try him there."

Moments later a number of men and a young boy were assembled in a ring around Sam Bellamy. The floor of the cellar was dirt, and bottles seemed to peer from shelves in the walls like an audience, craning their necks to observe what was about to happen. As the men stood around Sam, their sinuous shadows seemed to crawl up the cellar walls and move like ghosts. Young and frightened, Isaac would recall the motion of these shapes for the rest of his natural life. He was the one who had called the men to the tavern this night, who had revealed Sam's identity to Cole, who had betrayed his one-time friend. He had only wanted justice and revenge, but he could not know this evening that these shadows would haunt the walls of his mind until the day he died.

These men arrayed about him, the cool but choking air, the hard dirt beneath his boots, the impassive bottles mutely watching.... his immediate consciousness of these agents heightened Sam's sense of peril. But as he looked around himself, his eyes finally rested on Isaac

-- the young boy standing apart from the others – and something seemed to rise up within him: Was it the memory of Maria, lost now to him forever? Was it the lives of his men? Was it the vanished weight of his wealth still strapped tightly to his waist, and which would soon be taken from him? Was it the death of the man, Cole, whom he didn't know and for whose sake he was soon to die? As these thoughts washed over him, Sam felt a great ebbing sensation; resistance was no use, he knew that, and as he gazed at Isaac, whose hands were pressed against the wound that would soon be a scar, Sam smiled knowingly. Then he shrugged, as others have shrugged, as if surprised by the onset of death, and said, "Well, I'll be damned…" Then, looking more fiercely at Isaac, he said, "Remember me, boy."

At that instant a great wooden club broke into his skull. It was swung by Newcomb, the most stupid and violent of the lot, who muttered as he swung the club, "Now that will show the bastard, won't it?"

As Newcomb's club collided with Sam's brain, a small wave eased onto the Billingsgate Beach not far away, a red-tailed hawk descended upon an unsuspecting rabbit, massive thunderheads gathered over the uncolonized western plains, a tracery meteor now all but spent arced indifferently on its path, and in the Orion nebula many light years away stars burst into being. In the midst of all this vast cosmic activity Sam Bellamy's consciousness finally relented, relaxed, and subsided into the transitory order of things.

As abruptly as the scene had started, it was over. Cole bent over the body, felt for a pulse at the neck, and nodded to the others that the man was indeed dead. As he did so, he said, "Justice has been done, and my brother can rest in peace." At this, Newcomb looked around for approval and grinned with satisfaction at what he had done. Daniel Atwater averted his eyes, while, standing in a darkened corner of the cellar, Isaac stared in icy shock at the torch-lit and contorted shape on the ground. As he did so, he gently touched a blood-soaked towel to his tender cheek.

Before exiting the scene, the men dug a long, shallow hole in the hard-packed dirt and unceremoniously began to roll the body into it. In the slow rotation of the body toward the grave, a doubloon from Sam's sash shook free, and the low clinking of others alerted the men to what they might have suspected but no one had thought to seek.

"There's gold on the man's body," Newcomb shouted, "and now it's ours. We have earned it tonight!" In short order, the sash was unknotted, and a small pile of gold coins was glinting in the variable, flickering light. Cole, who seemed to hold sway over the others through the power of his intelligence and his tightly reined temper, was quick to take control of the moment:

"We will divide these coins evenly among us, but anyone who accepts a share is acknowledging that he is no longer an avenger but, instead, a brigand. What say you all?" The coins shone luridly on the hard ground of the cellar, seeming to smolder in the torchlight. The men – all except two – assented willingly to the bargain. The two who refused were Daniel Atwood and Isaac Doane. Atwood stared at the others standing in a semi-circle and said,

"To my great shame I have witnessed the murder of an old friend tonight. However, I strongly believe that had he not died here, he would have met a similar end somewhere else and soon. For this reason, I will allow him to be buried beneath this establishment. But I will not profit by his death, and I want nothing to do with his ill-gotten doubloons. For all I care, you can return the coins to the ocean where his ship lies…"

Isaac, who had been lost in the shadows until now, stepped forward and said more loudly than he intended, "I want no wealth from Sam Bellamy's corpse. He has paid his debt to others tonight, and I am sorry I was a part of it. I wish I could forget what has happened here tonight, and I do not want the coins to remind me of it. You may keep the money, Mr. Cole."

No others had such compunctions, and Cole quickly divided the pile among them. Upon finishing the task, Cole said these last words over the body, "Remember, gentlemen, there should be no need to discuss with others what has happened here tonight. We have evened our scores, and we need not bring any further attention to ourselves. Will you swear upon this?" All of the men, including Atwood and Isaac, rumbled their agreement.

With justice now done, the men looked at each other, almost as if surprised that the scene was over so quickly. As is often the case, moments intensely anticipated fail to satisfy the hungry imagination and in their aftermath leave the participants feeling vaguely alone and destitute. On this evening, however, each man found different forms of comfort in the conclusion, in part depending on the weight of the coins in his pockets. The men quickly dispersed speaking in subdued tones in twos and threes, but the principals seemed to choose their own paths: Isaac to cleansing his tender wound, Atwood to cleaning up the tavern, Cole limping back to his skiff, and Newcomb walking out into his accustomed darkness

All of those present that night would remember Cole's final injunction, and each would honor the oath he had sworn according to his own disposition. Such promises are easily made and often broken, however, and sometimes this fragility and the warping that ensues become the fodder for rumor, legend, and fiction.

Chapter Twenty Two
Epidemic
March, 1747

Years passed. Isaac was no longer a boy, nor was he young by any measure. The dull, temperamental throbs of pain in his back, in his knees, and in his hands reminded him that he was almost forty-seven years old and that his youth was behind him. Yet today was different. People were dying – friends and neighbors of his – and once again he was on his way, as quickly as an aging body could propel him, to Samuel Smith's tavern on the island, but this time his mission was different.

Earlier that morning, still blinking off sleep, Isaac had opened his cottage door only to be greeted by a large, wandering eyeball struggling keep him in focus. It belonged to Daniel Atwood, his old friend, who had been knocking firmly on the door and was anxious to speak with him.

"Mr. Smith needs you at the tavern, Isaac. The disease is spreading, and people are dying. Mr. Smith has transferred many of the James Island tribe to the tavern and declared that it will be an infirmary for those who are afflicted. Mr. Smith needs his friends to help him tend to the ailing on the island…"

Isaac simply nodded and said, "I will be there, and I'll be there soon."

Daniel smiled and said, "I knew you would. I told Mr. Smith you would, and now I must be off to find more volunteers."

"Farewell, Daniel," Isaac said as he closed the door, and within minutes he was dressed, out the door, and on the familiar path to the skiff.

****

At the sound of a closing door, she looked up from tending a sick child from the Pononakanet tribe who was lying on a makeshift cot beside the bar in the tavern. She was now in her mid-forties, but shadows of her youthful beauty still hovered about her, a twilight loveliness -- the curve of her jaw, her direct and intelligent eyes, her delicately turned lips. But thirty years of living amid the dunes, of walking the beaches, of turning her face to the sun and the wind had shaped her features as well. She was still a natural beauty but a weathered one, like a shard of sea glass rubbed smooth by the toss of the currents, cast up on the shore and glinting in the sunlight.

The interruption past, she now turned to tend to the child again, speaking softly to it and pulling a blanket up about its neck. It was a boy no more than ten years old, and he was crying soft, stifled tears. Isaac could see the blanket rising and falling with the rhythm of the child's labored sobs. Standing nearby but in the shadows was a tall, dark figure who, nevertheless, seemed familiar to Isaac. It was a man wrapped in a blanket with the colors and designs of the Pononakanet tribe on it. Then in an instant Isaac understood the scene. Thirty to forty people were being attended to, many of them very young, many of them Indians from nearby James Neck, and the tall, dark figure in the shadows was Running Water, his old friend. The child Maria was comforting was Running Water's son, and from the expression on his friend's face Isaac could tell that the child's condition was extremely grave. For some years now, Running Water had been the Chief of the Pononakanet tribe, and the sorrow in his eyes reflected the grief he felt not only for his child but for all the children of his people.

As Isaac slowly made his way across the room toward Maria and Running Water, he had to step around and over the bodies of the sick, many of them women and children and most of them Running Water's people. The stench of old vomit and rotting skin caused his throat to catch and gag, and he felt a flash of embarrassment. As he neared his old friends, his eyes were transfixed by the boy's skin: very small craters and lesions had spread out across his chest and arms, creating a moonscape of erupting flesh. Deep crevices had formed where the skin had separated on his face and his torso. Peelings of skin were attached to the rough sheet on which the child lay, and his eyes were glazed with exhaustion -- from nausea, from pain, and from sleeplessness. Death attended the boy.

Greeting his old friend, Running Water simply said, "The child's mother died two days ago."

Isaac said only, "I'm sorry," and as he did, his eyes fell upon Maria, who was holding a cool, moist cloth to the child's forehead.

"He's breathing so softly," she said to Running Water. "I fear he will not be with us much longer."

"I came to offer some help," Isaac said to neither one in particular, "but I had no idea there were so many who were so sick."

Within minutes Isaac was at work, bringing water and food, carrying towels helping to feed the sick, some of whom were mothers with their children. As he surveyed the tavern, a place so familiar to him, it seemed altogether transformed, almost unrecognizable. Gone were the merriment, the low rumble of male voices, the high ripple of female laughter, and in their place were the uncomprehending sobs of children, the jagged yelps of those in pain, and the soft purring voices of those offering comfort. Perhaps forty people were lying on the floor, on table tops, along benches; still others were housed in the upstairs rooms. A small group of ten to twelve people, whom Sam Smith had recruited to help, were moving quietly about the tavern or sitting by bedsides tending to the sick. Others, sick themselves, were nursing their afflicted children.

A voice behind him stirred Isaac out of his momentary reverie; it was Sam Smith himself.

"I am glad you have come, Isaac," he said, "The people here need our help, and I thought it best that we move them away from the town, from the tribe and even their families to slow the spread of the disease. More people are arriving every day, and we can use all the help we can get."

"I am glad to do anything I can," Isaac said to him, "and I only hope I can help."

Now almost sixty, Sam Smith had rounded with the years, his cheeks to reddish globes and his girth assuming a wider orbit. His beard curled in two great muttonchops, and his eyes glistened brightly. He was a serious man, one on whose shoulders a community or a country for that matter could be built. When he saw a need in his community, he addressed it; when he saw an opportunity, he took it. And now, approaching sixty, he was among the most respected men in the region. Isaac's regard for Sam had passed beyond respect and become love many years before. It was love not simply for a man but for an entire family. First the father and then the son had supported Isaac and his mother through the years and the hardest of times, so when Daniel had appeared at his front door saying that Sam Smith needed his help, Isaac had moved immediately into action.

Some twenty years before, another wave of the disease had visited Boston and the surrounding area, and during the previous century smallpox had ravaged Native American tribes reducing the Indian population in New England from 70,000 to less than 12,000. As the noted ecological historian, William Cronon, has noted, prior to the arrival of Old World pathogens, carried by humans, pigs, rats, and a variety of domesticated animals, the native population of the North American continent was remarkably healthy; protected by sparse population densities and a cold climate generally inhospitable to lethal microorganisms, the Indians of the seventeenth and early eighteenth centuries were especially vulnerable to the introduction of diseases like chicken pox, influenza, plague, and small pox among others. These formerly healthy people had established none of the antigens to counter the onslaught of Old World germs, and the results were devastating for them. One consequence of this was that entire villages were destroyed by disease, and the tribal social organization was radically disrupted. The first major outbreak of smallpox in New England occurred in 1616, and the tribes were still waging the battle over one hundred years later.

Once again, the figure of Cotton Mather looms in this narrative. On one hand, Mather was a voice preaching that by visiting disease on the Indians, "those pernicious creatures," the hand of God was at work "to make room for better growth" and improve the land for settlement by "the chosen flock." On the other hand, Mather had the vision and foresight, in the face of a Boston outbreak of smallpox, to promote inoculation against the disease in 1721, a pioneering measure, and one that forced him to reconcile, if only for the time being, the hand of

God with that of science. Against this background of disease and tribal
disintegration, Isaac made his way among the sick in the tavern.

There was danger in this place, and Isaac knew it. He recalled
the stories emanating from Boston some twenty years earlier, and
he knew enough to be frightened just to be breathing the tavern air.
As Isaac surveyed the room wondering where to begin and whom
to help, his senses revolted; his eyes squinted shut to avoid seeing
the lesions and blisters on the children's bodies. He began to breathe
through his mouth because the heavy aroma of rotting skin was too
rancid to inhale through his nose. He could feel the disease living
in the air. He could see its effects in the limp stares of the sick, and
when a young boy, wasted and lying on a hard mat, rolled toward
him, he could see a layer of the child's skin adhere to the mat.

As he set to work, his eye was drawn across the room once again
to Maria, and he longed to talk to her. Years had passed since they had
last spoken -- as if the death of Sam Bellamy and the circumstances
surrounding it had drawn down a curtain on their friendship -- but
Isaac had often thought fondly of her. He had never married nor been
tempted to, and his life had settled into a solitary, unencumbered
routine of tending to his small farm, doing odd jobs, and working
at the tavern when it was open for business. Seeing Maria again in
this place so familiar to him yet now grotesquely transformed was
so disorienting that he wondered if he would find words to say to her
if the chance arose.

****

The boy's name was Little Seahawk, that was what his father had
called him, and she despaired of his ever recovering. He was sleeping
now, and she wished him a peaceful rest. She was exhausted; this
was the tenth day she had come to the island to nurse the sick, and
she knew the dangers. No symptoms of the disease had yet appeared
on her body, and though she was tired, she still felt strong, strong
enough to help the women and the children especially. But the day
had been a long one, and after finding a chair on the porch of the
tavern, she lit the tobacco in her pipe and gratefully inhaled its

smoke. She felt the pleasure seep into her lungs and her muscles, and she let herself relax.

The winter was almost over, and the evening was uncommonly warm for mid-March. Behind her she heard the tavern door open and close, and when she turned, she saw Isaac coming slowly toward her. She had not spoken with him in the years since Sam Bellamy had died. She had lived her life, Isaac his, and she had felt no need to stir up the embers of rumor and recrimination. Sam Bellamy had now been dead for thirty years, and while his shadow still lingered for both of them, they had moved on.

"Hello, Isaac," she said, "It has been a long time."

"Yes, it has," Isaac said, "Do you mind if I sit here beside you for awhile?"

"Not at all," Maria replied. "It's been a long day, and you must be tired."

"Yes, I am," he said. "There are so many who are so sick, and it's so sad to see the sick mothers tending to their dying children."

She looked over at him and said, "And there seems to be so little we can do other than to make them more comfortable – and to comfort those who love them."

"That's true," said Isaac, and then after a pause, he added, "These days must be very difficult for Running Water."

"Yes, after losing his wife, he may well lose his son."

"I had not known of her death," Isaac murmured.

"Yes, she was a delicate one, and the disease took her quickly. Running Water is still standing tall against it, but who can tell how long he will last."

"And you, Maria, how long have you been here, and how do you feel?"

Maria looked at him, then laughed softly, "Ohhh, I am as well as someone who is over forty years old has any right to be. I have been here for more than a week, and I may stay for another if I am needed. More of the sick seem to arrive every day, so I suspect I will be here for some time."

The cool evening air had seeped into the threads of her woolen sweater, and Maria drew it around herself more tightly, rubbing her arms for warmth. Then looking directly at Isaac, she asked, ""Do you remember that Sunday tuck-a-nuck that you and I and Running Water went on so many years ago?" Isaac smiled and nodded. "So many things have changed since then, haven't they?" she said.

"Yes, things have changed," he said thoughtfully. "Events have swirled around us. But have you changed, Maria, or have I for that matter? I mean, are we really different from the young people we were on the beach that Sunday afternoon so long ago?"

The question hovered in the air for a moment or two, and then Maria said, "Perhaps you're right, Isaac, perhaps events don't change you. People can, however – people can change you profoundly I think."

Isaac wondered where her thoughts were at the moment: with Running Water and his family? With the three young people who had met for a picnic and whose lives had diverged in different ways? Or with the man whose life had affected her own so profoundly? Maria shivered again in the cool evening air, and then she said something very odd.

"I think money can buy freedom, but freedom is far from happiness."

Isaac who had been watching a gull make a lazy half-circle in the sky, settled his eyes upon her.

"Can you say more?" he asked.

"I was only thinking," she said, "about my old friend, Sam Bellamy, about what he did to make a fortune, and how close he came."

As she said this, she returned Isaac's gaze. "He was a good man, you know. For all that has been said about him, and about me too for that matter, he simply wanted the freedom that he knew money could buy. And he found that freedom on board a pirate ship. Perhaps if the crash had not occurred, he would have found the same freedom on land because he would have had all the money he needed," she concluded wistfully.

Time and weather had sketched their designs on Maria's face, and light shadows played down her neck; her skin was somewhat mottled like the pages of an old, well-read book. Sam had been dead for almost thirty years, Isaac knew that – he was witness to the fact – but he would not stay in the makeshift grave they had fashioned for him in the tavern's cellar that dark night. His shadows played along the edges of the memory and refused to depart.

"Do you think of him often?" Isaac asked as he inspected a schooner, small and white, coming into view on the horizon.

"Not as often as I used to," she said. "There was a time he occupied all my thoughts … even after he died," she said looking back at Isaac.

Isaac felt the accusation in the tone of her voice, and he fell silent for a moment.

Then, to answer her, he said, "I was present when he died, you know. It was right here in this tavern."

"There were many rumors."

"Yes," Isaac answered, "and there were rumors that he also got away."

"I knew those weren't true," she said, "because I am sitting here tonight with you."

Isaac sat in silence. As they had been talking, thirty years had dissolved like irridescent bubbles, and once again Sam Bellamy was walking along the shores of their minds and they were seeing themselves again in the refracting light of memory.

Then Isaac spoke again, "The past is dead, isn't it, Maria? The rumors, the mistakes we may have made. Yes, I was there the night he died," he continued, "and now many years later I regret it. Passions were high back then as you may remember, and some young men were tried, and a number died," he concluded as his finger slowly traced the scar on his cheek

"Were any women there that night?" Maria asked flatly.

"No, why do you ask?"

"I don't know," she said, "but I don't know what I would have done, whether I would have hurt him or tried to save him. It was all so long ago and so confusing. I was great with him at the time, but I can't say it was love, and I suspect that marriage was not for two such as Sam Bellamy and me," she said smiling wistfully.

A light puff of air, as soft as a cat's paw, ruffled a few wisps of her hair. She gently ran her fingers across her forehead, and a shadow crossed her face. Isaac noticed this and asked, "Are you well, Maria?"

"To say the truth, I'm not quite sure," she replied with a light laugh. "I have been helping the people of the tribe for about two weeks, and now that we're out here on the island, I keep waiting for the disease to strike me too. So far I have been fortunate, but you also, Isaac, have taken a risk in coming here, You have seen, haven't you, the empty eyes of the children?"

Shifting the conversation, Isaac looked directly at Maria and said, "I recall so well when we were younger, when time belonged to us, when I skated with you on the pond. Do you remember when you almost fell through the ice? And then the tuck-a-nuck with Running Water out on the island? I was very fond of you then, Maria. And after all the years, and sitting out here together now, I still am."

"After all these years, I'm an old woman," she said laughing, "an old woman who walks the dunes and brings men's ships to ruin – that's what they say," she continued laughing ruefully now. "What could a good man want in me?" She shivered imperceptibly in the evening air, hugging herself and rubbing her hands along her upper arms. With her right hand she pinched and kneaded the nape of her neck. "Yes, if I'm not yet an old woman, I'm getting older, for my muscles and head have done nothing but pain me, so much that I have wondered about it at times."

Isaac looked at her searchingly. Then he said, "Maria, our lives have been lonely ones. You came to my door many years ago when you needed help, and I can still recall the way your eyes shone when you looked at me that day. I loved you then, you know, and now, all these years later, maybe we could make a life together in the time that remains to us." Isaac then fell quiet, and Maria continued to knead her neck, considering what he had said.

The schooner both had been watching – seemingly freighted with the memories of each – had now disappeared from their view up the bay.

"Almost nothing in my life has been constant, Isaac, and I do not regret the fact. Few would welcome me at their door, and of those most are the tribespeople lying inside this tavern. Yet my life is my own. I have made it, and I owe nothing to anyone. I said before that I had questions about what is to come. In fact, I have fears, and I suspect I am ill-suited to living with you or with any man. I am jealous of the freedom I have earned, and I've paid for it." Then placing her hands in her lap, quivering a little as she did so, she closed her eyes and took a great deep breath of air. "Have you ever breathed in the night air, Isaac?" she asked as she turned toward him, "I mean smelled it, filled your lungs with it? Some nights when I am walking the beach, I feel as if I can touch the stars. On those nights the moonlight almost turns the night into day."

"At such times," Isaac asked gently, "do you think of the child?"

"Think of him?" she sighed incredulously, "The child would be thirty years old if he had not died that day in the barn. The fates took him from me. I cannot call them God, and the men of the church sealed the bargain and put me in jail for it. I was only a girl and so alone. In the name of God, how could they dare to do that? From the day the child died I have been alone, and that is the only life I have known."

"It doesn't have to be," Isaac said.

As she had spoken her last words, Maria's face had become a mask, hard like the one she had turned to the world for so many years, but Isaac's intrusion caused her features to soften. Then, choosing her words with great care, she said to him, "There are children here to be cared for. Perhaps we can make a difference for them, and then when this terrible disease has passed, if we are still here to see that day, let us meet here again on this tavern porch and speak of the future and what it might hold for us"

Isaac sealed the promise by curling his fingers and rubbing them across her cheek. It was the first time a man had touched her in years, and it was the first time Isaac had touched her since the day of their picnic years before. Having made this agreement, they rose, turned away from the bay now touched by fingertips of twilight, and reentered the tavern to tend to the sick, little knowing that they would not share such intimacy again.

****

Within days Maria's premonitions had become fact. The tell-tale lesions rose on her skin, her headaches intensified, and she was compelled to lie down heavily on one of the empty cots in the tavern. Pain and misery often lead us down the most solitary paths, reacquainting us with moments best forgotten, old regrets, the essential loneliness of long sleepless nights. So it was with Maria. When sleep came to her, it came as welcome oblivion, an unraveled thread, a friendly intruder. But on the fifth night of her illness, sleep drew no boundary between wakefulness and the dreamworld, between the past and the present.

Maria's Dream

As if from a great height, she saw herself walking in the summer heat on a beach she knew. As she walked, she was watching Wizard, who had died so many years before, running up ahead of her. Exotic flowers and palm trees spread out before her in lush profusion, and in a cove nearby, she could make out a large sailing vessel at rest at its mooring.

Now she was a young child, maybe five or six years old, standing on a high deck of a ship bound off to sea. From that deck she was waving farewell to her mother and father, to Isaac, to the town fathers of Eastham who had taken the child from her, to Running Water and his family, even to Cyprian Southack, the stern ramrod of a man she had met on the beach one morning. They, for their part, stood on the shore mutely, waving back to her slowly. But as she stood on the deck scanning the company, she grew more agitated because someone was missing, but she could not tell who.

Now Wizard was pulling at the hem of her skirt, and suddenly she did something curious: she stopped, stretched out her arms to the farthest reach of her fingertips, birdlike, stood on the very tips of her toes, closed her eyes, dreamlike, and rose lightly into the accepting sky. Within moments she was inscribing great circles and loops with increasing speed and joy as she mounted higher and higher in the summer air. As she rose yet higher, she delighted in seeing the outlines of the clouds. She then performed a great cartwheel, and after that, a great tumbling backflip. For a fleeting second she wondered if those below could see her and the fabulous figures she was making. She felt as if she had been loosed from the limb of a great tree, flung out into the pure emptiness of space, her lungs filled to overflowing with the joy of uncertainty. To no one did she owe a thing as she swung from cloud to cloud across the sky. And then the land below seemed consumed with fire; the woods were burning while all about her reeled images of loss and destruction. Then out of the fire there slowly rose a great arch, like a rainbow, extending high into the sky and beyond. After taking its measure, she began to ascend it, walking its dewy outermost edge and doing so alone. Yet as she went higher, she began to grow dizzy, and soon she was falling, falling through the saturated clouds laden with waterweight, swinging on them as she descended. As she tumbled through the sky, she wondered if she cast a shadow on the land below and if she did, could anyone see it? Still she continued to fall back to earth.

Then, at last, her back was resting against a familiar tree. The day was warm, not hot, and it was June, and she was young, maybe fourteen, and everything about her was strangely familiar: the grass moving lazily in the early summer breeze. And she was happy in her loneliness. Then as she looked down a long path before her, she discerned a dark figure in the distance coming slowly toward her. As it drew nearer, the mysterious shape assumed human features. It was walking, and in its arms the dark figure was carrying something, as if in offering, and as his face came into focus, she recognized him to be the father of her child…… and in his arms he was carrying her child, which he extended to her. "And perhaps," she thought, "this is what I shall know of heaven." As he stretched his arms out to her, her eyes glistened, her face softened, and a great smile blossomed on her lips and in her eyes.

Sitting by her bedside, as he had for the last three days, Isaac inspected once again the curvatures of Maria's face. Her once lovely skin had been blasted by the disease, and he knew that should she survive, her beauty would be gone forever; yet as he watched her so closely, he saw her cracked lips ever so slowly begin to form into a great expansive smile, and he wondered fleetingly if he was a part of the dream she was living in her sleep. He would never discover the answer, however, because before the night was over, she was gone.

Chapter Twenty-three
A Settling of Accounts
September, 1776

It was evening now. The British frigate was gone, and a shimmering peacefulness had returned to the bay. As pale blue smoke curled from the bowl of his pipe and diffused into the soft evening air, Isaac Doane considered the moment, the day he had just passed, and the passing of time. As he sat on the ruined porch of the tavern, he gazed at the sunset, glowing like hearth embers in the west over Plymouth, and he thought again, as he had so often, of the amber-haired girl he had loved but who had not loved him enough; he remembered the years in between -- filled with whales, hard men and women, and barroom stories; and he remembered especially the man whose bones still remained in the cellar beneath the Samuel Smith tavern. He wondered, too, about the life of the soul -- whether the souls of Maria and Sam, the two people he had loved, admired, and betrayed, had simply dissolved with their last breath, whether they continued to hover in the places where they had suffered most, or whether they had dispersed to heaven's reward or hell's inferno as Reverend Treat had promised so long ago. Isaac could not imagine that a soul could vanish, and even as an old man, he was vibrantly aware of their presence in his heart.

He had heard the many tales of Maria hovering above the Billingsgate dunes, luring men to their deaths on the shoals. In wildly animated sailors' yarns, her hair had been the grasses on the high dunes, her voice the turbulent and cacophonous wind, and the shoals on which their ships foundered, the instrument of her sworn vengeance against the world. Isaac remembered her wistfulness when they had sat together in these same rough-hewn chairs so many years ago, and he dismissed the hysteria of legend; but on this September evening, in his deepest heart, he wondered not whether Maria rested in peace but where her uncompromising spirit was biding its time.

About Sam Bellamy Isaac was less doubtful. He felt that the spirit of Black Sam had never abandoned this island or this very tavern where he had died -- that, in truth, his bones were still configured in the same unnatural position they had assumed when Isaac had last seen his bloodied skull almost sixty years before in the cellar beneath him. Isaac could still recall the glare with which Sam had fixed him, the flash of his knife, and the vastly different pain in both their faces -- one of sorrow and anger and the other of searing physical torment. While Isaac occasionally mused on the life of the soul, and Sam's especially, he knew that his own was cursed forever to recall the words, "Remember me, boy." Now as an old man he only hoped for the Lord's mercy when his spiritual accounts were finally settled.

The embers of the natural fire in the west flared briefly, smoldered orange, light blue, and pink for a few moments, then faded to darkness, and as he witnessed his day's end, Isaac Doane arose from his chair and prepared to complete his journey's purpose. The time had come to fulfill both his promise to Mr. Smith and a promise he had made to himself. An autumnal hush had settled over the island with the setting sun, and in the gathered silence Isaac conceived the voices of old friends, low and alluring, emerging seemingly from the interior of the tavern, whispering ghostlike in the tops of the trees, insistent and impatient like the call of a distant gull. These voices drew him from his chair into the darkened recesses of the tavern, where the captured air, the breath of the day and perhaps of many days past, seemed to rise up to meet him.

From his pocket Isaac withdrew a flint, a blackened length of cloth, a tuft of flax and a small piece of steel. From his other pocket he took the pine needles he had collected earlier and placed some of them in a pile next to the log wall. He then began to strike the steel against the flint in a methodical, practiced way until a spark flickered off the flint and landed on the cloth, identifiable as potential fire and glistening against the black fabric. Isaac immediately grasped the cloth in his hands, held it against the flax in front of his keen eyes and began to blow on it, nursing and coaxing it into flame. Once the flame had blossomed, he delicately lowered the smoldering flax to the pine needles, which in turn caught the flame and intensified it. In the darkness, Isaac watched as small fingers of flame curved around the wall's lowest log and began to curl upwards. Having begun, Isaac quickly walked across the rotten flooring of the room, knelt, and repeated the same process at the rear of the tavern, neatly piling the remaining pine needles, striking the flint, creating the spark, and giving it form. As he bent and touched the cloth to the needles, however, he thought he heard a noise below him -- low yet sibilant, a hoarse murmur. Perhaps it was a woodland creature living in the cellar that had been disturbed by the noise coming from above; perhaps it was the tavern's now fragile beams responding to the pressure of the old man's weight; or perhaps it was simply the circumambient autumn air reconfiguring itself in an old derelict building.

Be that as it may, until that instant when this eerie sound invaded his consciousness, Isaac had maintained a tenuous hold on his fears, his imagination, his entire nervous system. His hands had been steady as he set the first fire, but now as the flame leapt to the dried needles and quickly turned into fire, his thin fingers perceptibly quivered. He felt as if he had heard a dissatisfied voice out of a crypt -- as if the cellar below him had spoken directly and accusingly to him -- and his riotous mind was filled with doubts. He pictured the bones of Sam Bellamy reanimated, with flesh on them once again, and his black beard aflame. And at that instant he believed that he had been right all along, that Sam Bellamy's soul was present not only in the cellar of this old establishment, but in its very walls, in the air that Isaac was breathing at this very moment.

As the second flame began to lick against the wall, he turned to look at the first and was startled to see how it had grown so quickly. The flames were at least six feet high against the wall and moving higher, and when he stood up, his outline peopled the room with deformed shadows around the walls, all moving in a synchronized yet grotesquely gelatinous way toward the smoke-filled doorway. For a few seconds Isaac was immobilized by the ever-changing figures on the wall, which on closer inspection, seemed to coalesce into a presence both familiar and terrifying. In his mind Isaac saw the spirit of Sam Bellamy accented in gold and orange but essentially black -- risen from the cellar, liberated from its dankness, seeking to breathe the air of life -- and the vision made him reel. As if by accident, he turned toward the doorway, which by now was filled with flames and gathering smoke that had begun to circle within the low-ceilinged room. Upon seeing the door's vague outline, Isaac instinctively moved toward it, but as he did, the lurking shadow on the wall did so also, as an unmoored puppet might or a massive night-haunting moth. These few instants had taken place as if on a silent stage, so aware was Isaac of the brilliant golds, pinks, blues, and oranges in the room, the darkly moving figures on the wall, even the white stars that filled the doorway beyond the flames. But it was the fabulous misshapen figure of Black Bellamy, unhoused and silently stalking his imagination that made Isaac cry out in terror, simultaneously acknowledging his terrible debt to the man and expressing the long harbored sorrow over what he had done years before.

At the sound of his own anguish, this silent pantomime suddenly dissolved, and Isaac was shocked by the countless sounds surrounding him, the squeals of small creatures running on the floor at his feet, the snapping reports of the burning wood, the whirring rotation of the disturbed autumnal air. And he fled. Though his bones were old, he leapt through the licking fire, through the open doorway, and into the starlit darkness. Coughing spasmodically but barely singed by the flames, Isaac stumbled down the steps and away from the porch, where he fell to the soft ground. Far from feeling relief at his escape, however, he turned with a sense of foreboding to look at the tavern once again.

To people on the mainland and even as far away as Barnstable Harbor, the growing inferno must have seemed a suspended meteor in the sky, a celestial torch, perhaps some inexplicable omen of the war that was at hand. To Isaac, though, the hinges of hell were white hot, and its portals had opened wide. The exhalation of the flames reached out to enshroud the old man, but as he inhaled their heat, he also breathed in the soothing fragrance of the pine needles beneath him, and he recalled the days of his youth when such simple smells seemed to be everywhere. Slowly sitting up, he sensed the slow dance of the stars above: elegant Cassiopeia, Orion arriving late in the east, the bejeweled Pleiades, the Big Dipper hand-in-hand with Polaris. Then his eye descended to the bay below, which radiated outwards from him like a great moonlit counterpane, and in its elegant folds he pictured the years to come: the approaching war, the rise of a nation, the disappearance of the leviathans and the men who hunted them. In some strange way he felt as if he owned this universe -- the watery blue quilt spread out before him, even the past and future that were stitched into it, and he felt that as an old man, he had paid a high price for this possession, this wisdom. But he also felt as a bird must as it surveys the landscape in its solitary flights above the earth -- the tall pines, the woven waves, the shifting sands -- that no one could take this vision from him, that a poor man could own all the land and all the sea.

Having recovered his breath and calmer now, Isaac stood and watched the blaze rise higher and yet higher against the sky. He could see the flicker-flashes of the sparks borne aloft on errands of the wind, and he slowly recognized after seventy-six years where his life would end. As he stared at the blazing timbers, his face and the scar that marked it assumed the chiaroscuro hues created by the ghostly light and the golden flames. In the shape-shifting, lambent light, he saw figures beckoning to him -- Sam, Maria, Samuel Smith, Daniel Atwood, Running Water and his son, and countless others -- all lost forever to time and to him, yet not to the tides of memory, nor to the legends that humans would tell and need to tell about such shadowy figures.

However, Isaac knew that he would not be the one to pass on their tale. With this realization, he briefly bowed his head, perhaps in atonement, perhaps in supplication, and began to move toward the heart of the fire. Slowly but deliberately, he stepped across the threshold of the now glowing doorway and entered the blaze where rafters were beginning to fall and the high log walls of the great structure were signaling their imminent collapse. Too old to feel fear, Isaac reached out into the expanding inferno hoping to touch the figures he saw in the flames, to blend the images of those he saw in the fire with those he had carried in his heart for so many years; and whether he imagined the sensation or not, he felt their welcoming embrace. Then with a gesture of gentle propitiation, he smiled, lowered his hands, and felt the heat, the smoke, and the flames gather about him -- and so he pushed aside the veil separating the present from the past and completed the task of uniting the ashes of those long dead with his own.

Many years later, waves large and small continue to break against the shell-filled sands of Great Island. The skeleton of Mr. Smith's tavern has receded into the depths of the imposing dune that is still the island. Billingsgate Island to the southwest is no more, its countless grains of sand having given way to the demands of the tides and time. But in the sequent curl and ebb of the waves, in the intricate patterns of white foam inscribed in the waves and spread out so routinely on the sand, can be found the vast, ever-changing maps of the future. They were the same charts that Isaac saw one fire-lit evening two centuries before, which demarcated paths that led forward into the wilds of the western territories and backward to the inextricable knots of the past. The interlacings of foam written ever so briefly on the sand, and the sound of the waves that carried the messages seemed to offer a promise then -- and they continue to do so -- the whispered promise of love, of avarice, of history, and the mysteries of their unfolding.

Epilogue

As early as 1844, in his book "A Comprehensive History, Ecclesiastical and Civil, of Eastham, Wellfleet, and Orleans", Enoch Pratt speculated doubtfully as to the existence of the Smith Tavern on Great Island, a 600 acre piece of land protruding into Wellfleet Harbor. Some eighty-eight years later, in 1932, Earle Rich, a long-time native of Wellfleet who had heard countless rumors about the tavern, conducted his own search and was able to confirm not only the tavern's existence but the fact that it had burned down. He accomplished this detective work by locating an old path that scaled the sand cliffs on the eastern end of the island; then pursuing its traces, he found the remains of the tavern itself at the topmost point of Great Island bluff, a short distance from the edge of the cliff.

Upon discovering an oblong-shaped mound of sand covered by pine needles, he started digging and soon realized he had found the long-lost tavern. In addition to fire-blackened remains of timbers, he uncovered tablespoons of various designs and a well-preserved 1723 King George half-penny. His later excavations unearthed various other items including a matching fork and knife set, copper nails, fragments of Indian cooking pottery blackened by use, metal buttons, and especially intriguing, a lady's sewing thimble. Of additional assistance was a discovery made in the 1890's: Isaac Doane was wrong in believing the tavern's sign would never be read again when he flung it into the underbrush in 1776; in fact, a member of the Wise family who bought the property at the end of the nineteenth century rediscovered it and was able to make out its welcome in the words etched so deeply into the wood. However, the most perplexing object was not unearthed another thirty-seven years after Earl Rich's initial excavations.

From 1969 through 1971, an excavation project conducted by Plimoth Plantation, Brown University, and the National Park Service uncovered some 100,000 artifacts from the same plot. These remains established beyond any question that a tavern had thrived on the land from 1690 to 1740 and that it continued to operate until just prior to the Revolutionary War when the British blockaded Cape Cod ports. The archaeologists made their most interesting discovery, however, in the west cellar of the ruined tavern. There, nestled in the dirt, almost indistinguishable from whalebones, broken glass, and shards of brick, was the frontal bone of a middle-aged European male; more shocking to the excavators, however, was that the skull had been deeply cut and the brow fractured as if by a club.

Naturally, speculation as to the man's identity ensued, some believing him to be the victim of a barroom brawl, others that he had been murdered and transferred to the remote cellar. Whatever the truth may have been now rests with the man himself, with those who ended his life and deposited him there, and with the accidents of time and the fictions that interpret them.

Chapter Notes

Chapter One:

Page 7: **Grampus Bay** is now Wellfleet Harbor. The name **Silver Springs** appeared on early British maps of the Lower Cape Cod area but disappeared by the 19th Century. That area today is approximately where the Wellfleet Bay Wildlife Sanctuary is located. **Billingsgate** was considered the alternate name for the North Precinct of the Town of Eastham, which became the Town of Wellfleet in 1763. **Hither Billingsgate** referred to the southern half and **Yonder Billingsgate** referred to the northern half. **Fresh Brook Village** was a small settlement of the late 17th and early 18th Centuries that eventually wilted away to nothing. It was located in what is now South Wellfleet near the Oceanside of Route 6.

Page 9: **Duck Creek** still exists but it was much deeper in 1715 than it is today. There were several wharfs along its banks long before there was a "downtown" Wellfleet.

Page 11: **Barnstable Bay** is now called Cape Cod Bay.

Page 12: The sign for Samuel Smith's Tavern is most likely accurately quoted. According to a few accounts, it was still in existence and legible well into the 19th Century.

Chapter Two:

Page 15: **Great Island**, although fairly large, never became a choice location for the English settlers. Even when the land was parceled out to the original ones of Eastham in the early 18th Century, Sam Smith ended up buying out most of them. There were some native Americans living on the island as well, but the main tribe lived across Grampus Bay at James' Neck. Therefore, once the tavern ceased to operate, Great Island was essentially abandoned.

Chapter Three:
P17: **Great Pond** is still in the town of Eastham and it is still called Great Pond today.

P19: Maria Hallett is an elusive historical figure with very little written or known about her. There were several Halletts in Yarmouthport on Cape Cod including one named Mary but she was born in 1693 and would have been too old to have been Maria.

Chapter Four:
P26: **James Neck** is now called Indian Neck.

Chapter Five:
P39: A **tuck-a-nuck** is an old fashioned name for a picnic:

P45: **Billingsgate Island** did indeed vanish as Maria predicted and today it is only partially visible at low tide.

Chapter Six:
P53: **The Burying Acre** refers to the cemetery surrounding Eastham's first meetinghouse near Town Cove, which was used until c1720 when a new building was erected on Bridge Road.

Chapter Seven:
P65: **The Smith Tavern on Great Island** was most likely visible in 1715 to an observer standing on the shore at Rock Harbor. The distance was about 7 miles, as the crow flies.

Chapter Eight:
P78: The sailing trip from Rock Harbor to Town Cove extends more than 50 miles, but it is only 2 miles as the crow flies.

Chapter Nine:
P85: Captain Benjamin **Hornigold** was a well-known pirate at that time.

Chapter Ten:

P95: The early **Knowles** family members were among the original English settlers of Eastham. The same could be said of the **Smiths**, of whom Samuel was included.

Chapter Eleven:

P109: There is very little known about the **Eastham jail** in the early eighteenth century but most likely in was located close to the meetinghouse along the western shore of Town Cove.

Chapter Twelve:

P125: In terms of the political geography of 1717, the Whydah wrecked in the southern most part of Hither Billingsgate. In modern times that location corresponds to just north of the Eastham – Wellfleet border on the ocean side shoreline.

Chapter Thirteen:

P156: The Whydah would eventually see the **Billingsgate Cliffs** but only just before the vessel broke into pieces.

Chapter Fourteen:

P161: No one knows exactly where Maria's shack was located but most likely it was only a short distance north of where the Whydah met its demise. The irony here is undeniable.

P165: **The Pierce Tavern** was built in 1712 (later became the Pierce Stand) and existed until the late nineteenth century.

Chapter Fifteen:

P177: On today's maps **Pochet** is located just south of Nauset Beach in Orleans, Massachusetts.

Chapter Sixteen:

P185: Although the Smith tavern was on an island dividing Grampus Bay and Barnstable Bay, it was located so that it over overlooked Grampus Bay (Wellfleet Harbor).

Chapter Seventeen:
P191: **Great Pond** in Eastham proper was located about 5 miles from Maria's shack.

Chapter Eighteen:
P197: **The Boston News Letter** was the oldest newspaper in the English colonies and was published every week in the early eighteenth century.

P199: **Jeremiah's Gutter** was supposedly named for Jeremiah Smith, a settler who lived in the area.

Chapter Nineteen:
P213: Actually none of the survivors ever saw **Paul Williams** again, although he was able to retire from pirating a few years later.

Chapter Twenty:
P222: **Duck Creek** was much deeper in 1717 than it is today and ships then could navigate quite some distance up the creek. **James Neck** is now called Indian Neck.

Chapter Twenty One:
P246: **Billingsgate Island** was located about 3 miles due south of the Smith Tavern.

Chapter Twenty Two:
P250: The fate was sealed for the **Pononakanet tribe** with the smallpox epidemic of 1746-47, and there was no way for it to recover its losses after that.

Chapter Twenty Three:
P261: HMS Somerset would meet its own fate two years later when in wrecked in a storm of the outer side of Provincetown on November 2, 1778.

Selected References

Clifford, Barry. *The Pirate Prince*. New York: Prentice Hall / Simon & Shuster, 1993.

Batting, Douglas. *The Pirates*. Alexandria: Time-Life Books, 1978.

Coogan, Jim and Sheedy, Jack. *Cape Cod Voyage*. East Dennis: Harvest Home Books, 2002.

Cordingly, David. *Under the Black Flag*. New York: Random House, 2006.

Diggers, Jeremiah. *Cape Cod Pilot*. New York: Viking Press, 1937.

Dow, George Francis. *Every Day Life in the Massachusetts Colony*. New York: Dover Publications, Inc., 1988.

Echeverria, Durand. *A History of Billingsgate*. Wellfleet, Massachusetts, The Wellfleet Historical Society, 1993.

Ekholm, Erik & Dietz, James. *Wellfleet Tavern*. The Journal of The American Museum of Natural History, August-September 1971.

Kittredge, Henry. *Cape Cod; Its People and Their History*. Boston: Houghton Mifflin, 1968.

Lapouge, Gilles. *Pirates and Buccaneers*. Singapore: Hachette Illustrated, 2002.

Lowe, Alice. *Nauset On Cape Cod: A History Of Eastham*. Eastham, Massachusetts: Eastham Historical Society, 1968.

Oldale, Robert. Cape Cod, *Martha's Vineyard, and Nantucket: The Geologic Story.* Yarmouthport: On Cape Publications, 2001.

Pratt, Enoch. *A Comprehensive History, Ecclesiastical and Civil, of Eastham, Wellfleet and Orleans, County of Barnstable Mass, from 1644 to 1844.* Yarmouth, Massachusetts: Fisher, 1844.

Reynard, Elizabeth. *The Narrow Land.* Boston: Houghton Mifflin, 1963.

Rich Earle. *More Cape Cod Echoes.* Orleans, Massachusetts: Salt Meadow Publishers, 1978.

Snow, Edward Rowe. *Great Storms and Famous Shipwrecks of the New England Coast.* Boston: Yankee Publishing, 1943.

Rich, Earle. *The Story of the Old Tavern On Great Island.* Orleans, Massachusetts: The Cape Codder, October 24, 1968.

Schneider, Paul. *The Enduring Shore.* New York: Henry Holt and Co., 2000.

Synenki, Alan & Charles, Sheila. *The Great Island Tavern Site.* Boston: U.S. Dept. of Interior, 1984.

Thoreau, Henry David. *Cape Cod.* New York: Thomas Crowell, 1961.

Vanderbilt, Arthur T. *Treasure Wreck: The Fortune and Fate of the Pirate Ship Whydah.* Boston: Houghton Mifflin, 1986.

CPSIA information can be obtained at www.ICGtesting.com
262517BV00001B/105/P